"The

"Taylor is a consummate storyteller who captivates
and entertains from the first word."
—*Publishers Weekly* on *An Irish Country Girl*

"Taylor masterfully charts the small victories
and defeats of Irish village life."
—*Irish America* magazine

"Both hilarious and heartwarming."
—*The Roanoke Times*

"Charming, full of Irish wit and wisdom . . . and,
of course, all the village characters we've come
to love. For those just discovering the Irish doctor,
this book can stand on its own, but it will leave
the reader wanting more."
—*Booklist* on *Fingal O'Reilly, Irish Doctor*

"The cozy village of Ballybucklebo and its eccentric
inhabitants make the holidays bright."
—*Library Journal*
on *An Irish Country Christmas*

"Wraps you in the sensations of a vanished
time and place."
—*The Vancouver Sun*
on *An Irish Country Doctor*

ALSO BY PATRICK TAYLOR

Only Wounded
Pray for Us Sinners
Now and in the Hour of Our Death

IRISH COUNTRY BOOKS

An Irish Country Doctor
An Irish Country Village
An Irish Country Christmas
An Irish Country Girl
An Irish Country Courtship
A Dublin Student Doctor
An Irish Country Wedding
Fingal O'Reilly, Irish Doctor
An Irish Doctor in Peace and at War

The Wily O'Reilly
"Home Is the Sailor" (e-original)

An Irish
Country Wedding

PATRICK TAYLOR

A TOM DOHERTY ASSOCIATES BOOK
NEW YORK

This is a work of fiction. All of the characters, organizations, and events portrayed in this novel are either products of the author's imagination or are used fictitiously.

AN IRISH COUNTRY WEDDING

Copyright © 2012 by Ballybucklebo Stories Corp.

All rights reserved.

Maps by Elizabeth Danforth

Original etching by Dorothy Tinman

A Forge Book
Published by Tom Doherty Associates, LLC
175 Fifth Avenue
New York, NY 10010

www.tor-forge.com

Forge® is a registered trademark of Tom Doherty Associates, LLC.

ISBN 978-0-7653-6881-2

Forge books may be purchased for educational, business, or promotional use. For information on bulk purchases, please contact the Macmillan Corporate and Premium Sales Department at 1-800-221-7945, extension 5442, or write to specialmarkets@macmillan.com.

First Edition: October 2012
First Mass Market Edition: June 2015

Printed in the United States of America

0 9 8 7 6 5 4 3 2 1

To Dorothy

Acknowledgments

A friend recently remarked, "You always put acknowledgments at the start of your books. Why? Nobody ever reads them."

That may or may not be true, but without certain very important people you would not be reading the rest of this work and I would feel remiss unless I tendered my most unreserved thanks, and in no special order, to:

Simon Hally, Natalia Aponte, Tom Doherty, Carolyn Bateman, Paul Stevens, Irene Gallo and the art department, Gregory Manchess, Rosie and Jessica Buckman, Don Kalancha and Joe Meier, Patty Garcia and Alexis Saarela, everyone in sales, Christina MacDonald, and finally to all of you who read and enjoy this series and keep me at my keyboard.

Go raibh mile maith agat agus beannacht De agat, Thank you very much and God bless you.

AUTHOR'S NOTE

To old readers, it's grand to have you back in the village of Ballybucklebo, and to new readers, *cead mile fáilte,* a hundred thousand welcomes. Come in, sit down, and stay for a while.

This is the seventh book in the Irish Country Doctor series and in it I have made one important deviation from the usual. If you can bear with me, I offer this short explanation of why I have done so.

In all of *Country Wedding*'s predecessors, I skimmed over Irish politics. This deliberate refusal to weave the sad history through the stories applied equally to *Country Girl,* set in County Cork around the time of the Irish Civil War of 1922–23 (West Cork was a Republican stronghold), and to *Student Doctor,* set in Dublin in the 1930s, where the abortive Easter Rebellion of 1916, the subsequent 1918–1921 Anglo-Irish War, and the Civil War had all left unhealed wounds. Those works set in Ballybucklebo in the mid-'60s were only four years before the outbreak of thirty years of virulent internecine violence in the north of Ireland. Even then I barely alluded to the sectarian undercurrents that preceded "the Troubles."

I deliberately failed to do so for what seemed to me to be a cogent reason.

In the '90s I had written three gritty books set firmly in the squalor of the recent troubles in Northern Ireland. They are noted here on the page that lists my previous works. In all three I refused to be partisan because I believe that stirring the pot by fighting old battles over again—or worse, taking sides—is counterproductive.

I started the drafts in 2003 of what became *An Irish Country Doctor* and quite frankly have been more comfortable since then working in my version of an Ireland where such political matters do not intrude and where in the works set in Ballybucklebo an ecumenical spirit prevails. Such a harmonious Ireland is my wish for the future of the entire country and has been reflected in my writing.

Readers of the Irish Country series may remember that in *Country Christmas* I alluded to the historical fact of the lowering of Catholic-Protestant barriers in 1941 following the Luftwaffe's blitz of Belfast and Bangor. At that time, often in the country villages, evacuees and those bombed from their homes were taken in and cared for by strangers, regardless of the religious persuasion of either. In Ballybucklebo, the local priest and minister create a fictional tradition out of that real-life goodwill gesture of 1941. Since the separate Catholic and Protestant populations of children were too small to hold independent Christmas pageants, I have the two denominations coming together for a communal service of thanksgiving at Christmastide. In doing so, I was, I believe, giving voice to my desire to see all Ireland at peace.

My enthusiasm for that also led me to another piece of wishful thinking. I established the Bally-bucklebo Bonnaughts Rugby Football and Hurling Club. Such a thing would have been virtually impossible early in the twentieth century. The Gaelic Athletic Association (GAA), established in 1884 to preserve uniquely Irish sports such as hurling, camogie, and Irish football, frowned upon even mere attendance at a "foreign or garrison game" like rugby or soccer. Doing so could lead to expulsion from the association, so a club combining Irish hurling and the English sport of rugby would be unthinkable. I hope I will be forgiven by GAA purists, but in creating the Bonnaughts I was indulging, like Kinky Kincaid, in a little hopeful and, as it turned out, accurate foresight.

In 2005, the GAA temporarily relaxed its Rule 42, which prohibited the playing of games other than those deemed to be traditionally Irish on their facilities. The home and headquarters of Gaelic sports, Croke Park (Páirc an Chrócaigh) known to local Dubliners as "Croker," was thrown open to the Irish Rugby Football Union, whose facilities at Lansdowne Road, Dublin, were under reconstruction. The rugby team, even after the partition of Ireland in 1922 (which divided Ireland into the south—now the Republic of Ireland—and Northern Ireland), had refused to acknowledge the border and selected players from the entire island.

The team lost their first game in Croke Park to France in February 2007. The next, against England in March of that year, was awaited with some trepidation—and not only in regard to the athletic outcome on the pitch. Happily, there were no incidents and to almost everyone's delight Ireland beat England—by 43 to 13, which was the greatest victorious margin and the highest number of points ever scored by an Irish team against England since their first clash in 1875.

I watched on television that day in March 2007, and hearing the Irish crowd made up of those from both the north and the south roar out as one, and singing a triumphant, joyous "Fields of Athenry" gave me goose pimples and made the hair at the nape of my neck stand up. It also made me, an Ulsterman, proud to be Irish.

It is not to belittle the enormous efforts of all politicians on both sides of the border who strive to achive amity, but I couldn't help think that it is also such measures of tolerance and mutual support at grass-roots level that break down old barriers. I saw the Croke Park experience as an event much like the exchange of Ping-Pong players in the '70s between the United States and China, which paved the way for President Richard Nixon's visit to the People's Republic in 1972.

It has been my hope that in the first six Irish Country books I have been painting in microcosm an Ireland that should be.

But before the recent cross-border comings together, Ireland, and particularly Northern Ireland, starting in 1969, had to suffer. And strangely enough that anguish was in part inadvertently provoked by people of enormous goodwill, the civil rights workers who sought a more just state there.

Irish performing artist Phil Coulter said in "The Town I Loved So Well," a song about his childhood in Derry, Northern Ireland, "What's done is done . . . and what's lost is lost and gone forever"—and should be. I decided that for the sake of the authenticity for which I constantly strive, tempers in Ireland had cooled enough to let some Irish politics intrude into *An Irish Country Wedding*.

So I departed from my usual convention of skirting the sectarian question that has always been there like Banquo's ghost. Yet during the writing of this novel, the president of the Republic of Ireland, Mary McAleese (Máire Pádraigin Bean mHic Ghiolla Íosa) is an Ulsterwoman from Belfast, and tempers have indeed cooled enough. A little reality, I decided, could surface.

While regular readers will, I trust, be pleased to meet the usual cast of eccentric characters (and, yes, Arthur Guinness still likes his Smithwick's), and new readers will, I hope, find these folks amusing, I have for the first time allowed the doings of the nascent Northern Ireland civil rights movement to play a more central role, as would have been obvious to anyone living in Ulster at the time.

Perhaps what is true for life is also true for fiction.

No matter how hard one may try to avoid it, reality will always intrude. In this case, I hope it increases your enjoyment of the work and adds to your understanding of my native land.

PATRICK TAYLOR, 2011
Salt Spring Island
Canada

N

North Channel

County
Antrim

• Portmuck

• Whitehead

Carrickfergus •

Belfast Lough

Newtownabbey •

• Bangor

• Ballybucklebo

Belfast • ← The Kinnegar

Newtownards •

County
Down

Strangford Lough

County Antrim
and North Down

danforth ©

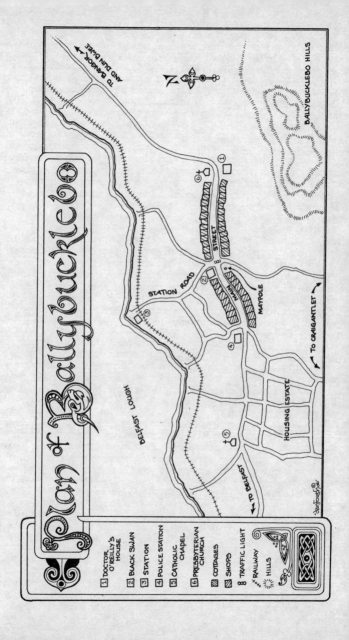

An Irish
Country Wedding

1

Diamonds Are Forever

"Kitty O'Hallorhan," said Doctor Fingal Flahertie O'Reilly, looking into those familiar grey eyes flecked with amber, "you don't look a day over thirty-five, and you're lovely." Her silver and black hair shone in the sunlight filtering down past the buildings on Belfast's Royal Avenue. Her tailored grey suit, with its slim, knee-length skirt, accentuated her figure. God, but she was looking well.

She shook her head. "You're an old flatterer, Fingal, a soft-soaper. You know I'll not see fifty again, but thank you."

"I'll always see you as twenty-two, the way you were when we were youngsters, always, and that's because," he hesitated, "I love you."

"Thank you, Fingal," she said. "Thank you for loving me, and thank you for telling me. I do love you so much."

He bloody well nearly bear-hugged and kissed her there and then. Instead, he continued walking with

Kitty at his side and thought about how on the drive here from her flat they'd discussed the progress of Donal Donnelly, one of Fingal's patients, who was being nursed by Kitty, a senior sister on the brain surgery ward of the Royal Victoria Hospital. It had made O'Reilly happy to discuss a patient with her. He was looking forward to these kinds of professional conversations when she became his wife, on July 3, 1965, and that was only a little more than two months away. He gave a hop and a skip, grinning as he did.

"Fingal," Kitty said with a smile, "will you stop acting the lig?"

"I'm happy," he said, guiding her through the mid-morning crowds of shoppers, office messengers, and delivery men. Traffic growled, and he heard the *ting* of the conductor's bell as a red double-decker bus pulled away from a stop. The air was heavy with exhaust fumes. A flock of starlings wheeled and jinked in unison across the sky. He pointed to a glass door on which SHARMAN D NEILL. JEWELLERS AND WATCH-MAKERS was etched in gilt letters. Watches, barometers, brass telescopes, and jewellery were displayed on velvet mounts in the window. "This is it," he said.

The lighting was subdued, the carpet thick. Glass jewellery cases were arranged around three walls. A door at the back led, O'Reilly presumed, to offices or storerooms. The air had only a trace of mustiness. Two staff members wearing short black jackets, pin-striped trousers, and highly polished black shoes stood waiting. The place exuded the confidence of a business that had catered to the upper classes for decades. Young men, O'Reilly thought, probably felt intimidated here, and their immediate concerns would be whether their budget might stretch. He was worried himself.

He and Kitty were the only customers.

An assistant glided across to them. He wore rimless spectacles.

"Sir? Modom?" His voice was reverential, his accent affected. "May I be of assistance?"

"Rings," O'Reilly said, surprising himself by lowering his voice.

"Certainly, sir." The man glanced at Kitty's gloved left hand. "Would that be dress or engagement?"

O'Reilly cleared his throat. His collar seemed to be tighter. "Engagement, please."

"How lovely. May I wish sir and modom every happiness?"

"Thank you," Kitty said.

O'Reilly wanted to tell the man to mind his own damned business and get on with selling them a flaming ring. He wanted to get this transaction completed. And it had been ages since, to his housekeeper Kinky Kincaid's amazement, he had refused the mixed grill she'd offered to cook and simply grabbed a quick cup of coffee and a slice of toast this morning in his hurry to get to Kitty's flat. Now he wanted his lunch.

The shop assistant moved behind a glass display case. "If I might enquire, would we be looking for a solitaire, a cluster, a trinity or bezel setting, a specific precious stone . . . perhaps modom's birthstone? Something," his lip curled, "semiprecious?"

Jasus, O'Reilly thought, in 1939 when I bought Deirdre her little ring it was just a gold band with one tiny diamond. Back then men bought the ring before they proposed, but today O'Reilly had brought Kitty to pick hers. He smiled at his soon-to-be wife and knew for certain that Deirdre O'Reilly, née Mawhinney, his young bride of six months who had died in the Belfast Blitz of 1941, would approve of Kitty, be glad for him and his newfound happiness. "Kitty?" he asked.

She smiled at him. "If it's all right with you, Fingal, I'd like something simple."

"It's your choice."

"It can be bewildering," the shop assistant said. "Might I suggest a nice cluster with a central half-carat blue diamond?"

O'Reilly heard the condescension in the man's voice. "Kitty?"

"No, thank you. I've really got my mind set on a well-cut solitaire, S12 clarity, I or J colour grade—"

O'Reilly's mouth fell open.

"—of slightly less than half a carat." She turned to him. "Blue diamonds are the most expensive. Prices rocket at the half- and full-carat mark. It takes a hell of an eye to tell the difference between a smaller stone and I don't want to bankrupt you, dear."

O'Reilly grinned. He'd ask her later where she'd learnt her gemology.

"Modom . . . modom knows her diamonds." There was awe in the shop assistant's voice.

Kitty inclined her head and said, "And I'm not fussed about the setting as long as it's platinum, the ring is gold, and the stone is good quality."

The man leant sideways and grabbed a set of sizing rings from the top of the case. "If I may?"

"Certainly." Kitty removed her left kid glove and gave him her hand. After using two rings the assistant said, "Size A and a half." He smiled. "I believe I have exactly what we need. If you'll excuse me?"

The second he'd left, O'Reilly asked, "Where in the hell did you—"

"Dublin's National College of Art and Design, remember? I was there before I started nursing, and I took a course on jewellery design."

He hugged her. "Do you know," he said, "I'd completely forgotten you'd been there. It is a year or two back." A year or two? More like thirty, he thought, but said, "And thank you for thinking of my wallet too."

"Fingal O'Reilly," she said, "not being extravagant on a ring doesn't mean you love me any less. You can't measure love in carats or colour. Pounds and shillings."

His throat felt tight and he swallowed. "Thank you, Kitty. Thank you for that." And he wasn't sure if he was thanking her for her understanding of how much he loved her, her solid business sense, or both. He heard a discreet cough and let Kitty go.

"I think this may be what modom requires."

O'Reilly watched as a ring was slipped on Kitty's finger. It fitted perfectly. He swallowed. From now on, Fingal would be the only man to put rings on Kitty's finger. Size A-½ at that. The second one, in July, would be plain gold. He'd pick that himself. Mrs. Kitty O'Reilly. He liked the sound of it.

She took it off. "It's absolutely beautiful."

"That's the ring you want?" O'Reilly asked.

"Yes, please. It's exactly what I had in mind."

"You don't want to look at any others?"

She shook her head.

"We'll take it," O'Reilly said.

"Just a minute, Fingal." Kitty spoke to the assistant. "May I borrow your loupe?"

"Certainly." He gave her a monocular magnifying eyepiece, which Kitty screwed into her right eye socket.

What the hell now? O'Reilly wondered.

She scrutinised the ring. "There's a tiny flaw in the stone," she said, handing the loupe and the ring to the man.

He examined the diamond. "Modom is right. I do apologise. Shall I—?"

"No need. I love the ring. We'll take it." She looked him in the eye. "But I'm sure you'll adjust the price."

"Of course."

"Good," she said. "Now, I'll wait outside while you take care of paying, dear." She lifted her glove and left.

Typical. O'Reilly had been going to suggest she go. He didn't want her to know what he paid.

"I'll box and wrap it, sir."

"Please. And the bill."

"Of course, and there will be a twenty percent discount because of the flaw."

"Thank you."

"And if sir doesn't mind me saying, he is a very fortunate man." The assistant looked at the door through which Kitty had vanished to a jangling of bells. "Your fiancée is a remarkable and very beautiful lady."

"I know," said O'Reilly, trying not to sound smug. "By God, I do know."

He paid, took his little parcel, thanked the assistant, and left.

Kitty linked her arm through his. "Thank you, darling. Thank you."

"Not yet," said O'Reilly. "We're going to Mooney's on Corn Market. It's not far. You can thank me after I've given it to you properly, you've put it on, and I've toasted you with a pint of black velvet."

"Black velvet?"

"Guinness and champagne. You'll love it." He set off at a brisk pace. "I'm buying lunch too."

"Sounds wonderful."

They crossed Royal Avenue and headed along Castle Place. "By the way," he said, "are you free this weekend?"

"I am."

"I'd like you to come down, show your ring to Barry and Kinky," he said, "the rest of the crew at Number One, Main Street, Ballybucklebo."

"I'd love to."

"Great." He pushed open the door to Mooney's Pub. "I know the barmen here," he said.

The place was packed, smoky, and noisy. "Black velvet. Two pints, Andy," O'Reilly roared in his quarterdeck voice, "menus, and a dozen oysters on the half shell to start with. My belly thinks my bloody throat's cut."

2

And Strangled in the Guts

What on earth was that clattering? Barry Laverty—Doctor Barry Laverty—was enjoying a cup of tea after lunch, but now he frowned and listened. Probably that demented cat Lady Macbeth knocking something over. He rose from the table wondering how O'Reilly was doing up in Belfast with Kitty. He'd been like a child going on a school outing, so impatient he hadn't even eaten a proper breakfast, which for O'Reilly was unheard of unless there was an emergency. And it would have to have been a life-threatening one at that for the big man to forgo his vittles.

The clattering stopped, but now he could hear

retching. A patient must have come into the house unannounced.

Barry crossed the hall and looked into the surgery. Empty. He hurried to the waiting room, but although the plain wood chairs and God-awful rose-patterned wallpaper were there, the room was deserted.

More sounds of retching were followed by a moan, and this time Barry knew where they were coming from—the kitchen. He ran to the back of the house and flung open the door. The room was warm and the stench of vomit smothered the cooking aromas. A saucepan lay on the floor with peeled and diced potatoes forming a small archipelago in a pool of spilled water. Mrs. Maureen "Kinky" Kincaid, Doctor O'Reilly's housekeeper, stood clutching the edges of the sink. Her silver chignon was in disarray, tears streamed down her cheeks. "Ohhh Lord Jasus," she gasped.

"Kinky, are you—" he began, then stopped. "Are you all right?" would be a bloody silly thing to ask, almost as stupid as "What's the matter?" He was a doctor, but it didn't take one to see that Kinky Kincaid was not well. He took a breath, resolved to behave like the doctor he was and sort out what needed to be done without wasting time mouthing platitudes. He moved to her and put an arm round her shoulders. "It's all right," he said. "It's all right. Let's get you sitting down."

"I'm sorry, sir," she said, and hiccupped, "but I've been taken over all funny, so, and I haven't finished getting tea ready for himself and you. And him with no breakfast." She dragged in a deep breath and shuddered. "I'll be grand if I could sit down for a shmall-little minute, so."

"Don't worry about tea," Barry said. Typical of Kinky to be thinking about "her doctors" and their next meal rather than herself. He knew he should get her into the surgery and onto the examining couch, or onto her own bed, but Kinky was what her fellow County Cork people would describe as "a powerful woman" and that did not imply slimness. He wasn't strong enough to oxter-cog her to the surgery or to her quarters in the next room. "Let's get you sitting down, Kinky Kincaid." He turned his head away as her shoulders shook and she threw up. "Sorry, sir," she said, and wiped her mouth with the back of her hand.

He felt her sag and with his hands under her armpits lowered her to the tile floor. He looked around. Laundry was piled nearby. He grabbed an armful and a plastic basin. Barry made a heap of the clothes, including, he noticed, a pair of his own trousers. "Lie back, Kinky. Put your head there." He set the bowl beside her.

"Thank you, sir." Her pinafore was splotched, her lips caked.

Barry dampened a tea towel, squatted beside her, and mopped her face. "Can you tell me what happened?"

She took a shallow breath, then said, "I was grand all together until about twelve thirty. I'd nearly finished getting lunch ready when I got a sharp pain. Mary, Mother of—" She clutched her lower belly and moaned. "There it is again."

"Tell me about the pain," he said. He took her pulse. The skin was clammy and her pulse rapid.

"It came on like a terrier pouncing on a rat, so, and it gnawed at me and kept on grinding, then it went away. That—" She inhaled. "—that was a blessèd relief for I was able to serve your luncheon on time, so."

Kinky, you're one brave woman, he thought, but asked professionally, "Can you show me where it hurts?"

She pointed to her left groin. "There, sir, and it does be back there now. And it's coming in spasms."

Barry glanced at his watch. One thirty-five. He frowned. Her vomiting had suggested the relatively innocuous acute gastroenteritis, often called stomach flu, or "the abdabs" by the locals. But while the disease might cause vomiting, clammy skin, and a fast pulse, it would not cause pain in the place Kinky was describing nor pain that came on so suddenly. "Have you ever had trouble there before?" he asked.

"Not like this. Once in a while if I've been lifting things or hoovering I'll get a bit of a grumbling there, but, och, sure don't I usually sit a while and then work it off?" She managed a weak smile. "My ma taught us that you should always try to work pain off, so. Not give in to it."

"And you've never mentioned it to Doctor O'Reilly?" He knew Kinky would not voluntarily consult him, Barry. She'd consider Doctor O'Reilly's assistant much too young.

"Och, Doctor Laverty, dear," she said, shaking her head. "Sure wasn't it only a shmall-little ache, and didn't it always go away, and amn't I at an age when you must expect such things? Another fourteen years won't I be seventy and if I'm spared I'll be playing in overtime then if you believe what the Good Book says about us being given three score years and ten?"

"Go on," he said, "tell me more about what's happening now." Her description of the pain and its situation had given a hint.

"Just a bit before you came, sir, I had another fierce one, a spasm like a hot knife in exactly the same place. I dropped a pan of potatoes. A few minutes later another one came and then—" A tear fell. "—I embarrassed meself. I threw up, so." She struggled to sit. "But I'm nearly better now—" She coughed. "—and soon I'll clean up."

Barry couldn't keep an edge out of his voice. "Kinky Kincaid, you'll do no such thing." She gasped and clutched her belly. He heard her stomach give an enormous gurgle. The exact words from *A Short Textbook of Surgery* sprang to mind. *Borborygmi are sometimes loud enough to be heard by the unaided ear. The sound of turbulent peristalsis coinciding with an attack of colic is valuable evidence of intestinal obstruction. The causes . . . which may be acute, chronic, or acute-on-chronic, are very numerous. The site of*

Kinky's pain and her previous history of a chronic ache brought on by exertion pointed to a hernia, a weakness in the abdominal muscles containing a sac of peritoneum. Spasms suggested a loop of bowel was trapped there, was being compressed, and causing pain every time a wave of peristalsis, the normal muscle contractions of the digestive tract, ran along the gut. He blew out his breath against partially closed lips. It was a logical explanation, but the other potential causes of obstruction were legion.

She groaned and used the basin. "Dear Lord," she said, and gasped. "Please can you make it go away, Doctor Laverty? Please. The pain does try a body, so." There was no strength in her voice.

"I'm sorry, Kinky," he said, rising to take the full basin away. I only wish I could, he thought, but what I think you need is beyond the capabilities of a country GP. He poured the contents into the sink. He didn't gag. All those years in the teaching hospital had inured him to many sights and smells. Before he turned on the tap to rinse the mess away he studied it. There was the greenish tinge of bile. That and the onset of pain immediately accompanied by vomiting, which by his guess was happening every three or four minutes, was typical of compression of the small intestine, probably the jejunem, that section of the small bowel immediately between the duodenum and the ileum. He was narrowing the list of possibilities. "I'll just be a sec," he called to Kinky as he rinsed the bowl.

Blockage lower down the bowel, he thought, usually produced pain that lasted for quite some time before the vomiting started.

Barry brought the basin back and squatted beside her. "Kinky," he said, "if you were anybody else I'd have to ask you a lot of personal questions, then examine you thoroughly. Last year Doctor O'Reilly taught me only to do the minimum to make a diagnosis if it spares the patient pain or embarrassment. He said when he was a student he'd learnt that from a surgeon in Dublin."

"Thank you." Her words caught in her throat. "But if you need to examine me, you fire away, sir. I'd not be any more ashamed than I already am for being so weak."

He felt a prickling behind his eyelids. "Kinky," he said. "Kinky, you mustn't be ashamed. You didn't bring this on." He stood. "Please, you just lie there. I'll be right back, but I have to make a phone call."

"Go ahead. I'll be grand if you leave me the basin. I'd not want to make any more mess on the floor." Her breathing came in gasps. "But don't be too long." Her voice dropped to a whisper and she looked him straight in the eye. "I'm mortal afraid, sir."

He pursed his lips and squeezed her hand. "We'll get you well soon. Don't be afraid. I'll be straight back. I promise." He rose, went to the hall phone, called the Royal Victoria Hospital switchboard, and waited for an answer.

As he did, drumming his fingers on the wall, he

couldn't help thinking how it was this having to refer difficult cases to specialists that made him question whether he was really cut out to be a rural GP.

"Royal Victoria Hospital."

"Doctor Laverty here. Can you get me Doctor Jack Mills please. It's urgent." Again Barry waited. Stop being so bloody selfish, he thought. You've more important things to worry about than whether you've made the right choice to go and try obstetrics and gynaecology. Important things like Kinky Kincaid being sick.

"Barry?" Jack's Antrim accent was clear. "What's up?"

"It's Kinky."

Jack laughed. "Hey bye, I like the sound of that, but what is? Ursula Andress in a white bikini in *Doctor No*? Or maybe Honor Blackman as Pussy Galore in *Goldfinger*. Remember when we used to watch her in *The Avengers* on telly in the students' mess? All dressed in that black leath—"

"Jack. Jack, be serious." Despite his concerns, Barry found himself smiling at his old friend. "I'm talking about our housekeeper, Mrs. Kincaid."

"Oh. That Kinky? Och, I am sorry. Is she sick?"

"Violent abdominal pain, and I do mean violent, of recent onset, concurrent bilious vomiting, previous history of groin aches—"

"Physical findings?"

"Clammy skin and tachycardia and that's all I know. Come on, Jack. Kinky's fed you often enough when you've come down here. You know how she looks after O'Reilly and me. It would be like examining my own mother."

"Fair enough. You don't need to anyway. It sounds like a strangulated hernia. Probably needs surgery," Jack said. "Shoot her up to us and we'll take care of examining her and doing any tests."

"I thought it might be a hernia," Barry said, "but getting her to you in a rush is tricky." It was gratifying to have his probable diagnosis confirmed by his friend who now had ten months of surgical training under his belt. Barry was happy to have the specialists take care of Kinky. She was family. It was the other referrals he'd had to make that were frustrating him.

"How soon can you get her to the Royal?" Jack asked.

With bowel obstructions, the sooner the constriction was removed the less was the likelihood of complications like gangrene of the bowel, perforation, peritonitis. Barry owed it to Kinky to move quickly, but— "I could run her up myself," he said, "but O'Reilly's not back from Belfast and if I do there'll be no one here if there's another emergency in the practice. She usually looks after the shop when the boss and I are both out. Makes not-so-urgent patients wait, gets an ambulance for the really sick ones and sends them to casualty."

"Not to worry. You're at home?"

"I am."

"I'll get an ambulance down pronto."

"Fine." Barry heard a distant low moan. "Jack, she's having a lot of pain. Morphine?"

"Better not, I'm afraid. Understanding the pain, where it's felt, what makes it worse, what relieves it, it's all part of making the final diagnosis in folks with acute bellies. Painkillers muddy the waters. We've known that since fourth year, Barry."

"I know. I just thought—" He bit off the words. He'd made the serious mistake of letting his concern for this special patient override what must be done. He also knew he hated to see Kinky suffering.

"We've made an informed guess that it's a hernia," Jack said, "but at her age, what, fifty, fifty-five? You could get those symptoms from a lot more things. Crohn's disease, ulcerative colitis—"

"I know, I know," said Barry. "You can spare me the list, Jack. Just tell the ambulance to be quick and ask one of the attendants to keep her company on the drive up to Belfast. She's in a lot of pain, and she'll be terrified. She shouldn't be left alone."

"Done, mate," Jack said, "and I'll talk to my boss, Sir Donald Cromie, at once. He's here in outpatients. He teaches that severe belly pain is either 'watching sick,' meaning you can observe them, try nonsurgical treatment, and perhaps they'll get better, or 'opening sick,' which means immediate surgery is indicated. And I'm sorry, Barry, but even sight unseen, your

Kinky sounds pretty 'opening sick' to me. If he agrees, he'll see her the minute she arrives on the ward. Save a bit of time."

"Thanks." Barry was going to say good-bye, but remembered, "One last thing. Kinky's hundreds of miles away from her family in County Cork. She'll be all on her own at the hospital. I'll have to let her folks know, but I'll wait 'til I hear for sure what's going on. Will you give me a call when you've seen her?"

"Sure."

"Thanks, Jack," Barry said. "I'd better go back and see how she's doing." And it won't be well, he thought, but at least I can offer her a bit of comfort while we wait.

3

"Plain Cooking" Cannot Be Entrusted to "Plain Cooks"

"What? You've sent Kinky to the Royal?" O'Reilly still had one arm in his wet raincoat as water from an April shower dripped onto the hall carpet. It was forty-five minutes since the ambulance had left. The house had felt hollow and empty to Barry without the stoic Corkwoman in her kitchen. He welcomed

O'Reilly's expansive presence now, even if he wasn't taking the news in exemplary fashion.

"Blue blazes. A bowel obstruction? Holy thundering Jasus, poor Kinky."

"I'm sorry, Fingal." His senior's nose tip had blanched, a sure sign the man was furious.

"No need for you to bloody well apologise." He hung up his coat so forcibly that Barry thought the coat-peg might be torn off the wall. "You didn't make her sick."

Barry said, "I wasn't apologising, Fingal. When I said 'sorry' I was expressing regret that Kinky's sick, not accepting blame for anything."

"I know," O'Reilly said. "I know, and I'm not angry with you, Barry. It's not your fault. You've got her in good hands, and I understand why you didn't take her to Belfast yourself. You could have panicked, but you didn't. Mind you, I'm not surprised you did the right thing. You've learnt a lot since you came to work here. I trust you, son. Implicitly."

"Thank you, Fingal." And he's right. I could have panicked, Barry thought. Seeing Kinky so sick and feeling helpless was scary, and I didn't let it beat me. Being scared by illness in others wasn't an emotion allowed to doctors.

O'Reilly continued, "I'm fit to be tied because she's sick. Poor woman. Kinky's had her share of grief."

"I know." Barry swallowed. "She asked me to pack a bag for her and put a stuffed toy bunny in it. I never knew she had one. She called it her *gorria mór*."

"Irish for 'big hare,'" said O'Reilly. "I suppose it's a comfort to her for some reason. None of our business."

But Barry knew the reason. He'd gone to her tidy room and seen her gallery of faded photographs—family, friends, a farmhouse. On her bedside table a book lay open to where a rosebud had been pressed between the pages, and done so long ago, judging by its dryness. Next to it, two sepia-coloured pictures shared a silver frame. In one, a grinning young man with long dark hair parted to one side sat in a small boat, holding two salmon. In the other, coatless, shirt-sleeves rolled up, he stood on a road between black-thorn hedges, right arm hanging low, ready to loft a "bullet"—a road bowling cannonball. The inscription was fading, but Barry could read it. *To Maureen from your* gorria mór, *with all my love.* It must have been the man's pet name. The lump in Barry's throat had nearly choked him. Maureen "Kinky" Kincaid, née O'Hanlon, had indeed had her "share of grief." He understood now why she'd wanted the toy, but decided O'Reilly was right. It was Kinky's business alone. No need to explain even to him. "She should be at the Royal by now," Barry said. "I wish we knew what's happening. My pal Jack Mills is going to admit her."

"The rugby player?"

"That's him. He promised to phone after he'd assessed her. Said he'd get an opinion from your friend Sir Donald Cromie too."

"In which case you and I must bide contented until we hear. I know you're concerned for her, Barry, damn it all so am I, but worrying never changed the price of turnips." O'Reilly turned. "Come on up to the lounge. I want to put my feet up." He headed for the stairs and Barry followed.

O'Reilly dropped heavily into an armchair by the fire and lit his pipe. Barry took the other comfortable chair. "You're right about being patient, but it's hard not to worry. I'd really like to hear what the surgeons think." Did he, he wondered, want to hear purely from concern for Kinky or was there an element of needing to know if his diagnosis had been right? He said, "I saw her into the ambulance, gave her her things. She looked me straight in the eye and told me, 'I'm going to be grand, so, never fear. Don't you worry your head about me, but I do worry about you, sir, and himself. What will you both eat, at all?' I told her she mustn't worry, we'd manage, and she grabbed my hand and said, 'There does be a steak-and-kidney pie in the fridge. Pop it in a medium oven and leave it for twenty-five minutes. It'll do for your tea tonight, but you'll have to do without the potatoes.'" Barry shook his head. "She'd dropped the pan and was still upset."

O'Reilly smiled. "Bless her. If she'd been on the *Titanic* she'd have been fussing about other folks before she'd get into a lifeboat."

"I know," Barry said. "Kinky Kinkaid's a remarkable woman."

"She's that, all right. She's been mothering me for

nineteen years, since 1946 when I bought the practice from old Doctor Flanagan's estate. Begod, I'd hate to lose her."

"Lose her?" Barry shook his head. "She's pretty sick now, Fingal, but if it *is* a strangulated hernia, once she's been operated on, I'm sure she'll be fine."

"Oh, no, I don't mean 'lose her' in that sense," O'Reilly said. "It's just that . . . you know I'm marrying Kitty in July and—"

"I know. I'm delighted for you both, Fingal. And I'm sure Kinky is too."

"Well, I *thought* Kinky was pretty chuffed. And she seemed genuinely excited about us buying the ring today. There was that bit of friction between them when Kitty first started coming down here—"

"But Kinky seemed happy for you both on Saturday. I'm sure she's over whatever bothered her. And one thing about being sick, it has a way of putting things into perspective very quickly."

"You're likely right." O'Reilly puffed his pipe. "But I remember an old saw about two women in one kitchen. Kinky's going to be a bit wobbly before she gets completely better and she may start to feel vulnerable again."

"I'm sure everything'll be fine," Barry said. "First we've to worry about getting Kinky back on her feet, and cross other bridges when we come to them."

O'Reilly raised an eyebrow. "Bridges? That's my line. Getting philosophical, Barry?"

"Well, I—"

"You're right," said O'Reilly. "When we come to them." He let go a blue cloud of pipe smoke. "There are a few practical matters which are more pressing though."

"Such as?"

"One. Once Kinky gets better and out of hospital she'll need to convalesce. Are you much of a nurse?"

"Me?"

"Nor me," O'Reilly said. "We'll have to let her sisters Fidelma and Sinead in Cork know about things as soon as we hear from Jack. They'll want to come up and see her, and when she's discharged they might want to have Kinky recuperate with them."

"That makes sense."

O'Reilly tamped the tobacco into the bowl of his pipe. "If not, we'll need to find someone here. Sonny and Maggie Houston have a big house and Maggie loves looking after folks."

Barry smiled. "If Kinky could put up with Maggie's stewed tea."

O'Reilly laughed. "Or her plum cake, but let's hope it doesn't come to that."

"Agreed."

"Number two," said O'Reilly. "How's your cooking? The magical thing Kinky usually does in the kitchen."

Barry laughed. "I lived at home, then went to a boarding school, student residence's refectory, houseman's mess, and now Number One, Main. I never learned how. I'd burn water boiling an egg."

Nor, he thought, had boys been expected to master the culinary arts. That's why only girls were taught "domestic science" at school. "Jack Mills showed me how to make a fried egg sandwich once when we were living in Royal Maternity if that helps."

"Hardly Cordon Bleu." O'Reilly smiled. "I learnt a bit when I was at sea, but it's pretty primitive. Spam fritters, corned beef hash, corned beef curry. I can fry up well enough and I can boil and mash, and fry potatoes. Make champ." He poked his pipe stem at Barry. "I thought being able to cook potatoes was in our Irish genes. I'm surprised Kinky was worried we'd have to do without them tonight."

Barry shook his head. "I've never trusted potatoes since An Gorta Mor, the Great Hunger of 1845." In truth he really didn't like spuds, unless they were roasted.

"Did you read the book?"

"Which one?"

"*The Great Hunger* by Cecil Woodham Smith."

"Never heard of him."

"Her," O'Reilly said. "This Cecil is a woman. She wrote about Florence Nightingale too, and the charge of the Light Brigade. She's a brilliant historian." He waved at the bookshelves. "Help yourself if you want to read the books."

"I will, and never mind famines. With your expertise, the magic tin-opener, and the humble sandwich," Barry said, "we'll not starve."

"True," O'Reilly said, "but it might mean you doing a bit more call if I'm going to be in the kitchen. At least when I am, I can field phone calls too."

"I'd be happy to do the visits," Barry said, and meant it. He enjoyed that aspect of rural practice, taking care of people in their own homes. He'd miss doing it when he left Ballybucklebo in July to take training in obstetrics and gynaecology in the Waveney Hospital in Ballymena.

"Good." O'Reilly tapped the mouthpiece of his pipe against his teeth. "Kitty's a great cook," he said. "She's coming down at the weekend to show you the ring I bought her today. I'll ask her if she'd mind making a few easy-to-heat dishes while she's here, or do some at her home and bring them down for us."

"Only if it's not too much trouble," Barry said.

"I did say I'd ask," O'Reilly said, "not order, but I'm sure she will. Kitty O'Hallorhan's a lovely woman."

Barry heard the deep affection in O'Reilly's voice. He could be envious of his senior's happiness, but even though Barry's own love life was in tatters he was delighted that Fingal had found Kitty.

The hall telephone rang. Barry flinched then rose. "That might be Jack Mills," he said, and raced for the stairs.

"I'm coming too," said O'Reilly.

4

Bones Are Smitten Asunder

He beat Barry to the receiver. "O'Reilly?"

Barry waited, tapping one foot.

O'Reilly listened. "Uh-huh. Uh-huh. I see. Uh-huh."

What did that mean? Barry held his breath. Was it Jack or Sir Donald Cromie calling about Kinky?

O'Reilly nodded, covered the mouthpiece with one hand, and shook his head. "It's Colin Brown's mother. He's done it again. Sounds like he's broken his arm this time."

"Oh." Barry stopped tapping and exhaled. He'd so hoped it was Jack with good or at least promising news. But other patients did need care too and Colin Brown had to be the most unlucky boy in Ballybucklebo. Last year Barry had stitched up the lad's hand. This year the boy had caught ringworm.

"Hang on, Connie," O'Reilly said. "I need to talk to Doctor Laverty." He looked at Barry. "If you'll nip round and see Colin, I'll wait to hear from the Royal, and start getting tea ready."

So, Barry thought, he'd not hear about Kinky for a while, damn it. "Fair enough. I know where they live. I'll get my bag, and splints." He took his coat off a peg, shrugged it on, and went to collect his gear. He heard O'Reilly say, "Don't worry, Connie. Doctor Laverty'll be round in ten minutes. Just keep Colin still and warm and try not to let him move the arm. If you have them, give him a couple of aspirin." The receiver tinged in its cradle.

Barry, packed doctor's bag in one hand, opened the front door. "I'll walk. It'll be quicker than getting my car."

"I'll see you when you get home. I'm sure I'll have heard from the Royal by then."

The pavements were drying in the late-afternoon spring sun. The April shower that earlier had drenched O'Reilly had passed and the air was crisp and felt freshly scrubbed. The Browns lived nearby in a thatched cottage next door to the tobacconist's, which was beside the Black Swan Pub, known to the natives as the Mucky Duck.

He paused at the traffic light beside the Maypole and waited for the light to change. Traffic was light on the Bangor to Belfast Road. The sign of the Duck creaked as it swung in a gentle breeze. A diesel lorry went by, belching black exhaust smoke, the stink of which smothered the usual mild attar of cow clap that always hung on from one weekly cattle market until the next.

"How's about ye, Doctor Laverty?" a man also waiting to cross said, raising his duncher. "Grand day for the time of year it's in, so it is."

The lights changed. "Afternoon, Gerry. Can't stop for a blether. Sorry, but I'm in a rush."

"You charge away on, sir."

Barry strode past Gerry Shanks, whose daughter Siobhan had recently recovered from bacterial meningitis. It was pleasant knowing your patients, their families, by name, not just as cases, and being greeted by them on the street. He'd miss that when he left in July, but Barry was looking forward to becoming a trainee obstetrician. And if he didn't like it, he had the option to return as a full partner here. It would be gratifying finally to answer the question, Where am I going? The question he'd first asked himself last July on his way to an interview with a certain Doctor Fingal Flahertie O'Reilly.

He stopped outside the red-painted door to the Browns' cottage, lifted the ring of a brass knocker cast as a lion's head, and rapped.

Connie Brown answered. "Come on on on in, Doctor," she said, and stood aside. She pointed to a towel wrapped round her head like a turban. "I must look a right mess. I was washing my hair, so I was."

"Don't worry about it, Connie. Where's your Colin?"

"I have him in the parlour. Poor wee mite, he must've took a ferocious purler."

It didn't surprise Barry that the boy had fallen down with a thump. Although he had just turned ten, Colin Brown attacked life with all the vigour of a terrier after a rat. Barry smelled boiled cabbage and fried bacon. Perhaps the Browns were going to have colcannon for their tea, a traditional Irish dish of spuds, cabbage, bacon, and butter.

"It's the doorway on your right," Connie said.

Barry went into a small room. Three plaster ducks climbed the whitewashed wall over a wood mantel above a coal fire. The room was warm and the light dim. Barry heard Colin's sobs before he made him out propped up on pillows, wrapped in a tartan shawl, sitting in a velvet-covered armchair several sizes too big for him. His legs didn't reach the linoleum-covered floor and his toes were turned in. He clutched his left forearm with his right hand.

"Nice Doctor Laverty's come to see youse, so he has," Connie said, and bent over her son.

Barry moved closer to the red-haired boy.

"Don't want him," Colin said, and sobbed. "Go away."

"What exactly happened, Connie?" Barry asked.

She fluffed her son's pillows and straightened up. "You mind his mouse, Maurice, died a wee while back?"

"I do."

"We were going to get a tortoise, but there weren't any at the pet store so his daddy got Colin a ferret instead, for a pet, like. He come home from school today, you know, done his homework, and went out into the yard for to play with Butch."

"Butch?"

"The ferret. Anyway, I heard a ferocious guldering and I rushed out and there was wee Colin, God love him, sitting up bawling his eyes out. He's yellin', 'Mammy. Mammy, it's me arm, Mammy. It's me arm.'"

She swallowed. "I didn't have the heart in me to look at it. I gathered him up, brung him in here, and got the fire going, so I did." She pulled in another deep breath. "And then I phoned. Thank God youse come so quick."

Barry's eyes had adjusted to the light. He could see no blood on Colin's shirtsleeve so there were probably no abrasions. More important, it was unlikely there was a compound fracture, where the jagged end of bone had torn through the skin. Such breaks were uncommon in children. The pain would be from a strain or a simple broken bone. It wouldn't be difficult to decide. "Let's have a look, Colin," Barry said, moving closer.

"You leave me be," Colin said. "It hurts." His voice was quavery and tears ran down his cheeks. Snot glistened on his upper lip.

"What hurts?" Barry asked.

"Me arm." He sniffed. "It hurts like buggery, so it does."

"Colin," Connie Brown shouted and wagged a finger. "I'll wash your mouth out with soap."

Colin's father, Lenny, was a notoriously foul-mouthed man, one who locally would be called a slubbergub. Barry ignored the little mother-son spat and asked, "What happened, Colin?"

Colin's lip trembled. The words tumbled out, punctuated by gasps of indrawn breath. "I was running to see Butch, and I tripped, and I fell down, and I put out my hand, like, and I got this ferocious stoon in my arm, and it still hurts, and Mammy brought me into the parlor, so she did. She said she wanted me by the fire, and then youse come."

"Can you wiggle your fingers?" Barry asked.

"No. It's too sore."

Pain. Loss of function. Two signs of a break. "Sure I can't take a look?" Barry was fairly certain he was dealing with a greenstick fracture of one or both of the forearm bones, the radius and ulna.

"My mammy won't let you," Colin said, inching back from Barry and turning piteous eyes on his mother.

"I think she might," Barry said.

As he had hoped, Connie came closer. "Come on, Colin, be a good boy. A big brave boy like a soldier. Doctor Laverty wants to make youse better, so he does. Mind when he fixed your wee hand?"

"No." Colin pouted. "Don't want to."

Poor little lad, Barry thought. Even if I'm unsure about choosing between GP and specialising, I know one thing. Whatever I do, it won't involve specialist paediatrics. He hated to see the wee ones in pain and terrified.

Connie moved closer, put her arms around her son, and adjusted the tartan shawl around his shoulders. "Doctor Laverty won't hurt you, son. Honest to God."

"No." Colin snuggled even closer against his mother.

Barry cast back to his hospital training. When persuasion failed, the child was pinoned by an orderly and examined while the nipper's screams and tears were ignored. That would not work here. He knew what O'Reilly would have done. Talked to the child. Tried to calm him. "So, Colin," Barry said, and he squatted so he didn't tower over the boy, "you've got a new pet."

Colin sniffed, but made no reply.

"Your mammy says you called him Witch." The mistake was deliberate.

"Butch," Colin said, peeping round past his mother. "Not Witch, you daft git. Butch. He's a boy ferret, so he is."

Barry saw Connie start to bristle again, but shook his head and smiled. "If you've got the energy to slag your doctor, you can't be feeling too badly, Colin Brown." Barry had no doubt the arm was broken, but there was no sign of shock if Colin could be so feisty. "What colour is Butch?"

"White," Colin said, "and he's ever so funny."

Barry waited.

"When he gets excited he goes lepping about all over the place hissing and making faces and hopping sideways. My daddy . . . he says . . . he knows about ferrets . . . he says that's called a weasel war dance, so it is."

"Could I come and get you to show me Butch one day, Colin? When your arm's better."

"Aye, certainly, couldn't he, Mammy?" Colin looked up at his mother.

"I'll make you a cup of tea when you do, Doctor," Connie said, clearly forcing a smile, then inclining her head toward Colin's arm.

"Tell you what, Mammy, could you help Colin roll up his sleeve?"

"I think so." Connie bent and unbuttoned Colin's shirtsleeve. His eyes never left his mother's face as she rolled the material one-third of the way up to where Colin supported the arm with his other hand.

"Now," said Barry, "did that hurt, Colin?"

The boy shook his head.

"If Mammy holds your hand and you hold your elbow, I think we can get the sleeve up a bit more so I can see the sore bit. Just to look at."

"Colin?" Connie asked. "Will we do what the doctor asks?"

Colin took a deep breath, and nodded.

"You'll need to let go of it," Barry said, and Colin obeyed. In no time Barry had carefully pushed the sleeve farther up. He could see that the forearm was bent out of its usual straight line into a curve. Another diagnostic sign. "Point to where it's sorest, Colin."

Colin's index finger hovered over the crown of the curve, the place where a moment ago he'd been cradling it. Local bone tenderness. Sign four. That was enough to confirm Barry's suspicions. He said, "I'm going to get a splint and bandages."

"Is it," Connie silently mouthed, "broken?"

"I think so."

She sighed. "Thank God it's not fractured, so it's not."

Barry had given up trying to explain that broken and fractured were the same thing. The entire population of Ulster, it seemed to him, was quite willing to accept a bone being broken, but the thought of a fracture filled them with dread. Perhaps because in pre-antibiotic days, compound fractures could become infected and gangrenous, and the limb would have to be amputated. Gangrene. For a moment Barry was distracted. If Kinky had a strangulated hernia, gangrene of the bowel was a risk. Concentrate, he told himself. Colin has a greenstick fracture where one side of the bone has cracked, but the opposite is intact. The same thing would happen to a young tree branch if you bent it far enough. The arm needed to be splinted to immobilise it and protect Colin from more pain. Later, in hospital, it would be set. "I'll just be a minute," he said. "Keep your arm still, Colin."

Barry took what he needed from his bag. His movements were deliberate, but in a short time, with Connie's help, he had put the forearm at right angles to the upper arm, thumb upward, palm toward the body, and had applied splints on the inner and outer sides of the forearm. "Now," he said, "bandages to hold the splints, and a sling." It was a good thing, he thought as he worked, that as a kid he'd been a Sea Scout and had passed his first-aid badge. This kind of splinting wasn't taught at medical school but was left to volunteers trained by the Saint John's Ambulance Brigade or to ambulance attendants, those who were usually first at the scene of any accident.

He stood, the job done. "How's that, Colin?"

"All right, so it is." The little lad wiped his nose along his right sleeve.

"Colin, use your hanky, for God's sake," Connie said.

Barry had a vivid image of one small boy in Belfast taunting another. "Hey, silver sleeves? Away on home. Your mammy wants ye."

"Now, Connie," said Barry, "can I use your phone?" He inclined his head to indicate she should follow.

"Aye, certainly. You be good for a wee minute, Colin." She led Barry into the hall. "Thonder." She pointed at a Bakelite receiver on a hall table. "Is it really bad, like?"

Barry shook his head. "Not really, but he'll need to go to hospital for an X-ray to be sure the bones are broken, and if they are he'll be given an anaesthetic so a surgeon can set the bone properly, pad the arm, and put on a plaster cast. Don't give him anything to eat or drink. He'll need to have an empty tummy for the anaesthetic and he'll have to stay in tonight, but you'll get him home tomorrow. The cast'll be taken off in six weeks. Don't be too worried. At his age kids heal perfectly."

"Thank God for that." She hesitated then asked, "We've no motorcar and my man won't be home from work for hours. Will I take him now on the train or bus up to Belfast?"

Barry shook his head. "That's what the country ambulance is for, but you'll have to get him home yourself tomorrow."

"Fair enough. I'm sure we can get a lift."

"I'll call for the ambulance. You go and keep Colin company. I'll be in in a minute."

Barry made the arrangements, went back into the parlour, and squatted beside Colin.

The little lad fixed Barry with an inquisitive glare. "Now what? Am I all fixed?"

Barry shook his head. "Did you ever go for a ride in an ambulance?"

"No," said Colin, pulling back. "Don't want to."

"Be a pity if you miss it," Barry said. "You could get the driver to go nee-naw on his siren."

"Right enough?" Colin leant forward.

"I'll bet you none of the boys in your class'll have had an ambulance ride."

"Aye." Colin managed a weak smile.

Barry said, "You've bust your arm, Colin. You need a plaster of Paris cast to hold it steady until the bones knit, and when you get back to school—"

"You mean I've to be off, like?" Colin brightened.

"I do indeed. Until next Monday."

"Wheeker," Colin said, and his grin was from ear to ear. "I can play with Butch all I want. Teach him tricks, like."

Barry chuckled. He knew that school was not Colin's favourite pastime. "And when you get back all your friends can sign your cast."

"Honest?"

"Cross my heart." Barry did.

"All except Art O'Callaghan. He's a right wee willick, so he is."

"Colin," Connie said.

Barry laughed, stood, and said, "When you get home, you tell your mammy if it still hurts or if your fingers swell up. And if Colin does, Connie, send for me. Sometimes if the arm swells a cast can get to be too tight and has to be split." Barry headed for the door, turned, and said, "I'll pop in later in the week, and I want to see Butch when I come."

"Och," said Colin, "could I not show him to you now?"

Barry shook his head. "Sorry," he said. "I have to get back to Number One. Doctor O'Reilly's making our tea."

Connie said, "Because Mrs. Kincaid's poorly."

Barry shook his head. He should have known word would be out in the village by now.

"I know because Aggie Arbuthnot, her that's Cissie Sloan's cousin, was passing Doctor O'Reilly's house a wee while back. She seen the ambulance and she said the attendants were putting Kinky in the back. Aggie popped in here to borrow some baking powder for to make biscuits before Colin took his purler." She looked Barry in the eye. "It's not serious with Mrs. Kincaid, is it, sir?"

He heard the concern in her voice and admired how Connie, who must be worried about Colin, could still find time to ask about Kinky. He knew Connie's question wasn't coming from idle curiosity. She cared. "I hope it's not," he said, "but you know I can't tell you any more. Kinky's family, but she's also my patient."

"I understand, Doctor, but if youse see her will you tell her I was asking about her?"

"I will, Connie." He went into the hall. "Now, I really must be running on. Try not to fret about Colin. He'll be fine," he said, and let himself out.

As he strode rapidly back to Number One he hoped to God O'Reilly had heard about Kinky so they had a clear idea about what was happening to her. When it came to family and friends, doctors were no better at dealing with medical uncertainty than a mother dealing with a hurt child.

5

Make unto All People a Feast of Fat Things

"I n the kitchen," bawled O'Reilly in answer to Barry's, "Where are you, Fingal?" He didn't wait to take off his coat, but headed straight in the direction of O'Reilly's roaring. The big man, stripped to his shirtsleeves, red braces crossed at his back, wrapped in one of Kinky's floral aprons, sat peeling a potato.

Despite his concern for Kinky, Barry had to stifle a laugh. A nearly empty glass of what he knew was Jameson's whiskey sat on the table beside a saucepan of water.

"Before you ask," O'Reilly said, "Cromie called. His examination and an X-ray have confirmed that Kinky has a strangulated inguinal hernia with a loop of jejunem trapped. The X-ray was quite clear. Classic concertina pattern."

"Now we know exactly what's wrong." Barry felt himself relax. "Thank goodness it's something treatable."

"And your diagnosis was right," said O'Reilly. "Good for you."

Barry dipped his head and took a certain selfish pleasure from having been right. "A strangulated hernia's not a great thing to have, but it could be worse. Much worse."

"It could," O'Reilly said. "Cromie asked me if I knew exactly when the pains had started, and I did, because you'd told me. He reckoned he'd time the onset of strangulation from when she started having pain at short intervals and vomiting. That gives him a start point of one thirty. He says he'll try conservative treatment for a while."

At least, Barry thought, part of that regimen was to give large doses of morphine. Finally she'd be getting relief from the pains.

"Cromie's none too sanguine. Six hours from onset will soon be up—"

"And if the bowel doesn't slip free by then, gangrene will set in." Barry knew he'd been right to worry about that. This time being correct gave him no pleasure. None at all.

"So it is likely they will operate." O'Reilly looked at his watch. "It's five thirty now. They'll go ahead at seven to give themselves half an hour's leeway." He dropped the peeled potato into the saucepan and grabbed another spud.

"Poor Kinky," Barry said. A tube would have been passed through her nose and down into her stomach to remove gastric secretions and any toxins that might accumulate above the blockage. With an intravenous dripping saline into a vein, she'd be nursed head down, feet up in the hope the bowel might slip free. He could imagine the pain going on until the narcotic at last took effect. "At least we know what's happening, and thank the Lord for morphine."

"Indeed," said O'Reilly. "Called after Morpheus—"

"Greek god of dreams," Barry said.

"Son of Hypnos, the god of sleep," parried O'Reilly, and with a flourish dropped another potato into the pot.

Barry smiled. This was a practised game between them now, Fingal spouting trivia and Barry rising to the bait like a trout to a fly to show he wasn't entirely unlettered. Barry decided it wasn't because of their lack of concern for Kinky, but rather relief at having had the uncertainty about her removed. Now that they knew the prognosis was good their emotional safety valves were blowing off steam.

"Cromie said he or Jack'll let us know if they've decided to operate and they'll phone us again once they've finished. I'll give one of her sisters a call after dinner."

"Decent of you, Fingal, and decent of the surgeons to keep us up to date," Barry said, knowing full well that few consultants made time to keep referring GPs apprised of their patients' progress.

"Cromie and I go back a long way. It's not what you know, Barry. It's who."

"My father often says that," Barry said.

"I learned it from him when we served on HMS *Warspite,* in the war." O'Reilly held a lit match over a ring on the stovetop. The resultant loud *pop* and ring of bright blue flames made Barry flinch, but O'Reilly seemed unconcerned. "Grub," he said, and blew out the match.

He put the saucepan of potatoes on the flames. "I've preheated the oven," he said. "Fetch that pie." He pointed to an oval Pyrex dish on a counter near Barry. "Put it on the counter here." O'Reilly dipped a brush into a cup. "Egg yolk," he said. "I've watched Kinky do this. Monkey see. Monkey do." He painted the yolk on the pie crust.

"Mmm, I think that's already been done, Fingal."

O'Reilly grinned. "Bit more won't hurt." He set the brush aside then opened the oven door and popped the pie in. "Thirty minutes and everything'll be done," he said.

"Kinky told me twenty-five minutes at medium," Barry said.

"Medium?" O'Reilly peered at the knurled wheel on the oven door. "I guessed that'd be about four hundred fifty. That's what it's at, and an extra five minutes won't do it any harm. I like my crust nice and brown," O'Reilly said.

Barry had a vague recollection of his mother using a setting of 350° to reheat already cooked food but decided to keep his counsel.

"Then at the start of the first dog watch, or if you prefer six o'clock, a feast fit for a couple of kings for us, lad." He dropped his bantering tone. "And not long to wait after we've finished eating to hear what's going to happen next in the Royal."

Barry recognised what Fingal was doing. It was primitive, probably a throwback to when their ancestors wore skins, but by refusing to mention Kinky by name, O'Reilly, like Barry, was trying to pretend nothing was happening to her, or could.

O'Reilly untied his apron. "In the meantime," he said, finishing the whiskey in one swallow, "I suggest we have a small libation, but unlike the ancient Greeks, refrain from pouring the sacrifice on the earth and use our throats instead." He set the apron aside. "Come on. Upstairs to the lounge."

"I'll get out of my coat and I'll be right up," Barry said.

He hung his coat in the hall and was heading for the stairs when the doorbell rang. Now what? Barry opened the door to find Maggie MacCorkle smiling her toothless smile.

"Hello, Doctor dear," she said. A limp daffodil adorned her hatband. "I'll only keep you a wee minute, so I will."

"Come in, Maggie."

"Och, no. I'll not be stopping." She proffered a brown paper bag. "John McIlderry, him that works at City Hall, came out to bring Sonny some townland records, you know . . . the oul goat's looking for a hill fort or a passage grave or some ancient ould thing near Ballybucklebo. You know what he's like about his archaeology." She raised her eyes to the heavens. "Anyways, John telt us Kinky was sick. He'd heard it from Cissie Sloan, so he had."

Who'd heard it from Aggie Arbuthnot, Barry thought.

"Sonny reckoned, no harm to yiz, but you and himself might not be the greatest cooks. Sonny's out in the motor—"

Barry leaned past Maggie and waved at Sonny, who was sitting in his parked 1954 Sunbeam-Talbot.

Sonny waved back.

"So we thought we'd bring youse this here cottage pie I'd made yesterday and had in the fridge." She shook the parcel. "And I put in a couple of slices of my plum cake for afters."

Barry accepted the bag. "That's very kind," he said,

hoping, ungraciously he knew, that Maggie's cottage pies were not as God-awful as her plum cake. "Thank you."

"Is Kinky going to be all right, sir?" Maggie had lowered her voice.

"She's in the Royal and she's comfortable," Barry said, knowing he sounded like an official hospital bulletin, "but that's all I can say. Sorry, Maggie."

"Och, aye. I know you're like priests, you doctors. Have to keep things confidential, like."

"That's it, Maggie, but we'll let her know you both were asking for her, and please thank Sonny."

"You and himself just let us know if you need anything," Maggie said, "and there's no rush to get the pie dish back when you've done." She turned, then called back over her shoulder, "Just drop it in some day you're passing."

"Right." You didn't get people like Maggie and Sonny fussing over you when you worked in a teaching hospital, Barry thought as he trotted through to the kitchen to pop the bag in the fridge.

He heard a roar from upstairs.

"Are you coming tonight, Laverty?"

"Take your hurry in your hand," he called back up and trotted to the staircase.

"Jameson or sherry?" O'Reilly was standing at the sideboard when Barry entered the room.

Barry hesitated then said, "Whiskey, please."

O'Reilly, who already had his own glass refilled, poured and handed Barry his. "Who was that?"

"Maggie and Sonny with a cottage pie."

O'Reilly nodded. "News travels," he said. "Come and sit down." He moved to an armchair, shooed Lady Macbeth out of the seat, sat, and made no objection when the little cat sprang into his lap and curled up in a purring ball.

Barry took the other chair. "*Sláinte.*" He sipped the smooth Irish whiskey.

"Cheers." O'Reilly drank. "How's Colin?"

"Greenstick. I splinted it and sent him to the Royal."

"Good man." O'Reilly scratched Lady Macbeth's head. "And I'll say again that you were absolutely right to send Kinky too so you'd be here if anybody needed one of us while I was out." He frowned. "It's dawned on me how much we're going to miss having her here to answer the phone or doorbell."

"We should be able to manage. One here, one out doing calls, like this afternoon."

O'Reilly frowned. "I'm not so sure. What if both of us are out? Or take tomorrow. Someone must go and see Kinky."

"She'd appreciate it if it's you, Fingal."

"I know. I'll look in on Donal Donnelly too. See how he's doing."

Donal. With all the anxiety about Kinky, Barry had forgotten that Ballybucklebo's arch-schemer had had a head injury last Saturday, been operated on that night for the removal of an intracranial blood clot, and was recovering well. "Say hello to him too."

"I will." O'Reilly paused. "Trouble is if you're out on a visit—"

"There'll be no one to answer if a patient calls here." Barry frowned. "Any chance we could get a temporary receptionist?"

"I doubt it," O'Reilly said, "but you never know." He took another swallow. "There's one thing in our favour. By now everybody in the village, aye, and most of the townland, will know Kinky's sick. They'll probably understand if they phone and there's no one here to answer." O'Reilly finished his whiskey and handed the glass to Barry. "Get me another, like a good lad. I don't want to disturb her ladyship."

Barry put his glass on a table and went to the sideboard. He sloshed a finger of whiskey into O'Reilly's glass. "Here."

"Cheers." O'Reilly raised his glass.

The front doorbell rang.

"Bugger it," said O'Reilly, rising, decanting Lady Macbeth, and putting his drink on the sideboard. "My turn, and I want to see how my spuds are coming on anyway. I'll be back in a minute."

Barry rose, sipped his drink, and wandered over to the bookshelf. It was all very well for O'Reilly to recommend a book about the charge of the Light Brigade. The man had absolutely no system of shelving his books. Two of Graham Greene's novels were separated by *The Wind in the Willows* and, Barry had to tilt his head to one side to read the upside-down title of *Rudyard Kipling's Verse. Inclusive Edition 1885–*

1926. He scanned book spines until he saw, on a shelf he could only reach by standing on tiptoe, *The Reason Why: The Story of the Fatal Charge of the Light Brigade* by Cecil Woodham-Smith. He pulled it down and read in the Acknowledgement, *This curious story has never been told before—* Good start, he thought. The author's got my interest. He was well into chapter one when Fingal reappeared.

"Spuds are coming on a treat," he said, "and I peeped in the oven. Talk about a scrumptious smell, and my egg yolk's browning the pastry to perfection. We'll eat in five minutes."

"Who was at the door this time, Fingal?" he asked.

"Alice Moloney," he said. "Bacon-and-egg pie for us and please give Kinky her love and wish her a speedy recovery. I put it in the fridge." He picked up his whiskey. "Bring your drink. It'll take me a minute to prepare things."

Barry rose and followed O'Reilly. As they reached the hall the doorbell and the phone rang. O'Reilly grabbed the phone and nodded to the door, which Barry, glass in hand, answered. "Cissie Sloan," he said, slipping the hand with the glass behind his back. He could hear the cadence of O'Reilly's voice, but not the words. Was it news about Kinky? "Come in," Barry said.

"I'll not, thanks, but my cousin Aggie, you know, her with the six toes, says Mrs. Kincaid's poorly and—"

"She is," Barry said, hoping to dam the verbal tide for which Cissie was renowned.

"I mind the last time Kinky got sick. I was telling Flo Bishop about it just there now. I seen her when I was walking over here, like."

Barry reckoned the entire population of the village must know about Kinky now.

"It was ages ago, so it was, 1954, the Coronation—" She stopped dead and tapped her temple with an index finger. "Amn't I the right eejit? The Queen was crowned in 1953 . . . anyroad Kinky was taken sick when they opened the festival of Britain."

"That was 1951, Cissie." Barry'd been eleven at the time and most impressed with the Skylon.

"Right enough? Then she must've got poorly in '52. Do you know, Doctor? See me? Some days my head's a marley. Full of hobbyhorse shite, so it is. I'd forget my own name."

Barry had two choices. He could agree that Cissie could indeed be absentminded or draw from his stock of kindly white lies. He chose the latter. "Nonsense, Cissie. Now, what can I do for you?" He really did want to know who was on that phone.

"Here y'are," she said, thrusting forward a grease-proof paper-wrapped parcel. "I got this recipe from my ma, and she got it from an Englishwoman who was in Holywood in the last war because her husband was a soldier stationed in Place Barracks there for a while. He was with the Royal Ulster Rifles, you know, their nickname's 'The Stickies,' so it is."

Barry accepted the parcel and quickly asked, "And

this is?" He reckoned he had to distract her before she could launch into a telling of all the regiment's battle honours since it was raised in 1793.

"In the old days it was a bugger, pardon my French, boiling down the pigs' trotters to make the gelatin for it, but you can buy that in the shops now."

"And *it* is?"

She grinned. "A couple of Melton Mowbray pies. They go a treat cold with Branston pickle, so they do."

"Thank you, Cissie. I'm sure they'll be lovely."

She dropped a tiny curtsey. "I'll be running along, then," she said, "but if there's anything youse and Doctor O'Reilly need?"

"Thank you, Cissie," O'Reilly said over Barry's shoulder, "and I'll be seeing Kinky tomorrow. I'll give her your love."

"Sir." She left.

"Good," said O'Reilly, peering up and down the road, "I don't see any three-legged asses, but that one could talk the hind leg off a donkey." He headed for the dining room. "Food. I've taken it through to the dining room. Come on."

With the drink he'd been hiding from Cissie in one hand and the Melton Mobray pies in the other, Barry followed O'Reilly into the dining room, sat, and put the pies on the table. "From Cissie," he said. "Pork pies. Now, who was on the phone?"

"Not the hospital. I'll tell you while we eat."

Barry glanced at his watch. Six ten. He should have realised it was too early to hear from the Royal. He looked at O'Reilly, who had put a tureen near himself. "Boiled spuds," he said, lifting the lid, "should have been floury things of beauty, but that phone call and Cissie held us up. They're a bit overdone now. Sorry."

Barry smiled. The big man was just like his mother, a superb cook who was forever apologising because she never felt her efforts were quite up to standard.

"And, *la piéce de résistance*." With a flourish O'Reilly waved his left hand above his head, wrist cocked, and with his right set a plate bearing the pie dish in front of Barry. "*Voila*. Note the brown beauty of the crust."

Barry thought perhaps the pastry should be a golden brown rather than deep mahogany.

O'Reilly sat at the head of the table. He handed Barry a large knife and a silver triangular server. "Do the honours, lad, and get a move on. As an old Dublin patient of mine used to say, 'I'm so hungry I could eat a farmer's arse through a tennis racquet.' I can taste those spuds soaked in the gravy from the pie."

Barry laughed as he sank the knife into the crust. A plume of steam escaped with the scent of cooked meat. Very well-cooked meat. He carved a wedge and placed it on Fingal's plate, already half full of potatoes. He started to serve himself when he heard a strangled noise followed by a loud "Bloody hell."

"What's up?"

"Look in your pie," O'Reilly roared. "Look in the bloody thing."

Barry peeled back the upper crust. Where there should have been tender steak and firm kidney surrounded by a rich gravy, only a few shrivelled pieces of meat sat beside black desiccated kidney slices. The gravy had congealed into lumps. "Oh dear," he said, and recalled that P. G. Wodehouse had famously remarked, "It is never difficult to distinguish between a Scotsman with a grievance and a ray of sunshine." Much the same could be said about a hungry Fingal Flahertie O'Reilly and a well-fed one.

"It's all Helen Hewitt's fault."

Barry shook his head. Sometimes O'Reilly's logic still lost Barry. "Helen Hewitt?" He remembered the young woman: pretty, green eyes, eczema—

"If she hadn't kept me on the phone so long. Still," O'Reilly said, "she's manna from heaven. We have a need and Providence has provided. You remember when Helen quit as Alice Moloney's shop assistant and got a job in a linen mill?"

"I do."

"The mill closed down last week. Helen's out of work. She heard about Kinky from Mary Dunleavy, the publican's daughter. Helen put two and two together and guessed we need someone to answer the phone—"

"Brilliant," Barry said, "and she was bloody quick off the mark. That shows initiative."

"I thought so too. She'll start tomorrow at lunchtime. Now, speaking of manna," said O'Reilly, "and in the culinary sense. Kinky makes her own Branston pickle." He rose. "I'll go and get some and we can eat up the pork pies. Starvation won't be on our agenda and I'm sure Arthur will enjoy the burnt steak and kidney." He took the remains of the pie and left.

The phone rang. "I'll get it," Barry said, sprang to his feet, and ran.

"Hello, Barry, just wanted to let you know the boss is starting to scrub. We'll be operating a bit earlier than anticipated," Jack Mills said.

Barry swallowed. "Has she got worse?"

"No. Sir Donald, and God knows how many of these things he's seen, feels we're on a hiding to nothing waiting for this to cure itself. We might as well get on with it."

"But at least she's no worse. Is she awake?"

"Anaesthetised, and I'd better trot. I'm assisting."

"Will you see her postop after she wakes up?"

"Sure."

"Tell her O'Reilly and I wish her—"

"Done, and I'll give you a ring once we've finished. Let you know what we found."

"Thanks, Jack. I'll go and tell O'Reilly." He hung up.

"No need to go. I'm here. I heard you and can work it out." Barry hadn't been aware of the big man's approach. "She's no worse, but they're operating," O'Reilly said.

"Right."

O'Reilly nodded. Pursed his lips. "I don't know if you're a praying man, Barry. I'm not, but if you are, say one for Kinky, and if you're not, close your eyes and think hard about her for a little while and I'll do the same."

Barry bowed his head. When he looked up, O'Reilly was standing stock still, eyes closed. He opened them. "Good luck, Kinky Kincaid," he said softly, and Barry silently mouthed, "Amen."

6

Under the Knife

O'Reilly heard the blue plastic doors slap shut behind him. The ward smells of human efflu-ent, powerful disinfectant, and floor polish must be universal, he thought. If he closed his eyes, Fingal O'Reilly could have been back thirty years ago in the teaching hospitals of Dublin. He strode along the hall to the long, narrow, twenty-four-bedded ward as a door to his left opened and a short man in a long white coat appeared. He was bald save for a fringe round the back and sides. He wore a Trinity College Dublin tie and his green eyes were smiling.

"Doctor O'Reilly. Good to see you," he said, offering his hand.

"Sir Donald." Fingal shook the hand. They'd been Fingal and Cromie for thirty-odd years, but in public the professional niceties had to be observed.

"Before you ask, she's doing fine." He nodded to the door. "Seeing she is who she is, I put her in the side ward by herself and she's out of bounds to the medical students."

O'Reilly knew that each unit had a single room, the side ward, where very seriously ill patients or those who needed to be isolated were nursed. By putting Kinky in there, Sir Donald was giving her a free private room. "Thanks for that, Cromie," he said. "I appreciate it and I know Kinky will."

"I'm pleased with her," Cromie said. "The surgery was straightforward and we'll keep a close eye on her postop. Should get her out by next week."

O'Reilly had already had a blow-by-blow description of the operation last night from Jack Mills. He was quite content to take his old friend's word for it today. "Thanks for looking after her—"

"It's what I'm here for."

"You and Charlie Greer."

"What's old Charlie been up to?"

"Did an extradural for a patient of mine. I'm going to see the man when I leave here. And that reminds me, I need to talk to you about something Charlie brought up about a class reunion next year, but I'll give you a call in a day or two to see if the three of us can get together to start planning it. You're busy now and I really want to see Kinky."

"Fair enough." Sir Donald looked at his watch. "Got to run, and don't worry, I'll have young Mills give you a daily update until she's ready for discharge."

"Thanks." O'Reilly turned to the door, let himself into the side ward, and closed the door behind him. "Mrs. Kinky Kincaid," he said, "good morning."

Kinky stared at him, blinked, and on her dry lips a tiny smile played despite the plastic tube that was taped to the side of her forehead and curled into a nostril. "Doctor O'Reilly, sir. Good of you to come." She was propped up on pillows and flapped one hand in the direction of a hard wooden chair. "Please sit down, sir." Her voice was weak and she was pale. As he sat, O'Reilly noticed that her silver hair had been neatly brushed and hung to her shoulders. He studied her pupils. Both were tiny, a sure sign she'd been given morphine. A red rubber intravenous line ran to a needle in an elbow vein from a glass bottle of saline suspended on a pole. "Well now, Kinky Kincaid," he said, "how are you feeling?"

"I am all the better for seeing yourself, sir, so. Thank you."

He took her free hand in his. The skin felt cool and dry. "You're not looking too bad yourself, Kinky," he said, "considering you've been through the wars." He took her pulse. It was normal.

"I'm mending now, sir. And those awful spasms have gone away, so. I don't miss them one bit. Not one bit. My tummy's sore where they cut me—" She winced. "—but sure you can't pickle a herring without killing the fish. That nice surgeon, Sir Donald, says I'll be charging 'round like a liltie in no time. I'll be back to running Number One before you and Doctor Laverty starve or run out of clean socks."

"Kinky Kincaid," O'Reilly said, "Sir Donald's idea of 'no time' doesn't mean in a day or two." O'Reilly didn't want to discourage her, but he didn't want her to have unrealistic expectations. "You were a very sick woman last night. You've had surgery. That knocks the stuffing out of anybody. It'll be a week before you're even out of here. And if you're worried about our socks, there's always Lilliput Laundry. They pick up and deliver."

"But," she said, struggling to sit straight up, "what'll you eat?"

"Not our socks, anyway," he said, and was pleased to see a smile return. "You lie still now." He laid a hand gently on her shoulder.

She sank back on her pillow, closed her eyes, and gasped.

O'Reilly waited until she looked at him again, then said, "We're managing fine. That steak and kidney last night? Delicious." Liar, he thought, but in a good cause. "And you know what Ballybucklebo's like. You'd need to beat our neighbours off with a big stick." He saw her relax and wondered if he could make her smile again. "I know what hospital grub's like. You're not allowed to eat yet, I understand, but when you are, I've two slices of Maggie MacCorkle's plum cake I could bring up." He heard a faint chuckle.

"Doctor O'Reilly, sir," she said with a little grin, "you do be a terrible one for taking a hand out of a poor Cork widow woman."

O'Reilly noticed that the toy hare Barry had mentioned was on the pillow beside her. "Doctor Laverty sends his love, says please get better soon."

"He's a nice young man."

"He is that," O'Reilly said, then, "I spoke to your sister Fidelma last night and Sinead was there too. She and Malachy send love. Fidelma said to tell you she's getting Eamon to drive her up."

"Thank you for letting them know. I've not seen them for a while." She frowned. "It's a brave stretch of the legs from Beal na mBláth."

O'Reilly laughed. "Your sister said you'd say that and to tell you to pay no heed. They're coming and that's that."

"Fidelma and me were always close."

"I think," said O'Reilly, "they've a half-notion to take you down to Cork to convalesce." He knew that six weeks was the generally recommended term, but he'd keep that to himself for now. "Let's see how you are next week, all right?"

She struggled forward. "But, sir, who'll look after Number One?" He heard her anxiety.

"Kinky Kincaid," he said firmly. "You will, but only

when you're on your feet. In the meantime, Barry and I can manage and I've already told you about the neighbours. We're coming down with pies, stews, roast chickens."

She lay back on her pillows. "I suppose."

"And I'm sure Kitty—"

"Miss O'Hallorhan?" She frowned. "In my kitchen?"

"Not at all." O'Reilly had been going to say, "will help." As tactful as a blow to the head with a ball-peen hammer, he thought, and instead said, "will be distressed to hear you're not well. I'll tell her when I see her." He rose and squeezed her hand before releasing it. "Now Kinky," he said, "I mustn't tire you out. You need your rest."

"Thank you for coming, sir, and please thank Doctor Laverty for seeing to me yesterday," she said. "Please look after yourself. All I've got here in the north is yourself and Number One." A tear trickled.

"We'll have you back there in no time," O'Reilly managed, but only just. His throat was tight.

Kinky lay back on her pillows and closed her eyes. Her breathing slowed and in moments she was snoring gently.

Fingal Flahertie O'Reilly bent and gently kissed her forehead. "Sleep well, Kinky Kincaid," he said. "Sleep well."

7

I Am Getting Better and Better

"Have you come to see Donal?" Sister Jane Hoey was sitting by herself at the Ward 21 desk in Quinn House, the neurosurgery unit of the Royal Victoria Hospital. The normally serious nurse smiled.

It was unusual for nurses to refer to patients by their first names. Donal Donnelly must have made an impression. "Please," O'Reilly said.

"Quite the character."

"I do know. What's he been up to?"

She laughed, and he could hear affection belying her words. "The sooner we get that buck eejit off my ward the better. He's been running a poker school, and making book on what time the tea trolley will get here."

"He's what?" O'Reilly couldn't help laughing. "He's incorrigible, that man. Still, it's a sure sign he's on the mend."

"We moved him to a four-bedded ward on Monday morning. By Monday evening it was a miracle he didn't have a roulette wheel working," she said. "Make sure you keep an eye on your wallet when you see him, Doctor O'Reilly. At least he's being discharged tomorrow."

Still chuckling, O'Reilly walked along the corridor of the octagonal building. Donal had been moved from a single room in the inner core, where the critically ill patients were nursed, to one on the outer side of the corridor, which meant he was getting better. Two of the other recovering patients in Donal's ward were playing cards at a table in the space between the beds. The third was in bed, snoring.

Donal, head swathed in a turban of white bandages, sat on a chair by his bed reading a tattered copy of *Reader's Digest*. A vase of wilted flowers kept a bunch of grapes and bottle of Lucozade company on a bedside locker. His bed was close to a window that gave a view across a lawn to the red-brick Royal Maternity Hospital.

Donal looked up and grinned. "How's about ye, Doc?" Donal's buck teeth had survived the fall intact.

"I'm fine, Donal. How are you?"

"I'm keeping rightly, so I am. Dead on. The ould dome still hurts," he pointed to his bandages, "but, och, I never worry." He indicated another chair. "Grab a pew, sir. Right decent of youse to come and see me, and that lady friend of yours, Sister O'Hallorhan? She's been a real corker. The way she looks after me is great, so it is."

O'Reilly was not surprised that Donal thought Kitty O'Hallorhan, whom he had met several times in Ballybucklebo, was outstanding. She was. And of course she'd give Donal a bit of extra TLC because he was Fingal's patient. He sat. "I'll tell her you said so next time I see her."

"Thanks, sir. I'm getting out the morrow," Donal said. "Julie's coming at ten for til take me home." He took a deep breath. "One of the nurses told her you saved my life. I'm very grate—"

"Wheest, Donal. All I did was get you into an ambulance."

"From what I hear, I've been one jammy bugger."

"You'd some luck, I grant you, but it's Mister Greer and Mister Gupta, the doctor who saw you first when you were admitted, you need to thank."

"No harm til youse, sir, but you're a hard man to thank, so you are."

O'Reilly made a guttural noise. "Bollix," he said. He'd only done what any doctor should have. "You'll be glad to get home," he said, changing the subject.

Donal's smile faded. "Huh. I'll not be sorry for to see the back of this place, though. That Sister Hoey. See that one? See her?" Donal's tone rose.

O'Reilly caught himself glancing in the direction of the door even though he knew that in Ulster, the expression didn't actually mean you could see someone. Donal was using "see her" for emphasis, and none too kindly either.

"Right spoilsport, so she is. Them three lads?" Donal nodded at his wardmates. "We had a wee poker school going, but she stopped it. And she made me give them back their money on the book I was making on the tea trolley, so she did, before it got here." He pouted. "I'd've made three pounds if she'd not interfered."

"You're no dozer, Donal Donnelly," O'Reilly said, chuckled, and leant closer. "As one betting man to another, how in the name of the sainted Jasus were you sure you were going to win?" Donal had a reputation for arranging for dogs to win greyhound races.

Donal shook his head and held a finger to his lips.

"All right, Donal. I understand."

"But I would have won. Sure thing." He winked at O'Reilly.

O'Reilly rose.

"Excuse me, sir, could I ask you a wee quick question, like, before you go?"

"Of course."

"When I get home and my feet under me, would you and maybe Doctor Laverty have time to look at a house?"

"A house? What house?" For many Ballybucklebo folks their doctor was, along with their priest or minister, the font of all wisdom and expected to render opinions on nonmedical matters too.

"I may be a bit hazy about the crash and what went before, like," said Donal, "but Julie told me I won a right clatter at the races and she's got a wee bit put by."

O'Reilly smiled. He'd helped Julie acquire some of that "wee bit."

"We'd like for to buy a house, so we would. Nothing special, like, but a place of our own, and I've heard, on the quiet like, of one that might be going cheap, you know. It's a lovely wee place, so it is," Donal said. "It's only a ways out of the village on the Bangor side. Where there's a big hairpin bend in the Bangor Belfast Road? It'd be close enough for me to ride my bike to work." He grinned. "Or nip into the Duck."

"You're a bloody menace when you're sober on that multicoloured bike," O'Reilly said. "I shudder to think of you with a skinful riding it on the Bangor Belfast Road."

Donal looked at O'Reilly in much the way, he thought, Arthur Guinness could, and said, "When the wean comes in another three months I'll be going dead easy on the booze."

"You're looking forward to being a daddy, aren't you, Donal?"

"It's going to be the best thing since sliced pan, so it is. Dead wheeker. And that's another thing about the house. Julie can get the bus for to go to the shops, do her messages, like, and there's a lovely kindergarten just up the road. For later, like, when the nipper's starting to grow up."

"You've it all planned, haven't you?"

"Aye," said Donal, "and there's one more thing. It's got a great wee garden behind a hedge where I can put in a kennel and a dog run for Bluebird."

"Still racing her?" O'Reilly asked. He had a soft spot for Donal's racing greyhound.

Donal shook his head. "I can't get decent odds no more, she's so bloody fast. All the tracks know the dog, but," he dropped a slow wink, "I've a half-notion how to—"

"Uh-uh, Donal. I don't want to know." O'Reilly had been involved in a few of Donal's harebrained schemes. Not this time.

"Fair enough, sir," Donal said. "What the ear doesn't hear, the heart doesn't grieve over."

"Finish telling me about the house," O'Reilly said. "I will have to be trotting soon."

"It's lovely and private, so it is. Quiet, like, you know? At the end of a wee lane. The hairpin bend's like a big 'U' and we're in the middle, between the arms, but you can't even hear the lorries and motor-cars going round the bend on the main road."

"Bejasus, I know the place," O'Reilly said. He did. It had been vacant for a year, since its owner, Myrtle Siggins, had died at 101. "It's a lovely cottage."

"You know the curve too, Doctor O'Reilly. Talking about me being a menace? You put me off my bike into the ditch there once, so you did, charging along in your big motorcar like your man Stirling Moss, the race car driver."

O'Reilly harrumphed and said, "I must have been on my way to an emergency."

"Aye. Or to the Duck," Donal said.

O'Reilly was so taken aback by Donal's newfound confidence he said nothing as the little man continued, "Least said, soonest mended. What was I saying about the house?"

For a second O'Reilly worried about short-term memory loss in a patient with a recent head injury, but his concern was allayed when Donal said, "I remember. I was on about the bend. There's a lane comes out at the top of the bend and it's only a wee doddle to the bus stop from there, so it is." He lowered his voice. "And here's the best bit. It's not dear. Them new wee bungalows down on Seymour Avenue in Carnalea are going for three thousand five hundred pounds. The estate agent says the one Julie and me likes is going for only two thousand pounds, and that's five hundred less than it's valued at, but it's been empty for a year and it needs a bit of fixing up, but sure amn't I good at that?"

"Five hundred less than appraised value? It sounds interesting," O'Reilly said. "How do you want me to help?"

"We don't know nothing about buying houses, Doctor. We thought maybe one day soon, when I'm allowed to go out of my house, like, you and maybe Doctor Laverty'd come with Julie and me and take a wee gander at it and see if you think it would be good for us."

"It's a promise, Donal."

"'At's dead on," said Donal, "and we don't want

til leave it too long." He inclined his head and whispered, "I heard tell somebody else may have an eye on it."

"Oh?" O'Reilly wasn't unduly concerned. "I'd not worry too much," he said. "As you say, it's been on the market for quite a while. We can probably wait a bit before we move. See if we can get the price down."

Donal smiled, but said, "I hope youse is right, sir. Julie has her heart set on it. If it's not too dear, like."

"Let's get you home first."

"I can't hardly wait," Donal said.

"And I'll sniff around a bit about the house."

Donal's toothy grin was from ear to ear. "That's wheeker, so it is. Thanks, sir. Away off now, Doc, and remember: if I don't see youse through the window, I'll see youse through the week."

O'Reilly was chuckling as he left, but it didn't prevent him overhearing Donal saying to the two card players, "Hey Hughie, Alfie, would youse quit that stupid beggar my neighbour? 'At's for kiddies, so it is. How's about a few hands of pontoon? Just for pennies, like?"

O'Reilly feared for the fortunes of the two when Donal involved them in what the French call *vingt-et-un* and the Americans, blackjack. Donal Donnelly was probably a card counter.

8

A Warmth Hidden in My Veins

"Have a pew, Aggie." Barry followed a limping Aggie Arbuthnot into the surgery. She was the fourth patient of the morning, Cissie Sloan's cousin, and famous throughout the village as the possessor of twelve toes. "Haven't had you in for a while," Barry said. "What's up? I've not seen you limping before either." He took his seat in the chair on casters in front of the rolltop desk.

Aggie Arbuthnot was short and skinny with a head of straw-coloured hair done up in a head-scarf knotted at the front. A couple of shocking-pink plastic curlers called Spoolies peeped from under the scarf.

"Never mind me," she said, sitting in the patient's seat. "What about Kinky? I near took the rickets when I seen her being put in thon ambulance yesterday. Here." She leant forward and gave Barry a cylindrical tin bearing a picture of the Coronation of Queen Elizabeth II. "Seeing Kinky's not here to look after you, and all, I brung youse and himself some of my Yellow Man toffee."

"That's very kind, Aggie," Barry said, placing the tin on the desktop. "Doctor O'Reilly's seeing her this morning in the Royal. I'm sure she'll be fine."

"I hope so," Aggie said. "She's a heart of corn that one."

"She's a very kind woman all right."

"If youse and himself needs anything?"

"Thank you, Aggie. I'll remember, but I don't think you came in today just to chat about Kinky?" He pointed at her leg.

She sniffed. "I've took an awful pain in my left leg, so I have. I think it's my very close veins playing up." She pointed to an elastic support stocking that O'Reilly had prescribed last year before her condition had deteriorated and she had been put on a waiting list for surgery.

Very close veins. Barry hid a smile. Nothing would persuade Aggie, and indeed many Ulsterfolk, to call varicose veins anything else. And it wasn't the only re-named condition he'd come across during his ten months of working in rural Ireland. He'd once over-heard a woman with uterine fibroids tell her friends that Doctor O'Reilly said she had "fireballs."

"When did the pain start?" he asked. Barry knew Aggie was single and worked as a folder in a Belfast shirt factory. He wasn't exactly clear about what a folder did.

"I was at my job on Tuesday and a fellah hit the back of my leg a ferocious dunt with a trolley. Since then it's been hurting something fierce, so it has. I tholed it, but now it's burning up so I come til see youse, so I did." She bent to rub her leg.

"It sounds like you may have a bit of inflammation. Come on over to the couch."

He took her arm to help her limp across the familiar room with its Snellen's eye testing chart on one wall, and examining couch against another, where a mercury-column sphygmomanometer was mounted. "Now," he said, "off with your stockings and climb up."

She started to hoist her skirt.

"Just a minute," Barry said, and pulled the screens across. Ulsterwomen were generally modest about such things. "Give me a shout when you're ready."

"You can come in now, Doctor."

Aggie lay propped on the pillows. Her skirt hem covered her to her knees. He noticed her extra little toe on each foot.

"See them?" she said. "Them there's special, so they are. My mammy when I was wee told me not to be bothered because I was different. Not to take any ould guff from anyone who tried to tease me, she told me, and she was right." Aggie chuckled. "When them two wee puppet pigs first come on TV in the '50s I give my spare toes their names. Pinky and Perky."

Barry laughed. "Good for you."

Aggie said, "Sure they've never been any bother, but this here calf?" She pointed, bent her knee, and rolled her leg sideways. "See that there? It hurts like the living bejizzis."

Barry could see the tortuous blue tracks of distended veins crawling under the patchily discoloured skin of her calf. An area half the size of a saucer was clearly inflamed. He laid the back of his hand there. It was hot. "That where it got bumped?"

"Aye."

Barry palpated the vein. He had no difficulty feeling the hard clot. The diagnosis wasn't difficult. "You've got superficial thrombophlebitis."

"Boys-a-boys, that's a quare mouthful," she said, and frowned. "If you put an air to it you could sing it."

"It means that the thump caused a clot to form in the vein and there is inflammation round the damaged area."

"Clot? It was a right clot what done it til me. Thon 'Sticky' Maguire's got two left feet, so he has. If there was a ten-acre field with one tree in it that great glipe would walk into the trunk."

Barry smiled. He'd no idea why people with the surname Maguire were always nicknamed "Sticky" in Ireland, just as Murphys were called "Spud."

Her frown deepened. "Is it serious, like?"

"Not really, as long as it's in the veins under the skin, and I'm pretty sure it is." Superficial disease was relatively innocuous. A clot in a deep calf vein posed risks that a piece might break off, be carried to the lungs, and cause a pulmonary embolism, a potentially lethal condition. That could happen any time in the first three postoperative weeks, he thought, wondering for the umpteenth time this morning about Kinky, lying in a hospital bed in Belfast. Stop worrying and concentrate, he told himself. "I want to be certain, though, Aggie, so could you straighten your leg for me?"

"Aye, surely."

He inspected the ankle. No oedema. Good. "I want you to tell me if this hurts," Barry said. He grasped Aggie's left heel in his left hand and with his right sharply pushed her toes and foot toward the ankle. If there was a clot in a deep vein this action could stretch the vein and cause pain.

Aggie shook her head. "Nah," she said, "that's no worser nor the pain that's there already."

The test wasn't foolproof, but it reassured Barry. For completeness, he examined her right calf. Other than the skin discolouration and the obvious varicosities, he could find nothing ominous. "I'll give you peace to get dressed," he said, "then come on through and we'll talk about treatment."

He returned to the desk and before he took out a sheet of practice letterhead and a sickness benefit form, he opened the tin of toffee. He picked an irregular, pale yellow lump and popped it into his mouth. The honeycomb sweetie crunched deliciously when he bit down. Back to work. Aggie would need a letter to her employer and a "sick line," as it was called, so she could draw benefits. He'd finished the Yellow Man and the form by the time she'd returned and taken her seat. "You'll need to rest with that leg propped up on pillows and wrapped in hot, damp towels and with hot water bottles. I'll get Colleen Brennan, the district nurse, to pop in."

"Thanks very much, Doctor." She leant forward and sniffed like a retriever searching for a downed bird. "You like my Yellow Man?"

Barry grinned. "It's lovely."

"Aye," she said. "I cook it by the great gross every August for the Lamass Fair. It's a traditional treat, like dulse, you know. Our fair here's not as famous as the one in Ballycastle, but the *craic*'s powerful."

"I'm sure it is," Barry said. "Now, Aggie, you really need to stay off that leg. Could anybody help you with cooking your meals?"

"Cissie. I'll phone her when I get home." Aggie smiled. "Talking of legs, she'd talk one of them off a three-leggèd stool—"

Barry smiled, and remembered her coming last night, blethering away like a spring tide rushing in. The Melton Mowbray pies she'd brought them had been delicious.

"—but sure aren't we family?"

He nodded. The whole village was one big family. His new family. "Have you aspirin at home?" he asked.

"I have, sir."

"One, four times a day. It will ease the pain and help the inflammation to heal. You're going to need time off, so I'll give you a line and a letter. Are they pretty decent about sick leave at your work?"

She snorted. "Them buggers probably had jobs as Pharaoh's overseers when the pyramids was getting built. It's lucky the union won't let them use whips nowadays."

Barry nodded. He'd heard about conditions in some of the Belfast factories. He leant forward. "What exactly do *you* do, Aggie?"

"Fold shirts. You know when you buy one it's all buttoned up and folded over cardboard with the sleeves pinned to it and packed in cellophane?"

"Yes."

"It's my job to stand at a board and do all that by hand on every shirt that the button-holers give us off their machines."

"You stand and do that all day?" No wonder she had varicose veins.

"Och aye. Five and a half days a week. I have done since I left school. I'm thirty-two now so that's sixteen years ago."

"That's nearly as long as Doctor O'Reilly's been practising here," Barry said, and pursed his lips. He recognised how ignorant he was of how the other half lived. He may be dissatisfied with the routine of his work, but to spend your whole working life folding shirts? "It's little wonder you've got varicose veins," he said, "with all that standing. Don't you get bored?"

"Not at all," she said. "Sure the *craic*'s powerful with the other girls, and after a while you could fold shirts with your eyes shut, so you could. It's wee buns."

"I wish you could sit down," Barry said.

She sighed. "I've kept asking for a job as a stitcher.

Youse get to sit down to do that, but och, there's always some excuse. Mind you," she scratched her cheek, "at least I still have a job. Poor Helen Hewitt. Her mill closed down."

"I know," Barry said. Fingal was going to interview her at twelve thirty. Barry decided to get a move on. There were other patients waiting. "What's your boss's name?" he asked.

Her lip curled. "Mister Ivan McCluggage. He owns the place along with some fellah he calls a 'silent partner.'" She lowered her voice. "Us workies call your man McCluggage 'Ivan the Terrible.'"

Barry didn't bother to hide his grin.

"Aye, I thought you'd like that," chuckled Aggie, "you being a learnèd man and all."

"I'll write to Mister McCluggage and tell him you need three weeks off, and I'll ask him to reassign you to a sitting job—you called it stitching?"

"I did." She smiled. "That's quare nor decent of you, sir, but I'll not hold my breath. You don't know our Tzar of all the Russias."

"It won't hurt to try, Aggie. We have to get you off your feet. And you'll need to stay off even after you've had your operation. We'll not want the veins coming back." Barry started to write.

He handed Aggie the sick line and letter. "Here you are." Barry stood. "Can you get home all right?"

"Aye, certainly. Archie Auchinleck, him what delivers the milk, lives fornenst me, you know. He has a wee motorcar. He give me a lift here and he's not working in the afternoons so he's in the waiting room ready to take me home."

"Good. I'll pop in to see you in a day or two, but if you get any pain in your calf or you're short of breath, no more of this 'tholing it.' You phone here at once." Barry wasn't overly concerned about the possibility of complications, but you never could be sure with veins.

Usually patients left by the front door, but he walked with her to the packed waiting room. Archie, who was standing because all the chairs were taken, said, "'Bout ye, Doc." He offered his arm. "Come on, Aggie. Let's be getting you home." He turned back to Barry. "How's Mrs. Kincaid, by the way?"

"She should be on the mend," Barry said.

"I'm main glad to hear that," Archie said. "Main glad, so I am. I've been dead worried." There was no doubting the man's sincerity.

Barry surveyed the waiting room. A heavyset man wearing a duncher was snorting into a pocket handkerchief. A recently born baby in its pram mewled gently. The God-awful roses on the wallpaper glared at him. "Safe home, Aggie," he said. "Right. Who's next?"

9

And a Good Job, Too

O'Reilly answered the door to a radiant Helen Hewitt. "Come in, Helen." He'd forgotten the sheen in her hair, the openess of her face. "Go on into the dining room." He inclined his head and followed, admiring the sway of her hips under what must be her Sunday-best skirt. By God, he may be past fifty and soon to marry the love of his middle-aged life, but he could still appreciate the sight of a pretty woman. "Have a pew." He pulled out a dining room chair, waited until she was seated, then sat opposite.

"How's Mrs. Kincaid doing?" she asked. "I'm desperate sorry to hear she's poorly, so I am."

"I'm just back from the Royal. She's doing well." He fished out his briar. "Mind if I smoke?" It was the accepted polite question, particularly in mixed company.

"I don't mind one wee bit. And I'm dead pleased to hear about Mrs. Kincaid getting better, so I am." She rummaged in her handbag. "Can I smoke too?" A smile played across her lips and lit up her startling green eyes.

Helen pulled out a packet of Wills Wild Woodbine. They were, along with Park Drive and Strand, the cheapest cigarettes available.

O'Reilly laughed. Not one patient in ten would have had the temerity to ask permission to smoke in his house. He admired her self-possession. But then he and Barry had known all about how feisty Helen Hewitt was ever since her run-in with Alice Moloney over some new hats. "Go right ahead," he said, "although I'm supposed to tell you that doctors think smoking's bad for you. That's what my research colleagues say." He struck a match, lit her cigarette, and fired up his pipe. "Didn't used to be a bad thing. Folks thought you were odd if you *didn't* smoke. Och well, 'Times they are a changin'.' They'll be picking on the drink next, or a good Ulster fry." He grinned at her and she grinned back, taking a quick draw on the cigarette. "You'll not remember, Helen, but years ago there was a song about life's good things called 'It's Illegal, It's Immoral, or It Makes You Fat.' I think we're getting there. Soon some eejit's going to start saying kiddies shouldn't have sweeties."

"Aye," she said. "They told us when we were wee smoking would stunt our growth, so it would, but sure I couldn't wear high heels if I was any taller. And I do remember the song, sir. Them Beverly Sisters sung it, so they did."

"Good for you, Helen, and you're right about the song," said O'Reilly, and rose. "I'll get you an ashtray."

"I hope, sir, you didn't mind me phoning up to see if you might need a bit of help, but I'd only just found out about my job as receptionist at the Belfast Mill.

I'm used to answering phones and I know that's one of the things Mrs. Kincaid did here, so I thought there might be a temporary vacancy. And the gentlemen buyers seemed to like talking to me when they called." She frowned. "I suppose I'm easy to talk to."

O'Reilly put a cut-glass ashtray on the tabletop beside her, sat, and looked hard at the young woman. He was sure the gentlemen buyers enjoyed chatting with such a good-looking girl, and probably not entirely because of her riveting conversation. And yet Helen seemed surprised that it should be so. "We could use help," he said, "at least until Kinky gets back on her feet, so it's likely you could be here for a couple of months."

"I didn't know she was that sick," Helen said. "If I'd known—" She sighed. "God, I feel like a vulture, so I do."

O'Reilly said, "No need, Helen. Kinky's fine. Honestly, but she'll need time before she can get back to work, and I need someone to answer the phone. You couldn't have come at a better time."

"Honest to God?"

He nodded.

"That would be great," she said.

"Just a couple of quick questions."

"Fire away."

"How old are you?"

"Twenty-two this August."

"Did you finish school?"

"Aye. Three years ago. I got my Junior Certificate

in eight subjects." She screwed up her face. "I hated Latin, but it was compulsory. Anyroad I went on and got Senior Certificate, and three Advanced levels too, in physics, chemistry, and biology."

O'Reilly whistled. He knew her widowed father was a builder's labourer with a big family. Helen was working class. Usually such girls left school at fifteen, but Helen had stayed long enough to complete university entrance requirements, and in science at that. "Did many girls do sciences at your school?" he asked.

She laughed. "At Sullivan Upper Grammar School in Holywood? Not at all. Most finished after Junior Certificate, one or two stayed on and did arts. Girls don't do science."

"Sooo?" He let the question hang. This was fascinating.

"There was this here science teacher—"

He heard the softness in her voice, saw a hint of mistiness in those green eyes.

"Mister Wilcoxson. I think I was a wee bit in love with him, so I was." Helen looked up suddenly and must have caught something in O'Reilly's expression.

"Och, no, Doctor. Nothing like that," Helen laughed. "He was the perfect gentleman. Just wanted to see me get on, you know. He give me no peace. I done science up to Junior Certificate. Got three distinctions, so I did. He kept after me until I said I'd do science for Senior. I was only sixteen," she said, "but anyroad, he gave me extra classes, kept me at it for two whole years." She shrugged. "He wanted me to go to university, but I never did." She shrugged. "That's for high-heejins, so it is. I could have gone for a secretary's course, but, och." She shrugged again. "I've done all right as a shop assistant and I liked my work at the mill, you know."

O'Reilly leant across the table. "Would you have liked to go to Queen's?"

She sighed. "Honest to God?"

He nodded.

"Aye. I would, but I'm the oldest. My da wanted us all to get our Seniors at least. Said with that none of us would have to do the kind of work he does. Me ma, she was a shifter in the mill. Brought in good money—".

And she died of ovarian cancer three years ago, O'Reilly thought. "I understand," he said.

"I know you do, sir. You were quare nor kind to her." A tear dropped.

He waited, sensing that Helen Hewitt would be offended if he tried to comfort her.

She took a deep breath, squared her shoulders, sniffed, looked him in the eye. "We could use a bit of the ould doh-ray-mi while I'm looking for a proper job, like."

"You can start right now, if you like," O'Reilly said. "The pay's not a king's ransom, but the work's light. I'll give you two pounds a week. Today's Wednesday so it would only be one quid this week. Cash. I can't afford to pay your benefits. I'm sorry. I still have to give Kinky her wages."

"That's right decent, sir," she said. "And we all want Kinky back. The job'll only be for a wee while anyway, but it'll help. I know that. Now, what does youse want me to do?"

"The phone's in the hall," O'Reilly said. "When it rings, you answer it, then you have to decide, as best you can, if the caller needs to talk to one of us doctors on the phone, whether they need to come here to the surgery at once, come to the next surgery, or wait a wee while until Doctor Laverty or myself can get to their house. If they sound really sick, then one of us doctors will need to rush out at once. You'll do no harm if you lean on the side of caution."

She frowned. "It doesn't sound too tricky." She puffed her Woodbine.

"It's not. Mind you, Kinky's had thirty years' experience and she knows everybody in the village and the townland." He shifted in his seat. "Most of the time one of us will be here, and if you're uncertain you can always ask. If we're both out, it's up to you to decide if the customer can wait or if you'll have to get an ambulance to take them to the Royal. The number of the ambulance is by the phone."

Her frown deepened. She crushed out her smoke. "I thought you'd have to be a doctor or a nurse to do that there stuff."

"Not at all." O'Reilly let his pipe go out. "If we're

not here, anyone who's bleeding, having trouble breathing, vomiting, having pains in their chest, or severe pain anywhere goes to hospital. Most of the rest, flus, backaches, rashes—"

"Like my eczema?"

"Exactly. They'll have to wait."

She leant back in her chair. "Sure I can give it a try. Do you, Doctor O'Reilly, have any notion of how many calls you get in a day?"

Fingal had to think. "I dunno. Half a dozen, maybe less, unless there's a flu epidemic on, then it's more, but this isn't flu season. Just at the moment, the bloody thing's hardly stopped ringing, but it's folks asking after Kinky, wanting to know if we need anything. Why do you ask?"

"I'm going to be bored stiff."

O'Reilly caught his breath. He'd been so sure she'd take the job.

She cocked her head to one side. "Would it be all right if maybe I done a bit of dusting and hoovering too?" She pointed at the table's mahogany top. "No harm to you, sir, but if you let all these here crumbs lie about," she bent and looked under before straightening up, "and on the carpet it'll be like sending the mice printed invitations."

O'Reilly guffawed then said, "No offence taken. I'd be more than happy to take you up on your offer." He hesitated, did some mental arithmetic, after all Kinky would not be eating at Number One, and said, "You do that, Helen, and I'll up your wages to two pound ten."

She shook her head. "I'd rather the two pounds and a wee favour, so I would."

"Go on."

"I'll be looking for full-time work, you know, but if I'm here I can't follow up on applications. I'd not tie up your phone, sir. I know it's for the patients to call in on and all, but if mebbe I could enquire about jobs once in a while?"

"I'll do better than that," he said. "If you land an interview, try to fix it for a morning when either Doctor Laverty or I are in the house and can answer the phone while you're out."

"I could have the time off for to go for it?" She stood, beamed down on him, and said, "The whole village knows you pretend to be an ould targe—"

He didn't pretend, he thought. He never hid his temper.

"But we've seen through youse. I have, anyroad, Doctor O'Reilly, you're the kindest man in County Down." She was grinning from ear to ear.

O'Reilly cleared his throat, blew out his cheeks, made a hah-hming noise—and blushed bright red. When he finally collected himself, he said, "Last details. You're on duty now until five. After that we can manage. I don't get too many calls in the evening, and we'll not need you at weekends." Kindest man? My aunt Fanny Jane. The cheek of the girl, and yet he really couldn't be angry with her.

Helen had returned to looking demure. "Yes, sir," she said, and bobbed her head.

"Exactly. Tomorrow I'd like you to start at eight. Surgery starts at nine so you give me a list before that of patients needing home visits from Doctor Laverty and myself. And bring it up to date at lunch time."

"I'll do that."

"And now," he said, "have you had your lunch?"

She shook her head.

O'Reilly's stomach grumbled. Still, the ready-to-grill Welsh rarebits that the bachelor undertaker Mister Coffin had shyly brought round last night would feed three. "You'll stay for lunch," he said. It wasn't a question.

With her mouth slightly open, she looked round at the dining room's elegant bog oak table and chairs, the matching sideboard, and then up at the cut-glass chandelier. Her voice was hushed when she said, "Oh, I couldn't possibly, sir," and he could practically hear her thinking, This is far too grand for the likes of me. It bloody well wasn't and although he didn't say it out loud, he was delighted by the chance of dining with a girl who had managed to rise above her station and qualify for university. The fact that she had worked so hard and wasn't going struck O'Reilly as a waste. A bloody awful waste. "Rubbish, Helen Hewitt," he said. "You're staying, but I am going to make you sing for your supper . . . or lunch."

"How?"

"Can you use a gas grill?"

She gave him one of those looks that say "Is the

pope Catholic?" "Would you ask a ship's captain if he could tie a reef knot?" she said.

"Grand," said O'Reilly. "Now, I don't usually put my guests to work but, under the circumstances, let me show you to the kitchen."

10

And O'er and O'er the Sand

"Sure you don't mind staying a bit longer, Helen?" Barry asked.

She looked up from a leather-bound book. "Away you go, Doctor Laverty. I'm happy here in your lounge."

Helen Hewitt had started work yesterday and taken to her duties like, well, like a retriever to water, Barry thought. "Doctor O'Reilly wasn't sure what time he'd be home," Barry said, "and Arthur needs his run."

"I'm sure Arthur'll enjoy that, Doctor Laverty, but see this one here?" She nodded down to where Lady Macbeth had taken up residence on Helen's lap and was purring mightily. "Never lets me be. I was washing dishes in the kitchen after lunch and she was weaving round my legs all the time. I hoovered the dining room and she got up on the sideboard, then she come straight up here with me and she's barely moved a muscle since. Wee dote, so she is."

Barry smiled. "She is, until she's not," he said. "She can be a regular tartar when the mood's on her."

"Och, sure, but can't all us girls?"

Helen's grin and the dimple that appeared in her left cheek seemed happily wicked. No doubt she was referring to an episode with Alice Moloney's hats. Barry coughed, remained noncommittal, but made a mental note never to irritate Helen Hewitt.

She held up the book. "Have you read this, Doctor Laverty?"

Barry looked at the title. *A Tale of Two Cities.* "I have."

"Your man Charles Dickens? He's a powerful writer, so he is. I've read *David Copperfield* and *Great Expectations* and I can always see the characters so clearly, but this here stuff about the French Revolution? It's dead exciting, so it is, but it must have been bloody awful to live in France then."

"It was, literally bloody," Barry said. "All revolutions are. We had one of our own here fifty years ago, you know."

"I do indeed," she said. "My da's a great man for his Irish history. He told us all about Padraig Pearse and James Connolly, Eamon Ceannt and the rest getting shot for taking part in the Easter Uprising in 1916. And your man Eamon de Valera being spared because he was born in America. My da always likes to tell us how de Valera went on to be president of the Republic and even greeted President Kennedy when he visited Ireland in 1963." She paused. "I think my da's right. It's a shame we didn't get taught Irish history at school."

"That's because Northern Ireland's part of Great Britain so we get British history." He shrugged. "I could have done without having to memorise the dates of every British king and queen since William the Conqueror."

"From 1066 to 1087, then William II, 1087 to 1100," she said, "and right on up til Queen Lizzie." They both laughed. "You should meet my da, sir, and hear him sing Irish songs when he's had a jar." Her dimple reappeared with her smile and Barry heard the affection in her voice.

"I've seen him in the Duck, but I've not heard him sing."

"He'd dead on, so he is. He sings rebel songs at home. He knows about the United Irishmen in 1798 and he even told me about the Cumann na mBan that was founded in 1913, the women's branch of the Irish Volunteers. I'll bet you didn't know that two hundred of them fought in that there Easter Rising? Margaretta Keogh was shot dead. Elizabeth O'Farrell was a go-between in negotiating the surrender of the rebels."

"You have a taste for rebellion?" said Barry.

"Och, aye. You're thinking about them hats, are you?" Helen chuckled, then said, more seriously, "and

not just about hats. We're lucky here in Ballybucklebo, there's no Catholic-Protestant rubbish, but it's
not the same all over Ulster. Us Catholics don't always
get a fair shake. There was good reasons for them
Irish rebellions, so there was. That's what my da
says."

Barry hadn't known Helen's religious persuasion
nor her political leanings. To him, particularly as a
doctor who had absolutely no right to let anyone's
religion or politics matter, they were irrelevant.

Before he could comment, she abruptly changed the
subject. "Do you think Doctor O'Reilly would mind
if I took the book home with me the night? I need to
know what happens next. I'll bring it back the morrow."

"I'm sure he'd not mind at all."

"Great," she said.

"Doctor O'Reilly has all twenty of Dickens's novels. I'm sure you can borrow any ones you want."

"Honest?"

Barry nodded. "But I'd avoid *Bleak House*. It's
awfully dry."

"I'll do that."

"All right, Helen," he said, "if you're happy enough,
you read away. See what Madame Defarge and
Charles Darnay get up to." Barry looked out through
the bay window, past the tilted spire of the Presbyterian church, and over its old yew trees to a cerulean
Belfast Lough. "At least we've no guillotine next to
the Maypole and it's lovely out there," he said. "I'll

see to Arthur and get back soon so you can go home and enjoy your evening."

"You take your time, Doctor Laverty. Me and her ladyship," the cat opened both eyes and yawned so mightily Barry thought she would dislocate her jaw, "are quite content, and I want to find out what happens to Sydney Carton." She winked at Barry. "I'd not mind having that boy's slippers under my breakfast table, so I'd not."

Barry stood on the hard wet sand near the sea's edge and felt the breeze ruffle his hair. The tang of seaweed filled his nostrils and wavelets pleaded with a sea-wrack tide line to allow them to come further ashore. Arthur Guinness sat at Barry's feet, the dog's gaze fixed on Barry's face. The big black Labrador quivered. Barry hurled a piece of driftwood and looked down to the dog, who tensed and stared straight out to sea, but otherwise didn't budge. Nor would he, Barry knew, until commanded. O'Reilly had trained his retriever well. "Hi lost," Barry said, and watched Arthur tear into the water and swim with powerful strokes and head high straight toward the wood. He snorted as he swam back with his prize in his mouth.

Pausing only to shake himself, the droplets sparkling, flying, and making tiny ephemeral rainbows, Arthur trotted on with the stick in his mouth and sat with his tail thrashing a fan shape in the sand. He put a paw up on Barry's leg.

"Good boy." Barry accepted the stick, brushed sand from his pants, threw again, and said, "Hi lost."

The dog bounded into the water and made a beeline. Old Arthur knew where he was going, which was more than Barry Laverty could say for himself for sure. He'd truly enjoyed his ten months here, but he was also looking forward to sampling life as a trainee specialist. He'd start his obstetrics and gynaecology in Ballymena's Waveney Hospital in July. He knew he was good at obstetrics, suspected that being a specialist could be a very satisfying career. Och, well. Time would tell which way he'd jump. He was young, had no commitments, and enjoyed the luxury of his professional world still being his oyster, or as Donal Donnelly might say, "The world's your lobster."

He watched Arthur grab the stick and turn for the shore. The big Lab could keep it up all day, the same task over and over, just like Aggie Arbuthnot folding shirts. Maybe the letter he'd given her might help her get a better job.

Arthur came ashore, gave Barry the stick, and looked up with longing deep in his soft eyes.

"All right. Once more." Barry threw. "Hi lost."

Away Arthur went.

Across Belfast Lough the cloud shadows played follow-my-leader over the Antrim Hills. There the Knockagh Monument stood; a solitary needle ready to pierce an eggshell blue sky. A freighter headed up-channel to the Port of Belfast. The sinking sun scattered spangles on the crests of wavelets and the squeals of gulls gave high counterpoint to the song of the sea on sand. This was going to be a hard place to leave, but Ballymena was no distance from the Glens of Antrim. He'd never been there, but they were said to have a wonder all their own. He intended to find out.

Arthur was panting when he arrived back. He was duly complimented and relieved of the stick. "Heel," Barry said, and the dog tucked in behind Barry's leg as together they headed home.

These sand dunes held memories; amusing ones of walking here with O'Reilly a couple of weeks back as they hatched a plot to stymie Councillor Bertie Bishop; sorrowful ones of a golden girl who'd blazed in Barry's life for a few short months then told him she'd met someone else. It didn't seem possible, now that she was so far away, that he'd ever kissed her here where the marram grass on the dunes' summits whispered secrets and the plaintive replies of curlew echoed on an evening breeze. Damn it, but losing her still hurt, not nearly as much, but memories of her were all around him. Going from here would dull the aching brought on by unexpected reminders.

A liver-and-white springer spaniel tore round a corner and skidded to a halt stiff-legged in front of Arthur, who regarded the newcomer and lowered his muzzle to sniff. The sniff was returned.

A woman called from the far side of the dune, "Max? Max? Where are you?"

Barry recognised the voice.

"*Max.* Come here, you witless oaf."

The spaniel bounced away, advanced with his belly close to the ground, yipped twice at Arthur, and dashed off, ears flapping, spurts of sand flying from his paws.

Arthur looked up at Barry as if to say, "Spaniels? They're all thick as two short planks."

"There you are, Max, you silly ass," came from round the sand hill. The voice was equal parts frustration and affection.

Barry bent and patted Arthur's head. "Good boy, Arthur. Now heel." He strode off and rounded the dune. A young woman with her back to Barry was stroking the spaniel and murmuring endearments. He noticed her waist-length plait of copper hair. He grinned and said, "Hello there, Sue Nolan."

Before she could turn and speak, the spaniel spotted Arthur and dashed across to greet his new acquaintance. Both dogs' tails thrashed.

"All right, Arthur," Barry said. "Go out." He watched the two animals bounding away, Arthur solid, sedate, the spaniel making short dashes, yipping and darting about.

The young woman turned and Barry was once again struck by the green eyes set in an oval face.

"Barry," she said, smiling, "how lovely to see you again." Her look was inquiring. He had said he would phone when they'd seen each other at the Downpatrick Races last weekend, and he had not.

"I was going to . . . phone you, that is . . ." he stammered, "but you'd not believe how busy we've been since last Saturday, and—" He stopped, not sure how to continue. He'd always been uncomfortable with girls, more so with very attractive ones like Sue Nolan. He admired the swell of her breasts under a grey cashmere sweater, her slim waist, the curve of her calves beneath the hem of a knee-length skirt. In the softening light of the late afternoon, her hair glowed. She was lovely.

"No rest for the wicked?" she said, and raised her eyebrow.

"Nor for me," Barry said, smiling, and quickly changed the subject. "What brings you here?"

"Max wanted his walk. The tide's in and Holywood Beach is under water so I came here."

"My boss, Doctor O'Reilly, is busy and Arthur Guinness needed his run."

"Arthur Guinness? That's a name and a half for a dog."

Barry laughed. "Doctor O'Reilly says it's because the big lad's Irish, black, and has a good head on him . . . like a well-poured pint of stout."

"Sounds like a character, your boss." She chuckled, a melodious sound. Barry liked it.

"He is," Barry said. "Indeed he is. I—" Barry had run out of things to say; his mind was blank. He looked at his watch to cover his confusion. "I . . . I should probably be running along. I'm expecting him home soon."

"I should be getting on too, Barry. I've homework to mark." She laughed again, looked directly at him, raised an eyebrow, and said, "I'd use just about any excuse to put off doing it for a while."

Say something, he thought, not sure whether he was referring to himself or Sue. In truth he'd certainly enjoy another few moments in her company, and Helen, back at Number One, clearly wasn't in a rush. "It is a lovely even—"

The two dogs suddenly tore over the dune's crest, sand spraying around them. The moment was shattered. "Here, Arthur," Barry called. "Sit."

The Lab came, planted his backside, and, tongue lolling, stared up at Barry.

"Max, Max, hold still, you goat." She bent and struggled to clip a lead to Max's collar.

Barry looked at the firm curve of her backside. Damn it, he hadn't held a girl since last Christmas. The worst she could do was refuse an invitation. "Sue," he said, "what are you doing on Saturday?" He knew Kitty was coming down and O'Reilly would be glad to have the place to himself, and it was his turn to take call.

She stood, straining against the springer's leash as Max practically strangled himself on a choke-chain collar. "Nothing after eight. I've a meeting to go to before that. It'll be over by seven thirty."

"How'd you fancy a late dinner?"

"I'd love it," she said. Then, arms stretched to full length, she was dragged away by the daft dog. "Phone me. I've gotta go."

"I will. Tonight," he yelled after her as she was dragged up and over the dune by Max. There, he told himself, that wasn't too difficult, was it? And he grinned when he realised how much he was looking forward to Saturday night now. He set off. "Come on, Arthur. Heel. Show me you've better manners than that unruly brute of Sue's." She might be a first-class teacher at MacNeill Memorial Elementary School, but she herself needed instruction in the art of dog training. Oh well, Barry thought as he moved onto the Shore Road, nobody's perfect, but Sue Nolan was very easy to look at. He wondered how it would feel to kiss her.

11

What Cat's Averse to Fish?

Barry, smiling at the thought of his end-of-week pint with O'Reilly, hammered on the Browns' door with its stern lion's head knocker. Helen Hewitt, who this afternoon had vacuumed the rooms and landings on the first floor, was now well into *Oliver Twist* and said she didn't mind staying at Number One Main to answer phones, even if it was a Friday.

O'Reilly, accompanied by the faithful hound, and Barry on his own, had agreed to make separate follow-up home visits and meet later at the Mucky Duck.

"Come on on on in, Doctor Laverty," Connie said "You've come for to see wee Colin? He's in the backyard."

"He's well?"

"Fit as a flea."

Barry followed her through the hall and into the kitchen, where two pots bubbled on top of a range and gave off mouthwatering scents. A loaded clotheshorse stood gently steaming in front of the range. He couldn't help noticing how many of the pairs of socks had been darned.

"Sorry about the clutter. It's right and sunny the day, but there's no drying in it. And with them wee squalls every now and then, I'd be going like a fiddler's elbow taking the washing in and putting it out again," Connie said.

"Please don't apologise. You'll have been busy enough since Colin came home from hospital."

She sighed and pushed her hair from her forehead with the back of one hand. "To tell you God's honest truth, I hope you do say he can go back to school on Monday. Anyroads, them Royal bone doctors was spot on, so they were. Had him fixed in no time, you know, and home here on Wednesday. He's been running round like a liltie, so he has. He has me driven daft sometimes. Och, but—" and she smiled fondly.

Barry laughed. Colin Brown would be a going concern all right, a regular Irish berserker.

"This way, sir." Connie unsnibbed a back door that led into a small yard enclosed between the house and three red-brick walls. Patches of moss sprouted from coping stones and the mortar between the bricks. An empty clothesline drooped overhead.

Colin was sitting on a wooden box on the tarmac. Beneath his short pants both knee socks were crumpled round his ankles. One knee was grazed. Barry saw how the lad cradled his pet ferret. The little animal twitched its whiskers and wrinkled its pointed nose, clearly scenting the newcomers. Colin turned and grinned. "How's about ye, Doctor Laverty? Come to see my Butch?"

"And you, Colin. How's the wing?"

Colin lifted the wounded extremity in its sling. "Dead on, so it is."

"May I see?"

"Aye, certainly." He slipped off the sling.

Barry looked at the white plaster of Paris tube that ran from Colin's wrist, past a flexed elbow, and halfway up his upper arm. The hand was neither swollen nor reddened. "Wiggle your fingers."

"See that there?" said Colin, waggling his fingers at Butch. "It don't hurt nor nothin'. And that ambulance ride was wheeker. Like you said he would, Doctor, your man, the driver, put on his 'nee-naw, nee-naw' just like one of them cops and robbers chases at the fillums."

Barry tousled Colin's hair. "Good man-ma-da." He turned to Connie. "You'll not even know there was anything wrong by the time the cast comes off."

"That's great. His daddy'll be pleased too."

Barry squatted. "And this is Butch?"

"Aye, and he's a wee cracker, so he is."

There was pride and affection in the boy's voice. Barry bent and stroked the coarse white fur of the animal's head and noticed the bright gleam in its beady eyes. In spite of himself he shivered. Those were killer's eyes. Ferrets were related to stoats, weasels, and polecats, and pound for pound they were some of nature's fiercest predators. "You take good care of Butch, Colin." Barry stood. "I'll be off, and you can go back to school on Monday." He turned and pretended not to see Colin sticking out his tongue.

"I'll show you out, Doctor," Connie said. "On Monday, Colin." She grinned as she turned to lead the way, and when they were in the kitchen said, "Excuse me, sir. You know I was dead sorry to hear about Mrs. Kincaid, so I was. I sent her a get-well card."

"That was thoughtful."

Connie blushed. "And if you don't mind me saying, sir, my Lenny's a great carpenter, but he can't cook for toffee apples. I've a notion not many men can, you know."

"You'd be right."

"If you'd not be offended, sir," she turned to a counter and picked up something wrapped in a tea towel, "this here's a Guinness beef pudding. I was going to bring it round."

"That's very kind." Barry accepted the parcel, feeling its weight. He knew Kinky's suet-crusted puddings were cooked in ceramic pudding bowls just like this one.

"Pop it as it is into boiling water for forty minutes, to heat it up, like."

"Thanks very much, Connie," Barry said. "I'll get the bowl back to you."

"No hurry."

"I'd better be running on," he said. "I'll let myself out."

It took him two minutes hurrying through the raindrops of a sun-shower to reach the Duck. He pushed through the swinging doors and walked into tobacco fug and the smell of beer in the low-ceilinged, oak-beamed single room where men in cloth caps and collarless shirts leant against a bar, pints of Guinness in their hands. Others, a few in suits and ties, occupied tables. The wooden tabletops were marked with cigarette burns and rings left by the bottoms of glasses.

No one noticed him come in because Helen Hewitt's da was singing. Although it was technically against the law in Ulster to sing in public houses, Willie Dunleavy, the proprietor and barman, let men with good voices perform, provided that they sang no sectarian songs. Constable Mulligan always turned a blind eye to a bit of music; indeed after he'd had a few, he could often be persuaded to recite "The Green Eye of the Little Yellow God" or "Cassabianca," stolidly declaiming, "The boy stood on the burning deck . . ."

The singer, middle-aged, stocky, blessed with a head of black hair and piercing mahogany eyes, stood with his thumbs hooked into the arm holes of his waistcoat. He was a fine baritone.

> One morning fair as I chanced the air down by
>   Black Water side
> In gazing all around me that Irish lad I spied . . .

Barry knew the folk song, a classic girl's lament for a lover's broken promise of marriage. The tune was haunting and its rendition deserved respect from its audience. As Barry listened, he glanced round the room and recognised most of the people. Councillor Bishop sat at the far end, loudly haranguing a man who was a stranger to Barry. Bertie Bishop was pointedly ignoring the singer. The councillor had never been known for his polished manners.

O'Reilly beckoned from a table near the front of the room then turned to the bar and signalled to Willie, who leant across the counter polishing a glass. O'Reilly pointed to his empty pint glass and held up two fingers.

Willie gave a thumbs-up, and started to pour.

Barry nodded a greeting to O'Reilly, sat, and the nod was returned accompanied by a smile. Arthur was under the table, happily lapping from a bowl that

Barry knew contained Smithwick's Irish ale. Barry had come to love this place—the rough plaster walls and oak beams, the easy smiles from folks he knew, and Willie's relaxed nature. And Helen's da wasn't the only one who could make soft music and enchant an evening. Barry set the beef pudding on the table and waited until the singing had finished.

And when fishes do fly and the seas run dry
It's then that you'll marry I.

He and O'Reilly joined in the applause.

"Jasus," said O'Reilly, "aren't us men terrible beasts? Leaving a poor girl like that? Who'd do such a thing?"

Not you, Fingal, Barry thought, as he reflected on his boss's imminent wedding. It may have taken him a while, but Fingal Flaherty O'Reilly was going to marry the girl he'd walked out with more than thirty years before. Now, in Barry's own case, it was usually the girls who left him, but after four months, the ache of the departure of a certain Patricia Spence was dimming, only surfacing when something like being in the dunes last evening brought back a particular memory. He shrugged.

"You'll recognise Helen Hewitt's da, Alan," O'Reilly said. He inhaled. "She got the hair and her eyes from her late mother. Lovely woman, Morna Hewitt. Shame about her. God Almighty, but I hate cancer." He curled his lip.

"Your pints, Doctors." Willie set the straight glasses on the table and collected O'Reilly's empty one. "Settle up when you're leaving, sir."

"Thanks, Willie. *Sláinte.*"

"*Sláinte.*" Barry savoured the Guinness. To change the subject he said, "Connie gave me a beef pudding."

"Sainted Jasus and half the apostles," said O'Reilly, his great eyebrows meeting above the bridge of his nose. "I don't want to be ungracious, Barry, but where in the hell are we going to put it? The fridge is full, the larder's overflowing, and we can't give things away. The donors would be mortified."

"True enough." The hurt taken would be irreparable. Barry had a notion. "Kitty's coming down tomorrow. I don't suppose she could take some things up to the Royal . . . dishes that aren't in anything that needs to be returned like this bowl." He indicated the tea-towel-wrapped bundle. "I'm sure the hospital could distribute the food to people who need it? That's one of the almoner's jobs, isn't it?"

O'Reilly brightened. "Bloody brilliant," he said. "Right you are, Barry. Kitty can take them to the almoner." His smile faded. "And, God knows there are plenty of folks in need in Belfast."

"And in Ballybucklebo. Helen's not the only one laid off by the mill."

"Another bloody shame," said O'Reilly, "but we can't help them all. Helen's different, though. Did you know she has all the marks in Senior that she needs to go to university?"

Barry whistled. "I did not. I've got the impression she's one smart girl, but I didn't know that. She could get entrance to Queen's?"

"Any university she chooses. I wonder," said O'Reilly, "if we could do anything about it. Maybe find a bursary or something."

There was such longing in Fingal's voice that for a moment Barry wondered if O'Reilly himself might establish one, but secretly generous as Barry knew his senior to be, he wasn't as wealthy as that.

O'Reilly had finished half his pint. "We can't do it here and now, but we can think about it." He pointed to Barry's, which was down by a third, but he shook his head. O'Reilly waved one finger and nodded at Willie and said to Barry, "How's your patient?"

"Colin?" Barry sipped. "His fracture's set and his arm's in a cast. Simple enough procedure for the orthopods in the Royal. Be easy enough to do here if we could give an anaesthetic, but I know these days that's considered too risky outside of a hospital."

"I set broken bones in my navy days, and sometimes, because we'd run out, not always with the benefit of any anaesthetic more powerful than rum." O'Reilly chuckled. "Knowing Colin, he'd probably have been happy to give a few tots a try, but I don't think Connie would have been impressed."

Willie set a new pint in front of O'Reilly.

"Cheers," he said, and took a long pull. "There've been a hell of a lot of changes since I started as a dispensary doctor in the Liberties of Dublin in the

'30s. Before I came north here to work for Doctor Flanagan."

Barry knew O'Reilly's history since he'd come to Ballybucklebo in 1939, but this was new and interesting. "Dispensary doctor?"

He took another drink. "Aye. Before the war, the Irish government employed GPs to work in the slums of Dublin and in the poorer country districts to provide a kind of basic medical care for the indigent. The system paid me a salary and the patients didn't have to cough up unless they had a job and could afford to." He took another drink. "I tell you, Barry, I was getting pretty expert at treating fleas, bedbugs, lice, scabies, and not always for the patients." Barry watched as O'Reilly suddenly began scratching his left side under his arm. "You've no idea how much DDT improved the lives of our troops in the war. Killed lice, fleas, mosquitoes. Cut down the numbers of cases of typhus, plague, malaria—"

"But have you read *Silent Spring*?"

"Rachel Carson? I have. I don't think we'll be using much DDT in the future. It's—"

Barry was aware of a figure standing at the table. He looked up to see Bertie Bishop, beer-barrel squat, legs braced apart. One thumb was hooked under the jacket lapels of his blue chalk-stripe suit, the other hand clutched a paper bag.

"A word, O'Reilly," Bertie said.

O'Reilly said, "Won't you have a seat, Councillor?"

"I'll stand, so I will. I told my friend I'd not be long."

Judging by the look on Bertie's face, Barry thought, the man was not a harbinger of comfort and joy.

"First Flo telt me if I seen youse to say she's very upset about Mrs. Kincaid and she's sent her a get-well card on behalf of the whole Women's Union, and a wheen of flowers. I'm sorry myself. We all hope she gets better soon."

"Generous, Bertie. Thank you. I'll be sure to tell Kinky. And please do thank your wife."

"Flo? That one? Do you know she wanted me to ask if youse two needed any laundry doing? No wife of mine's going to be like a common washerwoman, so she's not. I told her youse was big enough and ugly enough to look after yourselves and if youse wasn't yiz could use Lilliput Laundry."

"Indeed we could," O'Reilly said mildly. "Now if that's all?" He started to turn away.

"It's not. I've more, so I have. A whole lot more."

"Oh?" O'Reilly turned back. "Do go on."

Barry kept his counsel, but leant forward, drink forgotten.

Bertie's voice was harsh, belligerent. "Youse've a white cat?" he demanded.

"Lady Macbeth," O'Reilly said.

"I don't give a toss if you call her Queen Elizabeth II of the House of bloody Windsor. Keep the thing in your house." Bertie thrust his face forward.

"Whatever for?" O'Reilly leant back in his chair.

"You know I have racing pigeons? I've a loft over Steve Wallace's garage, like. Across the road from here."

"Everybody knows about your birds, Bertie, especially the ladies who have to redo their washing when your flock's gone overhead."

Barry saw the colour of Bertie's cheeks deepen. An artery throbbed at his temple. He spluttered.

"And I hear they've been doing very well. Won a couple of races recently," O'Reilly said.

Barry listened.

O'Reilly continued, "It must be very satisfying when they start coming back into the loft from a long way away. I'd think so anyway."

Barry recognised that O'Reilly was giving Bertie a chance to simmer down.

"Aye, well, there's two of mine won't be doing that no more. Your bloody cat got them, so it did." Little drops of spittle flew. "They're dead as feckin' dodos."

Barry sat straight up. Lady Macbeth certainly was never confined to barracks and cats did roam.

"Are you sure, Bertie?" O'Reilly asked, drinking slowly.

"Bloody right I am. Your man Steve Wallace, him that owns the garage, he seen her going in there this afternoon and by the time he got up the stairs, two of my champion birds was dead and your bloody cat had done a runner."

O'Reilly sighed. "But how can you be sure it was my cat? You didn't catch her in flagrante delicto."

"I don't know what the hell you're talking about, O'Reilly, but if I see her again near my loft I'll catch her in the backside with the toe of my feckin' boot.

She'll be wearing her arsehole for a necklace." He pounded a fist on the tabletop. "You keep your white cat to hell away from my pigeons. Do you hear, O'Reilly?"

"Unless I was stone deaf, Councillor, it would be difficult not to. I imagine they probably caught a word or two across the lough in Carrickfergus."

Barry noticed that although his words were measured, O'Reilly's nose tip was alabaster.

"If I get my hands on it—"

"I think you've made your point."

"Good night then to yiz." Bishop stumped away, turned, and came back. He slammed the paper bag on the table. "I near forgot. Flo baked these here gingersnaps. Said if I seen youse in here the night to give yiz them. She hopes youse enjoy them. I don't give a tinker's curse if you choke on them." He stormed off.

"Do thank her for me, Bertie," O'Reilly said to the man's departing back.

Barry'd seen colour photos of Antarctica where the ice was so white it had a blue tinge. So, it seemed, did the tip of O'Reilly's nose.

Willie Dunleavy stood by the table. "Excuse me, but I've just had Helen Hewitt on the phone. She says come home at once. It's urgent."

"Come on, Barry. Forget about Bertie. Leave that." O'Reilly didn't finish his pint either. "I'll settle up next time, Willie," he said, and charged for the door with Barry and Arthur Guinness in close pursuit.

12

Why Did You Answer the Phone?

"Sorry to drag you from the Duck," Helen said, "but when Jack . . . I mean Doctor Mills called—"

"Barry, get Mills on the phone. Now," O'Reilly said.

Barry dialled.

"Did he say why he was calling, Helen?" O'Reilly asked. He knew Jack couldn't tell her anything in detail about Kinky's condition. Even if young Mills had been seeing Helen for a month or two after Sonny and Maggie's wedding, she wasn't part of the medical fraternity. But perhaps Jack had given some hint, anything to let them know what this was about.

"No, sir. He sounded in a big hurry, and just told me to have you get hold of him as soon as possible."

Damnation. It must mean Kinky had taken a turn for the worse. "Sit, Arthur, and there's no need to apologise for sending for us, Helen. You did exactly the right thing."

Helen smiled. "Thank you, sir." She moved to the pegs and took down her coat.

O'Reilly fidgeted, tapped his foot, and frowned at the inevitable delay before one of the hospital operators on the understaffed switchboard could answer. Then Jack would probably have to be bleeped. "Give me the phone," he said gruffly, as if being on one end would speed things up. He couldn't bear the waiting. Barry relinquished the phone, and O'Reilly took it in time to hear, "Hello? Doctor Mills here."

"Mills? Fingal O'Reilly."

Jack Mills sounded calm. "I'm sorry to have to tell you, but your Mrs. Kincaid's gone downhill."

"Damn." He turned to Barry. "It's Kinky. She's had a setback. Mills, what's exactly wrong with her?"

"She developed a fever midmorning. The wound was a bit inflamed, but nothing else was obvious. Sir Donald didn't think it was serious enough for us to bother you and that we should simply watch her. Unfortunately, her temperature spiked a couple of hours ago and she's wheezy in her left lung base. We were pretty sure she'd got a postop bronchial pneumonia."

Or it could be an abscess under the diaphragm, lung collapse, or a pulmonary embolism, O'Reilly thought. Postoperative complications in the lungs did occur, but infrequently. And why Kinky Kincaid of all people? The woman had always seemed indestructible. On a number of occasions she'd had to nurse him through bad bouts of flu and a recent attack of acute bronchitis. It was unfair she'd been taken ill at all and doubly so that complications should set in.

Mills was saying, "We took a portable X-ray here

on the ward." O'Reilly read between the lines. Either Kinky wasn't well enough to be taken to the X-ray department, or bless her, a bit on the heavy side for nurses to wrestle on and off trolleys. He hoped it was the latter.

"There's involvement of the left lower lobe. Sir Donald started her on pen and strep."

Penicillin and streptomycin were the first line of defence against infection. Only if they failed were the newer antibiotics like tetracycline used.

"At least," Jack said, "her bowel sounds are normal, so we've taken her naso-gastric tube out and she's getting a liquid diet. She's still on a drip and getting plenty of painkillers. I'll give you an update if anything changes, but I'm sure she'll be grand. Unless you really want to, there's no need to come charging up here tonight."

"Thanks, Mills. We appreciate you letting us know." O'Reilly hung up. "I'm sure she'll be grand," those were Jack Mills's words, O'Reilly thought. Not a year into his training and already the young man was developing the confidence so characteristic of surgeons that armoured them to slice into their fellow beings—and lose some of them intra- or postoperatively without the doctor going into a decline. He glanced at Barry. There was another young man whose self-confidence had come on remarkably. "Looks like she has left lower lobe broncho-pneumonia, Barry. She's on the right antibiotics and Jack Mills says she needs a good night's sleep. Says there's no reason for us to race up there." Which of course was an unspoken message that Mills did not think Kinky was in any danger of dying. O'Reilly then realised that in his hurry to brief Barry he'd forgotten that Helen was standing there. "Helen—"

"I never heard nothing. Mum's the word," she said, and mimed pulling a zip across her lips, "but I hope Mrs. Kincaid gets better soon."

"Thank you, on both counts," O'Reilly said. "I know you'll keep it to yourself." He said to Barry, "Do me a favour?"

"Sure."

"Take Arthur to the back garden and on your way put the grub we were given in the kitchen."

"Come on, Arthur." Barry started to do as he'd been asked, then frowned as if remembering something and said, "I'd like to make a phone call when I've finished. I need to discuss something with Miss Nolan from the school."

"Go right ahead," O'Reilly said, and thought, And I hope it's nothing to do with professional matters. She's a pretty girl, that Sue Nolan, and it's time Barry started seeing young women again. O'Reilly rummaged in his pocket and turned to Helen. "Helen. Home. Thank you for sending for us. By just fielding that one call you've earned your keep this week." He gave her a pound note.

"Thank you, sir." She put the money in her handbag. "And I do hope Mrs. Kincaid does get well very soon."

"We all do. Let me help you on with your coat," O'Reilly said, and as he held it Lady Macbeth appeared from the dining room and began weaving against Helen's legs.

"The wee craythur hasn't left me alone all afternoon," Helen said. She bent and stroked the cat's head. "Night-night, your ladyship. Night, Doctor O'Reilly. And that *Oliver Twist* was great, so it was. I left it on the shelf. 'Please, sir. I want some more.'" Helen shook her head. "At least we don't have parish workhouses anymore."

"You're right." He opened the door. "Good night, Helen. See you on Monday, and don't worry about Kinky. She'll be fine." I hope. And before he realised it, he'd crossed his fingers.

As soon as he was in the lounge, O'Reilly poured a Jameson, plumped himself down in an armchair, set his booted feet on a footstool, and yawned. He rolled his shoulders, yawned again, and drank. Admit it, O'Reilly, you're no spring chicken anymore. You're tired. It was the worry about Kinky, he supposed. He was perfectly able, thank you, to deal with the day-to-day running of the practice. He sipped. Damn it all, he still felt twenty inside—well, twenty-four. That was how old he'd been when he met Kitty O'Hallorhan for the first time. Kitty. He glanced at the other armchair. Not long now until she'd be sitting there at his side, of an evening, after work. Him with his pipe and whiskey and her with a gin and tonic. He smiled, relished the thought, and recalled vividly a day when he'd walked with her down Dublin's O'Connell Street and a beggar had sold him the sheet music for "Star of the County Down." He sang,

—No horse I'll yoke and no pipe I'll smoke 'til my plough with the rust turns brown,
And a smiling bride by my own fireside is the star of the County Down.

That would be grand. Kitty up here, Kinky down below in her quarters, friends again with Kitty. Of course Kinky'd come round once she got better, and—

"You're in fine voice tonight, Fingal," Barry said.

O'Reilly harrumphed and said, "I didn't hear you come in." He nodded at the sideboard. "Help yourself."

Barry shook his head, but took a chair. "Do you think Kinky will be all right?"

"She should be fine," he said, and swallowed some whiskey. "Kinky's a tough old bird, you know. It could be a lot worse." He sipped thoughtfully. "I'm old enough to remember medicine before antibiotics, God bless them, and even back then lots of patients recovered from pneumonia. I'll tell you about a one-armed army sergeant, Paddy Keogh, one day." O'Reilly knew he was whistling in the dark. They both hoped Kinky'd be fine but also knew there were no promises. "I agree with Jack that we let her get a good night's sleep tonight, but how'd you feel about going to see her tomorrow, Barry? She'll appreciate a visit from one of us."

"Should it not be you?"

O'Reilly shook his head. "Your turn. I know she'd like to see you too, and Kitty's coming here and can answer the phone if I'm called out."

"I'd love to see Kinky, and I could use a trip to town. I'll pop into Robinson and Cleaver's. I need a new shirt or two."

O'Reilly wondered if new shirts and his phone call to a certain Miss Sue Nolan had anything to do with each other.

The door that Barry had not quite closed began to open and a white nose appeared. Lady Macbeth was letting herself in. O'Reilly recalled Bertie Bishop's accusations against her. "Barry," he said, "what did you think of what Bertie Bishop said about her ladyship?"

Barry frowned. "I hope it wasn't her, but all cats are bird killers. There is another possibil—"

"It couldn't have been this cat, by God," said O'Reilly suddenly. "Helen just said her ladyship had been here with her all afternoon. So Bertie can go and fly his kite. We have a watertight alibi." O'Reilly sipped his whiskey and wondered why Barry wasn't smiling.

"For her ladyship, yes."

"And isn't that all we need?"

"For her it is," Barry said, "but I've been thinking. I saw Colin Brown today. He lives across the road from Bishop's pigeon loft."

"And what has that to do with the price of corn?"

"Colin has a new pet, Butch, a ferret. A white ferret."

"And you think—?"

Barry shrugged. "Could be."

"Jasus," said O'Reilly. "And I'll bet Colin dotes on his pet and if it is the culprit, it doesn't bear thinking about how the young lad's going to feel if Bertie finds out and demands retribution."

13

Keep Thy Tongue from Evil

Barry had spent four and a half years working at the Royal Victoria Hospital, and each time he returned it was like coming home. He paused for a moment in the main corridor to listen to the bustle of uniformed staff, all, it seemed, hurrying on missions of the utmost importance. Cleaners sedately dusted, pushed brooms and electric polishers, clearly content to be in no particular rush.

Small groups of bewildered-looking civilians were coming in through the front entrance and heading for the wards. At this hour on a Saturday midmorning they'd be relatives arriving to collect discharged family members, and they'd be having mixed feelings. Barry knew it was considered unlucky in Ulster to be discharged on a Saturday, but there was always pressure to find beds for new admissions.

He turned onto the ward and went straight to the nurses' desk. A junior sister, recognisable by her navy blue uniform, had her back to him. "Morning, Sister. I'm Doctor—"

"How are you, Barry?" she said without turning.

He recognised the voice. Joy Lewis had been promoted since, as a staff nurse, she'd been one of Jack Mills's conquests. "Hello, Joy."

She turned. "You're here to see Mrs. Kincaid? Pity about her setback. Up until that she was doing well. But her temperature's down a bit this morning so the antibiotics are starting to work."

Kinky's temperature coming down was promising.

"She's in the side ward, but you may have trouble finding her, she's surrounded by so many flowers and get-well cards." Joy grinned. "And she's been given enough grapes to start a winery. She's not been well enough to see anyone but family, and we've turned away a lot of disappointed folks."

"She's much loved at home," Barry said. "I'll go and say hello." He headed for Kinky's room and wondered how many times he'd walked these units. They dated back to 1903, when the hospital had been opened by King Edward VII and named for his mother, Victoria Regina, who had died two years before. The layout had barely changed since then.

He let himself in. The scent of flowers was over-powering. Joy Lewis had not exaggerated. Long spears of gladioli protruded from profusions of multico-loured carnations. Someone had sent roses the colour of ocean coral. He recognised bluebells, wood anem-ones, and primroses, so some friends with not much cash must have collected bunches of wildflowers. Kinky lay propped on pillows, an intravenous drip in an arm vein, and the prongs of green plastic oxygen spectacles in her nostrils. One was red and irritated where her gastric tube must have been.

He heard the sounds of hissing oxygen, and her shallow breathing. Beads of sweat glistened on her forehead. Her eyes had been closed, but now they opened. "Doctor Laverty," she said.

"Kinky. How are you feeling? Doctor O'Reilly and everybody in the village send their love."

"That's very kind." She gasped. "I've been better, sir." It clearly took an effort to speak. "But my poor tummy's not as sore. It's my chest." She coughed and then collected herself. "Your friend, that nice Doctor Mills, is most attentive and the nurses are darlings, so." She wrinkled her nose. "It's not fair to say it, but the gruel I've to eat? I'd be better off having some of my own beef tea." She coughed again, a moist, con-gested sound.

Barry laid a hand on her arm. It was hot, clammy. The antibiotics might be starting to work, but she wasn't cured yet. "Don't tire yourself," he said, found a chair, and sat. "Did you see your sister?"

"I did, so. Fidelma came on Wednesday and again on Thursday, and Friday, but it does be powerful dear for her and Eamon to stay in that guest house on Eglinton Avenue, and the farm needs attending to. They're for home tomorrow." She lay back on her pillows. "It's a long way." She gasped and took shallow breaths. "I shall miss them."

Barry waited while she settled herself. "Sister told Doctor O'Reilly that the hospital would be needing a new switchboard for all the inquiries about you from Ballybucklebo."

"Sister said she'd to send a lot of folks away. I'll not lack for company once I'm feeling better." She forced a smile. "But I'm not sure I would wish to see anybody at the moment." She closed her eyes and her head lolled to one side. "I am tired, so."

"Would you like to sleep now, Kinky?"

She shook her head and stifled a cough. "Even my sleep has me weary, so. I suppose it's the morphine. Thoughts are buzzing around my head like angry wasps." She looked at Barry. "Memories. Lots of memories. Of myself, as a girl, a long time ago, in Cork. We lived on a farm near Beal na mBláth. And we did be close, so, even if my big sister Sinead was a bossy woman." She coughed. "But Fidelma and I really came together when the *dubh sidhe*, the black faeries, took her man Connor MacTaggart. In a blizzard it was . . . on Saint Stephen's Day."

Barry sat stock still. Kinky rarely spoke about her private life, but if she wanted—and needed—to talk, he was trained to listen. Besides, he was intrigued. He already knew Kinky was fey, had the sight. He himself found it difficult to believe in the Irish spirit world with its banshees and pookahs, thevshees and doov shees, but he knew many country folk believed implicitly.

She turned her head and must have caught sight of her stuffed hare. Barry heard a shuddering indrawing of breath. It caught in her throat and she made a tiny cry. When he saw the tears on her cheeks he wasn't sure if they had been caused by the pain in her chest or in her heart. "*Ochón, Ochón,* my poor Paudeen," she said softly, "my *giorra mór.*"

"It's all right, Kinky," he said, "it's all right. I understand." And he did. When Barry had been moping over Patricia Spence back in July, Kinky had encouraged Barry to see other young women, telling him about how, as a young woman herself, she'd been besotted with and had married a fisherman from Ring in County Cork. Six months later he'd drowned. She'd met other boys after that, but no one she'd loved as well as Paudeen Kincaid. Barry had been touched by the confidence then, and he was now.

She took another breath, not as deeply as the last, and said, "I'm sorry to be weepy, sir. I think that morphine must be like when the drink does be on some people. They can't help saying what is foremost in their minds, so."

"I don't mind."

"And I shouldn't be so selfish, thinking only about myself. I've had a grand home now at Number One."

She looked up at him, and said, "Tell me, sir, are you and himself managing?" He heard her concern. "Tell me the truth, now."

"The village has rallied round. We're coming down with grub, but we really miss your cooking, Kinky."

Her smile pleased him.

"And who answers the phone?"

"Helen Hewitt has been helping out. She's a very smart girl." He'd noticed how professionally she'd handled last night's worry about Kinky.

"I see." She took two short and shallow breaths. "At weekends too?"

Barry shook his head. "No, Kitty came down today. She'll look after calls if Doctor O'Reilly's out and that lets me have time off so I could come and see you."

"And your coming is appreciated."

There was a hesitancy in the words, even though Barry knew they were sincere. He wondered if a bit of local news might cheer Kinky. She was always able to take pleasure in the good fortune of others. "Do you remember Miss Nolan, the teacher?"

"I do, so."

"I'm taking her for dinner tonight. Picking her up at eight."

A smile passed over Kinky's face and she laid her hand lightly on Barry's. "It does do me good to hear it. You two have a lovely time. A young fellah your age should see lots of girls as long as you're not like the Corkman looking for a stick."

"A stick?"

"Aye, so. He went into a wood for to cut a walking stick, but every one he was going to pick he shook his head and said, 'Sure there'll be a better one further along, so.' And do you know what happened?"

Barry shook his head.

"He'd still not cut one until he was out of the wood entirely."

Barry smiled. "I'm not sure I'm ready to be getting married quite yet, but I appreciate the advice."

"I wasn't sure at first whether I was ready to get married either," said Kinky, her voice quavering. "But my Paudeen, well, he was—"

Barry was suddenly aware that the hand Kinky had laid on his was ice-cold. Gently he withdrew his hand, ready to take her pulse. "Kinky, are you all right?"

"Don't go, Doctor Laverty. I . . . last night, late, very late, I suppose about three o'clock, I saw something—"

Barry felt the hairs on his forearms lift. The Corkwoman's eyes had a glazed look; it was almost as if Kinky wasn't really in the room anymore.

"It might just have been a dream, or the morphine, but I could have sworn Paudeen was talking to me. I could see his long black hair and the creases round his eyes. 'Maureen,' he says to me, 'you do be a handsome woman. I do love you yet.' My heart near burst."

Barry felt himself close to tears.

"And Paudeen went on, 'And because I do, I wish you'd think again about finding another fellah. It would please me, so, to see you settled and happy.'"

Barry held his breath.

"And I reached out to him, but he was gone." She looked straight at Barry with a bittersweet smile. Then the smile faded, her eyes focused, and she said in her usual voice, "And you said Miss O'Hallorhan has come down? I suppose she'll cook, so?"

Barry exhaled and, mind still whirling with what Kinky had told him, said, "I surely hope Kitty will. It would be nice to have something that's not been re-heated." He heard a shuddering sigh, looked down, and saw another tear trickle down Kinky's cheek. Dear God, he thought, what have I said? Didn't O'Reilly tell me that Kinky was feeling vulnerable about her position at Number One? And haven't I just told her how her two prime functions can so easily be delegated— and to Kitty? "It's just a fill-in thing, Kinky. Honestly," Barry said. "Only until you get better. We need you back home."

"I am sure you're right, sir," she said. "Only temporary . . . until July, when Miss O'Hallorhan comes to live full time." There was a catch in her voice and she coughed.

Barry cleared his throat. He thought of O'Reilly's first law of holes: When you find yourself in a hole, for Christ's sake stop digging. He touched her hand and looked down into two black eyes that stared hopefully up into his. "Kinky, please don't worry. We all want you better and back at Number One running things. Now you save up all your strength and please, please get well."

She coughed and forced a grin that did not touch her eyes. "I think, sir, that if you don't mind, I'd like to take a nap now, so."

"Of course." Barry turned to go. "And if there's anything you need, ask Sister to phone us." He realised that Kinky, now clutching her toy hare, was already asleep. "Sleep well," he whispered, "and please don't worry." And he cursed himself for his carelessness. The Corkwoman with the heart of corn, who moments ago had mourned the loss of her Paudeen, who still felt she might like to remarry and have a home of her own, was terrified she was going to lose the only one she'd known since before the war. And he, Barry Laverty, had carelessly given her more cause for worry. Damn it. Damn it to hell.

14

But Lo the Old Inn

"I'm not quite ready," said Sue Nolan when she answered the door of her ground-floor flat in the Holywood terrace house. Something of an understatement, Barry thought. He took in her baggy Aran sweater, jeans, and bare feet. Most of her hair was hidden under a towel, curly wisps escaping at her nape. Yet she looked so charming Barry felt his annoyance softening. She showed Barry into a sitting room dominated by crowded bookshelves. "The meeting ran late, I only got in ten minutes ago. Have a pew. I'll be as quick as I can." She fled along a hallway. Max jumped off the couch, made a beeline for Barry, stood on his hind legs, and tried to lick Barry's face.

"Gerroff, dog." Barry tried to fend off the advances.

A door opened and Sue called from down the hall. "Max. Get down." The edge in her voice was tinged with exasperation. "Maximillian, get in here. Now."

The animal went back down on all fours, eyed Barry, then turned and padded down the hallway. A door opened, then closed. Silence.

Barry surveyed the wreckage. He'd gone to great pains with his appearance, and was wearing his only suit, one of the new shirts he'd bought after he'd seen Kinky, and his Old Campbellian tie. He couldn't remember who had said that first impressions were things you didn't get a second chance to make, but this was his first date with Sue and he'd been conscious of making a good one. He glimpsed his scowl reflected in the glass of a watercolour landscape. His tie was askew and long white dog hairs coated the front of his charcoal-grey jacket.

Damn it, he'd been on time, to the minute at eight o'clock, and their reservation at the Old Inn in Crawfordsburn was for eight thirty. They were going to be late. Four years of boarding school had instilled in him a near-obsessive respect for punctuality. Still, he thought, trying to wipe the hair from his jacket, he'd just have to be like Aggie Arbuthnot and thole things he couldn't change. It was hardly an auspicious start, though. Sue Nolan might be achingly lovely, but her idea of punctuality and her dog's manners could both use some work. He caught another glimpse of himself in the glass. "Eejit," he muttered. "Don't be so bloody pompous." This was his first Saturday night out in months. The maitre d' at the Old Inn would just have to forgive a little tardiness. Relax-ay-voo, in the immortal words of Dean Martin.

He was about to sit on the sofa, then thought better of it. The cushions were coated in Max's hairs. He wandered over to a bookcase. Several shelves were crowded with textbooks about education, as his own were with medical tomes, but Barry was more interested in what else Sue Nolan read. *Some Experiences of an Irish R.M.* by Somerville and Ross. He'd read it too, and enjoyed the eccentric characters. *Ulysses* by James Joyce. He'd read it, after a fashion, and had found the thing incomprehensible. Well-thumbed volumes of *Revolt in the North: Antrim and Down in 1798* by Charles Dickson and *A History of Ireland* by Edmund Curtis sat side by side. So she was interested in Irish history, even though she wasn't able to teach it to her pupils. This sat next to—he had to squint to read the title—*Go Tell It on the Mountain,* by James Baldwin. Barry recognised the name of the black American writer and civil rights activist. *Strength to Love* by Martin Luther King, Jr., kept Baldwin's work company. The world was well aware of the struggle for civil rights in the United States. The violently opposed march in Selma, Alabama, had been held only two months previously. The fight for racial equality must interest Sue.

Barry himself was apolitical. He had never had much time for the orange and the green, the Loyalist-Republican divide that bedevilled public life in Ulster. Fortunately, in the mid-'60s, it seemed to be quiescent in the province in general and certainly in Ballybucklebo. Long may it stay that way. Barry was convinced that good health was worth as much as any political ideology, but although no socialist, he was willing to admire the Labour Government for bringing in the National Health Service in 1947, under which he practised. Every working man and woman made a weekly contribution, so in times of ill health, they paid nothing for their care.

He moved along the shelf. A book by Sir Mortimer Wheeler, the moustachioed archaeologist whose TV appearances had done much to make his discipline popular. There was *The Lonely Girl* by Edna O'Brien; *Catch-22*; *The Chronicles of Narnia*, whose author, C. S. Lewis, had been born in Belfast; *The Sand Pebbles* by American author Richard McKenna; and several works by Barbara Cartland.

"I like books," she said from behind him. "All kinds of stuff."

Barry turned. His mouth opened and he had to swallow before he could say, "My word, you look stunning. Have you got a fairy godmother like Cinderella's back there to help you change?"

She wore a knee-length, sleeveless black dress. Black satin opera gloves complemented a patent leather clutch bag and low-heeled shoes. She spun slowly and he saw that between her shoulder blades there was a diamond cut-out neatly bisected by the single long plait of her hair. "Do you really like it?" she asked. "Dad and Mum gave me the dress for my birthday."

"Yes," he said. "Yes. I really do." He'd remember to ask about her birth date later, but now he moved to the door. "We'd better get a move on or we'll be late for dinner."

"Let me get my coat." She pulled it off a hook on the door. "I know I should wear a hat, but I hate the silly things." She chuckled. "I don't like false eyelashes either even if they are all the rage."

"You don't need them," he said, and meant it. As he helped her put on a lime green coat she lifted her plait over the shawl collar. Close to her he inhaled a gentle perfume.

"You be good now, Max," she said to the springer.

The dog looked at her with soulful eyes and jumped up on the couch.

She closed the door behind them.

When they were settled in Barry's Volkswagen he said, "We're going to the Old Inn at Crawfordsburn." He started the engine.

"Lovely," she said.

"We'll need to be quick. I was told when I made the reservation that they had a full house tonight. Don't want to lose our spot," he said.

"I'm so sorry I was late—"

"No apologies necessary, Miss Nolan, you are worth every minute of the wait."

"Thank you, sir," she said. "I like a man who can pay a girl a compliment."

Barry, entranced by the musk she wore and the nearness of the lovely young woman in the small car, tried to think of some kind of response, but found himself more than unusually tongue-tied. The traffic was heavy on the Belfast to Bangor Road. He would just have to pay attention to his driving. Every Irish village was a bottleneck to through traffic. In Ballybucklebo he stopped behind cars waiting for the traffic light.

She chuckled. "I like blue eyes too."

Barry glanced across at her. She was looking straight at him, one eyebrow raised. He glanced away. This was unheard of. Men were supposed to do the wooing. The best he could manage was, "I . . . um . . . I prefer green." The traffic moved on.

"Green eyes go with red hair," she said, "and red hair can be a sign of someone with a temper."

"Your hair's copper, and I don't believe for one minute you have a temper."

That laugh again. "Try me," she said. "Be cruel to an animal and just watch."

"I think Max is safe from me as long as he keeps his hairs to himself."

Sue reached over and plucked a long white one from the lapel of his jacket. "I see Max has greeted you." The gesture was natural and yet so intimate that he quivered. They passed Number One Main Street. "There's your house," said Sue.

"Well, not exactly mine," said Barry with a grin, "but it's where I live. Things are in a bit of an uproar there at the moment. Our housekeeper is in hospital . . . she's fine," he said quickly, catching a glimpse of Sue's look of distress. "She was quite ill but she's definitely on the mend. I can't tell you what was wrong . . . patient confidentiality. But she'll be fine. In the meantime, though, two bachelors are having to get along without her." Barry had phoned from the ward this morning to let Fingal know about Kinky's general state of health but hadn't mentioned the God-awful brick he'd dropped. He'd not had time to talk about it when he'd gone home to get changed this evening either, although O'Reilly had stuck his head out of the lounge to say that Jack had phoned and Kinky's pneumonia was improving.

"I'll bet the whole village is pitching in," said Sue.

"They are. Hang on." Barry'd let his mind wander and hadn't realised he was going too fast. He felt the rear slide and wrestled the car through a seemingly endless hairpin bend. He was sweating by the time they were back on a straight. "Phew," he said, "sorry about that."

"It was exhilarating," she touched his arm lightly, "but I think that's enough excitement for one drive."

"I'll pay attention," he said, and did, not speaking until he'd made the left turn onto the Crawfordsburn Road where there was no traffic. "There's a bit coming up I've always loved," he said, and drove round a gentle curve. "Just here." The car went from the low purple light of the spring gloaming into a dim tunnel as the road meandered between two rows of ancient elms. Hedge parsley bloomed pale against the darkness of the grass, and the bells of tall foxgloves hung along the verges. Barry glanced up to where the branches intertwined to make a canopy of freshly shot leaves. He let the car coast through and didn't bother to put on the headlights. "My dad, he's on sabbatical in Australia, used to drive me through here if we were going to Belfast. It's one of my earliest memories. It's—" He sought for the words, but when he glanced over at Sue, whatever had been forming in his mind dissolved.

"It's lovely, Barry. Reminds me of a place not too far from Broughshane in Glenarm."

"Which," Barry said, "is no distance from Ballymena. I'm going to be working there starting in July."

"Are you? So you're leaving Doctor O'Reilly's practice?"

"Yes, well, temporarily anyway. I'm going to get my obstetrics training at the Waveney."

The car moved into the velvet night as they left the trees behind. The moon had risen, gibbous, waxing, and silver.

"And I'll be home for the school summer holidays,"

she said. "When you get to Ballymena, where I live in Broughshane's just up the road. Don't forget that back at the Christmas pageant I invited you to come and see the Glens of Antrim. There's a spot called 'The Madman's Window' that's a great place for finding Neolithic things."

"I haven't forgotten the invitation, but I didn't know about the Stone Age stuff. I noticed you had a book by Sir Mortimer Wheeler."

"*The Excavation of Maiden Castle*," she said. "I've an aunt in Dorset and my family used to visit most summers until she died. I've explored that hill fort up and down, every rampart and ditch. It's fascinating."

"You'll have to meet one of our patients," Barry said. "I'll introduce you to Sonny Houston. He's a retired archaeologist."

"I'd love that."

Barry recognised that in making that simple statement he had already decided he wanted a second date with this bright, lovely young woman, one who by her reading tastes had interests ranging from archaeology to American civil rights.

He pulled into the car park of the Old Inn, stopped, and opened her door. He tingled when she, uninvited, took his hand in hers and started pulling him along. "Yes, I'd like to meet Mister Houston—"

Invitation accepted. Great, Barry thought.

"—and right now I'd love a glass of wine," she said as they went into the black-oak-beamed hall.

The dinner-suited maitre d' frowned at Barry, who

said with a straight face, "Maternity case. Sorry we're late, Bernard." Fingal Flahertie O'Reilly wasn't the only one who could bend the truth in a good cause.

"Of course, Doctor Laverty. Let me take the lady's coat."

Barry waited until it had been put in the cloakroom.

"Please come this way. Your table's ready." Bernard led them along a corridor to the dining room.

Sue chuckled and said sotto voce, "Was it a boy or a girl?"

"Twins, actually," and he smiled as Sue stifled a yelp of laughter. "It was the best excuse I could think of."

"For my lateness." She squeezed his hand. "I am sorry about that, but it was an important meeting."

They were seated, menus and a wine list were left, and Bernard discreetly withdrew.

"Was it a curriculum meeting?"

She burst out laughing. "Sorry, it's just that I can't imagine my colleagues meeting on a Saturday night. No, I belong to the Campaign for Social Justice. It was sort of an emergency meeting up in Belfast. The group's grown a lot since it started in Dungannon."

"Oh." Barry had heard of the organisation. Inspired by the civil rights movement in the United States, they'd been agitating for civil rights in Ulster for a couple of years. "One man, one vote and that sort of thing?" As apolitical as he was, Barry reckoned that having as many votes as the properties you owned was unfair to folks who rented and had no vote.

"Exactly," she said. "We've been writing letters to the British P.M., Sir Alec Douglas-Home. We've not achieved much. Tonight we were trying to decide what the next step should be."

She leaned across the table and took his hand in her satin-covered one. "But I don't want to talk any more politics tonight, Barry. Not tonight." She looked into his eyes and for Barry nothing mattered at that moment but those eyes and the satin touch on his hand.

"Tell me more about Barry Laverty." And as she spoke the flame of the candle between them released a curl of smoke that twined itself around two red roses in a slim Waterford vase.

15

They That Have the Power to Hurt

"Almost perfection," O'Reilly said, peering over a plate bearing traces of Hollandaise sauce. "It would have been total bloody perfection if you'd made me four eggs Benedict. You are one of the wonders of the modern world, Kitty O'Hallorhan." Not minding that Barry was also at the table, O'Reilly puckered a pretend kiss for her.

"Glad you enjoyed them. I've always believed Sunday breakfast should be special, but," she inclined her head in the direction of his tummy, "two is plenty for you, Fingal O'Reilly."

"It's also true," said O'Reilly, smiling at her and patting his belly, "that the way to a man's heart is through his stomach." He saw Barry grinning and hazarded a guess at what he was thinking. "Any remarks from you, young man, along the lines of 'for some folks it would be a hell of a long trip' will be treated with the disdain they deserve. Just because you must have had a good night out last night and are full of the joys of spring today there's no need for disrespect for your elders and betters."

Barry laughed. "How could you even begin to suspect me of such a thing, yer honour?"

"Because," said O'Reilly, chuckling, "if I was in your position when that remark was passed and you had a gut like mine, it's what I'd be thinking."

"You're a certified mind reader, just like Kinky, who—" Barry frowned and pushed away his plate.

"You all right, Barry?" O'Reilly asked.

Barry shook his head. "I need to talk to you both about Kinky."

"Kinky?" Kitty said. "But I thought Jack Mills said her temperature was falling and he was certain the antibiotics were working."

Barry took a deep breath. "Physically she's better," he said, "but . . ." He glanced from O'Reilly to Kitty and back to O'Reilly. "I made a gaffe yesterday. I'm sorry. I didn't want to talk about it on the phone."

O'Reilly sat back and waited.

"She asked me how we were managing. I told her how much we missed her cooking."

"After one forgivable error I've become a pretty damn good reheater," O'Reilly said, then smiled at Kitty. "But your fresh cooking has been greatly appreciated."

Barry sighed. "She was agitated from the morphine and very talkative. I think I got carried away . . . not only did I tell her Helen was answering the phone—"

O'Reilly nodded. "You told her Kitty'd be doing a bit of cooking."

"And fielding the calls at the weekend. I'm sorry. I should have kept my mouth shut."

O'Reilly sucked in his breath through his teeth. He could imagine Kinky feeling how easily she could be replaced. He had to get her to understand that Kitty, even after the wedding, would be working full time and that Kinky would be as important here as she had ever been. But simply telling her would not be enough.

"And Kinky was upset?" Kitty asked.

"Very. She cried. I told her not to worry, but, well . . ." Barry shrugged.

"Oh dear," Kitty said.

"You are not to feel as if you've done anything wrong, Barry," O'Reilly said. "Kinky will soon be allowed visitors who aren't family and she would have found out about Helen in no time. She knows Kitty's been coming here. You just confirmed what she must have suspected. In fact, I told her Kitty was coming for the weekend myself, and she knows I can't cook much. To a degree, what's happened now has only brought things to a head a couple of months sooner."

"I'm not sure I understand," Kitty said.

"When you move here in July, once we're married."

"And you think there'll be friction then?"

"For a while. Until she sees there's no threat. I've known Kinky Kincaid for a long time. This is her territory. A chap called Robert Ardrey has written a book about how primates behave. One trait is setting up pecking orders, another is protecting their territory. She's scared she'll lose her position. The concern had started even before the illness and, of course, she's worried. That was clear the day I saw her in hospital. If this hadn't blown up now she'd soon have seen in July that you were too busy with your own work and realized nothing had changed. But now her imagination can run riot."

Kitty asked, "So what can we do?"

"I'm not sure, but I'm glad you told her, Barry. Honesty is always best, and this way it doesn't look as if we're trying to hide anything." O'Reilly grinned and lit his pipe. "When she gets used to the idea that somebody else she can trust will be feeding me—you'll be gone to Ballymena by then, Barry—I might even be able to persuade her to take some decent holidays."

"That'll be the day," Barry said, but nodded and smiled. O'Reilly was relieved to hear him sounding more cheerful.

It was Kitty's turn to nod, if a little slowly.

"So you two try not to let it upset you. I'm not quite sure how to go about pouring oil on Kinky's troubled waters." He felt his eyebrows meet as he struggled with possible solutions. Finally he said, "For the time being, I think we should be comforting to her when we go to visit, but I think we're going to need a bit of action too. The Chinese say 'Talk doesn't cook rice,' and they're right."

"So what should we do, Fingal?" Kitty asked.

Sometimes, O'Reilly thought, being the font of all wisdom could be draining. "Honestly?" He shook his head. "I haven't the foggiest notion now, but I'm sure when we get her home, to her home here at Number One, we'll come up with something," O'Reilly said, then tipped his chair back on its two rear legs and looked at Barry. "Kitty's not going home tonight until after suppertime. How'd you like the rest of the day off?"

"I'd not mind a trip back to the Yacht Club," Barry said. "We start racing next month and there's still work to do on the boat I'm crewing."

He could have Kitty to himself with Barry away. "Off you go then," O'Reilly said, and rocked, teetering on the brink. Yes, something would come up. Kinky was feeling vulnerable now, but she was a sensible woman. A bit of reassurance and time to heal and the Corkwoman would be back in her rightful place here.

He took another long draw on the pipe and let

himself relax. Something white landed on his chest, and he felt his chair going backward, initially in slow motion but gathering speed. He whirled his arms like the sails of a demented windmill and roared, "Bloody cat."

Barry lunged forward. He missed.

O'Reilly clutched for Barry's hand, but grabbed the tablecloth.

Lady Macbeth, emitting an eldritch howl, leapt to the curtains as O'Reilly's chair hit the floor. His teeth rattled. Lady Macbeth continued up the curtains to perch on the pelmet and hurl feline vituperation. Her tail looked like a terrified cactus.

Above her spitting and yowling, O'Reilly could hear the clattering of plates. Forgetting Kitty's presence, he let go a stream of blasphemy that would have made a sailor blush. He was happy enough to accept Barry's hand and struggle upright.

"Holy thundering Mother of the Sainted Baby Jasus in velvet trousers," O'Reilly spluttered. "I'll marmalise that bloody cat. Jumping up on my chest and knocking me arse over teakettle. I'll skin her ali—"

"You'll do no such thing, Fingal O'Reilly," Kitty said. "She was only being affectionate."

O'Reilly glanced up to where Lady Macbeth sat. Her tail had subsided and the little cat was washing her backside. He took a deep breath. Kitty was right, and it wasn't an angry owner her ladyship needed. She already had Bertie Bishop after her hide even if she did have an alibi.

"All right," O'Reilly said. "You're forgiven, your ladyship." He dusted himself off. Nothing broken except a plate or two. Nothing wounded but his pride, and sure wouldn't that recover? "We'll say no more, and I think it would be pleasant to take our coffee upstairs. You can join us or go on any time you like, Barry."

"I'll be off," said Barry, "unless you want some help clearing up this lot."

"No need. Away you go." O'Reilly bent beside Kitty, who had started to pick up bits of broken china. He said, "There's a tray in the kitchen. I'll get it."

"Fingal. These plates are Belleek. Kinky'll know there are two missing. She'll never trust me in her kitchen again." Kitty straightened, holding up a handful of china pieces etched in green and gold shamrocks. "There's a shop in Belfast that carries discontinued patterns. I'm sure I can find replacements there."

"You, Kitty O'Hallorhan, are a gem without price." He straightened, still on his knees.

"She's practically been all the family you've had for years, Fingal. I want to come into it in July as gently as possible."

He bent and kissed her, an urgent yet tender kiss amid the plates and cutlery, the overturned chair and the sounds of Lady Macbeth purring from the pelmet. "Thank you, Kitty. Thank you for helping me try to put Kinky's pieces together again."

16

I Have a Dream

"You're sure you'd not want to get home now, Helen?" said O'Reilly. "It's Friday afternoon. You stayed late last Friday. We can chance not having anyone here to answer the phone for a little while." Helen, who had been washing and ironing all afternoon, was now in her favourite chair by the fire, and Lady Macbeth was in her usual position, curled up by Helen's right hip. He noticed she wasn't reading Dickens. "What have you got there?" he asked.

She held up a magazine. *Popular Science*. "There's a great article here about Professor Dorothy Crowfoot Hodgkin."

"Didn't she get the Nobel for chemistry last year?"

"Aye. Only the third woman to do it. She does this thing called X-ray crystallography and figures out the three-dimensional structure of molecules. It's very, very interesting stuff, so it is. Them two fellahs Watson and Crick would never have figured out the structure of DNA without it."

He heard the enthusiasm. And Helen did have Advanced Senior physics and biology. She probably understood the principles of the subject better than him, although he had been fascinated when the news broke that the two scientists and a Doctor Wilkins had unraveled what the press called "the secret of life" back in the early '50s. They'd got a Nobel in 1962. "I thought your interests were more literary," he said.

"I love reading, but I like science too."

"Good for you," he said, and meant it, "and you really should go home. The word's out about Kinky and most of the folks'll understand if there's no reply."

"Och, Doctor O'Reilly," Helen said, "I'm in no rush. My boyfriend," her lip curled, "the gurrier, took himself off a couple of weeks ago with a wee tramp from Turf Lodge up in Belfast." She shrugged. "I'd just be sitting at home helping my da watch TV. I really don't mind staying on here. Away you on off to see Donal and Julie, and give them my best."

"Bless you, Helen. It's important for the Donnellys. I'll try not to be too long."

"Can I ask you a question, sir, before you go, like? Do you have time?"

"Of course."

"You asked me a while back if I'd like to go to university." She gripped the fingers of her left hand with her right.

"I did."

"This last couple of weeks when you and Doctor Laverty have been out I've been phoning round, looking for a proper job, like you said I could."

"And?"

She shook her head. "I never knew you could be too qualified, but when I tell people I've my Advanced

Senior?" She scowled and shook her head. "They all say I'd cost too much. So I've been thinking."

"Go on."

"You'll not laugh?" Her tones were as serious as a priest giving the last rites and he saw the knuckles of her left hand blanch as her right tightened its grasp.

"Of course not."

"How'd I set about going to Queen's?"

"Queen's?" O'Reilly said. "And why the hell not? You have the marks, so you'll have no trouble getting admitted."

"I rung up yesterday," she said. "My subjects are enough all right, I could get in, but," she sighed, "people like me—"

"You mean women?"

"Naah. There's lots of women at Queen's. I mean . . . my da's a labourer and all." She looked into his eyes.

"And you think you're not good enough? Balls." He'd hated the class system since his student days. "Utter bloody balls. You, Helen Hewitt, are as good as the next man . . . or woman."

"Thank you," she said quietly, "thank you for saying that, but even if I am, it's going to be dear. I asked my da and he says if I really want to go I can live at home for free, but I'd have to travel to Belfast, buy books, clothes, and there's the fees. Seventy pounds a year."

"A lot of money. I know." He vividly remembered

his own student days when he'd had to live on the smell of an oily rag, count his pennies at every turn.

"I hear tell that in America you can get a loan to be a student. You've to pay it back after you qualify, but—"

O'Reilly frowned. "I don't know if you can here, but we can find out, or maybe you could work your way through. I have a friend in Belfast. His boy went to England last summer, to Grimsby. Worked in a frozen pea factory and made enough in his summer holidays to pay his fees."

"I'd not mind working," she scowled, "if I could get a bloody job." Her hand flew to her mouth. "Pardon me, sir. I shouldn't have said that."

O'Reilly chuckled. "Never worry. I used to be a sailor. I've heard a damn sight worse."

"A sailor? Like on a big ship?"

"After I left school. I was in the merchant navy for three years and spent another year on a Royal Navy warship." He grinned. "I needed money to go to university too. Just like you."

"I never knew." There was a hint of awe as she spoke.

"It's not important. What is is finding out about Queen's for you. There might even be scholarships."

"Will you help me, sir? Find out, like?"

"Damn right I will, but it'll take some time, that's all."

"Would you, sir?" Her eyes shone. "Honest?"

"Cross my heart."

"And we've lots of time. Applications don't close until September."

O'Reilly cocked his head on one side. "You've been doing your homework, haven't you?"

"My da says if you want something bad enough it's up to you to work hard enough to get it."

"Your da," said O'Reilly, "is a wise man." And this is one very determined young woman. "I will help you as much as I can, and we'll be keeping you busy here for a while longer while I do. We hope Mrs. Kincaid's coming home next week, but she'll still be taking it easy."

"I'm glad she's on the mend," Helen said, "and I can use the money until she gets back to her work."

O'Reilly grinned. "I'll start asking as soon as I can. Now, what would you like to study?" She had Advanced level passes in sciences, so what would suit a young woman with that background? Botany? Zoology?

Helen blushed, glanced down at the floor, then, straightening her shoulders, looked O'Reilly straight in the eye. Her voice was barely above a whisper. "I . . . I'd like to be a . . . I'd like to be a doctor." The last words came in a rush. "I've been watching you and Doctor Laverty and—"

"By God's Holy trousers," O'Reilly roared, and slapped his thigh. "A doctor? Sweet Jasus. I don't believe it. You, Helen Hewitt, really take the biscuit. I've not heard anything so bloody marvellous in years."

She blushed. "Someone's got to find out what cures

cancer. If that Professor Hodgkin can do research, maybe I could too. For my ma, like."

Oh, Helen, Helen, he thought, it's far too early for you to be thinking about that kind of thing. Let's get you into medical school first. After six years and your houseman's year you'll be like Barry, trying to decide what you want for a career. One step at a time. He hugged her, held her at arms' length, and said, "You have the Advanced entrance requirements, you told me you'd got Junior Latin too, so there's not a reason on God's green earth why you shouldn't go to medical school as long as we can raise the money."

"Doctor O'Reilly," she said, darted forward, pecked his cheek, and stepped back. "Thank you." Her smile was vast and from the corner of each green eye a single silver tear slipped. "Thank you very much."

O'Reilly took a deep breath before saying, "I'll do everything I can. That's a promise." He'd not tell her now, but almost certainly Cromie or Charlie Greer would know about scholarships or funds to help students from working backgrounds. When he met with the lads to discuss the reunion he'd find out. "I'll be back as quick as I can."

O'Reilly, still marvelling at Helen's determination, let himself into the backyard to be greeted by a joyous Arthur. "Come on, lummox," he said, looking up at the hospital-blanket-grey May sky and turning his collar against the steady drizzle.

He drove to Donal and Julie's rented cottage along the Shore Road. Oily rollers marched across a leaden lough. It had been a busy week, but he'd managed to run up to the Royal on Wednesday afternoon to see Kinky, whose daily progress reports from Jack had been, and continued to be, of steady physical improvement. She'd certainly looked much better, was eating solid food, and had only five more days of antibiotics to take. He hoped she would get home next week. Perhaps once she was home, he'd think of something to let her see how much she was needed.

He parked outside the Donnellys, told Arthur to stay, and headed up along the gravel path. He noticed that there were no weeds, which, given Ireland's climate, was remarkable. Someone had done the weeding. Donal and Julie were two house-proud people, considering they'd only been living here since they'd been married last Christmas and now were hoping to move out very soon into their own home. Lots of folks, he knew, would have let the path go for the landlord to sort out.

"Doctor O'Reilly." Julie smiled and said, "Come in. We're both ready." She was wearing a pac-a-mac, a plastic see-through raincoat. It could not hide her belly, neatly rounded with a—he had to think—a twenty-eight-week pregnancy. He followed her into the hall. Donal's bicycle of many colours, which he'd painted from the leftovers in half a dozen paint pots, stood propped against the staircase. A sleek greyhound pushed a questioning muzzle against O'Reilly's hand. "How are you, Bluebird?" O'Reilly stroked the dog's head and wondered when Donal would implement the plan to race her again. He'd mentioned it when he was in the Royal.

"How's about ye, Doc?" Donal appeared from a room to the left. His duncher perched rakishly on a small white bandage. He pointed to it. "Miss Brennan says this here comes off for good on Monday." He grimaced. "I'll be quare nor glad to see the back of it. I'd love to get a good scratch at my nut, so I would."

"Itchiness is a sign of healing," O'Reilly said. "A good sign."

"If you say so, Doc, but it's like I've got the whole of the Third Plague of Egypt under there, so it is."

O'Reilly had to think. What was the third plague Moses had visited on Pharaoh? Lice, that was it. "I can imagine," he said, and felt itchy himself. "Are we all set to go? Doctor Laverty would have liked to come but he's visiting Ag— I mean he's visiting a patient."

Donal dangled keys. "Oh, aye, I know all about that. Julie saw Cissie Sloan at the grocer's and she said Miss Brennan asked Doctor Laverty to take a look at Aggie's very close veins. She's got a temperature and a ferocious aching in her leg, so she has."

So much for patient confidentiality, thought O'Reilly with a grin. If Cissie Sloan knew something, the whole of the townland would know inside an hour.

"Your man Dapper Frew, the estate agent, him

that's Mister Coffin the undertaker's cousin, give me these here," Donal said, shaking the key ring. "Said for to let ourselves in."

"Grand," said O'Reilly. He'd heard that estate agents in North America showed potential buyers round houses for sale. Here in Ulster the owner did the showing, but Myrtle Siggins, who'd lived to the grand age of 101, had been dead for a year now. Clearly Dapper, a fellow piper in the Ballybucklebo Highlanders, trusted Donal to look round on his own. "Let's go."

"You be a good girl, Bluebird," Donal said to the greyhound, who looked from eyes abrim with adoration for her master. He turned to O'Reilly. "Lead on, MacDuff, sir."

17

The Fury and Mire of Human Veins

Barry parked in the housing estate and headed for one of the identical terrace houses. The drizzle had stopped and the pavement, decorated with the blurred chalk outlines of hopscotch, shone damply in bright contrast to the scummy puddles that had collected where the tarmac was cracked. Cigarette butts disintegrated in the gutters and kept company with discarded fish-and-chip wrappers.

Colleen Brennan opened the door. "Thanks for coming, Doctor Laverty. Aggie's in the parlour."

Barry hung his coat on the hall coatstand, the one he'd used three days ago when he'd popped in to make sure Aggie's superficial thrombophlebitis was getting better. It had been—then. "You think it's the deep veins?" That's what Colleen had said on the phone.

Colleen Brennan was a thickset, sandy-haired woman of thirty-five who had been the district nurse in Ballybucklebo for thirteen years. She nodded. "Aggie has a temperature of one hundred point two and says her leg hurts. It is tender."

"I see." Both were signs of deep venous thrombosis. "I don't like the sound of that," he said. "Let's take a look at her."

"This way."

Barry followed the nurse into a small room. A worn rug covered the linoleum in front of the grate where a coal fire had been banked with slack, little pieces of a low-quality coal. When dampened and put over the ordinary coals, it slowed the rate of burning and saved money. Aggie lay on a couch underneath a red blanket. "Afternoon, Doctor," she said. "I'm terrible sorry to drag youse out in this mucky weather, so I am."

"Don't worry, Aggie," Barry said. "Miss Brennan wanted me to see you."

"Aye. Well." She moved herself farther up the couch. "Before we start on me, how's Mrs. Kincaid? I knew

she'd been taken poorly but Cissie told me she's still
in the Royal and had to have an operation. It's terrible, so it is. Poor crayter."

"She was quite sick," Barry said, "but she's on the
mend."

"If youse sees her, tell her I was asking after her, so
I was."

"I will," Barry said. "I'm sure she'll be pleased." He
moved closer to the couch. "Miss Brennan says you're
not so well, Aggie."

She shrugged. "Them hot water bottles, and towels, and the aspirin all helped. The red bit's got much
wee-er, but I took an awful ache in my calf this morning, you know. It wasn't like the first one, but I didn't
want to bother you, sir. I waited until Miss Brennan
called by."

Barry resisted the temptation to remind Aggie that
he'd told her not to thole it, but call him if she was
worried. She'd not be the first of his patients who, out
of consideration for their doctor's time, had let their
condition deteriorate. "I'd better have a look," he
said. He waited until Aggie had thrown back the blanket. The hem of her tartan wool dressing gown was
pulled up. Barry crouched beside her. She lay so her
left leg was on the outside of the couch. The red area
he'd first seen last Tuesday had practically vanished.
"Show me where it hurts," he said.

She pointed to the centre of her calf. No superficial vessels coursed beneath the skin, but the deeper

posterior tibial and peroneal veins drained the calf muscles and were prone to clotting and causing pain. Her ankle looked swollen. "This won't hurt," Barry said, and pressed his fingertips into the swollen area above her ankle. Pits formed and were slow to disappear. That was oedema, fluid collecting there because the damaged vein could not carry it away. Another sign. "Tell me if this is sore," he said, and palpated her calf over the courses of the deep veins.

She sucked in her breath as his fingers probed.

"Sorry," he said and, before she had time to object, rapidly flexed her ankle toward her shin.

"Owwwwch." She gasped and screwed up her face. "That's right sore, so it is, not like the last time you done that."

A positive Homan's sign, which, while not infallible, if taken with all the other findings made Barry sure that Aggie did have a deep venous thrombosis. "You were right, Miss Brennan," he said. "You've got trouble in a deep vein, Aggie."

Colleen inclined her head but did not smile. Barry understood that her concern for the patient outweighed her professional satisfaction at having been correct. And she was right to be worried. Aggie was at risk of a piece of the clot breaking off, being carried to the lungs, and causing pulmonary embolism, a potentially lethal condition.

Treatment was straightforward, but although he could start it here, she would have to be admitted for follow-up and monitoring. "I'm sorry, Aggie," he said, "but you've got a deep clot. We call that phlebo-thrombosis."

"Fleebo . . . fleebo . . . I'd never get my tongue round the half of that," she said. "Is fleebo-whatsit bad? It certainly sounds as if it is, so it does."

He didn't like not telling the truth, but by the same token he didn't want to terrify her. "Probably not if we get treatment started straight away. I'll have to give you an injection." He stood up.

"I don't like them needles," Aggie said, "but if you must, you must."

"Miss Brennan, could you call the ambulance, please?"

"Of course." She left.

"Ambulance?" Aggie asked. "Can youse not fix me here, like?"

Barry rummaged in his bag. "I wish I could," and he did, "but you'll not be in long. I'll give you a medicine called heparin here. It'll work at once and stop the clot spreading."

"That's good," she said.

"You'll have to get five doses more of it."

"Needles?"

" 'Fraid so, but you'll get another medicine called warfarin in tablets to thin your blood, prevent more clotting. Once your specialists get the dose of warfarin right, they'll stop the injections."

She frowned. "Get the dose right? Should they not know already if they're specialists?"

"Everybody reacts differently," Barry said. "The doctors measure a thing called the prothrombin time. Once it's twice as long as normal, they'll know that's the right dose of the medicine for you and they'll let you come home. I'm sorry I can't do that for you here. The tests have to be done in a laboratory and you need nurses round the clock to give you the medicines." He found the bottle of heparin and a prepacked hypodermic syringe and needle.

"Boys-a-dear," she said, "modern science is a wonderful thing."

Barry dampened a ball of cotton wool with methylated spirits. The acrid fumes cut through the aroma of the smoking slack and tickled his nose. He turned his head away and sneezed. "Excuse me," he said, then swabbed the rubber cap of the heparin bottle and rapidly withdrew 15,000 units of the drug.

"They'll be here in half an hour," Miss Brennan said.

Barry hadn't heard her return.

"Good," he said. "Can you give me a hand?" He held up the loaded syringe. "IV," he said.

She moved to Aggie. "Hold out your arm, dear."

Aggie did and Colleen encircled it with both hands above the elbow. The antecubital vein began to distend.

Barry swabbed the elbow's hollow, slipped the needle into the vein, withdrew the plunger, and was pleased to see smoky turbulence. Blood had entered the barrel, proving the needle was in the vein. "Let go, Miss

Brennan." It took moments to inject the heparin. "All done," he said, removing the needle and pressing the cotton wool ball over the puncture.

"That wasn't too bad, sir," Aggie said. "Thank you."

Barry smiled. "They'll have you better in no time."

"They will," Colleen Brennan said. She turned to Barry. "I'm sure you've other cases, Doctor. I'll tidy up here. Get Aggie ready to go. Keep her company 'til the ambulance comes."

Barry did not have any more calls to make, but he did want to hear how O'Reilly had got on with the Donnellys. They were probably back by now. "Thank you," he said.

"Excuse me, sir," Aggie said, "before you go?"

"Yes, Aggie." Barry put the used syringe and heparin bottle back in his bag. He removed the cotton wool ball. Good. She wasn't bleeding from the puncture. He chucked the ball onto the coals, where it sizzled and burst into a tiny fireball.

"Colin Brown's mammy, Connie, looked in to see me. Her and me's in the Ballybucklebo Strolling Players, you know. She was a lovely Juliet last year, so she was. I was Nurse."

"I'm sorry I missed that," Barry said, marvelling at the depths that flowed beneath the surface of this place.

"Aye, well, we're doing Brian Friel's new play, *Philadelphia Here I Come,* this year. I'm Madge . . . at least I will be once my leg's better, and Connie's Kate Doogan." Aggie lowered her voice. "When Connie was here, and no harm to youse, sir, but—"

Barry knew a criticism was coming. Ulsterfolk always prefaced one that way.

"—she told me she didn't reckon you and Doctor O'Reilly were any great shakes as cooks."

Barry chuckled. "She's right."

"If you pop into my kitchen there's a cherry cake I baked, and before you get mad, sir, I mixed it all lying here. I only got up to put it in and take it out of the oven, so I did."

"That's very kind, Aggie. Thank you."

"It's just a wee thanks, sir, for seeing me and for trying to fix things up at my work."

Barry heard the emphasis on "trying." "What's wrong there?"

Aggie shook her head. "I sent them your letter. I got a phone call from Ivan the Terrible's secretary. She told me that Mister McCluggage and his partner had decided to reduce the workforce and were letting a folder and packer go. Me. I'm getting a month's notice and severance pay. Nothing to do with my being sick, like. No. No. Not at all." She curled her lip. "And if you'll believe that you'll believe fish walk on legs, but I can't do nothing, so I can't. I spoke to the shop steward and he told me the bosses was in their rights." She stifled a sob. "And me working there for sixteen years."

"I'm so sorry, Aggie," Barry said, wondering if there was anything he, or more likely he and the big guns of O'Reilly in full cry, could do. "I truly am."

"Thank you, sir. You're very kind." Aggie took a deep breath, squared her shoulders. "Doctor Laverty, when I'm at the hospital do you think they'd give me a brave wheen of that warfarin for to bring home?"

Barry frowned. "Why would you want a lot? I'll write you a prescription whenever you need more."

"Because," she said, and Barry heard the steel in her voice, "I know what warfarin's for. It's not just for thinning the blood. It's a bloody good rat poison, so it is, and I want to give some to Ivan the Terrible, so I do . . . and I'll tell you, that there silent partner? See him whoever he is? He'd be silent as the tomb all right, because he'd be in one, so he would."

18

A House with Deep Thatch

O'Reilly drove the Rover from the centre of the hairpin bend in the Bangor to Belfast Road to the end of a rutted lane. The tyres crunched on gravel in front of a single-storey thatched building. Patches of moss marred the straw. "Here we are," he said, and parked. The old cottage's whitewashed walls were grubby and the mullioned lead lattice windows needed washing. Red paint was peeling from the window frames and from the front door set in a narrow porch. Window boxes on sandstone windowsills had been invaded by blue-flowered birdseye speedwell and plantains. "Everybody out."

Donal leapt from the car and opened the back door for Julie and Arthur.

The drizzle had stopped, and high overhead patches of sky looked down between slowly drifting clouds. O'Reilly noticed branches of broom, already covered in bright yellow flowers, straggling through the gravel.

"That there has to go," Donal said, pointing to the weed. "Give that stuff an inch and it'll be all over everything like clap on a heifer's arse."

"Donal," said Julie, but her reproach was gentle.

Donal peered at an etched stone fixed to the wall beside the front door. "It says 1795. There's a thing," said Donal. "The house was built the year the Orange Order was founded. But what's the other say, sir? Can you read the Irish?"

O'Reilly scrutinized the lettering but although the carved date was clear, the letters were indistinct. He rubbed some of the moss away and thought he could make out *Dán Buídhe*. "Dawn Bwee," he said. "It's Irish for Yellow Poem."

"The wee place has a name, so it has. Just like the houses of toffs. Dawn Bwee? I like the sound of that, but I never heard of a yellow poem." He grinned and showed his buck teeth. "I've heard some blue ones, with the lads, like."

"Donal," Julie said. "Eejit."

He scratched his bandage under his cap. "Come on," he said, "let's take a wee dander round her before we go in."

"Heel, Arthur," O'Reilly said, and was happy to follow, listen, and watch as Donal pointed everything out to Julie. "That there gable end," he said as they passed, "needs new pargetting, but Buster Holland's a sound man with rough plaster, so he is."

O'Reilly could see bricks exposed where the old plaster had cracked and bits had flaked off.

"The back of the house is grand, just the door needs painting and the window frames. I'll do that, so I will. Do you see that there?" He pointed to where a spout ran from a roof gutter into a huge wooden tun. "That there collects rainwater, you know, and my ma says rainwater's so soft it's dead wheeker for washing your hair, so it is."

O'Reilly saw how fondly Donal gazed at his wife's waist-length blonde tresses.

"I can just see me giving you a hand with it on a summer's night, love," Donal continued, "out here in the back garden."

Unkempt grass studded with buttercups ran for fifty yards from the back of the house to a tall laurel hedge. O'Reilly guessed the lawn was thirty yards wide, bounded on each side by fifty-foot-tall leafless linden trees, known as limes in Ulster.

"See them there limes?" Donal asked. "I'd put Bluebird's run fornenst them to the right there." He glanced at Julie's tummy. "And when the leaves come there'll be great shade when you can put the wee lad out in his pram. And when he's bigger, him and me can kick a soccer ball about on the grass, like."

Julie said, "He might be a wee girl, you know."

O'Reilly watched the puzzled look on Donal's face turn into a huge smile. "Right enough she might, so she might. She can lie in her pram, and when she's bigger can't I make her a doll's house, maybe even a Wendy house for her to play in out here." He frowned. "Mind you, I'd have to flatten that there mound." Donal pointed to where a small hillock rose and fell, clothed in long unmown grass and a sunburst of myriad dandelions.

Donal laughed. "I'll tell you one thing," he said. "I never want to meet the mole that dug thon boy."

O'Reilly pictured Donal's supposed mole the size of a carthorse tunnelling under the lawn and throwing up the hill. "True," he said, and glanced at his watch. "Come on, Donal. Let's have a look inside the house. I'll have to get back home soon."

"Fair enough, sir." Donal unlocked the back door and lifted the snib to let them in.

"Stay," O'Reilly said to Arthur outside the door, and followed into a bright kitchen with a red tile floor. O'Reilly smelt the dry mustiness, but that wasn't surprising. The place had been empty for a year. "It's lovely, Donal," said Julie. "If we can buy the house and there's money left over, I could have a washing machine. I've never had one of my own and it would be great for doing nappies, so it would. I'd put it there."

"Aye," said Donal. "I'll plumb it in for you, darlin', but we'll need a sparks for to wire it into the mains. Boggy Baxter'd be the man for the job. He done all the electrics at Sonny and Maggie's house." Donal headed for an archway. "Come on 'til we see the rest of it."

O'Reilly followed them through the empty house. He held his peace, but watched and listened as Donal and Julie admired an alcove here, decided this wee room would be stickin' out a mile as a nursery, thought the parlour suite her ma had given Julie as a wedding present would be dead on in the front room. He envied them as they planned, dreamed.

Kitty wouldn't have that kind of pleasure—making a place her own. Not unless he sold Number One and let her start from scratch in her own house, but selling was not in the cards. No doubt she'd want to make some changes to their home, and Kitty O'Hallorhan was wise enough not to rush into that until she felt Kinky was comfortable with the presence of another woman. But, and the thought pleased him, handled in the right way, seeking Kinky's advice on any suggested changes might well be another way of making her understand that she truly was needed.

O'Reilly was still puzzling over Kinky and Kitty when he arrived in the small front hall and Donal announced, "Here endeth the conducted tour. What do you think, Julie?"

She took a very deep breath, held it, exhaled, and said, "It's lovely, so it is. I never thought in a million years, not a million, the likes of us could have a place like this. I love it. Are you sure we can afford it?" O'Reilly heard the longing in her voice.

"If we can get this house we'd be elected, so we would, and I think we've enough of the ould doh-ray-mi. What do you think, Doc?"

O'Reilly saw the pleasure in Julie's eyes. "It does need a bit of work, but it would be ideal for you . . . three." He pointed at Julie's bump.

She and Donal laughed.

O'Reilly said, "And they were asking two thousand pounds?"

"Aye, and we don't have it all, but what with Julie's five-hundred-pound settlement from Mister Bishop last year, my winnings on Bluebird, Julie's prize for nearly winning the hair model contest, and the dosh I got at the oul' gee-gees in Downpatrick, we can come close."

O'Reilly shook his head. "Hold your horses, now, even though I know it was a couple of horses, one called Arkle and the other Flo's Fancy, that helped get you some of the money. Two thousand pounds is not all you'd have to pay if you give the full price."

Donal frowned. "Why not?"

It was O'Reilly's turn to inhale before he said, "You have to settle the estate agent's commission, stamp duty—that's a tax on all house sales—and you'll need a lawyer to sort out the deeds." For a moment O'Reilly thought of asking his brother Lars, a solicitor in Portaferry, to conveyance the house as a favour, but realised if he did they'd soon be flooded with requests for favours every time someone bought or sold a house. "And you'll need money to insure the place, pay the rates . . . the county council taxes . . . and money to fix it up and finish furnishing it." He saw the smile flee from Julie's face and watched Donal put his arm around her. Uh-oh. O'Reilly hadn't meant to discourage them, but they did have to face the facts.

"Thank you for being honest, Doctor O'Reilly," Julie said. There was a catch in her voice. "It was nice to dream for a wee minute there, so it was." She turned her face into Donal's shoulder.

"Wait a minute," said O'Reilly. "It's not as bad as that. I didn't mean you couldn't afford it. I was trying to explain what it takes to buy a property. Now that's one of the reasons you asked me to come, isn't it?"

"It is," Julie said. She looked at Donal for reassurance. "And we know you're helping us, don't we, Donal?"

"We do indeed," Donal said.

"So," said O'Reilly, relieved that his little faux-pas had been forgiven, "with what Donal earns working for Councillor Bishop, you can get a mortgage, a loan from the bank, if you don't have quite enough money."

"Honest to God?" Donal said. "Me?"

"You, Donal Donnelly. You pay it off every month, just like paying rent, but one day you'll own the house lock, stock, and barrel."

"Like buying on the never-never?" Julie asked.

"Like hire-purchase," O'Reilly said, "and I'm not sure you'll need to offer the whole amount the estate's asking anyway."

Donal frowned. "Why not?"

"The house needs work. Nobody's bought it in a year. Maybe the people who inherited it are getting tired of paying rates and the upkeep and would be glad to get rid of it for a bit less. They're already asking five hundred pounds below what's called the 'appraised value.'"

Donal's frown vanished. "Do you think so, sir?"

"I do, Donal. Offer one thousand seven hundred but have a word with your bank manager about a mortgage first. What with the repairs and furnishing, things could be a bit pricier than you expected. The manager will look at what you've got, what you earn, and work out the details of financing

"That would be great," Donal said, "and I would ask, sir, honest to God, but I don't have a bank, never mind a manager."

Donal wasn't the only countryman who mistrusted banks and in truth rarely had enough money to need an account. "I'll speak to Mister Canning at the Bank of Ireland," O'Reilly said. "You go see him next week. He'll take care of you."

"By God, I will see him, sir." He scratched his bandage. "First thing after this yoke comes off." He spun to Julie, and Donal Donnelly's words came tumbling out. "We're going to get the wee house, Julie." He grabbed her and waltzed her round the hall. "Our wee house. You, me, and the chissler." He sang off-key,

—the roof was thatched with yellow straw,
the walls were white as snow.
The turf fire boiled the pot. I see it still . . .

O'Reilly recognised "The Little Old Mud Cabin on the Hill."
Donal stopped singing and released Julie. She stepped up to O'Reilly and kissed his cheek. "Thank you, sir. Thank you very, very much." There were tears in her eyes. "I'm so happy."
That was twice in an hour he'd made a woman cry and been kissed. O'Reilly stepped back, cleared his throat, and said, "I didn't do anything, Julie."
Her look said "Like hell you didn't," and he imagined Julie Donnelly, née MacAteer, rarely swore. All very embarassing, this effusive thanking. "And there's one other thing, Donal."
"Yes, sir?"
"You go to Dapper Frew, tell him you want to offer one thousand seven hundred pounds. He'll present that offer to the sellers. Dapper'll make all the arrangements, get you a solicitor, that kind of stuff. If they make a counteroffer and want more money,

or if there are any complications, come and talk to me."

"I will, sir. In soul, I will."

"And Donal? Julie? Keep this all to yourselves. I don't want to spoil your day, but buying a house is a complicated business. It's not guaranteed until contracts are exchanged and a deposit's paid. Before that someone else might bid more."

"I'd not like that," Julie said.

"On principle then, the less anyone knows the better, and you know how the word gets out around here," O'Reilly said. "Now come on. Lock up. I have to fetch Arthur from the back garden. I want to get you two home and then get to Number One Main and sort out what Barry and I are going to have for our tea."

"I don't know what you're having for yiz tea, Doctor, but I do know what you're having for pudding. Cissie Sloan said Aggie baked one of her cherry cakes this morning for the doctors. She's quare nor clever with preserved fruit," Julie said.

"Did she, by God? That's very kind of her. In that case I'll nip down to Bangor before going home. I've a notion that Doctor Laverty and I'd appreciate ice cream with Aggie's cherry cake." The Mencarellis', Capronis', and Togneris' sweetie shops all made wonderful ice cream, but no one, in O'Reilly's opinion, made it quite like Paola Lucchi and her sister Ada.

19

The Time Has Come to Talk of Other Things

O'Reilly was sipping his pre-dinner Jameson and listening to Tchaikovsky's Sixth Symphony when Barry walked into the upstairs lounge. "So, what's the word on Aggie?" O'Reilly said, then, pointing at the sideboard, "Help yourself. He was delighted how things were going for Donal and Julie Donnelly and his mood was light.

"Aggie's on her way to the Royal," Barry said, pouring himself a whiskey. "Deep venous thrombosis. I gave her heparin." He sat in the other armchair. "*Sláinte.*"

"*Prost,*" said O'Reilly. "Did you know *prosit* is the third-person singular present active subjunctive of the Latin verb *Prosum,* or the Maltese *prosit,* meaning bravo."

"No, Fingal, I can say with an absolute degree of certainty that I did not know that. How do you?"

O'Reilly chuckled. "I learnt the Latin grammar at school, and a good thing too, because when I was a student at Trinity some lectures were delivered in Latin. I picked up the Maltese word when I was in the local equivalent of a pub in Grand Harbour in the war."

O'Reilly raised his glass. "Aggie'll be all right once they get her stabilised on warfarin."

Barry shook his head. "Your eruditon, Fingal, is astounding." He put his glass on the coffee table, scratched his chin, and said, "And medically you're probably right about Aggie, but damn it, Fingal, it's not fair."

Was Barry going to object to having to refer all interesting cases? O'Reilly hoped not.

Barry said, "Half the reason the woman has varicose veins is because she's had a job for years where she never got a chance to sit down. I wrote a letter to her employer asking if she could be switched to something sedentary and do you know what he's done?" Barry's face had reddened. One hand was clenching and unclenching and O'Reilly was sure the lad was unaware he was doing it. "He's given her notice. He's laying her off. That's not bloody well fair." Barry lifted his whiskey.

"No," said O'Reilly, "it's not." He waited. Six months ago Barry'd probably have thought that people losing jobs was no concern of their physician. Nor would he have sworn. Now?

Barry stood, paced, and turned back. "Something'll have to be done about it, that's all."

O'Reilly set his drink aside, rose, clapped Barry on the shoulder, and said, "Good lad. I hoped you'd say that. And you're right." He fished out his pipe. "Any suggestions what that 'something' might be?"

Barry shook his head. "At this moment? No. Apparently her employer is quite within his rights legally." He swallowed whiskey. "All I know is that the shirt factory is owned by a Mister Ivan McCluggage and a partner."

O'Reilly frowned. He lit up and puffed out a cloud of blue smoke. His pipe always gave him time to think. "Seems to me there's a couple of options—"

Barry interrupted. "If you're going to say I could have a word with her boss, see if he'll change his mind, I've already thought of that."

"I was." Good for you, Barry, O'Reilly thought, and I like the way you said "I," not "we." He lifted his drink. "But, I tell you, Barry," he said, "I know about Belfast factory owners. They're all tough as nails. McCluggage would probably tell you to run away off and feel your head, if he was feeling polite."

At least that made Barry smile. "I'm not going to bother."

"Who said, 'Give me a lever and, with a place to stand, I will move the whole world'?" O'Reilly asked, and drank again.

"Archimedes. But that might have worked in ancient Greece, and it certainly works here in Ballybucklebo where you know everybody and can usually find the fulcrum, something to help you force them to do what you want. But we don't know this McCluggage or his partner. How can we find something to put pressure on them?"

O'Reilly puffed again. Lord, but Barry Laverty

learnt fast. "Search me, but I do have contacts in Belfast. Give me a bit of time. You never know what I might discover." He ambled to the sideboard. "Ready for another?"

Barry shook his head.

"I've often told you about birds not being able to fly on only one wing," O'Reilly said, and poured for himself. "And talking about Belfast and birds—" He stopped when he saw Barry's look of irritation. "No, I am *not* changing the subject, as it happens. I want to go up there tomorrow. I've two birds I want to kill with one stone."

"Did you know the Chinese say one arrow, two vultures?" Barry said, his expression softening.

O'Reilly laughed. "I didn't know that. I'm not sure Kinky would like to be called a vulture," his voice lost its bantering tone, "but I want to go and see her. Make sure she's on the mend." Try to reassure her about her place here, he thought. "I've had a notion about trying to set her mind at rest."

"Oh?"

"What do you know about planning weddings?"

Barry laughed. "About as much as I know about the local sports in Ulan Bator, Mongolia. I thought you said you weren't changing the subject."

"Horse racing, archery, and Mongolian wrestling," O'Reilly said. "Read about the place in the *Times* just last week. I'm not changing the subject. I'm going to ask Kinky to take charge once she's back here and more on her feet."

Barry whistled. "You mean plan your wedding? Make her feel indispensable, is that it? That's brilliant."

"It's worth a try, so that's job one in the city."

"And job two?"

O'Reilly puffed hugely. "You are not going to believe this."

Barry chuckled. "With you, Fingal, if you said the earth was flat I'd probably believe it."

"Helen wants to go to medical school."

"Helen Hewitt?" Barry asked, sounding surprised.

"No, you goat, Helen of Troy. Of course Helen Hewitt."

Barry frowned, started to say something, and then shut his mouth. O'Reilly could imagine what was going through the young lad's mind. In Ulster, very few working-class kids went to university, never mind to professional schools. The rest went to technical school if they went at all. Helen Hewitt's dream of medical school was a huge leap any way you looked at it, and Barry Laverty clearly needed time to digest the information. But then he said with a smile, "And we're going to help her, aren't we? What can I do?"

"Good man-ma-da," O'Reilly said. "I knew you'd agree she should. Thank you, but actually there's not much you can do. We already know she's qualified for admission. The problem is, how can she afford it?"

"It cost my dad seventy pounds in fees every year for six years," Barry said, "but he was making three thousand a year. Helen's father's a builder's labourer . . . Lord, I only get one thousand eight hundred a year before deductions . . . and I'm not complaining."

"I know you're not. I've been on the phone while you were out. I'm meeting two old friends. You know them. Charlie Greer and Donald Cromie. We're going to start planning a reunion for our Trinity medical class of '36 next year. Do you know we'll be thirty years qualified then? Where the hell has the time gone?"

"You don't look a day over forty, Fingal," Barry said, and laughed, "but what's that got to do with Helen?"

"Less of your lip, young Laverty," O'Reilly said, laughed mightily, and thought, You'd not have teased me six months ago, boy. Well done. "I'll bet senior consultants will know of any scholarships. Helen's hard up right now. Keeping Kinky busy as our wedding planner'll let me keep Helen Hewitt on to answer the phone and help with the heavy housework. Someone needs to do the hoovering, although I'll bet Kinky's back cooking before the week's out. That'll get Helen a few bob for a while and if we can find a scholarship for her, well—"

"Brilliant," Barry said. "Bloody brilliant. I really hope your friends can help. Now what about Aggie?"

O'Reilly inclined his head. "You know how tight a community Ulster is. While I'm at it, I'll ask if by any chance either one of them knows this Ivan—?"

"McCluggage." Barry chuckled. "You said something about killing two birds. That's three."

"Och sure, who's counting," O'Reilly said. "But it's all worth trying, so it's me for Belfast tomorrow. You'll be on your own, but don't worry about having someone to answer the phone if you get called out—"

"Fingal, would you mind if I brought a girl here?" Barry asked.

"Not at all. Who is she?"

"Sue Nolan. I took her for dinner last week and I want to see her again, but reckoned I couldn't until next weekend when it was my turn to be off. I could phone her and ask her to come down. There's plenty of grub in the fridge. BBC telly's showing *Our Man in Havana* with Alex Guinness that evening so she'll not be bored if I have to go out. If she can come, she could field phone calls."

"Barry, I'm delighted, and you're right. She could do just what Kitty did last weekend." O'Reilly moved to where Barry stood. "Give me that glass. You've time for another before tea. It's Mairead Shanks's Irish stew tonight. I have it in the oven."

Barry released his glass and O'Reilly poured. "And Aggie Arbuthnot's cherry cake to follow," Barry said. "It's in the dining room."

"I know about Aggie's cherry cake. Julie saw Cissy in the village. We'll have it a la mode with some ice cream I bought."

Barry said, quietly, "The neighbours, and how they've all wanted to help?" He shook his head. "You know—thanks, Fingal." Barry accepted the glass. "I'm going to miss this place—a lot."

"I do understand, Barry." He hesitated then said, "I may have mentioned to you that when I was at your stage in my career I flirted with obstetrics, but decided that I preferred GP work."

"You did say something. About the Rotunda Hospital in Dublin."

"I was there for a while, but I've been here for nineteen years." O'Reilly took his chair. "Sit you down," he said. "Cheers."

Barry sat and sipped.

"We all have to find our way," O'Reilly said. "You'll find yours, and I've already told you if you want to come back—"

"Thank you, Fingal."

"I'm not trying to influence you, Barry. Honestly." Liar, O'Reilly thought. He'd grown fond of the lad, who was turning into a first-class GP. "I'd welcome you as a partner if you find specialising's not all it's cracked up to be and that you're missing this place, the people, things like helping the Donnellys buy a house."

"How did it go this afternoon?" Barry said.

"Very well. It's a sound cottage, dry, well-built, good plumbing, indoor toilet. It's got two bedrooms. Julie has one picked out for a nursery already."

"Sounds ideal."

"It is. And they can afford it." O'Reilly sipped his whiskey. "Donal didn't have a clue about things like mortgages, conveyancing, house insurance, but I've pointed him in the right direction. I've phoned

Mike Canning of the Bank of Ireland. He'll talk to Donal on Monday about a mortgage. The estate agent, Dapper Frew, will take care of them. He's a good skin. Used to play on the wing for the Ballybucklebo Bonnaughts rugby team. I'd love to see the Donnellys get the place. Julie has her heart so set on it."

Barry sipped his drink. "Fingal, can I ask you a question?"

"Fire away."

"Does it never get you down? It's one thing, ministering to individual patients' medical needs, but from what I've seen since I came here you've taken the whole damn village under your wing. Don't you find that tiring? I know you don't show it." Barry laughed. "You hardly ever show that you're tired, but not showing and being aren't the same thing."

O'Reilly set his glass on a table. Folding his hands like a praying supplicant, he rested his elbows on the arms of the chair and his chin on his fingertips. "I think it was the war," he said, his pipe still clenched between his teeth. "Often when my old battleship *Warspite* had been in action or had picked up survivors, the medical department worked round the clock. You came to accept it as normal. Learned to take catnaps." He let go a cloud like old *Warspite* did when she was cleaning her boilers, and wondered why he found it so easy to be open with Barry.

"My dad—"

"And my friend, Tom Laverty," O'Reilly said, picturing *Warspite*'s navigating officer.

"He never talks about the war, but once, when I was a student, I was complaining about all the night work." Barry looked down.

"Go on," O'Reilly said, quietly thinking about what Tom might have told his son. O'Reilly didn't mention the war often, nor did most of the ex-servicemen he knew. Like John MacNeill, the marquis of Ballybucklebo, or his butler, Thompson, who'd both been decorated for gallantry.

"Dad said during one battle when he had to keep the navigational plot updated constantly for thirty-eight hours he learned that you only were permitted the luxury of being tired when you didn't have other people's lives in your hands."

"That must have been the Battle of Matapan in 1941. A lot of that fighting was at night." Four Italian cruisers had been sunk, O'Reilly remembered, and half the officers on his ship had been kept going with liberal doses of the amphetamine stimulants he'd handed out. "Said that, did he, by God? Smart man, your dad." O'Reilly straightened up and took his pipe out of his mouth. "I think, Barry," he said, "you've answered your own question."

"But what about this business of looking after the whole village? Do you see it in the same way?"

O'Reilly grunted and stroked his chin with the web between thumb and forefinger.

"Well?" Barry said.

"I've never really thought of it like that, but now you come to mention it, I suppose I do, don't I?"

"Too true."

O'Reilly grinned. "But it's fun too," he said, thinking about Donal and Julie again. "I know you aren't happy having to send Colin Brown to hospital. You can set a greenstick fracture. You know how to establish a dose of warfarin for a patient like Aggie. I used to feel that way myself, years ago, but now? Instead of getting satisfaction from doing a, I don't know, a Caesarean section for a stranger, I get to help with the lives of my friends. Make a difference sometimes. It's very, very good for the soul."

"And you don't feel a bit Godlike when you do?"

O'Reilly could tell from Barry's tone he was curious, not critical. "Me?" he said. "Me? Godlike?" He laughed until he felt tears start. "I couldn't possibly. Oh dear." He controlled his laughter and said, "If I did, I'd be taking my own name in vain far too beJeezusly frequently and—" He finished his whiskey. "—if you believe what certain parsons round Ulster preach, the Almighty wouldn't go within a beagle's gowl of a drop of the hard stuff." O'Reilly rose. "Come on, Barry. Let's get stuck into that Irish stew and between the pair of us get next week organised."

20

We Will Pardon Thy Mistake

"I t's decent of you to come down from Holywood at short notice, Sue," Barry said as he let her into Number One half an hour after Fingal had left for Belfast. "Not everyone would reckon answering the phone was an exciting way of spending a Saturday."

"Happy to help out," she said, taking off her coat and hanging it on the coatstand.

The cashmere sweater she wore fitted her perfectly and Barry admired the swell of her breasts beneath. "You really don't mind missing your sail-and-learn class at the Yacht Club?"

She shook her head. "I told you on the phone, silly, today's part two of diesel engine maintenance for beginners." She laughed. "I've done pretty well on the theory of sailing, coastal pilotage, anchoring, chart reading, buoyage, all the boating stuff, but I don't think I'm cut out to footer about with fuel injectors, piston rings, oil filters, oil changes. Far too messy and you always end up stinking of diesel. Anyway I enjoyed our dinner last week." She looked him right in the eye and smiled. "A lot. And I was thinking having to wait until next weekend when you were off duty again was quite a while. Seemed to me a trip here beat skinning my knuckles footering about with a torque wrench on a banjo bolt, and it gives me a chance to see you too."

Nice to know how you're rated, Barry thought, second to avoiding skinned knuckles, and he smiled. "Um . . . I did . . . enjoy our dinner last week too. Very much." And the moonlit drive home, he thought, remembering their kisses when he'd parked on a farm lane near Holywood to say goodnight. He was delighted she felt as he did—that waiting until next weekend was far too long. "It's great you've come today. I just hope I don't get many calls."

"If you do," she waved a leather briefcase, "I brought my reading and I'll not mind catching up with some work and answering the phone if I have to." She moved closer.

He inhaled that soft attar she wore and tingled when she kissed him.

"We had such a marvellous dinner at the Crawfordsburn," she said. "I certainly had fun." She kissed him again. "And I found out when you said goodnight, that for such a shy boy, you're not a half-bad kisser."

Barry blushed and wondered if he'd ever be able to be relaxed around any girl until he'd got to know her properly, but he hugged Sue and returned the kiss, tongue on tongue. He trembled and when they parted his breath came in short gasps. "Can I . . . um . . . can I show you around the place?" he said.

She laughed. "I think you'd better." Her colour was high and her eyes bright. Sue Nolan was no demure schoolmarm, but this was O'Reilly's home, and certain social conventions should be maintained. Still, Barry knew that much more of her nearness and her kisses and— He imagined a fragment of a song, "—as I lifted her petticoat easy and slow."

Sue was wearing snugly fitting black Capri trousers.

"Penny for them?" she said.

"What? I'm sorry. You know the way, for no good reason, a tune pops into your head?" He didn't want to tell her exactly what the tune was and the images it had brought forth.

"And won't go away?"

And in his mind he heard,

Girls . . . are well made for holding, and most of
    them are
But any young fellah is only a fool
If he tries at the first time to go a bit far.

And Barry knew it was going to be difficult not to try to with this sexy young woman. He swallowed and said, "Our prof of ENT said it's called an earworm."

"I never knew it had a name, but I read a short story once called *Rum-Titty-Titty-Rum-TAH-Tee* where someone wrote music so powerful it took over the whole world until somebody else developed a counter rhythm."

"Easy and Slow" was the old Irish tune, and described exactly in three words how he knew he had to behave. After all it was their second date, and ten in the morning, but, Lord, not only was Sue Nolan easy on the eye, she was lovely to hold and to kiss. He inhaled, pointed, and said, "Right, then, there's the phone."

"And I know what to do if anyone calls. You explained last night."

"Great." He opened the door. "And this is the dining room." He crossed the floor. "And this—" He shooed the cat from where she was perched on the sideboard tucking into the remains of a kipper Barry hadn't had time to clear away. "—this, in the absence of our housekeeper, Mrs. Kinky Kincaid, who really runs the place, is the other mistress of the domain, Lady Macbeth."

"Purryeow," said her ladyship. The "yeow" was accentuated as she landed on the carpet, arched her back, stuck her tail straight up, and wove around Sue's legs. She bent and stroked the cat. "Pretty wee thing," she said, and straightened.

The animal left white hairs on her black pants.

"I," Sue said, "am a human magnet for hairs." She laughed.

Barry piled the dirty breakfast plates on a tray. "I'll take these to the kitchen. Follow me. Surgery's in there," he said as they headed down the hall. "And that's the waiting room," he added, rebalancing the tray while she peered in.

"Good Lord, who on earth chose the wallpaper? I've never seen roses like that in my life."

Barry chuckled. "It was here before my time. I saw it first when I came for the job interview. I couldn't believe anyone could pick such a dreadful pattern. That, of course, was before I got to know O'Reilly. 'Orthodox' and 'Doctor O'Reilly' don't always fit in the same sentence."

"But you do like the man?"

"Very much. He's hard not to like," Barry said seriously, "unless you've crossed him."

"I'll try not to," Sue said, and chuckled. She followed him into the kitchen. He put the dishes in the sink and then, reaching for her hand, said, "Come on, let's go upstairs."

"Doctor Laverty," Sue said. "I've my reputation to think of."

"Huh?" Barry frowned, then it dawned on him exactly what he'd implied. Who'd said that a double entendre only ever had one meaning? He knew he'd turned beetroot red. His hand, as it always did when he was embarrassed, flew to his tuft and smoothed it down. "I didn't mean to go to . . . that is I—" First law of holes again, he thought. Don't say "bed," idiot.

Sue Nolan was now heaving with what must be suppressed mirth. "Oh, my," she said, and then laughed out loud. "I am sorry, Barry. I didn't mean to embarrass you. Honestly."

Barry could feel his colour fading. "And I didn't mean what it sounded like. That I was suggesting, well, that I was trying to—"

Sue was still smiling at him.

"Oh, hell," he said, laughing at himself now. "The lounge is upstairs. It's where we're going to be for most of today until Doctor O'Reilly gets back home."

"Well, let's get up there," she said. "Which way?"

Barry led her up the stairs. She hesitated in front of a photo on the landing. "Is that *Warspite*?"

"How did you know?"

"My dad was a junior gunnery officer on her in 1940, then he went to destroyers."

"I don't believe it," Barry said. "Doctor O'Reilly was one of her medicos during the war and my father served on her in 1939, before we were born." He opened the door and said, "The lounge. Make yourself at home."

"My dad's pretty sure he knows yours," Sue said. "He and your mum are in Australia, aren't they?"

"They are. He's on sabbatical in Melbourne. He's a mining engineer."

She dropped into the armchair nearest the unlit fire and set her attaché case on the floor. "I told my folks about you after you took me to the Inn. Dad reckoned there could only be one Doctor Barry Laverty of your age from Bangor. My dad had a letter from his friend Tom when his son graduated from medical school in 1963. And that had to have been you."

"It's weird, isn't it?" But actually it wasn't. Ulster was small and within half an hour of their meeting any two native strangers could usually find they knew many people in common. "Before I park myself," he said, "can I get you anything? Tea? Coffee?"

"No, thanks, Barry. This is fine."

He was halfway into the chair when the phone rang. "Bugger," Barry muttered, well aware that the longer he stayed working here the more he grew like his mentor. "I'd better see who it is."

21

Not Ecstasy but It Was Comfort

"**D**octor O'Reilly," Kinky said with a smile when he arrived at her bedside, "it's very decent of you coming to see me. And on a Saturday too." Her oxygen spectacles and the IV line had been removed. Wearing a pink crochetted bed jacket over her nightie, she sat propped up on her pillows reading a copy of last night's *Belfast Telegraph*.

O'Reilly noticed the headline, *Chinese Detonate Second Atom Bomb*. The world was going to hell in a bucket, but there was bugger all an Ulster country

GP could do about it. He could, however, help his friends, friends like Maureen "Kinky" Kincaid. "How are you today?" he asked.

"I'm a deal more at myself, so, and I'll be shot of those needles tomorrow," she said. "And thank the Lord because they sting sore even if they are doing me good. Penicillin's not too bad, but that streptomycin." She grimaced. "At least they are feeding me more than gruel now, but to tell you the truth, sir, and I don't mean to be ungrateful," she lowered her voice, "when I was a girl on the home farm in Beal na mBláth our pigs were fed better, so."

O'Reilly chuckled. "I know." He handed her a bottle of Lucozade. "Here you are. Tonic drink for those recovering." He was willing to bet there wasn't a bedside locker in any hospital in the British Isles that didn't have a bottle of Lucozade on it, such was the faith of the populace in the drink's restorative powers. He also gave her a parcel wrapped in greaseproof paper. "Sister says you can have these." Today the senior nurse on duty was a woman O'Reilly hadn't met before. A narrow person—narrow-nosed, narrow-lipped, probably narrow-minded—she'd been as starched as her apron, and when he'd asked if Kinky could have a food parcel had refused to allow any such breach of rules. "She can have the Lucozade, that's permitted, but food from the outside on *my* ward? Nonsense. Take it away. Now. At once."

Despite a chill feeling in his nose tip, a sure sign of its blanching, O'Reilly had reminded himself that "a soft answer turneth away wrath," and had explained how Miss Florence Elliott, the matron of the hospital, was his personal friend of long standing. And if the sister subsequently discovered that it was quite untrue, that he didn't know the most senior nurse in the hospital, would it matter? Not at all, but by invoking her name and explaining how upset she would be if she thought a sister had interfered with the care of one of his patients, he'd been able to overcome the resistance and get the grub to Kinky. The poker table wasn't the only place where bluffing was a winning tactic.

As Kinky unwrapped the paper he noticed that her cheeks were pale, but her eyes were bright, and her hair was up in its usual chignon. O'Reilly's first law of medicine was, *Never let the patients get the upper hand.* His second law was, *When patients who'd been seriously ill start taking trouble about their appearance they're on the mend.* He was delighted. "I like your jacket," he said.

She stopped unwrapping and glanced at it. "It was a present from Flo Bishop. She's a mighty crochetter. Now," she said, "that's a thing I cannot do. I'm a dab hand with the knitting needles, and I can tat, but I've two left thumbs with a crochet hook."

O'Reilly nodded. "We can't be experts at everything, Kinky. That gansey you knitted for me years ago still keeps me warm when Arthur and I go wildfowling." Her smile pleased him.

Kinky finished unwrapping. She sat rigidly. "And

who made these sandwiches?" she asked. "Miss O'Hallorhan in my kitchen, I suppose?" She started to hand them back.

Uh-oh. "Not at all, Kinky." He pushed them to her. "Kitty hasn't been near Number One since last weekend and she's down in Tallaght in Dublin today visiting her mother. Alice Moloney gave us another ham and Mary Dunleavy from the Duck brought slices of a roast of beef she'd cooked. Barry made the sandwiches for you." O'Reilly winked. "He said they'd be all the better because he'd put on some of your home-made mustard."

"That's all right, then," she said, patting her chignon. "Please thank Alice, and Mary, and Doctor Laverty."

"I will." It was O'Reilly's turn to lower his voice. "You know, Barry lived in this hospital when he was training, and the students' mess was supplied by the same kitchen that's feeding you. I've worked with the lad for ten months and we've been through some dire emergencies together, but the only time I've ever seen him shudder was when he mentioned the hospital's Cornish pasties and mashed turnip. He said he'd bet you were famished and would appreciate a change."

"That was very thoughtful." She set the package on the narrow Formica-topped table on casters that spanned the bed. "And how are you both managing, sir?"

"We're getting by, but we miss your cooking." He

laughed. "By now I think we've sampled the cuisine of everyone in the village. They've all been kind, but there's not the one of them can hold a candle to Kinky Kincaid in the kitchen."

Kinky smiled. "Get on with you, Doctor O'Reilly, sir. You're an old soft-soaper, so."

"Flattery's nothing to do with it," he said, "and we need you back. You hurry up and get better." He touched her hand. "I miss you, Barry does, and I've a special job for you."

She cocked her head. "Special job?"

"You know how busy the practice is. And Kitty's working long hours here at the hospital . . . and will up to and then after we're married." He stole a glance to see if that news had had any effect, but Kinky's expression was deadpan. "Someone's going to have to be in charge of arranging the wedding."

Kinky narrowed her eyes.

"Will you take that job on, Kinky, once you're better and back home?"

She pursed her lips.

"I know it would be a big load on top of cooking—"

"I'll manage," she said quickly, and a small smile played on her lips.

"And you'll have to put up with Helen Hewitt underfoot. I'm keeping her on to answer the phone and do a bit of dusting."

The smile fled.

"Now, Kinky, I've told you Helen lost her job." He decided not to tell Kinky about Helen's aspirations yet, and ploughed on. "Two pounds a week for her won't bankrupt me, but it means an awful lot to her, until she gets settled. And once the wedding's over and you have more time to take up all your old jobs, we'll not need her, and by then you'll be completely your old self." He chuckled, then said, "And Mrs. O'Reilly's going to be far too busy nursing here to help you with your work."

"There does be truth in what you say, sir, and keeping Helen on is a Christian charity, so."

"Nothing of the kind. She earns her keep." While O'Reilly enjoyed performing acts of kindness he preferred for them to go unremarked upon by other people, but, he smiled, Kinky could see through him every time.

"When I was a girl I helped with my sister Sinead's wedding, aye, and Fidelma's. I'd enjoy the planning of yours. I would, so. Menus, and flowers, and seating, and the like, but I think you and Miss O'Hallorhan should pick the hymns, so."

He'd sown the seeds, now he wanted to let them germinate without more discussion. "It's a great relief to hear that you will." O'Reilly lifted the chart from the end of her bed. "Let's see how you're doing." The inky lines crawling across graph paper showed him that her temperature, pulse, and respiratory rate were all normal and had been for two days. "I think, Kinky," O'Reilly said with a grin, "we're going to have to shoot you." This was a very different woman from the seriously ill patient who had been admitted twelve days ago. "You've made remarkable progress. I'm delighted."

"That nice Doctor Mills says I'll be out of here soon. They took out my stitches on Thursday and the wound has healed nicely. The nurses have been getting me up to walk about."

That was to prevent venous stasis that could lead to the same thing Aggie had, a deep venous thrombosis and its potential successor, a pulmonary embolism.

"And I'm getting much stronger."

"I'm delighted to hear that."

She lowered her voice. "They do weigh me, you know. I've lost nearly a stone since the operation." She glanced down, then back at O'Reilly. "I think when I'm home, if it's all right with you, sir, I'll be cutting some of the fat and starches out of our meals. I'd . . . I'd like for to be just a bit slimmer, so."

"Good for you, Kinky. You fire away at what you think will be best." He patted his own tummy. Kitty wouldn't mind if there was a bit less of him, he was sure.

"I put my hair up this morning. I'll very soon be able to take care of myself completely, sir, and get back to Number One."

"We can't wait to get you home." O'Reilly understood the significance in that one word. Home. "It's where you belong." He was pleased to see her smile. It was the look that the old Kinky would have given him when he complimented her on one of her dishes.

"You'll have to take it easy at first, but you can start thinking about the things you mentioned and hotels for the reception."

"I think the Culloden would be lovely, sir, indeed it would. The grounds are *álainn*—"

A musical way of saying "beautiful," O'Reilly thought.

"The grounds are so well kept with all those acres of emerald-green lawns, and it does have one of the best views of Belfast Lough and the Antrim Hills in all of County Down. Or maybe the Crawfordsburn Inn would be nice. I love the old thatch roofs and the dark wood beams inside. I just want—" She took a deep breath and asked, "And are Lady Macbeth, the wee dote, and Arthur well?"

O'Reilly swallowed. Her eagerness and her attempt not to seem overly so touched him. "They both miss you," he said. "You go on getting better so that we can have you home as soon as this place will let us have you back. But you may have to put up with your neighbours' cooking for a while. The larder's still full to the gills. We've enough steak-and-kidney pies, chicken hot pots, roast hams, and cold boiled tongue to feed the whole of the Royal Ulster Rifles and probably the Royal Iniskilling Fusiliers as well. I don't think the ladies of the village believe Barry and I could cope. Flo Bishop even offered to do our laundry. The councillor threw a purple fit."

"I'm sure we'll survive," she said, "as long as we

don't get too much from Maggie MacCorkle." Kinky laughed.

O'Reilly laughed with her. "Maggie has a heart of corn, but I'd class her cooking not so much Cordon Bleu as Cordon Grey."

"It'll be good to be back, sir. And you may find I'm going to be a bit changed."

O'Reilly frowned. "In what way? I want the old Kinky back."

"You'll have that, sir, but I may be asking you for a little more time off."

"That won't cause any difficulty. Do you mind me asking why?"

She hoisted herself up from her pillows and said, "Being in here has given me time to think. Seeing you and your lady got me to pondering that you, sir, are living proof that there's many a good tune left in an old fiddle, so."

O'Reilly grinned and wondered where this was leading.

She frowned and said seriously, "I do think I have been spending too much of my free time in the company of women."

O'Reilly grinned mightily and said, "And you're going to start mingling with the men of the parish, is that it?"

"You'll tell no one, sir?"

"Not a soul."

"Mister Archie Auchinleck, the milkman, he's a

widow-man like yourself. He had asked me out twice before I got sick, but I'd said no. Now if he asks again, I've half a notion to accept."

"By God, Kinky, you must. You dance at my wedding and I'll dance at yours."

"Go 'way, sir," but the smile dimples were there on her cheeks. "It does be nothing like that, but still—" She let the words hang and he heard the wistfulness.

O'Reilly knew the details of her past. He did not hesitate to say, "And I'm sure your Paudeen would have approved."

"He does, sir. He told me so."

O'Reilly felt the hairs on the nape of his neck rise, and he had no doubt that Kinky Kincaid meant what she said about her long-drowned husband. "I'm glad for you. I truly am."

She sat up straighter and said, "And if I'm going to get home soon I need to build up my strength." She lifted a sandwich.

"As you'd say yourself, Kinky, 'Eat up however little much is in it.'"

"Thank you, sir," she said, taking a large bite.

O'Reilly knew she was being thankful for more than the food. "Right," he said. "I've got to go, but Doctor Mills will keep us posted down at Number One, and the minute he says you're ready for home, Barry or myself'll be up here to fetch you as fast as one of those Yankee Agena rockets."

Before he closed the door behind him, he turned back. "How is it?" he asked.

She swallowed, frowned, then said, "It was most generous of Mary Dunleavy . . . but I do believe the joint could have taken five minutes more in the oven, so. And Doctor Laverty could have been more generous with the mustard." Kinky looked O'Reilly straight in the eye. "It is a fair sandwich all right, but it does be time I was back at Number One."

"It does indeed," O'Reilly said. "Cheerio, Kinky." He was still chuckling as he walked down the main corridor to visit Aggie Arbuthnot. It certainly seemed to him that the Corkwoman was truly on the mend, and in many more ways than one.

22

Politics Is Not an Exact Science . . . But

"Did you save a life?" Sue asked when Barry came into the lounge and headed for the fireplace, blowing on his hands. He turned his back to the fire as a gust of wind rattled the glass of the bow windows. He noticed that the coffee table was strewn with papers. Lady Macbeth was curled up asleep on a red folder. Sue sat in an armchair, reading glasses on the end of her nose. Very schoolmistressy, he thought. "One life?" Barry said, and grinned. "Only one? Single-handedly I have cleared up a raging epidemic—"

"You sound like Peter Sellers trying to impress Sophia Loren in that song . . . what was it called? It was a big hit a few years ago." She sang,

—with one jab of my needle in the Punjab, How
   I cleared up beriberi—

" 'Goodness Gracious Me,' " said Barry.

Sue made a face. "Was my singing that bad?"

"Silly. That's the name of the song." He smiled and moved to the side. The backs of his trouser legs were becoming uncomfortably hot, but overall he was feeling warmed up. The unseasonal May gale must have come screeching down from somewhere north of Spitzbergen. As he'd once heard O'Reilly remark, "Any Ballybucklebo brass monkeys would be singing treble."

"I'm teasing you, Barry Laverty." Then she laughed and to Barry's ear it was even more musical than her singing. "All right," he said, "no epidemic. It was one of our regulars. Lives up on the council estate. Chap has chronic bronchitis and it had flared up into an acute attack. That bloody place is so damp it's a wonder not everybody on it has bronchitis. Anyway, penicillin and Friar's Balsam inhalations should do the trick for Ronan."

"*Rónán*," she said, lengthening the vowels to its Irish pronunciation, "Gaelic for little seal." She patted the chair beside her. "Come and sit down. And, by the way, there were no other calls while you were out." She took off her glasses and popped them into a handbag.

"Good." Barry collapsed into the chair. "Bloody cold out there," he said.

"Would you like a cup of something?"

Barry shook his head. "It'll be lunchtime soon. I'm warmed up now. I'll wait."

"If you're allowed a wee tot on call?"

"I am."

"I put a bottle of Entre-Deux-Mers in the fridge to have with lunch. I hope you don't mind. I hope it's all right. I'm not much of a wine expert."

"Lovely," he said, "and thank you." He looked at the light dancing in her copper hair, the smile in those eyes and on her most kissable lips and thought there was nothing he'd rather be doing than sipping a glass of chilled white wine over lunch with Sue Nolan. And after? Things would be "easy and slow," but up here in the lounge, alone? Perhaps more than just kisses? Barry inhaled deeply and was barely aware that he was making an expectant growling in his throat. He noticed a basket of turf a patient had given O'Reilly, and the earthy scent of a couple of pieces on the usually coal-burning fire would certainly add to the atmosphere when they came back up here.

Lady Macbeth yawned, stood, arched her back, and looked at Sue.

"I always thought white cats were standoffish, but

this wee thing seems to have taken a shine to me. She's been up here with me since you left," Sue said.

Her Ladyship jumped down and dislodged papers that Barry bent to retrieve. He read, *Minutes of the May 1, 1965, meeting of the Campaign for Social Justice* and handed the papers to Sue.

"I'm secretary," she said. "Mrs. Patricia McCluskey is chairman, and Mrs. Olive Scott and Mister Peter Gormley are some of the committee."

"Peter Gormley's a surgeon. Decent chap. I've met him," Barry said. He remembered Sue saying last Saturday that she'd been at the CSJ meeting, but she hadn't wanted to discuss politics over dinner, a statement of which he had heartily approved. He'd be perfectly happy to leave such discussion in abeyance today too, but Sue had picked up one of the papers and was clearing her throat. "Our purpose, and I quote, 'is to bring the light of publicity to bear on the discrimination which exists in our community—' "

"Very interesting, Sue. I'd . . . I'd love to hear more, but I think I'll just go upstairs and wash my hands before lunch—"

"Just a bit more." She took a deep breath. " 'The discrimination which exists in our community against the Catholic section of that community, representing more than one-third of the total population.' "

"Good Lord, that's a mouthful."

"Barry," she shook her head, "if I didn't know better, I'd think you were patronizing me." Her voice was stern but there was still a playful light in her eyes. "Seriously, though," she said softly, "do you have any idea how bad it is here? Do you?"

Barry hung his head. "I'm sorry, but no, not really. I mean, I've seen plenty of patients like Ronan in those God-awful council estate places, and I know it's important, Sue, I know it's out there. I just treated a fellow who was well on his way to breaking a rib, he was coughing so violently. But my job's to fix individuals, not whole communities." He tried to lighten the tone by grinning and saying, "I'm not sure I'm ready for this, not before lunch."

She shook her head. "But that's what's wrong. No one knows about the problem, and no one wants to know. They prefer to pretend it doesn't exist, and that's why somebody has to do something."

She wasn't going to be deflected. Barry admired people who had principles—and stuck to them. "Like your society?" he said, deciding to hear her out.

"Yes, and the other group, the Campaign for Democracy in Ulster." She lifted a pamphlet and handed it to him.

He read the title: "'Northern Ireland: The Plain Truth. February 1964.'"

"Or that."

"'Londonderry: One Man No Vote.'"

"We put those two out." She sat, arms folded across her chest. "The Catholics in this country are treated as badly as the blacks in America, but at least over there they're starting to rear up and get results. We need a Martin Luther King." Her eyes shone. "I saw his 'I Have a Dream' speech on television two years ago. Such powerful thoughts."

"And that's what got you interested in civil rights? I saw your library," Barry said.

She nodded. "People should be treated fairly."

And certainly in modern Ulster when there was discrimination it was the Catholics who suffered, and they of all people would be the ones most motivated to agitate. He hesitated. Certain questions were taboo in Ulster, but if Barry was going to go on seeing Sue Nolan, there was one that must be answered, and answered now before things between them, as he was beginning to hope they might, got serious. It wouldn't mean an end, only that things would be in the open. The question had plagued the whole country for four hundred years. As a doctor, he knew that, ethically, a patient's religious persuasion was not permitted to matter, regardless of the doctor's personal beliefs. Even before he'd become a physician Barry had not cared about what side of the religious divide anybody stood. He had two classmates who'd had mixed marriages, though. One lad and his wife were in Canada now, and Finoula O'Gara and her Protestant husband were in New Zealand. Ulster society on both sides didn't make it easy for such couples. "Sue," he said, "I hesitate to ask, but are you—"

"Am I a Catholic?" One eyebrow rose. He could imagine he might get that look if he were a schoolboy who had failed to do his homework. He found it attractive despite the edge in her voice. "No," she said, "no, I'm not. Would it have mattered, to us?"

Barry had already decided what his answer was, but he was also aware of the instant sense of relief that swept through him. Old tribal folk beliefs died hard no matter how liberally one tried to think. It didn't, however, lessen the anxiety of knowing that if answered incorrectly that would be the end of any further friendship or any deepening of feelings. "No," he said unhesitatingly, "it wouldn't. Not one bit."

"Put those pamphlets down and stand up," she said, and rose.

He obeyed and she came to him, kissed him long and hard, and said, "I took a shine to you, Barry Laverty, before Christmas at the kiddies' Christmas pageant. I warmed to you last Saturday over dinner, and if you really mean that . . . really mean it, I think I could get very fond of you. Very fond indeed." And she kissed him again. "Now, how about lunch and that wine?"

Barry tried to catch his breath. Too fast. The whole thing was going too fast, but swept up in her mood he trotted after her, nearly tripping over the cat, who was heading downstairs.

The phone rang. Not now, damn it all, not now.

Sue was passing the phone. She turned around and pointed. "Shall I?"

He nodded and she answered, "Doctors O'Reilly and Laverty?"

He watched her frown, turn pale, and say, "There's

no need to be rude." Making no attempt to cover the mouthpiece, she handed Barry the receiver while saying, "It's a Councillor Bishop and he is not a nice man."

"Hello?"

A voice roared over the phone, "What the hell do you mean, not nice?"

If the boot fits, Barry thought, but said, "Can I help you, Councillor?"

"Laverty? Where the hell's O'Reilly?"

There were days when Barry wished he were not bound by Hippocratic tenets and could tell Bertie Bishop to go to blazes, but he said, "In Belfast. Can I help you?"

"His bloody cat's been at my pigeons again. I just seen it running away there now, so I did."

Barry waited.

"Are you still there, Laverty?"

"I am, Councillor, and so is Doctor O'Reilly's cat."

"Away off and feel your head. I told you I just seen the bloody thing not five minutes ago."

"I'm sorry, you can't have. She's been here all morning, and you don't have to take my word for it. I have a witness. You spoke to her a minute ago. And the last time this happened, the cat had been with our receptionist, Helen Hewitt, the entire time."

"Huh," Bertie grunted, and said, "well, something white got two more of my birds, and by Jesus I'm going to get it, so I am."

Barry's ear tingled from the crash of Bertie's receiver being slammed down. He put his on the cradle, grinned at Sue, and shrugged. "You're right. Not a nice man, our Bertie Bishop," he said. "I'm sorry you had to take abuse from him."

"I've heard worse," she said, then moved to him and asked, "What's for lunch, Doctor?"

"I honestly don't know," he said, "but we can go and look in the fridge."

As they walked hand in hand along the hall to the kitchen, Barry gave a moment's thought to Colin Brown's ferret, Butch. That would have to be looked into before Bishop put two and two together, came to a conclusion, and rightly or wrongly demanded retribution. But not today, not until after lunch and a bottle of chilled white. Not until, telephone willing and O'Reilly not coming home too soon, Barry had spent time alone with Sue Nolan in the comfortable, cosy, private, upstairs lounge.

23

In That Case, What Is the Question?

"Sorry I'm late, lads," O'Reilly said as he opened the door to one of the ten snugs in the Crown Liquor Saloon on Great Victoria Street, not far from the Royal. "I had to pop in with a couple of patients."

Aggie Arbuthnot had been surprised and pleased to see him and was indeed doing well, physically, but was still worrying about finding a job. She should be discharged soon. "Move over in the bed, Charlie." Charlie Greer slid along the cubicle's deep U of smooth black leather benches with button backs. O'Reilly sat beside his friend.

"Better late than never," Sir Donald Cromie said. "Did you call with Mrs. Kincaid?"

"I did," said O'Reilly, "and thanks to you, Cromie, she's out of the woods and well on her way." Ever since they had been students together in the 1930s, "Cromie" had been his friend's preferred form of address. "And thanks to you too, Charlie, and your Mister Gupta, Donal Donnelly's running round like a bee on a hot brick."

Charlie Greer laughed. "Do the sheep in your neck of the woods still have fleeces? Before we discharged him, Jane Hoey had to make him give back the money he'd won playing pontoon."

O'Reilly shook his head. "That's Donal. But as far as I know he's behaving himself now he's back home."

"So," said Charlie, sipping his pint, "God's in His Heaven and all's right with the world."

"The hell it is," O'Reilly said. "You two have drinks. I haven't." He pushed an electric bell mounted on the wall of the booth. The dark wooden panels were each surmounted by stained-glass windows adorned with shells, fairies, pineapples, fleurs-de-lis, and clowns.

Conversations from the other booths and the open bar were subdued, and the place was mercifully unpolluted by the piped musical rubbish that was starting to infiltrate Irish bars. Traffic could barely be heard outside. A tobacco-smoke cloud hovered beneath an ornately carved ceiling. By peering over the snug's half-wall, O'Reilly could read, etched in glass over the bar, *Bonders of Old High Class Whiskies and Direct Importers of Sandeman's Reserve Port.*

"It's not the same as Davy Byrne's in Dublin," Cromie said. "It'll never have the memories of us there when we were youngsters, but the Crown keeps its pints in very good order." He drank from his.

"It's probably the most stylish pub in Belfast," O'Reilly said. "Founded by Felix O'Hanlon as the Railway Tavern and refurbished by Patrick Flanagan in 1885." O'Reilly splayed his hands on the dark wood table in front of him. "That was the same year the prince and princess of Wales were booed in County Cork and General Gordon was killed in Kartoum."

"And you know about that because you were here in 1885 for the reopening, weren't you, you old fart?" Charlie said.

"Go 'way, you young puppy," O'Reilly said, grinning. They were all in their fifties now and had been meeting regularly for years. The easy teasing, the comfort of being with real friends was always a delight and O'Reilly smiled at the two men. It was what he had asked them here to discuss—old friends and acquaintances, and the possibility of gathering them all together in one place next year for a class reunion. "Just because I'm a few years older than you two doesn't mean I'm senile. I've already told you I'm marrying Kitty O'Hallorhan in July and I expect you both there as ushers."

"Yes, sir. What'll it be?" An aproned barman opened the door to the snug. "Och, it's yourself, Doctor O'Reilly. How's about ye?"

"Overall, I'm fine, thanks, Knockers." The man's name was Knox Ritchie, but everyone called him Knockers. "But did you know that under ancient Irish Brehon laws, your estate can declare a grievance if you die of thirst in a public house? Make you forfeit all your sheep? My tongue's hanging out."

The young man laughed. "Can't have that. Anyroad, where'd you find a free Gael to administer the law? The usual?"

"Aye."

Knockers left.

"I must say you rocked me when you first told me you were going to walk down the aisle," said Cromie, "but Charlie and I are delighted for you both. As this is our first get-together since you broke the news, it calls for me to order another jar as soon as your man gets back."

"She's quite the woman," Charlie said. "Always was."

"True on you, Charlie Greer. True on you," O'Reilly said. Kitty with the grey eyes. Kitty with her gentle "I wish you'd drive more slowly." Kitty who knew her diamonds, Kitty with her soft lips. Quite the woman indeed.

"I hope I'm not going to lose my damn fine ward sister," Charlie said.

O'Reilly shook his head. "She intends to go on working."

"I'm relieved," Charlie said.

"Here's to the pair of you, Fingal." Cromie lifted his glass and drank. "Long life and happiness."

"Hear him." Charlie drank too.

"Thanks, lads." O'Reilly grinned at them both and was grateful there weren't any remarks about it being bloody well time he'd made up his mind about the girl he'd walked out with thirty years ago. His friends knew about Deirdre. And they also knew not to reopen old wounds with banter about his new wife-to-be. "I'll make sure you and your missusses get formal invites. The service will be in the Ballybucklebo Presbyterian church, but we haven't decided on the venue for the reception, yet. But you'll both hear in good time."

"Grand," Charlie said, "and I suppose it'll be top hats and tails? I hope to God mine still fit."

O'Reilly laughed. "I'll certainly have to get my old naval number one uniform let out. Kitty wants me to wear it for old times' sake."

"I doubt there's many of our class could fit into their graduation suits now," Cromie said, "and I believe that we're here to talk about a reunion."

"True," said O'Reilly. He glanced at the snug door.

"I wish Knockers would get a move on. Anyway, about the reunion, we should discuss it, and lads, while we're together, I want your advice with a couple of other matters. Shirt factories and scholarships. They'll keep 'til later, but I do need help."

Charlie said, "Shirt factories and scholarships? Doesn't sound as romantic as 'Moonlight and Roses,' but whatever we can do we will."

"What are you on about, Charlie?" Cromie asked.

"You know I sing in a choir. It's one of the numbers we're doing in a concert."

Cromie knit his brows and feigned bafflement. "I've never heard of a tune called 'Shirt Factories and Scholarships.' Will you be singing it?"

"We're doing 'Moonlight,' you eejit."

"All right, you two," said O'Reilly, laughing, "if you've finished acting the lig, back to the agenda. We all remember Hilda Manwell. She wrote to Charlie from Australia and suggested a thirtieth class reunion next year and we've all agreed it would be a good thing."

Two heads nodded.

"And we'd be the steering committee?"

"Agreed." Two voices spoke.

"We'd pick a meeting site, contact the class, and make sure there's lots of interest, perhaps arrange a little scientific program so we can get tax concessions for the ones who have to come a long way?" O'Reilly said.

"Chase the pharmaceutical companies for grants. Invite some of our old teachers if they're still alive, and set up the social events," Cromie added.

"And," said O'Reilly, "I suggest we divvy up the jobs. I'll look after a place. It has to be in Dublin because that's where it all began. I'd suggest the Shelbourne as the meeting hotel. I'll work through the Trinity Alumni Association. They'll have a class list of addresses."

Charlie said, "When you get it, Fingal, send it to me. I'll dictate a letter to the whole class, see who's interested, what dates would suit. My secretary can run off copies. We've just got one of those new Xerox machines, beats the hell out of the old Gestetner. And the letters can go out with the rest of the hospital mail. They'll be addressed to a bunch of doctors, after all."

"Good," O'Reilly said.

Cromie added, "Charlie and I'll take care of the science, the pharmaceutical companies, and see who of our old profs are still around. I know Victor Millington Synge is and that surgeon Mister Kinnear."

"He let me do my first appendicectomy," O'Reilly said. "He's a good skin."

"He is," said Charlie. "I saw him last year at the Royal College, and old Synge was pretty decent too. Do you remember when the . . . damn it, I've forgotten their name . . . the visiting society came?"

"The Pilgrims," O'Reilly said. "All those senior doctors. The ones we set Ronald Hercules Fitzpatrick up for a fall in front of. Ronald was an arrogant bollix, but he practises near me now. He'll have to be invited."

Cromie said, "Maybe he'll have forgotten that day, but I haven't. Embarrassed the hell out of Fitzpatrick, but Doctor Synge turned it all into a laugh and even got Doctor Micks to see the funny side."

"I came close to giving myself a hernia, I laughed so much," Charlie said, "and Bob Beresford had tears in his eyes."

"Good old Bob," O'Reilly said quietly. "Sad what happened."

"Aye," said Charlie, "very sad."

The door opened. "Here y'are." Knockers set a pint on the table. "That'll be two and tuppence, sir."

"You're an angel of mercy, Knockers. *Sláinte,*" O'Reilly said, and sank one-third of his pint. "I think you've just saved a life."

"Here," said Cromie, handing the barman a half crown and waiting for his change. Tipping was not a custom in Belfast pubs. "And bring another round, please."

The hinges of the swing door creaked as Knockers left.

"Right," said Charlie, "now Fingal is getting himself refuelled, is there anything more about the reunion?"

O'Reilly shook his head. "I think that's it, isn't it? We've all jobs to do and we can report back when we've made progress."

"My kind of meeting," Cromie said. "Short,

sharp, and to the point. Not like some of the hospital ones."

"You can say that again," Charlie said. "You were at the last surgical operating theatre committee. Went on for bloody hours."

"It's an advantage of being a GP," O'Reilly said. "No medical committees and the rugby club executive is different."

"Do you miss playing the game?" Charlie said.

"Do you?" O'Reilly said, remembering he and Charlie Greer playing together, proudly wearing their country's green.

"I do." Charlie nodded, but said, "We'd fun, but the world moves on. I reckon the Irish team are going to be hard to beat next season. Willie John McBride and Syd Millar will be back in the forwards and Michael Gibson in the backs."

"I hear there's a real prospect playing for Queen's," O'Reilly said. "Medical student called Ken Kennedy."

Cromie coughed. "If I might try to get you two mighty athletes to stop getting dewy-eyed over a game of legalised mayhem and come back to the questions at hand, I'd suggest we get together here next month for reports?"

Two heads nodded.

"Now, about shirt factories," O'Reilly said. "Do either of you know anything about the ones here in Belfast?"

"Faulat and Latimer have a band, the Faulat Girl Pipers, very pretty they look in their short kilts, and they're damn fine pipers too," Charlie said. "But that's all I know. I'm sure it's not much use."

O'Reilly shrugged. "Can't be helped. Cromie?"

He shook his head. "Why the sudden interest?"

"We've a patient, one I was seeing today, who lost her job at the Beresford Street factory. The owner's a man called Ivan McCluggage. He has a silent partner. I'm trying to find out more about them, see if there's a way to persuade them to rehire Aggie."

Charlie said, "McCluggage?" and frowned. "There's a Robin McCluggage, a surgeon at the Belfast City Hospital. He's a member of Royal Belfast Golf Club like me. Once in a while he brings his brother as a guest. I've a half notion his name's Ivan. I could have a word with Robin. It's pretty thin, Fingal, I'm sorry, but it's the best I can do."

"Och," said O'Reilly, "every little bit helps. I'd be grateful if you would." He finished his pint.

Someone must have told a good story out in the bar because a gale of men's laughter swept through the place.

"Sounds like they're happy at their work," Cromie said. He drank and said, "You'd another question, Fingal. About scholarships?"

O'Reilly, his Guinness now finished, glanced longingly at the door of the cubicle. It did take time to pour a good pint. "About scholarships in general and to medical school in particular," he said.

Cromie frowned. "In general you can win them in

our national examination, Advanced Senior. I can't remember the exact marks you need, but one level in a clatter of subjects earns you a County Scholarship, paid for by your county, and higher marks get you a State Exhibition, paid for by Her Majesty's Government. That's the one with the most money. My Jennifer—"

"Your daughter who married the pathologist?" O'Reilly said.

"Aye, she had a County. Saved me a few quid while she was getting her B.A."

"Good for her," O'Reilly said, "but I'm pretty sure my lass doesn't qualify for either. She'd have told me if she had, but do either of you know of any ones aimed at less privileged kids?" He waited.

Finally Cromie said, "I think there are a couple. They're not awarded every year. I've not got a notion about the details, but I know the bursar, chap called George Burland. I could find out."

"I'd be grateful, Cromie."

"I'll ask next week. Call you."

The door swung open and Knockers, bearing a tray of pints, came in and set them down on the table. "Here yiz are. Six shillings and sixpence."

"My shout," Cromie said, and paid.

As Knockers left, two pints were raised and Cromie said, "Here's to you, Fingal and Kitty. Every happiness, you old bollix."

"Thanks, lads," O'Reilly said. "Now if you two will join me in our old goodnight blessing?"

In unison, three voices called, "Here's to us. Who's like us? Damn few and they're mostly dead."

"Aye," said O'Reilly, wiping froth from his upper lip, and thinking fondly of the old days. "Damn few."

"Do you remember a folk group called the Limelighters?" Charlie said.

"'Wabash Canonball'? 'City of New Orleans'?" O'Reilly said.

"That's them, but I was thinking of another number. 'Those Were the Days.'" He sat back. "Trinity 1931 to '36, five years, but for us three those *were* the days. Five bloody good years."

"I wonder," said Cromie, "how many of the rest of the class feel that way?"

"We're going to have to wait to find out," Charlie said, "but as soon as we start getting replies to our letter to the class we'll know."

"Patience," said O'Reilly, "is a virtue which I'll try to exercise while I wait for any answers you two can get for me on those other matters, but for the meantime I'd like to propose another toast." He raised his glass. "To absent friends," and as the others repeated the toast and raised their glasses, Fingal O'Reilly thought with bittersweet fondness of Bob Beresford, the man who in Trinity had been the fourth member of their Fearsome Four, and, of them, O'Reilly's closest friend.

24

Home Sweet Home

"Get a move on," O'Reilly muttered as he drummed his fingers on the steering wheel. The car was becoming warm so he wound down the window. He knew he should be used to the inevitable delays of the Thursday cattle market in Ballybucklebo, but he wanted to get Kinky to Number One, and he understood how she was aching to be there. Seventeen days was a long time to spend in hospital. He turned and looked into the rear of the Rover. "All right in the back? Sorry about the holdup."

Kinky, wearing a tartan dressing gown, lay across the seat, pillows propping her against one side of the car, fluffy-slippered feet sticking out from under the red rug that covered her legs. Her face, though pale, was wreathed in a beatific smile. "I'm doing very well, sir."

An Aberdeen Angus bullock lowed as it and two companions ambled their way past the car. A cattle smell made more powerful by the mid-May heat drifted in through the car's open window.

"City folks might find that awful," said Kinky. "But I'd rather get a whiff of a good beast in the country than the stink of motorcar fumes in the city, and I've had my fill of the smell of disinfectant, so. Don't you fret, sir. Up ahead now I can see the Maypole so we're nearly home."

"We are that," O'Reilly said, managing to edge past the last of the herd and accelerate through the traffic light just as it was changing from amber to red. He parked outside Number One, came round, and opened Kinky's door. "We have arrived, madam," said O'Reilly, bowing and extending his hand. "Can I help you out?"

"Take you this, sir." She handed him the rug and her overnight bag. He noticed the toy hare's droopy ears sticking out through the half-open zip. Puffing, and hauling on O'Reilly's hand, she managed to slide out of the seat, get her feet onto the pavement, and stand.

With the rug and the bag tucked under one arm, O'Reilly offered her his elbow.

She took it and said, "I do be like a great lady being squired on the arm of a gentleman, so."

"Hang on," he said as he twisted, managed to slam the door, and turned back. "I'll get the pillows later." He took a deep breath. "Now, Kinky? Ready?"

She nodded.

He measured his steps to hers, feeling her weight as she leaned against him, and together they walked along the path, past the rosebushes, and up to the green-painted door. This wasn't the old Kinky. She had to stop once to catch her breath. Her dressing gown seemed to be a size too big. O'Reilly frowned and sought for the right word. That was it. Kinky seemed to have shrunk.

But not, it seemed, when it came to accepting her responsibilities.

She stopped, pointed, tutted, and said, "Would you look at your brass plate, sir. Just look at it. Mother of God, but it's a disgrace, so."

He glanced at the offending object.

DR. F. F. O'REILLY, M.B., B.CH., B.A.O.
PHYSICIAN AND SURGEON

"All tarnished. It should shine like—"

"Kinky Kincaid," O'Reilly said, chuckling, "we are going to get you into the house, into your quarters, and tucked up. The bloody plate can wait."

The door opened. Cissie Sloan stopped in the doorway, her mouth opened, then she beamed and said, "Welcome home, Kinky, and good morning to yourself, Doctor dear."

"Morning, Cissie," O'Reilly said. "Now, if you'll give us room, I need to get Kinky into the house."

"Certainly, sir." Cissie didn't budge. "I was just seeing that nice Doctor Laverty, so I was. I needed a prescription for more of them there thyroxine tablets to take care of the little thingys in my blood that—"

"Cissie." It wasn't his force-ten bellow, but O'Reilly spoke sharply.

"Right enough, sir. Sorry, sir." She got out of the way. "Get you better soon, Kinky. All the ladies at the Women's Union wants to see you. Flo Bishop says, so she does, says she—"

Cissie was still talking on the intake of breath as O'Reilly helped Kinky into the hall and closed the door. She stopped as soon as they were across the threshold and he heard her whisper, "Home. Thank you. Thank you."

And Fingal O'Reilly knew to whom Kinky, who went to church every Sunday, was speaking. He nodded in agreement. "Not far now," he said, and helped her down the hall. The surgery door was shut, but he could hear Barry's tones. The door of the waiting room was open. Hughey Gamble, the octagenarian known to all as "Shooey," who must have been in because of his arthritis, spotted them. "Kinky's back," he called, and from the waiting room came a solid and prolonged round of applause.

Kinky grinned. "Thank you," she called, and said to O'Reilly, "I know Flo'll have spread the word. I told her two days ago when I was getting home."

O'Reilly stuck his head round the corner and, as always, admired the puce-coloured roses on the wallpaper. "Thank you all. It's good to have her home."

When they reached the kitchen, Helen Hewitt turned from the stove. "Doctor O'Reilly," she said, "and Mrs. Kincaid. Lovely to see you home."

O'Reilly saw Helen deliberately place herself between Kinky and the stove, where a saucepan filled with steaming water held a sealed jam jar. Something brown was being heated over a low flame. "Helen's doing me a favour," he said. "Before she goes back upstairs."

Kinky smiled and cast a searching eye round her kitchen. "I approve, Miss Hewitt. And thank you for helping out while I was away. Doctor O'Reilly has explained, so. I will be pleased to have you in this house until I'm back on my feet, and I do hope you find the perfect job soon."

"Thank you, Mrs. Kincaid," Helen said. "I hope so too."

O'Reilly heard how flat her voice was. So far she'd had only one interview, for a salesgirl position at Robinson and Cleaver's department store in Belfast. It had been unsuccessful. They were looking for someone younger and, of course, cheaper. Helen, with her Junior, Senior, and Advanced Senior certificate subjects was entitled to a higher starting wage than someone younger who'd left school at fifteen with no qualifications. He wished Cromie would call again, but on Monday he'd rung to explain that the bursar was away until next week so Cromie had no news about any potential scholarships. "You'll be with us for a few more weeks," he said. "Isn't that right, Kinky."

"If you say so, sir." But Kinky was smiling. "That pneumonia does knock the stuffing out of a body. We're happy to have you here, Helen, to help my doctors, so."

And O'Reilly was delighted to hear that, and pleased by how quickly Kinky had moved from the formal "Miss Hewitt" to an informal "Helen." "Come on," he said, "let's get you settled." He steered her through the kitchen and into her tidy sitting room. "Where would you like to sit?"

Kinky didn't answer.

O'Reilly waited as she looked round the room—at the black enamelled fireplace with its crenellated semicircular arch over the top, at the brass fender round a tiled hearth, at the fire screen with its tapestry behind glass standing beside the fire. O'Reilly knew Kinky had embroidered the galleon in full sail. And she'd tatted the lace antimacassars on the two maroon armchairs. They were arranged near the fireplace but angled so she could watch her TV, which sat on a mahogany table. Both armchairs were flanked by circular wine tables, each with three legs and a spiral pedestal. A brass handbell sat on one table. On the far wall, beside the door to her bedroom and bathroom, two framed prints of Percy French watercolours depicting the Mountains of Mourne hung over a mahogany tallboy with ash trim and brass drawer handles. It shone in recently polished splendour, courtesy of Helen Hewitt, and was topped with a vase of freshly cut red, yellow, and maroon tulips, beside which a large placard announced, WELCOME HOME, KINKY KINCAID.

"I . . . I'll sit here, please," she said, starting to lower herself into an armchair. "Oh, my," she said softly, "but it does be very, very good to be home."

He could tell by the way her voice and her lip both trembled that Kinky was having to fight back her tears.

"And I do so love tulips. Did yourself do the card, sir?"

"You've seen my handwriting, Kinky Kincaid," said O'Reilly with a smile. "No, it was Barry who did the lettering, but it was Kitty's idea. So were the tulips." She'd told him when they'd last spoken on the phone, although rather than specifically mentioning tulips she had suggested "Kinky's favourite flowers." O'Reilly had known of the Corkwoman's fondness for their bright colours.

"Well," she said, "Miss O'Hallorhan is a thoughtful woman, so."

O'Reilly was disappointed at the formality, but he knew that it was going to take more than a hand-lettered placard and a bunch of flowers to restore Kitty to Kinky's good graces.

"Please thank her for me, sir. In fact, I'll thank her myself when next I see her, which I hope will be soon if we're to get this wedding planned."

That was promising, he thought, but said, "Kinky, I am delighted you're going to work on that, but you've to get your feet under you first." He put her bag on the floor and tucked the rug over her knees. "Are you warm enough? I could light the fire."

"I'm toasty, sir, thank you." She frowned. "And planning can be done without getting out of a chair.

I am not as strong as I was, not yet, but I'm not an invalid, sir."

"Kinky, you're wonderful." O'Reilly then laughed before he said, "No one thinks you're an invalid, but, and I'm speaking as a doctor, people who overdo things after an illness can have relapses. I'm delighted to have you home and I want to keep you here so I'll be the judge of when you can start work." He nodded at her TV. "And it won't be until after you've had a chance to see your favourites on Saturday night."

Kinky's frown fled. "I've missed two whole episodes of *Z-Cars*," she said, "and I want to know what's happening to that nice policeman from Belfast, Bert Lynch."

Someone knocked on the door.

"Come in," Kinky said.

Helen Hewitt entered, carrying a steaming mug, and set it on a mat on the wine table with the bell.

"That," said O'Reilly, "is something I believe you told Doctor Laverty you'd like."

"I've just made it fresh, so I have," Helen said.

O'Reilly chuckled. "Helen was warming it on the stove when we arrived. We wanted it to be a little surprise."

Kinky inhaled. "By the good Lord," she said, "beef tea." She lifted the mug.

"Careful," said Helen. "It's very hot."

"And shouldn't it be drunk hot if a body's to get the goodness of it?" Kinky sipped. Her face creased into a massive smile. "Helen, I couldn't have done better myself. Thank you." She sipped again. "I can feel the power of it, so."

O'Reilly hid a smile. He'd looked out Kinky's own recipe for Helen to try, but given Kinky's fierce possessiveness about her kitchen and everything in it he'd felt it best not to tell her. "Right." He gestured to Kinky's bag. "Helen, would you please take that through to Mrs. Kincaid's bedroom?"

"I'll see to unpacking it in a shmall-little minute, Helen," Kinky said.

Helen returned and said, "It *is* good to see you home, Mrs. Kincaid."

Before Kinky could answer, O'Reilly heard the ring of the front doorbell. "I'll see to it." Helen left at a trot.

O'Reilly frowned. "Wonder who that could be? When surgery's open the customers are meant to come in through the waiting-room door."

Helen soon returned with a huge bunch of lilacs and the room was filled with their perfume. She handed Kinky a card. "Mister Auchinleck brought the flowers and the card."

"Well," said Kinky, "that did be very thoughtful." A small smile played on her lips. "Be a good girl, now, and take them into the kitchen. There's a Waterford vase in the cupboard to the left of the sink."

"I'll see to it," Helen said, and left.

Kinky opened the envelope, removed the card, read, then slid the card back in the envelope. "I must write Mister Auchinleck a thank-you letter." Her smile was vast. "He does be quite the gentleman, so."

"You do that, Kinky," O'Reilly said, smiling himself, certain that Kinky had a suitor and was going to accept his overtures. He was delighted for her. He said, "By all means write a letter, but for right now, Mrs. Maureen 'Kinky' Kincaid, you sit there at your ease, drink up your beef tea while it's still hot, and if you need anything, give that little bell a shake and Helen or Barry or myself will come. Helen collected some books from the lounge that she thought you might enjoy reading. You concentrate on getting better. We've missed you, and we're delighted to have you back where you belong. At home."

He saw her eyes mist. Not wishing to embarrass her by seeing her tears, O'Reilly didn't wait for a reply but left her to savour her homecoming—and no doubt ready to issue a string of orders to Helen about what needed doing as soon as she returned with Archie's flowers in the vase. And O'Reilly knew the first direction would be for Helen to polish the brass plate on the door of Number One, Main Street, Ballybucklebo.

25

I Am Disappointed by That Stroke

"It does," said Kinky, "seem different, sir, me sitting up here taking tea with yourself, so." She and O'Reilly were both on their second cup yet she continued to look round as if she had never set foot in a room she must have dusted and vacuumed thousands of times.

O'Reilly, in the other upstairs armchair, laughed. "We should have started doing this years ago, Kinky. We need to plan, and doing it over a cup of tea makes it that bit more pleasant." And it's a none-too-subtle reinforcement of how important you are to me, Mrs. Kinky Kincaid, he thought. He handed her a piece of paper. "I've started my list for my half of the guests. Please take a look."

She scanned his handwriting, tutting and muttering about inky spiders. "I can see why you'd have your two surgeon friends as ushers," Kinky said, but then frowned. "I am surprised, though, that your brother, Mister Lars, is an usher too and won't be your best man."

"Lars Porsena O'Reilly is absolutely terrified of public speaking," O'Reilly said, leaning back in his chair. "I'd go as far as to call it a phobia, Kinky. Our father may have been a professor of classics and English literature and a recognised orator, but Lars did not inherit that talent."

"And the best man has to make a speech." Kinky nodded. "I do think sparing him that is a great kindness, so."

O'Reilly pursed his lips. "It was the only way to be sure he'd actually come. Lars would normally be going to his place in Villefranche for the summer, but he was so tickled when I told him back in April that I was getting married again he's delayed going until after the wedding. But I had to promise him he wouldn't have to get up on his hind legs and make a speech. I've known Cromie and Charlie for more than thirty years. Which one could I have picked without possibly upsetting the other? But Barry's like family. He'll do a great job." O'Reilly poured himself another cup.

"You haven't seen Mister Lars since March, have you, sir?"

O'Reilly shook his head. "Between the practice here and his legal work and his hobbies we haven't been able to make time."

"I think the pair of you should make time. If I may say, it seems a lonely life for your brother in that wee town on Strangford Lough."

O'Reilly shook his head. "I don't think Lars is happier than when he's in his greenhouse with only his orchids for company or tramping around Strangford bird-watching, but your point's taken, Kinky. I will be taking a trip down the Saturday after next."

"I am glad to hear it," she said. "Family is the most important thing of all, so."

"And you're family too," O'Reilly said.

She made no acknowledgement. "And Miss O'Hallorhan, will she be arranging the bride's side soon?"

"She's working on her list. Her father died three years ago and she's been worrying over who to ask to give her away. There aren't any close male relatives. Only a distant cousin, Brendan. I thought I'd ask the marquis. He'd be coming anyway as my guest and he and Kitty hit it off so well at his pheasant shoot. Of course we'll invite Myrna, his sister, too."

"Grand, so, Doctor. And I'll make a note," Kinky said, picking up her fountain pen. "Now. I don't see Councillor and Flo Bishop's names."

From below came the double rings of the telephone. Helen, whom O'Reilly had last seen working in the dining room, would answer it.

"You're right." O'Reilly grimaced, but said, "The bloody man's a councillor. Can't avoid it. Put 'em on there." He watched Kinky inscribe "Mr. and Mrs. Albert Bishop" in her neat copperplate.

"And we'll have to have my old classmate and colleague, Doctor Fitzpatrick from the Kinnegar."

Kinky sniffed. Fitzpatrick had made the mistake of crossing her—once.

"Two classic cases of 'trapped by courtesy,'" O'Reilly said, "but, noblesse oblige."

"Excuse me, Doctor O'Reilly," Helen said as she

came through the door. One of Kinky's aprons and a pair of yellow rubber gloves could not hide how attractive she looked in a rollneck sweater and blue jeans. Her hair was up in a fashionable beehive hairdo. "Excuse me, it's a Sir Donald Cromie's secretary on the phone." There was a hushed tone to her voice. "She's getting her boss and asked me to fetch you."

O'Reilly stood. "Thanks, Helen. Excuse me, Kinky." He took the stairs two at a time.

A woman's voice came over the phone. "Sir Donald will be with you in a moment."

"Fingal?" Cromie said.

"Cromie? What the hell are you on about? Is *Sir* Donald Cromie too bloody important to pick up the phone and dial?"

"Not at all, but you should see the stack of calls I've to make and you know as well as I do how much time you can waste waiting to be answered. My Joyce is a good lass. She calls ahead." He chuckled. "I think she's more impressed with my knighthood than I am and loves to use it when she calls."

"My Helen is in a state of shock. I think she reckons a knight of the realm is next to royalty."

"Far from it," Cromie said. "Look. I finally got hold of Mister Burland, the bursar. I was right. There are two scholarships available to working-class kids from Ireland to go to medical school. But I'm afraid they both may be nonstarters. They're like the Rhodes, specifically for young men."

"Damnation." O'Reilly pursed his lips and glanced up to see that Helen had followed him down the stairs. What a waste of those extra years of study. What a bloody awful waste.

"One's watertight. Only an act of Parliament can change the terms of the bequest, but there may be a glimmer of hope in the other."

O'Reilly brightened. "Go on."

"There's been a MacNeill Bursary since Queen's was opened in 1849."

"MacNeill?"

"The Lords of Ballybucklebo," Cromie said.

"My marquis?" O'Reilly's eyes narrowed.

"Apparently."

"Good Lord, I've never even heard of it." He frowned. Surely the winning of such a prize would be instantly the only topic of proud conversation in the village. Of course, few if any children here completed the university entrance requirements. Most went to work at fifteen, on the family farm or in Belfast's shipyards and linen mills.

"Mister Burland says that it is in the gift of the head of the family, and it's only for potential students from County Down. It hasn't been awarded for some time, and it's presently open."

Helen grinned at him as she went into the dining room and closed the door. He heard the Hoover start up. There had to be more in life for such a bright young woman than low-paying jobs, then marriage to a workingman and years of motherhood.

O'Reilly pursed his lips, then said, "But it's only for boys, isn't it?"

"Burland thinks that is in the original will, yes. But he also thinks there might have been a codicil. He's not sure."

"Go on." O'Reilly nodded to a patient who had come from the surgery and was leaving by the front door. The older man knuckled his forehead.

"Unfortunately, Burland doesn't possess the original documents."

"Who the hell does?"

"The marquis."

"Thanks, Cromie. I'll follow up on that." O'Reilly decided it would be worth a visit to Lord John Mac-Neill at Ballybucklebo House. He noticed Barry coming from the waiting room, heading for the surgery, and being followed by Donal and Julie Donnelly.

"Still there, Fingal?" Cromie asked.

"Sorry. Mind was wandering."

He heard a chuckle, then, "Be sure to be nice to it if it ever comes back."

O'Reilly smiled. "Bugger off, Cromie, and thanks for the gen."

"One other thing. I bumped into Charlie this morning. Told him I'd be phoning you."

"Oh?"

"Aye. He asked me to tell you that he's had a word with the surgeon, Robin McCluggage. His brother Ivan does own a shirt factory. Robin used to be in it too, old family business, but he sold out his share."

"Who to?"

"Charlie's sorry, Fingal, but Robin's not at liberty to say. It's a silent partnership. He did let slip it's someone from your part of County Down."

Fingal sighed. "Be nice to know exactly who. I have a half notion, but I'd like to be sure. Thanks for letting me know."

"You're welcome, and good luck with whoever you're trying to get a scholarship for. I'm off. See you next month." The connection went dead.

O'Reilly rubbed his hands. "At least," he said to himself, "I'll bet John can help Helen. I just know he can. Pity there doesn't seem to be any real information about McCluggage that Barry could use to help Aggie."

"It does be said," he heard Kinky remark, "that grown men who talk to themselves—"

He spun and saw her standing in the hall. "What are you doing here? I left you hard at work on that list upstairs. And *sitting down*."

"Doctor O'Reilly," she said, "the nurses at the Royal told me that I had to walk about every day so I'd not get clots in my legs, so."

"It's twenty-three days since your operation. When folks get DVTs it's usually within three weeks," he said, knowing he was not going to persuade Kinky Kincaid to take it easy any longer.

"I am glad for that. Now, sir, I finished your list and left it on the lounge table. I enjoyed our tea, but if you'll excuse me I'm sure the silver needs polishing, so."

"If it does, ask Helen to take care of it." He pretended not to notice her "don't be silly" look.

"Fingal." Barry stood frowning outside the surgery door. "Something's come up. I need your help."

"Sure." O'Reilly crossed the hall and went into the surgery. Donal and Julie both half-turned in their chairs and stared at him. Julie was tearful. Was something wrong with her pregnancy? She was due on July fifth so she'd be—he did a quick calculation—thirty-four and a half weeks. "Doctor Laverty, is Julie all right?"

"Julie's fine and the pregnancy's fine," Barry said. "Donal, explain to Doctor O'Reilly what you told me." Barry hopped up and sat on the examination couch, legs dangling, as he had on the very first surgery they'd taken together last July.

O'Reilly walked past Donal to sit in the swivel chair. "I see your thatch is growing back nicely, Donal," O'Reilly said.

"But it's still dead itchy," Donal said, scratching the stubble over his recent surgical scar. His other hand held Julie's. "But never mind a bit of irritation. It's the wee house. It's desperate, so it is, sir. I done everything like you told me, and thanks a million for putting in the word with Mister Canning at the bank, and all. He was dead on, so he was. We seen Dapper Frew first thing last Monday and made an offer of one thousand seven hundred . . . just like you said to, sir. It was contagious on us—"

Julie, who'd stopped crying, managed a weak smile and said, "Contingent on us, love."

"Aye, right enough, contingent. Thank you, Julie." He beamed at her. "Julie keeps me right, you know. Contingent on us getting a mortgage. We trotted over to the bank. Dapper'd phoned and give your man Mister Canning all the details. He explained a lot of stuff about monthy payments, insuring the mortgage, but at the heels of the hunt he said if we could put eight hundred pounds down, and we could manage nine at a pinch, you know, he'd give us up to nine hundred at three and a half percent over twenty-five years. I can pay that off every month, wee buns. Mister Canning was dead up front, so he was. He said seeing what I earn, and all, and Julie not going to be working after the wee lad comes, nine hundred was the very best he can do, but it was enough, we thought."

That would certainly buy the house, and if Donal and Julie could get it for £1,700 O'Reilly knew they'd enough in their nest egg to pay the incidental expenses and furnish it. Donal would have no trouble making the monthly payments from his wages. "So what went wrong?"

"We seen a lawyer and he was for taking care of what he calls exchanging contracts, because we heard the estate was going to accept. Then, there now, about an hour ago . . . I'm still on 'the sick,' so I was at home . . . Dapper comes round, says he til me, 'Youse two's up the creek. There's been an offer for the whole two thousand pounds, and cash too.' Sellers, says Dapper, always prefer that to mortgages. Says I til him, 'They can't do that to Julie and me. We're British objects. We've our rights, so we have.' "

O'Reilly glanced at Julie, who was shaking her head, but clearly deciding not to correct her husband even though her lips framed the word "subjects."

"Ould Dapper, he says he's sorry, but unless we can top the two thousand pounds we'll not get the wee house." He squeezed Julie's hand. "Julie here's all upset and I'm not too happy myself, but Dapper says, and he knows these things, that it's not worth more than two thousand at most and we'd be daft to offer any more."

"I'm sorry, Julie," O'Reilly said, "but I have to agree with Mister Frew."

She nodded her head, dashed the back of a hand across her eyes, hicupped, and said, "I do understand, sir. I shouldn't have got my heart so set on it." She patted her swollen tummy and took a deep breath. "I'd the nursery all planned and I could see the wane in her pram in the back garden under them lime trees."

"It's all right, love." Donal leant across and kissed her forehead. "I'll find us another place. Never you worry." He forced a smile. "At least I'll not have to level that big mound in the back garden."

Barry said quietly, "That's only the half of it, Doctor O'Reilly. Go on please, Donal."

Donal's face reddened and an artery throbbed at his

temple. "I asked Dapper if there was any chance the other fellah, whoever he is, might change his mind." Donal clenched his teeth before saying, "There's about as much chance of that as there is of Rathlin Island floating over to Scotland for a weekend."

O'Reilly sat forward in his chair. "Why?"

Donal looked at Barry and back to O'Reilly. "You and Doctor Laverty'll keep it to yourselves. I know that, but Dapper's not supposed to give away names. I told youse he's a right good head. He told me, on the QT like, the other is a fellah from Belfast. He owns a shirt factory. He's got pots of money. His name's Mister Ivan McCluggage."

O'Reilly stiffened. This shirt factory owner suddenly seemed to be intruding into life in Ballybucklebo. Why? And who was his silent partner? Cromie'd said Charlie hadn't been able to answer that question, but had gleaned a hint that he was a North Down man.

Donal straightened his narrow shoulders and looked O'Reilly in the eye. "Doctor, sir, it's only about a month since youse sorted things for me and my mates over that there horse. Now me and Julie don't want to be any trouble, you know, but youse two being learnèd men, is there any way youse could help Julie and me?"

O'Reilly looked at Barry, who held up his hands palms up and hoisted his shoulders.

"It's all right, sir," Julie said. "We know you can't fix everything."

Donal patted her belly. "I'd do anything for you and the wee fellah in there."

"And all I can do is make some enquiries," O'Reilly said, "but honestly I'm none too hopeful."

"We understand," Julie said, rising to her feet. "Come on, Donal. We've taken too much of the doctors' time, so we have." She smiled at Barry. "I'll be back in to see you in two weeks for my next antenatal visit. Not long to wait now."

"Not long at all," Barry said, slipping off the couch and opening the door for the couple.

Donal crammed a woolly toque on his head and pulled it down over the tops of both ears. "I'd not want nobody to think I'd met a Sioux on the warpath, so I'd not." He closed the door.

"Bugger," said O'Reilly. "Hellfire and damnation. What are we going to do?"

"Sorry," Barry said. "I've no ideas."

O'Reilly scratched his chin. "All right," he said, "what do we know? For sure only that a man called Ivan McCluggage wants the house. He has a silent partner in his shirt factory and he's suddenly getting interested in property in Ballybucklebo. I've just heard from Cromie, from a man who knows a man, that McCluggage's partner comes from near here." O'Reilly scratched the nape of his neck. "I can only think of one man here who knows a great deal about property and always has an eye out for the main chance when it comes to making a fast few quid."

"Bishop?" Barry pursed his lips and exhaled through his nose. "I suppose—"

"I know, Barry. There's not a scrap of evidence to connect the two, but . . . but, damn it, I can feel it."

Barry laughed. "Don't tell me you're getting like Kinky?"

O'Reilly shook his head. "Not me, but humour me, Barry, let's assume for a minute I'm right. What would a shirt factory owner want with a house here that he's willing to pay probably more than it's worth to get it? Who told him about it?"

Barry said, "Bishop's a builder. Perhaps he wants to fix the place up and sell it for a profit and doesn't want folks to know he's interested?"

O'Reilly shook his head. "I doubt it. He'd know to the penny what the place should fetch. The estate agent'll have disclosed what Donal had offered. They have to. And why involve his partner? Bishop would make a damn sight more money if he bought it himself. So McCluggage's upped the ante to be sure Donal's out, no one else offers, and he gets it, but by the time a couple of hundred's spent into really doing it up . . . ? It doesn't make sense, so why, damn it, why in the name of the wee man do they want the place? Why?"

Barry said, "It's just a thought, but the cottage is in the hollow of that God-awful hairpin bend. I wonder if council has any plans to straighten it? I nearly went off the road there driving Sue to the restaurant last week. I was . . . a little distracted."

O'Reilly frowned. "And you reckon that because he's on council, he might be planning to get them to do just that and then he'd make a lot of money when the place came under a compulsory purchase order?"

"I hadn't thought it through, and you know Bertie better than I do. But he could be using McCluggage as a front so he can't be accused of using inside information."

O'Reilly shook his head. "Yes, I do know Bertie, by God," he said. "Indeed I bloody well do. I've seen him at the rugby club committee. If he wants something done he's like a flaming juggernaut—"

"Unstoppable," Barry said.

"Exactly. If Bertie sees a chance to make a few pounds he'll have the council eating out of his hand. They'll be begging to be allowed to straighten the bloody road. Jasus, Barry." O'Reilly wagged a finger. "I think you're dead on the money. Councils that buy property have to pay the assessed value, that's two thousand five hundred pounds, and add a hundred or two to compensate the owners for the inconvenience of buying another house or renting while they're house hunting. It would certainly be worth his while. Hell, Bertie may even get the contract to demolish the very house he's bought *and* do the road straightening."

"Do you really think the councillor would?" Barry stopped and turned to stare at the Snellen's eye chart on the wall as if trying to decipher hieroglyphics. "Good Lord, Fingal. It does make perfect sense."

"This is just the kind of swindle Bertie Bishop loves. Do you know, he'd not even have to pay any tax if the council buys the house? And he's smart enough to have covered his tracks. Using McCluggage as a front is a stroke of genius even if he's going to have to split the profits." O'Reilly took a deep breath and blew it out. "But I'm buggered if I can see what we can do about it. It's pure supposition that Bishop's even involved, and if we accuse him all he has to do is deny it . . . and he would."

26

In the Neolithic Age

"Are you sure you don't mind me bringing Max?" Sue Nolan was peering into Barry's Volkswagen and eyeing the backseat. "I'd feel awful if I had to leave him at home all day on a Saturday again. He'll be no bother."

"Of course I'm sure. Pop him in the back."

"Just be a tick." She ran back into her flat, reappearing with the mad spaniel bounding behind her. She tipped the front passenger seat forward and the animal charged in. "Stay put, Max." Readjusting the seat, she climbed in herself and leant across to kiss Barry. "I've been looking forward to today," she said. "How was your week?"

Barry savoured the kiss, smiled, and headed to the Belfast to Bangor Road. "Medically it was pretty routine. Most of the work in general practice is. I did deliver a baby on Thursday night though. Nice wee boy."

"Heavens," she said, "that must be satisfying."

"It is. At least I think so. That's why I'm going to give specialising a try."

"Starting in July." She squeezed his arm. "And I'll be home in Broughshane then, just down the road. Two whole months of summer holidays. Wonderful."

"It's all right for some," he said with a grin, "but most of us have to work. I don't know what my on-call schedule will be yet, but when I do get time off, you promised to show me the Glens of Antrim." Still tingling from her kiss and memories of her soft body against his last Saturday after lunch, he thought about taking long walks in those rugged valleys with Sue. He hoped there were lots of secluded places there. "Yacht Club today though, and we've a detour first. Then on to Ballyholme for lunch and your sailing course and last-minute boat work for me."

"Detour?"

"You know our housekeeper was in hospital. She came home on Wednesday and is meant to be resting, but try to get Mrs. Kincaid to rest? The best of British luck." He shook his head. "While she was sick the villagers made sure Doctor O'Reilly and I were well fed. We haven't been altogether efficient about returning things like pie dishes, which she wasn't slow to point out once she started sniffing about in her kitchen. I've taken most of them back, but I've one more to drop off."

"Fine by me."

"I think you'll enjoy Sonny and Maggie Houston," Barry said. He steered the car wide of a man trundling along on a woman's bicycle. Barry might be taking on some of O'Reilly's traits, but forcing cyclists into the ditch wasn't one of them.

He waited until a stream of cars being led by a slow-moving rust-pocked Massey-Harris tractor had passed, then made his turn and parked a short distance along the narrow country road near a two-storey Georgian house, grey with green window trim. Sonny Houston's Sunbeam-Talbot was parked to one side. Unusually for somewhere as damp as Ulster, there was no moss on the clean roof slates, and Barry knew why. Although the building dated back to the early nineteenth century, the slates had been installed less than a year ago. "Come on," Barry said, "but leave Max. The folks here have five dogs and a cat." He chuckled. "The cat's called General Sir Bernard Law Montgomery because he's from Ulster and likes a good fight."

Sue laughed. "Quite the town for noble cats. Doctor O'Reilly has her ladyship and now Sir Bernard. The real Monty's a lord too, you know."

"Viscount Montgomery of Alamein." Barry lifted a paper bag containing the pie dish, got out, and took her hand. "Maybe we should ask Maggie to elevate the General to the peerage."

"Eejit."

He led her through a cast-iron gate in a low stone wall and along a path of flagstones between two small manicured lawns. Window boxes on the lower sills were ablaze with geranium blooms, pink and orange and red. Between two stems, the dew-spangled filigree of an orb-weaver's web caught and reflected the sunlight.

Barry knocked on the door. A chorus of barks rang out and over it a man's voice. "Quiet, dogs. Into the kitchen." The barking stopped and the front door was opened. "Doctor Laverty. How are you?" There was a genuine warmth in Sonny Houston's voice that Barry always appreciated. Sonny's silver hair was neatly combed and Barry was pleased to see that the man's cheeks showed none of the duskiness of his chronic heart failure, so the drugs O'Reilly had prescribed were still controlling it.

"Sonny Houston," Barry said to Sue. And turning to Sonny, "I believe you know Miss Nolan."

"One of our schoolteachers. We've never actually been introduced so I'm delighted to meet you properly." He inclined his head.

"Pleased to meet you, Mr. Houston."

"Please," he said, "call me Sonny."

"And it's Sue."

"Thank you, Sue," he said. "Do come in. Maggie's in the lounge." He opened the door completely and ushered them into a wide hall. Barry noticed the familiar blue oar with gilt lettering hanging in the hall. Sonny had been a Cambridge University rowing blue. For a second Barry's thoughts drifted to a more recent Cambridge student, one Patricia Spence, but the memory was driven away by the happy enthusiasm in Sue's voice. "Those pictures, Sonny. That's Petra in Jordan, isn't it? Wherever did you get them?"

"I was there in the '30s," Sonny said.

"Sonny's the archaeologist I was telling you about, Sue." He said to Sonny, "Sue's interested in the Stone Age."

"Are you, my dear? How wonderful. I may have something very exciting to show you in a minute, but . . ." He opened a door and said, "Maggie, Doctor Laverty's here and he's brought Miss Sue Nolan."

Maggie Houston née MacCorkle was in a wing-backed armchair with the one-eyed, one-eared General on her lap. A rotund dog of indiscernible breed lay at her feet. Maggie put down a copy of the *Belfast Newsletter* and smiled her toothless grin. "Nice to see you both. Would you like a cup of tea in your hand and a biccy? I've no plum cake the day."

"That would be lovely, Mrs. Houston," Sue said before Barry could stop her.

"I'll only be a wee minute," Maggie said, and stood.

The General made a deep-throated growl as he was decanted onto the floor and Maggie headed, Barry presumed, for the kitchen.

"Hang on, Maggie. I brought this back," he said, and gave her the pie dish. "The cottage pie was wonderful."

She took the dish. "And we hear that Kinky's home. We're all very pleased, so we are. You give her our love, now." She trotted off.

Sonny bent to pat the dog. "Normally I don't allow them in the sitting room, but Missy here was a naughty girl. She got out on her own when she was in heat. Silly of me. She's the only one of my five who isn't neutered. She's due to whelp very soon and we like to keep an eye on her." He straightened. "I don't suppose either one of you would like a pup of indeterminate lineage?"

Barry shook his head. "Arthur Guinness is enough dog for Number One."

"My Max is out in Barry's car," Sue said. "Sorry."

Sonny smiled. "Perfectly all right. Please sit down. Now, Sue, you're interested in the Neolithic period, Doctor Laverty just said."

"I am. I had a wonderful teacher in Broughshane. She did her job teaching the English history that's compulsory, but Miss Tipping always left a wee bit of time at the end of class to tell us about Irish mythology . . . the real people and the times that gave rise to the legends. I've never forgotten her, or the prehistory. It's been a hobby ever since."

"The Neolithic peoples were the first ones here," Sonny said. "Then they were subjugated by bronze users from the Mediterranean, the Firbolg. They were dark, small folks who were in turn displaced by the Picts."

"In Irish the Cruithne," Sue said.

"I never learned any of this at my school," Barry said.

"I wouldn't have either if it hadn't been for Miss Tipping, bless her," said Sue. "It was those first people that really captured my imagination. In our Irish folk tales we call them the Tuatha dé Danaan, they're the ones who built the *lios* and *ráths*, those are the forts, and also the *crannógs*, the man-made islands, and the underground passage graves called the *sidthe*."

"Isn't there a big one in County Meath near the Boyne River?" asked Barry.

"Indeed there is," said Sonny. "Newgrange is one of the most important megalithic structures in Europe. It was built between 3,100 and 2,900 B.C. There's evidence of the Stone Age culture all over Ireland." Sonny leant forward. "I believe we've overlooked some interesting sites right on our own doorstep. Outside Newcastle on the southeast coast of County Down there's Legananny Dolmen and in the southwest corner of the county at Lough Island Reavy there's a stone ring fort or *ráth*. We know about those ones, and some others," he lowered his voice, "but I'm certain I'm on the track of one close to Ballybucklebo."

Sue whistled. "Honestly? How exciting. What makes you think so?"

"The old Irish monks were wonderful cataloguers, and I have a friend, John McIlderry, who gets me photocopies of ancient manuscripts." Sonny pointed to a folding card table covered in printed papers. "Come and see," he said. He handed Sue a sheet. "That's the first page of one that was illuminated by monks at Bangor Abbey about the time Saint Comgall founded the place in the sixth century A.D. It's in Latin, of course, but perfectly legible." Sonny's tone was that of one who would have been surprised to learn that not everyone was a fluent Latin reader. "It's not as old as the Stone Age, but it and documents like it are clues I'm following."

"Because the old monks may have described things they saw, but aren't obvious today?" Sue said. "I've read about the technique. Piecing their evidence together, and using it to uncover actual structures. Real detective work." Barry thought she looked wistful when she said, "Sometimes I think I missed my calling."

Sonny shook his head. "Most of the time it's pretty dry, but the occasional discovery is what makes it exciting."

Sue smiled. "A bit like getting a pupil to understand something for the first time."

"I imagine that is exactly correct. Now," he said, producing another paper, "this one is from another source."

Sue, eyes bright, bent to look at the ancient words.

"It alludes to a *lios,* a ring fort, or a *sidthe,* a passage grave, three miles east of a monastery where a Brother Finnian wrote the description." Sonny picked up a magnifying glass and bent over the photocopy. "Can you see, Sue?"

She peered through the glass.

"There," Sonny said, "'Sanctum Lignum.' It's quite clear. Finnian worked at the monastery there. Do you think, Doctor Laverty, that might be a reference to the place we now call Holywood or Holy Wood?"

"I think it's one literal translation," Barry said, remembering with a certain amount of distaste the Latin exam he'd had to pass as a prerequisite for admission to medical school.

Sue said, "You know, Sonny, in Irish, Holywood was called Baile Doire, Ballyderry, the place of the oak. I know because I'm living there and the ruins of the old priory on the site of the original church are just down the road from my flat, not far from the remains of Norman Motte near Brook Street. I've visited them both and done a bit of reading."

"Indeed," said Sonny, "well done, Sue." He frowned. "Unfortunately I've very little Irish, but if I come across that name in my reading it might help pinpoint what I'm looking for. I'm hoping to use Holywood as one of my reference points." He tapped a finger on the tabletop, then said, "For now though, I'll continue working on the assumption that I'm right about the old Sanctum Lignum being Holywood. My source predates the coming of King Henry II's men to Ireland by a good four hundred years, and the old Celtic disciples of Saint Patrick did use ancient Latin back then. There's been a church on the site of the Holywood Priory since 640 A.D., you know."

Maggie returned, a smile on her face and carrying a tray. Barry noticed that she had taken the opportunity to put in her teeth. "Can you move your papers, Sonny?" Her dentures clicked. "Lord," she said, "I wish thon dental technician would get my new teeth finished. With these ould ones in I sound like I've a mouthful of castanets."

Barry stifled a smile.

Sonny made several neatly stacked piles, leaving room for Maggie to set the tray down.

"Him and his archaeology," she said. "Your woman Agatha Christie was on the telly. Her hubby's an archaeologist, you know, and she said, 'An archaeologist is the best husband a woman can get. The older she gets the more interested he is in her.'" She pecked Sonny's cheek. "Isn't that right, you ould goat?"

Sonny beamed at her. "Come and sit down, everyone," he said, and led them back to the armchairs while Maggie poured. "If I can find a cross-reference that says the founder of the monastery that Finnian cites was a Saint Laiseran, that will confirm it *is* what we call Holywood today. There is solid evidence that old Laiseran built the first church here, and if it is where Finnian wrote then there's a neolithic structure three miles east." Sonny's smile was as wide and as innocent as a child's on seeing its first snow. "Finnian was quite specific." He frowned. "Of course I'll have to hazard a guess he was working in Roman miles."

"Why?" Sue asked.

"Because," he said, "the English statute mile of one thousand seven hundred and sixty yards didn't come in until 1592. The old Roman mile was one thousand six hundred and seventeen yards, and the Irish mile could vary from county to county." He smiled. "I could be wrong, but I am confident the old monks would think in Latin measurements, *mille passuum,* a thousand paces."

"How will you find out for sure?"

"If I can find a similar reference in the papers from Bangor Abbey—and I've got lots here—giving a distance west of Bangor, it'll be like working from two cross bearings. And if I'm right about their being in Roman miles the arcs drawn on a map will kiss each other without overlap."

"That's very exciting. You will keep me posted, Sonny, won't you? I'd love to hear." Sue frowned and said, "I don't know if it helps, but another Irish name for Holywood was Ard mHic Nasca, and that means 'the heights of Nasca's son.' "

"What?" Sonny's voice went up. "Are you certain? I didn't know that. Nasca was a princess here. She sent her son to study under Saint Comgall in Bangor and then near Cork. When the son came back he founded a church. I'll have to check it, but I'm almost certain that Laiseran was that son."

Barry watched the two, who clearly because of

their excitement had forgotten there was anyone else present.

"Does that give you your first coordinate, Sonny?" Sue asked. Her voice had dropped to a whisper.

Sonny frowned. "I'd like documentary proof," he started shuffling through papers, "but if you're right about Laiseran, and once I get the information from the Bangor material it would be easy enough to use them and work on the assumption that you're right, Sue. I could plot a cross bearing, find a location, and go out and look at it. Thank you. I think you've given me exactly what I need."

She smiled. "And you'll let me know what you find out, won't you? I'd love to know."

"It would be my pleasure."

Maggie, who had been pouring, interrupted. "Sonny, would yiz stop footering about with those blooming papers? If thon yoke's been there for a couple of thousand years it's not going to run away while we have a cup of tea." She turned to Sue. "Here yiz are, Miss Nolan, and help yourself to milk and sugar, and seeing you're the only lady guest, yiz can have the last piece of plum cake. I thought I was out, but there was a wee taste left."

Barry, knowing full well that Sue, in sampling Maggie's cake, was about to have an encounter with something as hard as a relic from the Stone Age, rushed to the rescue. "I know Sue's too polite to refuse, Maggie," he said ostentatiously, looking at his watch, "but we're going for lunch and she'll not want to spoil her appetite." He stared at Sue and made a miniscule shake of his head. "Will you?"

"It's all right, Barry," Sue said, accepted the plate of cake, lifted the slice, and bit.

Barry could hardly bear to watch, and his admiration for Sue Nolan grew as not only did she manage to eat the whole thing, albeit chewing mightily, but she accepted a second cup of Maggie's famous stewed tea, which was known throughout Ballybucklebo and the townland to be strong enough to cure leather.

27

Where There's a Will . . .

"One hundred and forty over ninety, John. Bit better than after Christmas," O'Reilly said to Lord John MacNeill, twenty-seventh marquis of Ballybucklebo. "Not bad for a man of sixty-three." O'Reilly removed the blood pressure cuff, put his stethoscope back into his jacket pocket, and rummaged in his bag to produce an opthalmoscope. "Quick look at your retinas." He half-turned and pointed. "Stare at the cock pheasant in the Milliken painting over there beside the bookshelf and try not to blink."

The marquis, sitting in a leather button-backed

chair in his study in Ballybucklebo House, fixed the picture with a hawklike glare.

O'Reilly bent and shone the light through the lens of the left eye, peered through the eyepiece, and spun the focusing wheel until he had a good view of the inner lining of the organ. The scarlet retina contained the cells, called rods and cones, that were responsible for picking up images that were transmitted through the lens and feeding them to the optic nerve. He could see the nerve end as a regular white disc, the macula, in the centre at the back of the eyeball. Over the surface of the retina snaked small arteries and veins. He paid particular attention to the arteries, looking for any evidence of narrowing or nipping of the veins where an artery crossed. If such distortions were visible, it was because the arteries' walls had become thickened in response to the patient's raised blood pressure and were pressing on the vein beneath. "Vessels and that disc are okay," he said, moving to examine the right eye. "Now, as a disc jockey would say, 'Let's have a look at the flip side.'" He hmmmed to himself. "Looks grand," he said. O'Reilly straightened and switched off the opthalmoscope. "You'll do for another six months, John. Carry on with the chlorothiazide five hundred milligrams daily and go easy on the salt." He busied himself writing a prescription, which he left on a table.

"I will. Thank you, Fingal." The marquis rose, rolled down his shirtsleeve, pushed one end of a gold cuff link back in place, and took a tweed hacking jacket with scuffed leather elbow patches from the back of his chair. "I didn't think I was due for your ministrations for another couple of months." He slipped the jacket on and stroked his neatly trimmed grey moustache with his index finger.

"You weren't," O'Reilly said, "but I was passing and wanted to call and ask you if you could help me."

"Naturally. If I can." He glanced at an ormolu clock on the mantel of a marble Adam fireplace. "I've to go out in half an hour."

"Won't take that long."

The marquis ambled across to the sideboard. "Would a whiskey ease our discussion along?"

"Indeed it would." O'Reilly put his instruments back in his bag. Needing no invitation from a friend of long standing, O'Reilly sat in an armchair. "I do have a couple of questions," he said.

"Here." The marquis handed him a Waterford cut-crystal glass and, with his own drink, a small whiskey and water, in his other hand, retook his seat. "Cheers."

"Cheers, and praise and blessings be on Mister John Jameson and sons. Although why you insist on putting water in yours is beyond me. Have you ever seen what water does to the outside of a boat?"

The marquis laughed. "You never change, do you, Fingal?"

"Well, actually, I do, or I'm about to, and you know it." He gave his friend a lopsided smile. "I told you I'm getting married."

"You did, and at first I thought, good Lord. You, O'Reilly? Married? I thought you were completely set in your ways, like me, but you surprised me and it's wonderful news. I am truly delighted for you." He sighed and glanced at an oil painting of a striking woman mounted sidesaddle on a black gelding. A long ponytail escaped from under a John Bull top hat. Piercing blue eyes smiled straight at the artist—and the beholder. "I still miss Laura, you know. She's gone nine years in August."

"The first time I met her, and you, back in '35, she looked just like that. She looked as if she was a female centaur, she was so comfortable on her horse."

"Before the Portaferry Hounds Boxing Day hunt. I remember it. We were just back from India. I was a captain then."

"She'd sprained her ankle and I was a medical student. You asked me to take a look."

The marquis smiled. "And she swore to me blind that you'd said it was all right for her to hunt. Bloody thing swelled up like a barrage balloon." He sighed and took a sip of his drink. "She was a game one, my Laura," he said softly. "Even if the war took a chunk out of them we had twenty-two wonderful years and a son, Sean, to follow me into my old regiment." He paused and looked Fingal in the eye. "Perhaps I shouldn't have mentioned that. I do know what the war did to your—"

"Don't worry, John. I'll always carry a soft spot in my heart for my Deirdre, but I'm certain she'd approve of Kitty. Want me to be happy. I expect your

Laura would have felt the same if the right woman came along for you."

"Not likely at my age, but thanks for the thought, Fingal." The marquis cleared his throat, offered a hand, and said, "It's not the custom to say congratulations, but may I wish you and your bride-to-be every happiness?"

"You may, John." He shook the proffered hand.

"I first met your Kitty at my Christmas party and last at the Downpatrick Races a month ago. Dublin lass. Nursing sister. Remarkable eyes with amber flecks. You're a lucky man, Fingal." The marquis lifted his glass. "To you both."

"*Sláinte,*" O'Reilly said, and thought, Lucky man? By God I am. "The big day's Saturday, July third. Kitty's father is dead and she has no close male relatives. Would you, as a favour to us, stand in for him, walk her up the aisle, John? Give her away?"

"Why, I'd be honoured. Truly honoured." He stood, went to a mahogany escritoire, and consulted a desk diary. "In the morning?"

"Aye. Eleven thirty. And there'll be a reception after the ceremony. Your sister Myrna'll get her invitation to both through the post."

The marquis frowned. "I'm supposed to be attending some damn meeting. It'll wait. I'd not miss your big day, my friend. Not for anything." He lifted a pen and wrote.

"Thank you." O'Reilly took a swallow of his drink.

"My friend." It was true. They'd become reacquainted here in Ballybucklebo after the war because of a mutual love of rugby football. They'd both played for Ireland, and John MacNeill, once the social gap between a commoner and a peer had been bridged, was a very easy man to like.

"That's taken care of." The marquis turned. "Formal dress, I presume?"

Fingal chuckled. "Kitty wants me to wear my naval number ones."

"Lord. I don't think even my butler, Thompson, knows where my Guards' kit has got to."

"Don't worry, John. Top hat and tails'll be fine."

"Good. Thompson will know where those are. Poor chap has to do double duty as my valet these days. Had to let Smithers my valet go three years ago. Taxes, you know. I was able to get him a position, but I was sorry to lose him." The marquis shrugged. "Now, you did say you'd a couple of questions? What's the other?"

One thing, O'Reilly thought, about John MacNeill. He comes straight to the point. "It's about the Mac-Neill Scholarship."

"The what?" He frowned.

"MacNeill Scholarship. According to the bursar at Queen's it's specifically for kids from County Down, kids from poor backgrounds, to go to Queen's medical school."

A smile creased the marquis's face. "Of course, of course. Unfortunately we don't get many applicants." He tapped his temple with one finger. "Sometimes things do slip my mind, but you're absolutely right. I remember my father granting it once or twice. As I recollect, I gave one in '56. Nice young man from Banbridge, Arthur . . . Arthur Furey. He's in Canada now. Surgeon in Toronto. I get a Christmas card from him every year." He stood.

"I have a candidate I'd like to recommend."

"Do you?" The marquis stretched out his hand. "Here. Let me refill that." He took O'Reilly's glass and moved to the sideboard. "Tell me about him."

O'Reilly said, "I'm afraid the him is a her, but she's a remarkable young woman."

The marquis came back and handed O'Reilly his refilled glass. "Oh." He sat. "That's a bit tricky."

"I do know," O'Reilly said. "I've been told that it's specifically for young men, but I've also been told there may be a codicil, and apparently the whole thing is in your gift."

The marquis folded his arms and supported his chin with his left hand. "Tell me about her."

"Her name's Helen Hewitt. She's single, she'll be twenty-two this August. Helen left one position in a dress shop, then lost her job last month when a linen mill closed down. At the moment she's my temporary receptionist."

John frowned. "She doesn't seem academically well qualified. Am I missing something?"

O'Reilly grinned. "She has three Advanced level subjects—physics, chemistry, and biology. She reads Dickens for pleasure, understands X-ray crystallography, and thinks she wants a career in medical research. *And* she's had the gumption to enquire about the admission requirements."

"Sounds like a regular polymath, by jove. Just the type the original bequest was looking for." The marquis smiled. "I should have known you'd not be recommending someone who wasn't special, Fingal."

"She's that, all right. She can go to medical school . . . if she can afford it. That's the rub. She's been with us for four weeks. She's bright as a bee, hard-working, keeps her head. She wanted to go to university three years ago when she left school, but her mother had just died. That's why the thoughts about research. Helen wants to discover the cure for cancer. Her da's a workingman, but between him and his missus they probably could have afforded to send Helen, but once there was only one wage—"

"And that's the kind of thing the scholarship was meant to put right. Pity she's a girl, but of course folks did think differently about the sexes back in Victoria's day."

"And when I was a student at Trinity in the '30s. The women students had their own dissecting room and anatomy lectures in deference to their sensitive natures, but these days things have moved along a bit."

The marquis shook his head and said, "I do know that, but it still might not allow me to alter the bequest. I'm not sure if there's anything I can do. As far as I know the law protects the terms of most wills. I'm truly sorry, Fingal."

"Could you perhaps look at the original bequest? See exactly what was specified?"

"I fully intend to do that, but I can't today."

O'Reilly was going to ask Why the hell not? But he took a slow sip of his drink and realised that would be impertinent and instead said, "I'd be very grateful, John. You'll let me know?"

"The documents are with my solicitor. Unfortunately he's up in Ballymoney for two weeks' salmon fishing on the Bush River. He'll be back the second week in June. I'll ask him to take a look as soon as he is and I'll phone you, or better still, don't we have a rugby club executive on June eleventh?"

"We do," O'Reilly said.

"I'll see you there, then." He glanced at the clock. "Now, I don't want to rush you, Fingal, but—"

"You've a meeting to go to." O'Reilly finished his whiskey and stood.

"It's the fourth Thursday of the month. County Council. Some business about roadworks." The marquis raised his eyes to the heavens and said with a smile, "You have absolutely no idea how utterly, positively riveting discussions of roadworks can be."

"Rather you than me," O'Reilly said. "I'm sure the next rugby club executive will be much more fun. I'll see you there, John."

28

A Place for Everything

"Keep Mairead in bed and don't let her eat or drink anything," Barry said into the phone. "What? Gerry, don't be daft. Of course I don't mind coming out on a Saturday morning. I'm on call. I'll be right over." Barry put the phone down and headed up the stairs to where O'Reilly, Kitty, and Kinky were deep in conversation. He was impatient to be on his way to the Shanks's, but knew important decisions were being made.

"I do be sure you are right, sir," Kinky was saying, "only close friends and family in church, and you'll both need to speak to Mister Robinson the Presbyterian minister about the ceremony, so. He may want to change the service."

Kitty said, "I can't see him going on about 'the procreation of children—'"

O'Reilly roared with laughter then said, "'Then Abraham laughed and fell on his face and said in his heart, Shall a child be born unto him that is a hundred years old?' Genesis 17:17. Come on, Kitty. I'm not quite a hundred yet."

Kinky smiled and said, "No sir, but you are no spring chicken either, so."

That teasing of her boss was more like the old Kinky, Barry thought. He looked at Kitty and wondered how she really felt. Would she have liked to have been the mother of their children? He'd never know and it was too late for that now.

"And I'd like the 'obey' bit taken out, Fingal," Kitty said. "It *is* 1965."

"Consider it done." He reached over and touched her arm.

Kinky said, "That's the decision about the service taken care of, but you still have to decide what you want to do for a reception."

O'Reilly pursed his lips and said, "The whole village won't mind not being invited to the church, but the do after's a different matter. I'd prefer to keep it small, but—"

"Me too," said Kitty. "The folks who've been to the ceremony, maybe a few others."

"But then we have to think of the rest of the village," O'Reilly said. "What happens if we invite Bertie and Flo Bishop, and Cissie Sloan because she'll be playing the harmonium in church, but not Aggie Arbuthnot? We could put a lot of noses out of joint among the folks who think they should have been asked, but haven't." He looked up and noticed Barry standing in the doorway. "What do you think, Barry, about who we should ask to the reception?"

"You know the village a lot better than I, Fingal. All I can tell you is that I had a damn sight more fun at Seamus and Maureen Galvin's going-away party in your back garden where the whole village was invited than I had at Bertie Bishop's Boxing Day do, where the guest list was more select." He had every reason to want completely to forget Bertie Bishop's Boxing Day party.

"True." O'Reilly scratched his chin, eyed Barry, and then turned to the women again. "Kinky? Kitty?"

"Excuse me," Barry said. "That was Gerry Shanks on the phone. Mairead's period's two weeks late, and she fainted. I'm off to see her. Just wanted to let you know. Probably only a touch of what my old prof described as 'Oh, pregnant women get that a lot,' when he couldn't make head nor tail of the not-very-specific symptoms of early pregnancy." Barry didn't like the sound of the faint, but there could be a simple explanation.

"Off you go. We'll take care of things while you're out." O'Reilly turned back to Kinky. As he left, Barry heard, "Come on, Kinky, you've been here longer than any of us. Small crowd or free-for-all?" Fingal O'Reilly was certainly working hard at reminding Kinky Kincaid how important she was to him and Number One Main.

"Doctor Laverty," said Gerry Shanks as he opened the door. He bent to two children who were peeping round his legs. "Angus. Siobhan. Run away on over to your auntie Gertie's. Tell her Mammy's poorly and needs you minded for a wee while. Go on. Daddy and Mammy has to see Doctor Laverty, so we have."

Barry stood inside the hall and remembered that O'Reilly had delivered a breech-birth baby for Gertie Gorman last year.

"Here, Angus. Here's sixpence," said the boy's father. "Buy you and your wee sister some dolly mixtures or midget gems." He shooed his two children out.

Two shrill voices chorused, "Thank you for the sweeties, Daddy," and the children ran off.

Gerry shut the door. "Good of you to come, sir."

"Not at all, Gerry. Where's Mairead?"

"In bed. Come on, I'll show yiz, sir."

Barry followed along a hall decorated with black-and-white photographs of rows of men in sports gear all looking purposefully at the camera. In each photo, the central seated figure, presumably the captain, held a soccer ball with the year's date painted on it. Gerry, Barry remembered, was a keen supporter of the Glentoran Football Club.

"In here." Gerry showed Barry into a tidy bedroom where Mairead lay covered with a pink candlewick bedspread on a double bed. "Hello, Doctor Laverty. Sorry to bring you. I'm feeling much better, so I am. I think I'm mending."

"I'm glad to hear it, but seeing that I'm here I'd like to ask you a few questions. Examine you."

"If you'll excuse me, Doc, I'll wait outside," Gerry said.

It was customary for men to absent themselves when their wives were being examined.

"Put you the kettle on, Gerry," Mairead said. "Doctor Laverty might like a wee cup of tea in his hand when he's finished with me."

Barry said, "Thank you, but let's see to you first, Mairead."

Barry studied her face. She was very pale. Tiny sweat beads stood out on her forehead. Her eyes were bright and focused. "So tell me what happened," Barry asked, beginning to wonder, simply because of her pallor, if it was more than "Oh, pregnant women get that a lot."

Her voice was firm, steady. "I was doing the ironing. I had the radio on. 'Housewife's Choice,' you know, the program that plays requests? Them Beatles was doing 'I Want to Hold Your Hand' when I took this ferocious cutting stoon down in my right side. I let a roar out of me and the next thing I knew Gerry had me tucked up in bed and was patting my hand and saying, 'Wake up, love.' Then he said he was going for to get the doctor, so he was."

Gerry hadn't mentioned pain on the phone and one word, "cutting," now took Barry's attention. His text, *Operative Obstetrics*, observed that in cases of tubal pregnancy the pain was usually aching, but severe episodes, probably caused by blood dripping onto the peritoneum, were, he could picture the words, *usually described as "cutting."* "So," he said, "you were feeling fine and suddenly you got a pain and fainted?"

"Aye."

"Tell me about the pain."

"I'd not never had nothing like that in my life. Just like someone stuck a knife in me."

"Can you show me where?"

She threw back the bedspread—she was fully dressed—and pointed to a spot on the right between the centre of her skirt waistband and her hip bone.

"Thank you. And have you been noticing anything else?"

"Like Gerry told you, Doctor, my monthlies are two weeks late."

"What date?"

"I should have started on Friday the fourteenth of this here month, and you could set your watch by mine. Every twenty-eight days and the one before was on April seventeenth."

Today was the thirtieth of May. That was slightly more than six weeks since her last period. Barry could imagine hearing Doctor Graham Harley, lecturer in obstetrics and gynaecology at the Royal Maternity Hospital, saying, "If you learn nothing else from me, remember this: Every woman is pregnant until proven otherwise. Even if they've not even missed a period. Then you'll not make silly mistakes like ordering lower-back X-rays and irradiating an early embryo until you're sure it's safe." Sound advice, and from the time Gerry had phoned, Barry had assumed that Mairead was pregnant. Now he must consider all the possible causes of her pain in the light of that assumption.

Even though it was early she might have some more symptoms of pregnancy. "Any morning sickness? Sore breasts?"

"No, sir. Just the pain and the fainting, but I was sure I was up the spout. I was so excited. You know me and Gerry's been trying for number three for a brave while. And here hadn't it happened just like Doctor O'Reilly said it would if we just took our time. Now this? I hope to God there's nothing wrong." She managed a weak smile. "I've heard tell lots of pregnant women swoon."

A few still did, but not in the numbers they used to, Barry thought, when women wore tightly laced corsets with whalebone stays. He didn't comment. His text had remarked, *Sudden faintness . . . is a characteristic symptom of ectopic pregnancy.* If he'd known about the pain when Gerry had phoned, Barry would not have taken the other symptom so lightly, or spent as much time listening to Fingal's wedding plans.

"Have you noticed any bleeding down below?" A small amount of vaginal bleeding could be a sign of impending miscarriage, but it too was associated with ectopic pregnancy.

She shook her head.

Bleeding wasn't vital in order for him to make a working diagnosis. Barry was as certain as he could be on the three facts so far available that Mairead was pregnant and something untoward was happening. It could be a threatened miscarriage, but the absence of bleeding made that unlikely. With the pain in her right side, it might be a bowel condition like appendicitis and unrelated to the pregnancy. Or it could be a disease of the ovaries or Fallopian tubes, once again unrelated. But there, at the forefront of his thoughts, was a growing belief that she was pregnant, that the early embryo had failed to reach her uterus, and now was growing in her Fallopian tube. This condition could not continue. The greatest risk was that the tube would burst and the resulting haemorrhage would be lethal.

He reached over and took her wrist. "Your pulse is nearly normal," he said. "Tiny bit fast at ninety-two, and I don't think you've got a fever. You feel cool enough. Now, I just need to take your blood pressure and have a look at your belly and down below."

Her blood pressure was normal, her abdomen not unduly tender when he palpated it. Barry turned his back, ostensibly to take rubber gloves from his bag, but also to give Mairead a moment of privacy to remove her knickers.

"Ready, Doctor," she said.

He turned. She lay on her back, knees flexed, thighs parted. Barry squeezed some K-Y Jelly onto the first two fingers of his right hand. "I'll be as gentle as I can," he said, knowing that it was going to be impossible not to hurt her. He was looking for one last diagnostic sign. In so early a pregnancy, he probably couldn't tell if the uterus had, under the influence of pregnancy hormones, become enlarged, nor would he be able to feel a distended tube if one did contain the fetal sac. The tube would be too soft and too small, but if there was blood on the sensitive peritoneum, his exploring fingers would produce what was graphically described as "yelling tenderness."

They did.

Mairead shrieked and Barry rapidly withdrew his examining fingers, pulled down her skirt, and covered her with the bedclothes. "Sorry, Mairead," he said, thinking what a hollow word it could be. "Sorry." But that scream had clinched it in his mind. Mairead Shanks, who so desperately wanted a third child, almost certainly had a tubal pregnancy.

She took a series of deep breaths, blowing each out through partially closed lips.

Gerry rushed in. "What's up?"

Barry said, "I'm sorry, Gerry. I was examining Mairead and touched a sensitive spot."

"It's all right, Doctor," Mairead said. "I understand youse was only doing what youse had to. I'm over it now." She took a huge breath. "Can youse tell us what's wrong?"

Barry stripped off his glove. He stared at the floor and thought, Get on with it. It's your job to break bad news. He sat on the bed and took Mairead's hand. "I think you *are* pregnant," he said.

"But it's gone bad," Mairead said. "I knew it."

"I'm afraid so. I believe it's not in the right place."

"An ectopic, like?" she asked.

"How do you know about ectopics?"

"When I was still at school, a wee girl in my class, my best friend, got knocked up, so she did. But nobody knew until she collapsed in class and they had to rush her to the Royal for an operation, you know. They took out the tube with the pregnancy in it. She told me all about it when she came back to school." She looked up at her husband. "It's all right, Gerry. She got married two years later and has two lovely weans, so she has. This doesn't mean I'll not be able to have another, does it, Doctor Laverty?"

Barry marvelled at the stoicism and the optimism of his patient. "Women do get pregnant after tubal pregnancies," he said, and reckoned that this was not the time to tell the Shankses that such patients did run a risk of having another ectopic in the remaining tube. "We'd better see about getting you to the hospital," he said. He knew exactly what would have to be done to confirm his diagnosis, and the kind of surgery Mairead would almost certainly need. In another six weeks, he'd be learning to do that surgery. He was looking forward to that. "I'll go and phone for the ambulance."

Gerry bent and kissed his wife's forehead. "It's going to be all right, love, isn't it, Doctor Laverty?"

And despite the uncertainties that surround ectopic pregnancies and any kind of major surgery, what else, Barry thought, could he say? "Of course it is, although I am pretty sure you'll need an operation, Mairead." He put a hand on her arm and stood. "I'll wait until the ambulance comes." If the bloody thing ruptured while they were waiting, there wasn't much he could do, but he could ask the despatcher to make sure there were four pints of O-negative blood on board. Just in case. "So I'll make that call, and if the kettle's boiled, a cup of tea would really hit the spot, Gerry."

29

Of Manners Gentle

"I must say," said O'Reilly, pushing away a plate where only a couple of bones remained of what had been a lunch of cold poached salmon garnished with parsley, slices of lemon, and leaves of crisp iceberg lettuce from his vegetable garden, "since we finished the overflowing benificence of our neighbours yesterday, it is indeed a great relief to have Kinky back in her kitchen." Even, he thought, if she is keeping her promise about cutting back on starch. Ordinarily there would have been a cold potato salad and her oh-so-creamy homemade mayonnaise. Och, well.

"It is that," Barry said. "Doesn't seem like nearly six weeks since her operation. She's recovering very well." He dislodged something with his little fingernail from between two teeth. "And she hasn't forgotten how to cook."

"It was absolutely delicious," Sue Nolan said. "I wonder if she'd show me how she gets the fish so firm?"

"I would take pleasure in that, Miss Sue," Kinky said, coming in from the hall. She set a tray on the table and started to clear. "It was my own mother-in-law showed me how when we lived at her house in Ring in County Cork. When you're married to a fisherman you'd better learn how to cook fish, so."

Interesting that Kinky would mention her past in front of Sue, O'Reilly thought, and the "Miss Sue" was a sure sign of acceptance too. Of course, Sue Nolan posed no threat, and Kinky was a good thirty years older than the schoolmistress. That age difference gave Kinky the right to be familiar and use the younger woman's Christian name, but as she was accompanying Barry, there was a social gap, so Sue still must be accorded her title, "Miss." Och, O'Reilly thought, the rules of etiquette, they're so bloody archaic, but it pleased him enormously to watch Kinky being her friendly self and seeing how the colour had returned to her usually rosy cheeks. He knew she'd lost weight, but, like himself, she could afford to. He gave a small, wry smile. But it was a pity about the mayonnaise.

"Let me help," Sue said, getting to her feet.

"Stay where you are for now," Kinky said, "but

thanks for the offer." There was a clattering of plate on plate. "I'd appreciate it if you'd come with me in a minute. The coffee's ready and it would be a favour to me if you'd take this tray downstairs and the coffee up." She smiled at Sue. "Climbing them stairs still does be an effort, so."

"You, Kinky Kincaid," said O'Reilly, "get your kitchen tidied and then take the rest of the day off. I'm going to Portaferry after coffee to see my brother. You'll not mind giving Mrs. Kincaid a break, answering the phone, Sue, if Barry gets called out and you're on your own?" He was curious to see how having yet another stranger doing her job would affect Kinky.

Sue said, "I'd be delighted. I've paperwork to do for the CSJ, so I won't get bored if I am left on my own."

Barry had told O'Reilly about Sue's political work for civil rights. Like Barry, O'Reilly distanced himself from sectarian politics, treated everybody the same, but had said he thoroughly approved of Sue's involvement.

"I'd be very grateful if you would, Miss Sue," Kinky said. She looked straight at O'Reilly. "I have become used to having Helen do part of my duties during the week, and it is a load off not to have to be interrupted at my new job. Since we decided the reception is going to be in the back garden here I have a great deal of work to do arranging the food and drink, so, and a marquee. We'll ask the Highlanders pipe band for the loan of theirs like we did for Seamus and Maureen Galvin's going away last July."

"We're happy to leave that to you, but not this afternoon, Kinky," O'Reilly said. "I want you to rest."

"Wellll," she said, "it does be the first Saturday in June, there's always horse racing at Goodwood, and it'll be on *Grandstand* on the telly." She chuckled. "I might have a flutter with the bookie, Mister McArdle."

"I saw how you did at Downpatrick," O'Reilly said. "I could feel sorry for Willy." And he wondered, as he often had, if Kinky's being fey in any way influenced her remarkable successes at the betting.

"I've always loved the horses, so. My brother-in-law, Malachy Aherne, is very good with them. In fact, his name in the Irish is Ó Echtigerna, which means 'grandson of the lord of the horses.' I do believe his understanding of the animals rubbed off on me."

"Kinky?" Barry said. "Could you possibly field calls at suppertime for a couple of hours? I'd like to take Sue to the Culloden. It'll only take me fifteen minutes to get back if anyone needs me."

"Doctor Laverty, dear," she said, "off you young people trot whenever you like. Just let me know when you go and where to find you."

"Thanks, Kinky."

"Now if you'd give me a hand with the tray and come with me, Miss Sue? Gentlemen, upstairs with you both, the coffee'll be on its way, all of you enjoy your afternoons, and if you hear the phone tinkle once it'll be me on to Willy. There does be a very good filly, Maureen's Magic, from the National Stud in the Curragh of Kildare running in the third. I like her form and I always bet on any horse that carries my name."

Fingal O'Reilly chuckled to himself. It was grand to have the old Kinky back, and he was certain, absolutely positive, that it wouldn't be too long before Miss O'Hallorhan, soon to be Mrs. O'Reilly and now on duty on Ward 21, would be, in Kinky's eyes, her friend Kitty, at least in private when social convention permitted.

O'Reilly turned the Rover right at the T-junction in the middle of Greyabbey and passed the police station, a sombre grey building set back from the street. He knew that the original Cistercian monastery here, for which the village was named, had been founded in 1193 by Affreca, daughter of Godfred, King of Mann and the Isles. You couldn't turn a corner in Ireland without being reminded of the country's history. And, praise be, thanks to the government in Ulster, every effort was being made to maintain the old buildings and artefacts. Preservation orders were issued that prevented the ancient relics being bulldozed to make way for progress. A country, he thought, must cherish its past or, like Ur of the Chaldees, be utterly swept away to be remembered, if at all, in name only.

He took a sharp left at the Orange Tree Hatchery, where they raised chickens, not baby trees as Fingal had thought when Lars had brought his thirteen-year-old younger brother down here for his first day's wildfowling.

Passing the lake on the Mount Stewart Estate to his left always signalled the halfway mark on this familiar journey to Portaferry. A family of coot, dumpy black waterfowl with white bills and white, featherless, frontal shields on their foreheads, glided sedately above their reflections, leaving tiny wakes on the otherwise unruffled surface.

His view as he skirted the estate was uninterrupted across acres of shining silver mud flats, regularly rippled in long, continous, sinuous lines where the waves of the ebbing tide had scrawled their signatures on the sea bed. Oystercatchers, probing with their long red bills, ran from seaweed clump to seaweed clump. Flocks of buff-pated widgeon browsed on the eel grass. With the window open he could hear their whistled conversations, smell the bladder-wrack and kelp drying in the hot sun. He glanced over South Island, Chapel Island, the blue waters, and on and up to Scrabo Tower, a lonely sentinel perched high above the town of Newtownards.

Arthur had been dozing in the back, but must have picked up familiar scents. O'Reilly heard happy murmurings coming from deep in the big dog's throat. "Go back to sleep, lummox. We're not going shooting." He recognized disappointment in Arthur's sighed response.

For the last ten miles to Portaferry, the winding narrow road, as it skirted Strangford Lough to O'Reilly's right, was bordered by drystone walls and blackthorn hedges. The car swooped up and down small rounded hills, passing fields of gorse with flowers bright yellow and thorns dark green. Fields were dotted with sheep and their adolescent lambs, or cows and their calves. Inlets of the lough meandered between banks of coarse grass, the mud waiting for the incoming tide, flotsam and jetsam piled on the shore.

He crossed the Saltwater Brig, as the locals called the bridge over the Blackstaff River. He and Lars had spent countless chilled hours at the mouth of that stream waiting in the half-light for the dawn flight. He passed the old white church at Lisbane, from the Irish *lios bán*, the white fort, with its leaning Celtic cross. The house of worship had been built in 1777 and still contained a statue of Saint Patrick brought from Scotland and carried here by horse and cart from the east coast of the Ards Peninsula.

Next door to the church was Davy MacMaster's farm and pub. After a day's fowling, nothing could equal the pleasure of a man thawing his outsides in front of Davy MacMaster's huge, peat-fired, black iron range, a hot Jameson flavoured with sugar, cloves, and lemon juice in his hand warming the inner man. He'd have to discuss his love of duck hunting on Strangford Lough with Kitty, but he was sure she'd not mind him slipping away occasionally in the season. She hadn't when they'd been young in Dublin.

O'Reilly wrapped himself in his memories of pleasant days gone, dreams of good days to come, and, at home in the familiar countryside and at peace, sang softly to himself as the car ate up the last few miles.

> If my health be spared I'll be long relating
> Of that boat that sailed out from *anac Cuan* . . .

Lough Cuan, the peaceful lough. That's what the Celts had called the place, and that it was on this langorous day in the merry month of June.

30

A Noble Pair of Brothers

Lars's grey, pebble-dashed, two-storey house had a view over the water to the Castleward demense on the Strangford Town side. O'Reilly parked the Rover then watched as the little car ferry crabbed sideways across the Narrows, pushed upstream by the inrushing tide. In the distance the Mourne Mountains bulked against the sky. Slieve Donard, from the Irish "Sliabh Domhanghairt," Saint Donard's Mountain, rose nearly three thousand feet above the sea. The pre-Christian Celts had called the peak Sliabh Sláinge after Sláinge mHic Partholóin, who reputedly was the first physician in Ireland and who lay buried under a cairn there. O'Reilly smiled and thought, when the time came, they could plant a man in a worse place.

He let Arthur out.

The brown front door was opened. "Finn. Great to see you." Lars O'Reilly stood in the doorway. "I heard your car in the drive. Good run down?"

Arthur, tail thrashing, trotted over to Lars and was affectionately patted.

"Grand altogether. How are you, big brother?" As they shook hands, O'Reilly thought that Lars seemed a little stooped. His once dark moustache was flecked with grey. Still, considering he'd turned sixty this year his eyes were bright and his handshake firm.

"All the better for seeing yourself. And I know I've told you on the phone, but I'll say it again, it's great news about the wedding. I'm sure you're sick and tired of being wished every happiness—"

"Not at all, but I'll consider it said."

"And thank you for not asking me to be best man," said Lars, bending to pull a burr from under Arthur's chin. "You know how I get tongue-tied speaking in public. It's why I never wanted to be a barrister." He shuddered. "I couldn't argue a case in court. I don't think Father ever understood that."

"No, he did not. But I do," O'Reilly said, thinking to himself, And you were never a driven man, Lars O'Reilly. You always seemed content doing the routine work of a country solicitor. I suppose in the same way I never specialised. Country general practice was far too appealing. "I'm no great shakes at the speechifying myself, but it's a small price to pay for being the groom. I never thought, Lars, I'd get wed a second time, but," O'Reilly took a deep breath, "Kitty's a remarkable woman. Hard to believe four weeks today she'll be Mrs. O'Reilly."

Lars smiled. "You deserve every happiness, Finn. Too early for a celebratory drink?"

"Even for me," O'Reilly said. "Why don't we take a stroll, give Arthur a run, and you can bring me up to date with what you've been doing?"

"Let me grab a jacket."

As O'Reilly waited, his gaze was immediately attracted to a greenhouse attached to one gable end. Through the glass he could see a blaze of colour.

"Admiring my orchids from afar?" Lars asked. "I'll show you my new ones when we get back. I've been really lucky with a hybrid I've been working on. With her permission I'd like to make it a present to Kitty and call the bloom 'Kitty O'Hallorhan.' It is truly beautiful, just like your Kitty."

"I'm sure she'd be tickled," O'Reilly said. "It's a great honour."

"It's not really," Lars said. "There's already about twenty-five thousand recognised species, but I hope it might please her." He smiled his slow smile and started to walk. "Come on. We'll go out the back gate and over the fields."

"Heel," O'Reilly said, and he and Arthur followed

Lars across a lawn, through an ornamental lychgate covered in climbing roses heavy with buds about to burst, and into a small valley.

Lars closed the gate.

For a moment, O'Reilly stood and savoured the day. The sun was warm and the white clouds and blue sky formed a painted backdrop where swallows soared and dived in a never-ending aerial ballet. His nose was filled with the almond scent of whin flowers. A tractor grumbled, and somewhere a donkey brayed. "Hey on out, Arthur," he told the dog, and watched as the big lad, nose to the ground, ran ahead quartering, scenting in red ben weeds and clumps of reeds. A single long-billed snipe rose and jinked away, hoarsely scolding.

"My old springer, Barney, loved this field," Lars said. "When he died in '46, I buried him in the far corner there, under that big sycamore."

"He was a great gun-dog," O'Reilly said.

"And he's got his successors Kris and Dirk to keep him company. I'd given up wildfowling by the time Dirk died so I didn't bother getting another retriever, but I like to think my old friends can still watch the rabbits," Lars said, and smiled.

"I should have brought my gun," O'Reilly said. "Kinky makes a lovely rabbit stew."

"Not from the rabbits in my field," Lars said. "Sorry."

O'Reilly remembered that his brother had turned from a keen shot to a conservationist. "But aren't you up to your neck in the creatures if you don't cull them?" He watched Arthur disappear over the hill's crest.

"I preserve them for an old friend, Jimmy Caulwell. He has exclusive rights to take them and sell them to the butcher."

They crested the hill.

"He likes a shot?"

Lars shook his head. "Butchers prefer them taken by other means. The customers don't like biting lead pellets. Jimmy'll tell you himself how he does it. There he is talking to Arthur."

Farther down the slope a little man holding the shaft of a spade in one hand was bending and patting the dog's head. Fresh earth was heaped in a pile at his feet. He looked up and waved. "How's about ye, Mister Lars? Sound day. Sound day."

"Grand, thank you, Jimmy," Lars called back. "Jimmy lives near here, works on a couple of the farms, and does odd jobs for me."

As they approached, O'Reilly appraised the man. He couldn't be more than five feet tall and about seven stone. His face was weathered at the forehead with deep creases round his blue eyes, and above a stubbly chin his cheeks were the colour somewhere between scarlet and purple that is typical of Ulster farm folk who must spend a lifetime braving the elements. His ears were thickened and stuck out.

He wore a tweed duncher from under which sweat dripped. The cap on his bald head was set so far back it looked to be in imminent danger of falling off. A red flannel undervest was open at the neck to expose a deeply tanned V. His arms, bare from the short sleeves down, were equally bronzed and the sinews stood out like cords. Moleskin trousers and black rubber Wellington boots completed his outfit. The boots were crusted with cow clap.

"My brother, Doctor Fingal O'Reilly," Lars said.

"Pleased to meet youse, sir, so I am." Jimmy knuckled his forehead.

"Jimmy," O'Reilly said.

"What are you up to?" Lars asked.

The man's face split into a grin revealing four front teeth in his lower jaw. "Before youse two and this here big dog come, I was by myself here. I was number one." He waved an all-encompassing arm. "I was outstanding in my field, so I was." He cackled mightily.

Lars chuckled. "Outstanding in your field. Jimmy, that one has whiskers."

O'Reilly laughed out loud. "And you were digging. Looks like you're getting some help now."

Arthur had stuck his backside in the air, and with his front paws working like steam shovels, was hurling a stream of sandy earth behind him.

"More power to him, sir. Bejizz, but it's heavy going on a hot day. Keep up the good work, dog, but can you make him stop, sir, when I say so?"

"Sure. Why?"

Jimmy pointed uphill. "See them nets?"

Scattered apparently randomly on the hillside were pieces of fine mesh held in place by pegs driven into the ground. "I do."

"Them's all over rabbit bolt holes. This here's one big warren, so it is."

O'Reilly nodded. Now he knew how Jimmy Caulwell hunted rabbits. With a ferret. Put nets over all the escape tunnels, slip the predator through the main entrance, and wait until the fleeing, panicked rabbits had netted themselves, deal with them, then recover the ferret and feed it by way of thanks and to reinforce that its hunting was always rewarded when it surfaced. Very clever, except that once in a while—

"Killed underground, has he?" O'Reilly asked. If such were the case, the animal would gorge, fall asleep, and could be lost forever unless the owner waited, often for a couple of days, until the animal surfaced, or someone dug it out.

"Aye, silly bugger that he is." Jimmy pointed to where Arthur still toiled away. "Your dog scents him and his kill. I was digging him out, so I was, but I reckon your big fellah must be pretty close by now."

"Arthur," O'Reilly called. "Come."

Arthur, with his eyebrows working furiously, looked at his master, sighed audibly, and obeyed. He could almost hear the lab thinking, Spoilsport.

"Sit."

"Likely sensible, sir," Jimmy said. "Your man down there's a polecat ferret, dead fierce, so he is. He's no' big, but neither was Rinty Monaghan, our Belfast boxer, and he packed a hell of a punch for a flyweight. My fellah'd likely give your . . . Arthur is it?"

"Aye."

"If your Arthur dug him up, my boy'd likely give the dog a terrible tousling, so he would. Just like Rinty done to Jackie Paterson in 1948. I was fifteen then. Rinty was my hero, so he was."

"You box?" O'Reilly said.

"Aye. I did. Mini-flyweight." He squinted. "And, no harm til you, sir. So did you."

O'Reilly laughed. "I did." He pointed to his bent nose. "That's what you get if you let your guard down."

"I'll not here." Jimmy bent and picked up a pair of heavy leather gloves. "My ferret can't bite through these." He donned the gloves and hefted the spade. "Now, sir, Mister Lars, the *craic*'s been great. Thank youse very much, Arthur, but I've got to get on with this here job, so I have." With clearly practised ease, he drove the shovel blade into the earth.

"Good luck, Jimmy," Lars said, "and if you've time next week, I've more shelves I need hung in the orchid house."

"I'll see to it, sir."

O'Reilly fell into step with his big brother, and Arthur, after one soulful look over his shoulder to where Jimmy was chucking up more spadefuls, walked at his master's side.

"If we cut over the stile at the far side of the field,"

Lars said, "there's a pleasant, not-too-taxing two-mile walk that goes past the castle, through a couple of woods, along the sea front, and fetches up at the Portaferry Arms."

"In that case, I'm your man," O'Reilly said, striding out, "and now, brother, it's been a few months. It's time you brought me up to date with all that's been happening in your life."

31

The Flowers That Bloom in the Spring

Barry walked into the upstairs lounge in time to hear Kitty say, "We'll have to make a decision about the honeymoon soon, dear. There's only twenty-five days to go."

"Sorry to interrupt, you two," Barry said. "I'm off to Sue's for dinner."

O'Reilly barely raised his head from where he and Kitty were poring over gaudy brochures of the Balearics, Malta, Crete, Rhodes, and the other Dodecanese Islands. "Have fun," they said in unison, then laughed and returned to the brochures.

"I'm not so sure about Malta, Kit," O'Reilly was saying as Barry headed for the stairs. "The last time I was in Valetta, the Germans were making it bloody hot for the Royal Navy and the Maltese. I've lots of memories of the place . . . and not all happy ones. Let's take another look at Rhodes. Sonny Houston would like the place. It's covered in all kinds of ancient relics."

"In twenty-five days from now it could have a couple more," said Kitty.

Barry couldn't stop a snort of laughter.

"I heard that, Doctor Barry Laverty," roared O'Reilly, then more laughter from upstairs.

Barry headed along the hallway, and on his way to his car met Kinky in her kitchen. "You're looking well this evening, Kinky Kinkaid," he said. She was, in a floral mid-calf dress, half-heeled brogues, and kid gloves. Her handbag, Barry knew, had been a gift from Kitty in April. On her head she wore a bottle-green caubeen tilted to the left, and over her right arm she carried a folded beige woollen cardigan. "Women's Union meeting?"

"No, Doctor Laverty, dear. 'Tis Tuesday. The WU meets on a Monday, so. I've been given the night off." She smiled. "It's a rare treat I'm going to have. It's six weeks to the day since I was taken poorly and Doctor O'Reilly says I am well enough to go out of the house for a while." She cleared her throat. "I've left them a chicken pot pie and I do think that he and Miss O'Hallorhan can manage the rest well enough on their own, so."

Barry heard no bitterness, but it was still "Miss

O'Hallorhan." "I'm going to Holywood. Can I give you a lift anywhere?"

She shook her head. "That's kind, sir, but I am being collected. In fact, I—"

There was a knock on the kitchen door and Kinky answered. "Come in, Mister Auchinleck."

Barry frowned. Funny time for a milk delivery. Then he noticed that Archie was carrying a posy of primroses. Barry smiled and stepped aside. Hadn't Kinky told him in the hospital that her Paudeen had wanted her to move on? Was this the first step?

Archie Auchinleck, the milkman, was wearing what must be his best, or perhaps his only, navy blue serge suit, white shirt, tie, and highly polished black shoes. His dark brown wavy hair was as shiny as his shoes, probably because he'd used Brylcreem, Barry thought. It was precisely parted to the right. His cheeks had a freshly shaved look and there was a faint odour of Old Spice. "Good evening, Doctor Laverty, sir. Good evening, Mrs. Kincaid," he said, bowing a little to both.

"Evening, Archie," Barry said. "How's your back?" Last August, O'Reilly had given the man a verbal tousling for coming to the surgery on a Sunday morning to complain of a sore back he'd had for weeks. At that time, Archie's son had been serving with the British Army in Cyprus during the Cypriot state of emergency. The EOKA, the Greek partisans who wanted union with Greece, were making it hell for the Turkish Cypriots and the security forces caught in between the two factions, but Corporal Auchinleck was now safely back in Palace Barracks outside Holywood—and Archie's back the better for it. But it didn't hurt to let patients know you hadn't forgotten their concerns.

"Och sure, it's great, so it is. Thanks for asking." He turned from Barry and said, "You're looking very well, Mrs. Kincaid, if I might be permitted to say so. Very well indeed. It's a great relief to me . . . well . . . to everybody in the whole village and townland, so it is, that you're back on your feet. You was sore missed, you know."

"It is nice to be home." Kinky smiled. "Very nice."

He thrust the flowers to her. "I brung youse these," he said, and Barry could have sworn Archie blushed.

"Thank you, Mister Auchinleck." Kinky brought them to her face, inhaled deeply, then ran water into a glass in the sink and placed them in it carefully. "They're very pretty and they'll be fine there for a while, so, until I can get them into a proper vase when we get back. I don't want to keep you waiting."

"So we're all set?" Archie turned back to Barry. "We're for going to the Tonic in Bangor to see *My Fair Lady*. It won a brave wheen of them Oscars." He winked and continued, "The music's lovely and see that there Audrey Hepburn? She's a wee cracker, so she is."

Barry saw how when Archie turned back to Kinky and offered her his arm he looked into her face and said, "I've always liked dark eyes, so I have."

"You two have fun," Barry said. "Enjoy the picture." For a moment he had a mischievous notion of saying something like, "And don't you keep her out too late, Archibald Auchinleck," as a protective father might say to his daughter's swain. Silly idea. Kinky Kincaid was no teenager. But Barry had seen how she glowed when Archie gave her the bouquet and he remembered a dried, pressed rosebud between the pages of a book on her bedside table.

As he watched them leave, the sound of O'Reilly and Kitty's laughter filtered in from upstairs and he felt a wave of inexplicable melancholy he couldn't explain. Or could he? If a certain young woman hadn't decided to move to Cambridge, it might have been him upstairs planning a honeymoon. He straightened his shoulders and reminded himself that another lovely young woman was cooking him dinner and if he didn't get a move on, he'd be late. And he hated being late.

The scent of Kinky's primroses wafted up from the sink. If the little florist's in Holywood was still open when he got there he'd buy some flowers for Sue.

"For you, Sue." Barry handed her a bunch of mixed dark red and white carnations the moment she opened the door of her flat. "You look lovely," he said. And she did. Her short-sleeved cream dress was pinched at the waist by a patent leather belt. The knee-length skirt was a swirl of pleats. In her heels she stood as tall as Barry.

"Thank you, sir," she said, and sniffed the flowers, "and thank you for these." She kissed him. Hard.

Barry, clutching a bottle of wine in his other hand, still managed to enfold her in a hug, feeling the firmness of her breasts against him. He returned her kiss with interest and was breathing rapidly when they parted.

Sue ran a hand over her crown, swallowed, and said, "How did you know I was born in January?"

Barry's hand mirrored Sue's as he smoothed his cow's lick. "I didn't." The night they'd gone to the Inn he'd meant to ask her when her birthday was, but he'd been so entranced by her company he'd quite forgotten. "But come to think of it, carnations are your birth flower. My mum told me about the language of flowers." He smiled. "Although I'm not so sure the red goes with your hair. Sorry about that."

"They're lovely."

"And I brought this." He gave her a bottle of Nuits Saint George. "You said you were cooking beef tonight and it's the same one the sommelier recommended we have with our beef Wellington in the Culloden on Saturday." He thought of the drive home after the meal and the lingering kisses in this room.

"Lovely," she said. "I'll open it now. I think red wine is supposed to be left to 'breathe,' whatever that means. I'm cooking a beef stroganoff. My mum's recipe." She took a pace back. "Come in."

He followed her into the bookcase-surrounded living room.

"Back in a jiffy," she said. "Would you like a glass of white or rosé? We're having prawn cocktails to start."

"White, please."

As Sue disappeared through a door, amazing smells came from the kitchen.

Max, who was lying on the sofa, lifted his head, looked at Barry, and promptly went back to sleep. Familiarity may not always breed contempt, Barry thought, but he was at least now saved Max's formerly lavish welcomes. It also served to keep Max's hairs on Max and not on Barry's good suit. He gave the springer a pat on the head and looked around. The table was set for two. Sue already had the appetizers on the table, glasses of lettuce bearing prawns in a pink Marie Rose sauce.

On a desk in one corner, papers were carelessly strewn. He wandered over to take a look. One was entitled *Northern Ireland: Why Justice Cannot Be Done–The Douglas Home Correspondence*. Another, *Northern Ireland: What the Papers Say*. Both were dated 1964.

He smiled and shook his head. Please, no politics tonight, Sue. And perhaps not too much of the "Easy and Slow" either, he thought, still feeling the softness of her lips on his, the firmness of her breasts. They were well past their first date now and Barry recognised that the more he saw of Sue Nolan the more he wanted to see her. After Patricia he still hesitated to call what he was feeling love. Perhaps, he thought, I'm a bit gun-shy. But it was something damn close.

Her voice called from the kitchen, "Barry, can you give me a hand? I got the white poured, but I can't get the cork out of the red."

He went through. Sue stood with her back to him, arms akimbo as she struggled with the corkscrew. He stood behind her, wrapped his arms round her waist, and dropped a kiss on the nape of her neck. She leant back against him and murmured in her throat. Barry let his hands slip slowly up until he cupped a breast in each palm.

"Nice," she said softly, and tucked her head down into her shoulders, rolling her head from side to side. Turning in his arms, she kissed him long and hard, then stepped back, breathing in short gasps. She held the bottle of wine between them. Her eyes shone. "Later, Barry," she said, "later. Here. Please." She handed him the bottle with the corkscrew attached.

Barry took a deep breath, savouring the promise of that "later." Gripping the bottle between his knees, he hauled on the corkscrew. Slowly, slowly the cork began to budge. Barry clenched his teeth and pulled harder. "Open Sesame," he said as the cork left the neck with an audible pop. "There." He handed her the bottle and the cork.

"Thank you, Sinbad." She laughed and put the bottle on the counter. Handing him a glass of cold white wine, she picked up her own and a vase with the carnations. "Come on through and sit down."

She put the flowers on the table as a centerpiece, and Barry pictured the two red roses and a curl of candle smoke that symbolized for him that perfect evening at the Crawfordsburn Inn.

Once they were seated at the table, she lifted her glass. "Cheers."

"And here's to your bright eyes, Sue." And bright they were, shining emerald and looking into his. He sipped and the wine was crisp on his tongue. "Sue—"

"Barry—"

They both laughed. "Go ahead. You first," he said, relieved not to be the one starting the conversation. He'd had no idea what he was going to say. He put one hand on the tabletop.

"I'm so glad you were able to come over tonight." She covered his hand with hers.

He turned his hand and entwined his fingers with hers. "So am I."

"You see," she said, "there's something I want to ask you."

"Go right ahead." He wondered what was coming.

"I think . . . I think you're getting fond of me."

"Very," he said without a second's hesitation. He squeezed her fingers.

The squeeze was returned. Sue tilted her head to one side, gazed straight into his eyes, looked down, then back up. "Me too and I . . . I'd like it to go further—"

"So," Barry said, "would I." And he knew he meant more than her promise of what might come "later."

Sue took a deep breath. "There's one thing, I don't think it's a big thing, but I need to know."

Barry had a vision of his asking her if she was a Catholic. They'd surmounted that. "Go ahead. Fire away."

"What do you think of the work I'm doing for civil rights?"

Barry frowned. Since she'd mentioned it on their first date more than five weeks back, the subject had come up only once, when she'd come to Number One a couple of weeks ago and he'd told her he'd rather not take sides. But they hadn't discussed it in any great depth. They'd simply been two young people having fun and getting to know each other. He sighed. He'd hoped the whole thing was a hare she'd let sit, but if Sue felt it *must* be discussed? Perhaps he could head her off. "To be honest I haven't given it a great deal of thought."

He felt the grip of her fingers relax on his.

"You should, you know."

Barry's frown deepened. The evening had started out so gently, now why were they heading in this direction? "Tell me why?" he asked.

She sat back in her chair and as if suddenly weary put her hand behind the nape of her neck. "Because what's going on in this little country of a million and a half souls is wrong. Plain wrong."

He frowned. "But I don't see what it has got to do with me."

She put her hands on the tabletop and leant forward. "Do you know what Edmund Burke said?"

Barry shook his head. He sipped his wine, but it had lost its crispness.

"'All it takes for evil to flourish is for good men to do nothing.' Barry, I'm trying to do something. We all are in the CSJ. The discrimination against the Catholics is appalling. They don't get hired, they can't get subsidised housing because the Council flats are two bedrooms . . . and Catholics have big families. They can't vote unless they're property owners, and if they don't have work how can they buy property? Even if a constituency ever does look like it's going to have a majority Catholic electorate, the boundaries are changed so they're a minority again. That's called gerrymandering."

"Sue," he said, wanting to change the subject, but at the same time feeling a need to defend himself and not being quite sure why, "I do know about gerrymandering. And I'm not a bigot. I have heard what you're telling me before. But it's been forever thus, since partition in 1922. You know as well as I do that the religious divide goes back to when Protestant settlers were imported to the north in the early seventeenth century in the Plantation of Ulster. And it's not a one-way street. The Orange Order was formed in 1795 to protect Protestants from Catholic violence. It takes two sides to make an argument." And, he thought, an argument's the last thing I want tonight. He looked down at his plate, then back up. "I think we should try to understand a little of the Protestant attitude, then perhaps you and I can leave it at that. I can see how deeply you feel about this, I do. But honestly, Sue, I believe there's right and wrong in both parties. And I'd rather not take sides." He smiled at her. Maybe they could drop it now?

"Go on," she said, "I'm listening. What do you understand about how the Protestants feel?" There was an edge to her voice.

Barry shook his head. Should he agree with her, declare himself to be on her side, placate her, or should he stick to his middle-of-the-road guns? He said slowly, "I can't pretend to speak for every Protestant, but I've met enough hard-liners from both camps. The Royal Victoria Hospital stands between the Catholic Falls and the Protestant Sandy Row districts. The medical staff and nurses didn't, don't, care what persuasion someone is. They're simply sick people."

"That's commendable. It's how it should be in every aspect of life, but it's not. So please, tell me what Protestants feel. I am one. I should know but I'd be interested to hear you describe it."

Barry sighed. "Okay. In Ulster, the Protestants are the majority. The hard-line Republicans, who are mostly Catholic, want nothing short of a reunion of the six counties here in the north with the twenty-six counties of the Republic of Ireland." He tried to keep his voice level, his tone patient. But he could feel the impatience creeping in. He had not come here tonight to get—or give—a history lesson. "The Republic, of course, is an officially Catholic country with the church having a place in its Constitution. If Ulster were to unite with the Republic, that would put the one million Protestants in the minority in a country of four million. You see the same in South Africa with the white South Africans. They're massively outnumbered so they've tried to segregate the races."

Sue shook her head. "Apartheid. Barry, it's bloody nearly like that here. It's wrong."

Barry didn't want the argument to continue, but damn it all, he did have an opinion and it wasn't, he half-smiled at the unconscious pun, as black and white as Sue seemed to think. "I agree," he said, "but I'm willing to try to understand both sides. The committed Loyalists want to stay part of Britain. So it's not just Catholic-Protestant, it's to do with class, national loyalties that have been manipulated for political ends, desire to hold on to power. I believe people are frightened, and frightened people do irrational things."

"And we want to change that." She folded her arms across her chest. "I wish you could see that."

Barry took a deep breath. "Okay. I'll try, Sue. I promise." He inclined his head to his prawn cocktail. "Now, I'm a bit peckish." Liar, he thought, his appetite had fled. "Should we perhaps start having our dinner? You've gone to a great deal of trouble."

He looked at Sue, who was looking down at her food with about as much enthusiasm as he felt. The vase of carnations, dark red and white, seemed to be taunting him. Dark red for deep love, and white for pure love and good luck. The bloody things might as well have been Loyalist orange and Republican green. And he didn't understand how things seemed to have gone so horribly wrong.

32

The Road Through the Woods

"And that concludes the agenda for this Friday evening. Thank you all very much," the marquis said to the other six members. "The next session of the executive committee of the Ballybucklebo Bonnaughts Sports Club will be after the summer on the second Friday in September, but for now I'll entertain a motion to adjourn unless there is any other business."

"Mister Chairman." Fergus Finnegan was rising to his feet and addressing the marquis. The bandy-legged little man was captain of the rugby team and the marquis's jockey. "There's one wee matter, sir. It's not official, like, but if I could have the floor for a wee minute, and I know Dermot Kennedy has something to say too." He nodded to a man sitting across the long mahogany table.

"Carry on, Fergus," the marquis said.

"And get a move on," Bertie Bishop snapped, "I've not got all night." He fiddled with the Masonic Order fob on his gold watch chain.

O'Reilly stifled his annoyance. He'd been delayed by a patient with a nosebleed and had arrived late. He'd still hoped to have a quiet word with Bertie after the meeting, ask about the man's possible interest in the shirt factory, test Barry's ideas about the cottage, but it wasn't to be.

Fergus ignored Bertie's remark. He was holding a brown-paper-wrapped parcel. "On behalf of all the rugby players, we'd like for to give this here wee present to Doctor O'Reilly and Miss O'Hallorhan to mark the occasion of their upcoming wedding."

Father O'Toole, sporting an egg stain on his rusty black cassock, said with a grin, "Having met your Miss O'Hallorhan, Doctor O'Reilly, I think you are a lucky man, bye." His Cork accent was as soft and musical as Kinky's.

Fergus handed the gift to O'Reilly and before he could say thanks, Dermot Kennedy rose and spoke. O'Reilly moved to face the captain of the hurling team. Dermot had a turn in one eye, making it tricky to determine to whom he was speaking. "This here's one from all the hurlers, sir, you know. It comes with our wishes for a long and happy life for both of yiz, so it does." He too thrust a wrapped gift at O'Reilly.

There was a prolonged round of applause. Jasus, O'Reilly thought, if any eejit starts singing "For He's a Jolly Good Fellow" I'll die of embarrassment, but he felt a lump in his throat.

The applause died and O'Reilly rose. "Thank you both, and please thank all the players. I know Kitty will be delighted too so please thank them on her behalf as well. I'd like—"

"Move to adjourn," Bertie yelled, heaving himself out of his chair.

"Sit down please, Councillor," said Mister Robinson, the Presbyterian minister, "and when the doctor's finished I'll second your motion."

Bertie subsided onto his chair, muttering to himself.

O'Reilly gave Bertie a frosty smile and continued, "I'll come straight to the point so Councillor Bishop can get away. We all know what a busy man he is. Kitty and I would love to invite everyone to the church." O'Reilly inclined his head to Mister Robinson, who earlier had agreed to this little subterfuge. "But Mister Robinson would rather not have standing room only, so we're keeping the guest list small, mostly family, but . . . but everyone, and I do mean *everyone* is invited to the after-service ta-ta-ta-ra at Number One. The festivities'll be starting at about twelve thirty Saturday, July third."

Another round of applause.

"Is that it, Doctor?" the marquis said.

O'Reilly nodded.

"Motion to adjourn seconded," the minister said.

"I call the question," Father O'Toole said so the chair could ask for a vote.

No one waited for the marquis to speak. Six hands instantly were raised.

"Carried," said the marquis.

"About bloody well time," Bertie Bishop said, and headed for the door without so much as a "good evening."

Damn it, O'Reilly thought, but said, "One minute please, Mister Chairman. Unless anyone else has pressing business elsewhere, in view of the generosity to me and Kitty this evening, I'd like to invite everyone still here through to the bar."

"That," said Father O'Toole, "is a brilliant notion. I'm your man, Doctor O'Reilly, and just by chance, as secretary-treasurer, I do happen to have the keys with me, bye."

O'Reilly and the marquis were the last to leave the room with its head-and-shoulders photos of all the Bonnaught rugby players who had represented Ulster, and the hurlers who had played for County Down. The marquis fell into step. "I think I may have some good news for you, Fingal."

"Go on."

"My solicitor has looked at the MacNeill bequest. Initially he feared we were right. Young men only when it was set up by my great-great-grandfather in 1849, but it seems my great-grandfather, William Mac-Neill, changed it in 1899."

They turned into the main function room, with its high ceilings, wood floors, and plain folding tables and chairs randomly arranged or stacked against the walls. At the far end, Father O'Toole was opening sliding doors halfway up the wall to reveal a small room where the drinks were kept.

O'Reilly could barely control his excitement about the scholarship, but waited as his lordship continued.

"Seems the agèd ancestor was in the Royal Horse Artillery. The family didn't start serving in the Irish Guards until after Queen Victoria founded the regiment in 1900. He was wounded during the seige of Sevastopol in the Crimean War, and nursed in Scutari. He was mightily impressed by Florence Nightingale and Mary Seacole. Thought they both should have been doctors, but of course—" He shrugged.

When they arrived at the bar, O'Reilly called, "My shout, Father O'Toole," and as the others gave their orders asked, "Whiskey, sir?" Calling his friend "John" was for private conversations.

The marquis nodded. "Please. With water."

"Jameson's and a pint."

"Anyway," the marquis said, "the original will said that the incumbent trustee, always the current marquis, could at the family's discretion alter its conditions. Great-grandpapa William, the twenty-fourth marquis, persuaded the family to agree to an alteration," he pulled a piece of paper from an inside pocket of his jacket, "and I quote from this copy of the relevant page, 'If no suitable young men have come forward by July the First of any given year, and whereas the medical faculty of the Queen's University of Belfast has in this the year of our Lord eighteen hundred and ninety-nine near the dawn of a new millennium approved the admission of women into the faculty of medicine, and if a suitable candidate of the fair sex can be identified as possessing the necessary character and intellect and as attested to by two medical men is of sufficiently robust spirit to withstand the rigours of a medical education in the aforesaid faculty—'" He smiled widely at O'Reilly.

"Jasus," said O'Reilly softly. "Jasus Murphy, the first of July's only three weeks away, and Barry and I can certainly give Helen whatever medical certif—"

"Here." The marquis handed O'Reilly his pint and picked up his whiskey. "I hate to tempt Providence, Fingal, but it looks very like your Helen Hewitt is going to be the first female MacNeill laureate, and I'm delighted. Maybe she will find a cure for cancer."

"By God," said O'Reilly, "I'll drink to that," and by God he did, sinking half his pint in one swallow. "Thank you, sir. I know we're all going to be very proud of that girl, but I'll say nothing to her until you give me the go-ahead."

"I think that's wise, Fingal. 'Many a slip,' and all that."

The four other members of the committee had settled themselves at a table, and as far as O'Reilly could discern from scraps of their conversation were good-naturedly debating the relative merits of rugby and hurling, a subject which had provided a constant source of discussion since he had joined the club nineteen years ago.

"I must say," the marquis remarked, changing the subject, "I do find these sports club committees a good deal more entertaining than the county council ones."

"You have the pleasure of Bertie's company on both," said O'Reilly, barely keeping the sarcasm out of his voice.

"He's not my favourite man, and I know you don't trust him, Fingal, but I think he does take his community duties seriously."

O'Reilly nodded. "I suppose."

"Take the last meeting. It'll be common knowledge by now because the report was released for last night's *County Down Spectator,* so I'm not breaching any confidence. Council are considering straightening that bad hairpin bend on the Belfast to Bangor Road. There'd been some vague talk of it before, but Councillor Wilson introduced the motion under 'any other business.' We'll vote on it next month, but I'm pretty sure it'll go through then."

O'Reilly stiffened. It may have been guesswork, but Barry might just have been right about why Donal and Julie had been outbid for the cottage in the loop of the bend.

"Our Councillor Bishop disqualified Bishop's Builders from tendering," said the marquis, taking a sip of his whiskey. "Apparently there's land that'll have to be expropriated and a cottage demolished. He said being on council meant he was in a conflict of interest, that he had plenty of work, and that his support for the project was a simple discharge of his civic duty."

"I see," said O'Reilly drily. He wasn't impressed by Bertie's "discharge of civic duty." It was quite possible that Bertie had prior knowledge of Councillor Wilson's motion. Or perhaps Bertie had nothing to do with McCluggage? One thing was certain, however: McCluggage was going to make a pretty profit when the cottage and land were purchased by council. It didn't allay O'Reilly's suspicions when the marquis continued.

"He even asked why, if council had had notions to straighten the bend, they hadn't moved sooner and bought it from the estate. The house has been on the market for a year and now some chap from Belfast has an accepted offer on the place."

O'Reilly frowned. Was that all smokescreen? And yet where was any real evidence to link Bertie to McCluggage?

"Now," said the marquis, "I suppose the fact that his actions will be recorded verbatim in the public report and that council elections are not too far away—" He let the thought hang.

O'Reilly inclined his head. "I knew Bertie would have an angle," he said aloud, but thought to himself, I'm certain it's more than simply playing for votes. Now, how can I get proof? O'Reilly finished his pint and nodded to the marquis's glass. "One for the road, sir?"

"Just one, and I think we should join the others."

They moved across to the table where the rest were finishing their drinks. "It's all right, Father. Sit where you are," O'Reilly said. "I can pour a pint and it's still my shout. Anyone else?"

"I'm fine thanks, Fingal," Mister Robinson said, nursing his half-pint shandy.

Both Fergus and Dermot held up nearly empty pint glasses. "Please, Doc," they both said.

"Right, and a half-un, Father?"

"Please."

O'Reilly fished out his pipe and fired it up on his way to the bar. The tobacco was burning splendidly by the time he had seen to the whiskies and had three pints of Guinness on the pour. He released a huge cloud of smoke, relishing the flavour of the Erinmore flake tobacco. He'd smoked that brand ever since old Doctor Micks had given young Fingal a tin for a Christmas present back in 1934 when he was a student.

O'Reilly turned the spigot's tap and topped off the first pint, making sure the head was creamy smooth. Thinking of medical school brought the marquis's news back to his mind with renewed pleasure. It was going to take all his willpower not to tell Helen until it was absolutely certain that she'd get the bursary.

He topped off the second pint then his own, found a tin tray, and carried the drinks over to the table. "Here we are," he said, "help yourselves."

He pulled up a chair and, pint in hand, sat. *"Sláinte,"*

he said, and as the rest replied, drank deeply, quietly mulling over how to find out more about Bishop and McCluggage. If his and Barry's surmises were right, he wanted to stop Bishop in his tracks right now, but anyone with the temerity to accuse the man without proof would be the recipient of a suit for slander. Even if it became common knowledge that the two men knew each other, tongues might wag, and public suspicions be raised, but it would be a nine-day wonder and soon forgotten.

Fingal O'Reilly smiled and drank. "Well," he said to no one in particular, "it will make that road a damn sight safer." He lowered more of his pint. But he doubted very much if that civic-minded goal had even crossed the councillor's small and narrow mind.

33

Visit Us in Great Humility

Barry whistled off-key. Roger Miller's "King of the Road" had topped the British pop charts four weeks ago. It was a catchy tune and its title suited what he was doing this Tuesday afternoon, driving round Ballybucklebo making follow-up home visits.

He remembered the first time Fingal had driven them both round these bucolic byways familiarising Barry with the layout of the local roads so he could plan future visits with as little backtracking as possible.

It was a straightforward route today, up to the estate, back down to a street running parallel with the main Bangor to Belfast Road, and finally on to Station Road to see Colin Brown, who had been up at the Royal this morning having his plaster cast removed, six weeks after its application.

He parked outside a familiar council house, got out, and knocked on the door. A little girl with flaxen pigtails, cornflower blue eyes, and snot on her upper lip was pushing a doll's pram that had, he noticed, several spokes missing from one of its wheels and a torn navy blue canopy. She paid no attention to Barry, but wagged an admonitory finger at the dolly inside and said with a lisp, "If youth's not a good boy, Mammy will thpank your botty, tho she will."

"Doctor Laverty." Barry turned to see Aggie Arbuthnot standing in the doorway holding a paperback copy of *Philadelphia, Here I Come!* "How's about ye, sir?"

"I'm fine, Aggie, but I thought I'd pop in. See how you're getting on."

"Come on in," she said, and led the way into her parlour. "Cup of tea?"

"Better not. I've more calls to make, but thanks."

"Well, sit you down anyroad." She lowered herself in an overstuffed armchair and put the book on a table. "I was learning my lines and my blocking, so I was," she said. She'd told him on his last visit that she was to act the character of Madge in Brian Friel's new play. Here she was rehearsing her part and the moves, her blocking, she would have to make on stage.

Barry parked himself in another comfortable chair. "How are you?"

"Och, Doctor dear," she said, "I'm bravely, so I am. No more pain in the oul' hind leg." She pulled up her skirt and turned her lower leg so Barry could see the calf. Apart from the old varicose veins, it looked healthy. "I was up at the Royal last week, you know. I'd more blood tests."

"I do know," Barry said. "I'd a letter from your specialist, Doctor Crozier, saying your prothrombin time is spot-on. Keep on taking the warfarin, and you've nothing to worry about. You've not noticed any bruises?" Warfarin interfered with the body's clotting system and bruising was a sign of overdose.

"Not a bit," she said. "I'm right as rain, so I am, but—" She shrugged and sighed. "Only, my 'sick' runs out July fifth. Then I'll have to go on the burroo and they cut your benefits in half." She sniffed. "I've still a bit of the severance doh-ray-mi, you know, but I'm not sure how I'll get by when it runs out."

Barry pursed his lips. Since he'd written that letter to her employer when first she'd come in with superficial thrombophlebitis he'd not done much to help her find a job, despite his protestations of good intent to O'Reilly. Aggie had been receiving state sickness insurance, but now her illness was better she was expected to go back to work or sign on for benefits at the Unemployment Bureau, or "burroo" as the locals called it, where the weekly payments were less. There was one option, but it was a slim one. "I could send a recommendation to the medical referee, see if we could get you more time on the 'sick.'" The referee's main function was to weed out malingerers who were abusing the system, but he could also grant extensions of benefits.

She shrank in her chair. Her eyes widened. "The Big Doctor?"

"Aggie, you know your 'sick' is finished soon anyway. I'd be asking for an extension, trying to get you a bit more cash. That's all."

She frowned. Seemed to be mulling it over.

Barry knew that patients hated having to see the physician employed by the Ministry of Health and Welfare to resolve questions about who really was sick and who was well enough to return to work. This removed the onus for making such decisions from GPs, who stood to deal with a great deal of anger from patients they refused to certify as sick. For many, a trip to "the Big Doctor," meant being cut off from benefits and was regarded with trepidation.

"If you say so, sir," Aggie said, "but I'll not count my chickens. I'm still looking for work, so I am."

"I do understand," Barry said and, remembering one of his father's adages, "Never promise unless you know you can keep it," made no further unrealistic offers. "If the referee decides to see you, you'll get a letter and an appointment. He may even simply write and say your request has been approved," he said. He rose. "Time I was off."

"Thanks for coming," she said, and picked up her book. She smiled at him. "Learning these here lines puts in the day, so it does," she said, and smiled. "Good afternoon, sir. I'll be fine, so I will."

Fine? With no job and her money running out? Barry shook his head. As he drove to his next call he wondered if it might be worth going to see Mister Ivan McCluggage despite O'Reilly's warning that Barry would almost certainly be told to "go and feel his head." And if, as O'Reilly also suggested, McCluggage was in cahoots with Bertie Bishop? Not promising. Not promising at all. They were probably two of a kind. Mercenary and as hard-hearted as Pharaoh in his dealings with Moses.

Barry parked on a street of semi-detached houses behind the main road, got out, and knocked on the door. Overhead a flock of starlings darkened the azure sky as the birds, whistling and chirping, made their way to their roosts on the gantries of Harland and Wolff's shipyards. From not far away, he could hear the burbling engine of the little diesel train rattling over the rails beside the Shore Road and see the faint blue cloud of its exhaust.

He turned. "Hello, Mairead," he said when Mairead

Shanks opened the door. "How are you today?" He was pleased to see that she was dressed, a good sign she was not feeling sorry for herself and slopping about in her dressing gown. It was two weeks since her surgery and she'd been discharged three days ago.

"Doctor Laverty, how nice," she said. "Come on in. Come in."

"Who is it, Mammy?" Barry recognised Angus's high-pitched voice coming from the kitchen.

"It's the doctor, so it is."

"Is he going to send youse away like the last time?" Barry heard the concern in the little lad's voice. "Me and Siobhan don't want him to, so we don't."

"Not this time," Mairead said. "He's come for to make sure Mammy's all right, isn't that right, Doctor?"

"It is."

"Come into the parlour then," she said, and called, "You two run out and play now."

Barry heard the slam of what must be the back door and followed her into the front room.

"They're two great wee nippers, so they are," she said. "Gerry and me was all tickled when we thought I was up the spout with number three . . . but, och, it wasn't to be. Not this time."

"I'm sorry, Mairead," Barry said, "but you're feeling well now?"

"Och, aye. Bit tired. They give me a blood transfusion in the ambulance, and when I was getting discharged they said it would take a wee while for my body to make up the blood I'd lost so they prescribed me a wheen of iron pills for to take." She sat on the sofa. "Sit down, Doctor. Take the weight off your feet."

"In a minute," Barry said. "Can I have a look at your wound?"

"Aye, certainly." She lay up on the sofa and pulled up her skirt and petticoat.

Barry would have liked to have had a blanket or a rug to cover her now exposed suspenders and stockings, but there didn't seem to be one handy, and anyway, checking her wound wouldn't take long. He sat on the edge of the sofa beside her and said, "All right?" as he pulled down the tops of her knickers.

"Go you right ahead, sir."

A dusky stubble of pubic hair was growing back from being shaved off preoperatively. The scar was obvious, a red line slightly curved down and running horizontally across the bottom of her belly an inch and a half above her pubic symphysis. Good. Her gynaecologist, Doctor Harley, had made the transverse Pfannenstiel incision now being used more frequently rather than the more traditional pubic-symphysis-to-belly-button vertical one. A teacher of Barry's referred to it as "splitting the patient from stem to gudgeon," a nautical expression indicating the entire length of a vessel. "Nice bikini incision," he said, laying a hand over it. It was cool, and obviously Mairead was feeling no discomfort. He palpated her lower abdomen. Once again she did not complain. "You're healing up well," he said, pulling up her knickers and standing.

Mairead stood and let her skirt fall, adjusted it, and sat. "Thank you, sir," she said, and inclined her head. "Can I ask you a wee question? And please sit yiz down."

Barry sat in a rocking chair. "Fire away."

She rummaged in her purse and handed him a thin sheet of aluminium foil regularly studded with little transparent plastic bubbles, each containing a tablet. "Them there's called Conovid," she said.

Barry recognised the oral contraceptive that had been introduced into the United Kingdom four years ago. "The Pill," he said.

"Doctor Harley says he doesn't want me getting pregnant for six months. Give my innards a chance to heal up."

"That makes good sense," Barry said. The hospital had sent him a copy of the operative report and he knew exactly what had been done. "Doctor Harley's a great man for new techniques. I know because he taught me. He's specially interested in helping women get pregnant when they are having trouble. Most gynaecologists would have taken out the damaged tube with the pregnancy in it. Then you'd only have had one tube left for you to try to get pregnant again."

She nodded hard. "And me and Gerry want another wee one, so we do."

"And I reckon you've been given the best possible chance, because Doctor Harley was able to save the damaged tube, so you still have two." Barry did not tell her that statistically she now had a reduced chance of conceiving at all. And if she did, of women whose tube containing a first ectopic pregnancy had been conserved, fifteen percent of those next pregnancies would be another ectopic. Even so she would have been even less likely to suceed with only one tube. By not telling Mairead these statistics he was following the precepts of his teachers who believed that if the future for a patient was unclear, there was no need to worry them further with uncertainties. It was believed to be the kindest way. Perhaps, Barry thought, but I know if it was me I'd like to be told exactly what was going on; but then, I speak the language of medicine.

"So why can't I try to get pregnant at once? I'm not getting any younger, you know, and there's already a powerful gap between my two and the next one."

Barry, humbled by her optimism, sought for the best words to explain. "Your tube, the one that was operated on, it's not completely better yet. It'll still be raw in places, and when an egg tries to get along it it might get stuck—"

She smiled. "You mean I'd be like an egg-bound hen?"

"Sort of," Barry said. Typical of a countrywoman to pick a familiar example to help her understand. Occasionally a hen's egg became trapped in the oviduct causing the unfortunate bird great pain. "But human eggs don't have hard shells and are so tiny it wouldn't harm you, but if it got fertilised there and couldn't move to the womb, it would grow until—"

She grimaced. "I'd rather not have that again."

"So you do as Doctor Harley suggests. Take your pill for six months and then away you go . . . and Mairead, if you do get pregnant, and I sincerely hope you do . . . you let Doctor O'Reilly know at once."

Her face fell. "Can I not come to you, sir? I mean Doctor O'Reilly's very nice and all, so he is, but I've heard about how good you are delivering babies, you know."

Barry blushed. God, but there were some lovely advantages in being known and respected in the local community. He'd miss it. He'd forgotten that it wasn't common knowledge in the village that he'd be moving on soon. Once he told Mairead, he knew it wouldn't be long before the word was out. And his patients had a right to know. "Mairead, I've really enjoyed working here, but come July I'm going away to take more training."

"Honest to God? Och."

Och. The universal Ulster sound that could convey any emotion from surprise to disappointment to amazement. This one was definitely disappointment. "But I'm going to learn more about delivering babies and treating ectopic pregnancies," he said.

She sighed. "If you must, you must, I suppose—" She looked at him, head slightly to one side. "But might you come back, sir, once you've finished training, like?"

"You never know," Barry said. And it was the truth. He himself didn't know for sure and only time would tell, but he was certainly looking forward to finding out. "And if I do and the timing's right, I'll look after you." He glanced at his watch and stood. "Now, if you'll excuse me, I've one last call to make."

He had and then it was home to get tidied up. He'd not seen Sue since Saturday, ten days ago, and that had been a less than successful evening. Their difficult conversation over her political activism had put a decided damper on the entire dinner and her goodnight kisses had lacked warmth.

Barry got into the Volkswagen and started the engine. Oh well, a long time ago Billy Shakespeare had said something about the course of love never running smoothly. Barry drove away from the kerb. And it wasn't that he was in love with Sue Nolan, now was it? But damn it all, he'd missed her like hell since that night and was sure, now things were back to normal at Number One in the evenings and Fingal had given Barry tonight off, that the dinner for two he was taking her to at the Crawfordsburn Inn would see them reconciled. Of course it would.

34

Is Murder by the Law?

"Aye," Colin Brown said, showing Barry a split grubby plaster cast covered in scrawled signatures and childishly drawn pictures, "the nice doctor at the Royal said I could keep it as a sou . . . sou . . . keepsake, so he did." He grimaced. "Mind youse, when your man the cast fellah got out the wee electric saw to cut the plaster, I thought he was going to take off my whole bloody arm—"

"Colin," Connie said. "Language."

"Sorry, Mammy."

Barry was sitting at the kitchen table. "They do look scary and they make an awful buzzing noise." Barry remembered the finely toothed wheel attachment that was powered by an electric drill motor. "But the little saw doesn't spin round and round. It just rocks back and forth very very quickly and it only divides the plaster."

"And it tickles, so it does," Colin said. "By the time your man was finished I was laughing like a drain." He held up his arm. It was deathly white where it had been hidden from the light for six weeks. "Good as new," he said, wiggling his fingers. "Just like youse promised my mammy, Doctor Laverty."

"Say thank you to Doctor Laverty," Connie said, "for coming specially for to see youse again today."

"Not just Colin," Barry said, not relishing what he wanted to ask next. "How's Butch?" There had been no more complaints from Bertie Bishop about Lady Macbeth since the Saturday Sue had come down from Belfast, and neither Barry nor Fingal had had the time to make enquiries. But it wasn't only to satisfy his curiosity that Barry wanted to know if Colin's ferret could be the instigator of the pigeonicide.

Colin frowned, looked down at his shoes, scuffing a toe on the tiles.

"Come on, Colin," Connie said, "it's not like you to get shy all of a sudden. Tell Doctor Laverty what happened. He'll not tell nobody, isn't that right, sir?"

By the way Connie moved to her son and laid a protective hand on his shoulder, Barry had a fairly good idea about what might be coming next, so he quickly said, "Cross my heart," and did so. Among the children of Ulster and indeed among many of the adults, there was no more binding promise.

Colin swallowed, looked up at his mother, back to Barry, took a deep breath, and said, "Butch must've got out last night, so he must. I said night-night til him at my bedtime, put him back in his cage, and when I went out to give him his brekky—" Colin stared at the floor.

"Go on," Connie prompted.

"He was sitting in our yard. I didn't know how he'd got out, but Daddy found a hole in the chicken wire at the back of Butch's cage." Colin brightened. "My daddy fixed it, so he did. Butch'll not get out again, honest to God. He'll be good, so he will." His look at his mother was full of pleading. "He'll be good."

"It's not all," Connie said.

Barry heard Colin sniffle and say, "I'll tell him, Mammy."

"That's a good grown-up boy. Always tell the truth, even if it hurts," Connie said.

"When I took a hold of him his nose was all bloody, and—"

Oh dear, Barry thought, dreading what was coming next.

"And I found two feathers in the yard."

"I reckon Butch'd killed a seagull or something," Connie said, and as she looked at Barry he heard the hope in her voice and knew she was asking him to corroborate her statement. "God knows," she said, "there's lots of them round Ballybucklebo."

Barry was torn between wanting to go along with the fable and being in no doubt as to the real source of the feathers. And, he suspected, nor were Connie and Colin. News of Bertie's earlier losses would have been all over the village.

"We're waiting for Colin's daddy to come home, so we are."

"Daddy'll know it was a seagull," Colin said. "He will. He will."

Connie nodded. "I hope so—"

There was a hammering at the front door. "Excuse me," Connie said. "I'll just go and see who that is."

Barry slipped off his chair and squatted in front of Colin. "You love Butch, don't you?"

"Aye, I do." He was close to tears.

Before Barry had time to console his young patient, a pounding of boots along the hallway forced him to look up, only to be confronted by a scarlet-faced Bertie Bishop. The man hadn't even had the courtesy to remove his bowler hat. "Councillor," Barry said, his heart sinking, "what brings you here?"

"None of your business, Laverty."

Barry flinched, straightened his shoulders, and, remembering something O'Reilly had said about bullies, stood his ground. "You're interrupting a medical consultation. I'll thank you to wait outside." He could see Connie standing behind Bishop, trying to get past him to be with Colin.

Bishop clenched his teeth, growled deep in his throat, and Barry watched as the man's chest swelled not unlike one of his own pigeons. "I've come here to say something, I'm going for to say it, then I'll let you finish with your patient," said Bishop. "Youse bloody quacks think youse is more important than anybody else, so youse do. Well, you're not."

Barry ignored the jibe. "Say your piece, then out." He pointed to the hall. Inside he was trembling, but with suppressed rage or amazement at his own temerity he did not know. It was what O'Reilly would have said. Barry even managed a tiny smile. Bertie Bishop wasn't the patient today, but Barry was in principle invoking O'Reilly's first law, *Never, never, never let the patients get the upper hand.*

Bishop thrust out his chin. "Youse know bloody well, Laverty, that something's been getting at my birds."

"You accused Doctor O'Reilly's cat . . . twice, and you were wrong," Barry said with a quick glance at Colin, whose lower lip had started to tremble.

"Aye, well, I'm not wrong this time, so I'm not." Bishop's grimace was feral. "I'm just back from Belfast. I went to see the new birds I got on Saturday, so I did. Both of them were dead. Looked like they'd been put through a combine harvester and them still with their feathers on before they went in."

Barry heard a catch in the councillor's voice. Miserable gobshite, as O'Reilly would call the man, he might be, but there was a sense of loss in his tone.

"And there was pawprints in the bloodstains all over the place. Clear as the nose on your face."

Barry heard a small sob and looked to see tears streaming down Colin's face. "Could it have been a fox?" Barry asked, trying to divert the councillor.

"Jasus, you're no countryman, Laverty. Fox gets into a henhouse it'll kill every bloody thing in there, and anyroad these weren't fox's prints. Much wee-er. And the animal has five toes, foxes have only four on their back paws."

Barry tried desperately to find an alternative. "Perhaps a stoat or a . . . a weasel got in?"

Bishop barked a single "Huh," then said, "youse've no notion, son. Them's one and the same thing, just different names."

"I believe," said Barry, determined not to let Bishop score a point, "the term 'sable' is also applicable."

"That's as may be," Bishop ploughed on. "There's no pure white weasels, certainly no white foxes in Ireland, but there is ferrets, and one of them lives dead close to my feckin' loft, so it does. Your man Steve Wallace, him that owns the garage the loft's over, him what mistook the animal for O'Reilly's cat . . . I'm glad you put me right on that, Laverty . . . that bloody cat was nothing but a red herring."

Barry felt a peculiar sense of guilt because by his exonerating Lady Macbeth Barry had put Bishop onto a hot scent.

"Steve saw a white thing this morning, and everybody knows about that wee lad there's ferret. And it's just a doddle across the road to my loft from here."

"I don't think that proves anything," Barry said, but knew he was clutching at straws.

"I want to see that ferret," Bishop shouted, "and it's none of your business, Laverty. I don't give a tinker's toss what you think. I'm sure it's been murdering my birds." Bishop tried to stride past Barry, but Barry moved to block the man's progress.

"Mister Bishop, you've made your point."

"I want that there feckin' ferret. If there's blood on its paws—"

Barry took a deep breath. His mind raced as he

tried to formulate an emergency plan. "Connie," he said, looking her in the eye with a gaze that probably went right down to the soles of her feet, "will you please ask the councillor to wait in your lounge. I'll be finished with Colin soon." He turned his back on Bishop and bent to Colin.

Bishop said, "All right. All right. I'll wait, but youse remember what it says in the Bible. 'An eye for an eye, a tooth for a feckin' tooth.' If I find that—" He was still protesting as, judging by his fading tones, Connie showed him into the lounge and shut the door. "Colin," Barry said in a stage whisper. "Do you trust me?"

Colin nodded.

"Take me to Butch. Quietly." Barry snatched a large tea towel off the drying rack and followed Colin, who unsnibbed the back door. Together they slipped out, Barry carrying his doctor's bag.

"Do you ever carry Butch in your pocket or in a box?"

"Aye. He's well used to it." Colin pointed to a cage with a wooden door in one side, a wooden floor, and chicken wire sides and top. "There he is."

The ferret reared up on its hind legs and put its forepaws on the wire. Barry noticed what could be blood-staining on the pads. "All right, Colin," he said, "get him—" Barry opened his bag, spread the tea towel over the contents. "—and pop him in there."

Colin hesitated.

Barry said, "You told me you loved Butch."

Colin nodded and looked solemn.

"We've not much time. I'm going to save his life, but you're going to have to let him go."

Colin nodded. His tears were tripping him. He bent, unlatched the door, gently took hold of the little animal, dropped a kiss on its head, popped him into Barry's bag, and said, "Bye-bye, Butch. Take you care, now."

Barry shut his bag. "Your mammy was right, Colin. You are a grown-up man." He cast around and saw a stick, grabbed it, and used it to tear a rent in the chicken wire. "Come on, Colin," he said, "back inside."

Once in the kitchen, Barry pushed his bag under the table, took a deep breath, and called, "All right, Connie. I'm finished."

Connie reappeared with Bishop in hot pursuit.

Again Barry looked deep into her eyes and nodded nearly imperceptibly. Please understand, Connie, he thought.

"Where is it?" Bishop demanded.

"I'll show you," Connie said, and opened the back door.

Barry craned to see Bishop storming out, bending over the cage, peering inside, fingering the rent in the wire, and yelling, "The bloody thing's not here. Where the hell is it?" He charged back into the kitchen. "The feckin' thing's got away, Laverty."

Barry thought Colin could have got a place with Aggie's amateur dramatic company, so realistic was his "Noooooo," and the increased floods of tears that followed.

"I think, Councillor," Barry said as stiffly as he could manage, "you may have been right about Butch. But if the animal has disappeared, you won't be able to prove it, ever, so I am afraid, just like Shylock, you won't be able to collect your pound of flesh."

Bishop spluttered, veins standing out on his forehead. "If that bloody ferret shows up here again and I find out, Mrs. Bishop's going to have a white fur trim on her best coat collar, so she is."

Colin howled on.

"I think," Barry said, "you've caused quite enough upset for one day. The little lad's heartbroken. Making threats doesn't help. Perhaps—" He indicated the hall to the front door.

"And I suppose you think I'm laughing my leg off because the damn thing killed a wheen of my birds?" Bishop thrust his face into Barry's. "If you do, Laverty, you're a feckin' bollix, so you are." Spittle flew.

Barry recoiled and as he did he saw that his bag was mysteriously jerking across the tiles and moving out from under the table. He had to distract Bishop before the man noticed. Barry stepped closer to Bishop. "Mister Bishop, there is a lady and a child present. I'll thank you to moderate your language." He grabbed Bishop by the elbow and hustled him across the room so the bag was no longer in the councillor's line of sight. "Out," he said as soon as they reached the kitchen door. "Out."

He closed the kitchen door. As Bishop came to a halt his bowler fell to the floor. His face was puce as he roared, "Who the hell do you think you are?"

"Mister Bishop, I know you are upset, but there's no need to scare a little boy, swear in front of his mother."

"Aye. Well." The councillor's voice had returned to nearly normal.

"I think," said Barry, "you should be running along." He bent, retrieved the hat, and handed it to Bishop.

"Good afternoon, *Doctor*." The councillor crammed his hat on his head and stamped away.

As Barry turned to go back he heard the front door slam. He opened the kitchen door and saw Connie standing with her arm round Colin's shoulder. Colin had stopped crying and held the bag to his chest. "Sorry about that, Connie," Barry said.

She smiled. "I don't know how youse done it, Doctor Laverty, but I knew by the way youse looked at me youse was up to something." She bent to Colin. "Here. Blow your nose," she said, and gave him a hanky. "Colin told me while youse was out of the room, but I didn't let him open the bag in case the wee craythur got out and Mister Bishop came back and seen him."

"Very wise," Barry said, "but we can take a peek now." Barry opened his bag a fraction and a small black nose peeped out. "I'll not let him out, Colin," Barry said.

Connie laughed. "That was dead brill, so it was, hiding Butch in there."

"Our fugitive ferret may be safe for now," Barry said, "but it's only half the battle won. You heard what Mister Bishop said. If he ever hears that Butch has come home . . . I didn't like what he said about fur collars."

Colin sniffed and blew his nose.

"We're going to have to arrange for Butch to disappear. He'd never be safe here, you understand, Colin?"

"Yes, Doctor Laverty." The little boy took a couple of deep breaths. "Can I hold him just once, like?"

Barry felt the lump in his throat. "Mammy, can we shut the kitchen door?" He had visions of an all-out ferret pursuit if Butch tried to escape.

Connie shut the door, and Barry held his bag close to Colin and opened it more widely. Colin reached inside and withdrew the ferret from the folds of the towel. He wrapped the little animal in both arms and held it to his chest for a long minute, without speaking, then he gave Barry a wistful look and put the creature back in the bag.

Barry shut the clasp.

Connie moved to Colin and put her hand on his shoulder. She too was crying.

Barry came close to tears himself, but managed to say, "I'm sorry Butch has to go, but I promise I'll find him a good home." He touched Colin on the head. "You're a very brave boy," he said. "Very brave." And as he turned to go, he hoped to God that O'Reilly would know where to lodge a fugitive ferret so Bertie could never find the animal.

35

Be Bruised in a New Place

"**G**et down, Arthur." Barry let himself into the back garden. He had forgotten about the dog's extraordinary sense of smell. "Down." Arthur stood, put his paws on Barry's shoulders, and tried to grab the medical bag Barry held above his head. "*Down,* you great lummox."

Arthur subsided, sat, threw back his head, and yodelled.

Barry was amazed by the noise coming from the Labrador and gave thanks for the small mercy of now being unencumbered. He scuttled for the back door, let himself into a kitchen redolent with the scent of boiling ham, and slammed the door.

"It's yourself, is it, Doctor Laverty? And in a powerful rush, so." Kinky turned from a bubbling pot. "And Arthur sounds beside himself." She opened the door and said, "Do you be quiet now, Arthur. There's a good dog. Go back to your kennel, bye."

The yodelling stopped as if turned off by a switch.

She closed the door. "Whatever can have upset him?"

"I've got a ferret in here." Barry set his bag on the table. "Arthur wanted to get at it."

Kinky chuckled and her chins wobbled. "Don't be teasing a poor Corkwoman, sir. I know you youngsters listen to that silly BBC program *I'm Sorry, I'll Read That Again* with that John Cleese who's always going on about ferrets."

It was Barry's turn to laugh. "You're right. And he sings that song about having one sticking up his nose. But I'm not teasing you. I really do have a ferret in there and I need Doctor O'Reilly's advice about what to do with it."

She frowned. "And may I ask how, sir, did it come to be in your bag?"

"It's a long story, Kinky."

"Well, I have nowhere to go, Doctor dear, and I think it will be worth hearing how a wee wild craytur came to be inside your medical bag, so."

"It's not wild, Kinky," Barry said, eyeing the bag, "although it may well be by the time it gets out. It's Colin Brown's pet. It killed some of Bertie Bishop's pigeons, and Bertie wanted his pound of ferret flesh. I stuffed it in my bag to get it out of the Browns' house before Bertie found it."

She took a step back. "I'm sure that was very kind

of you, sir, but I'd rather it was not in my kitchen. You'll find himself in the dining room." She frowned. "He's not in his best of moods."

"Oh?"

"I'm behind in my wedding arrangements so he's doing me a favour by completing and addressing preprinted invitations, and you know how he hates filling in forms." She raised her eyes to heaven.

"I do," said Barry, "but I'll risk bearding the lion in his lair." He lifted the bag.

"I'm sure Doctor O'Reilly will be able to help. Himself is always at his best in a crisis."

The lid of the saucepan rattled.

"Now if you'll excuse me, the hambones are knocking to get out," Kinky said with a sniff and a sidelong glance at the medical bag. "I'm making stock."

Barry felt his mouth water. Kinky's soups were delicious. "You carry on, Kinky. I'll go and see what Doctor O'Reilly thinks."

As he walked down the hall Barry smiled to see how Kinky, now seven weeks postop, had bounced back to being her old self, albeit pounds lighter. Keeping Helen on to answer the phone in the daytime and help with the heavier chores had certainly speeded Kinky's recovery. Pity Helen would have to be let go at the end of the month, and Fingal hadn't mentioned anything more about getting help for her to go to Queen's.

Barry had only half-opened the dining room door when he heard O'Reilly roar, "Go away." He did not look up from where he sat writing at the head of the dining room table. "I'm busy. Go . . . away."

To O'Reilly's right was a box of embossed cards. The top one was tucked under the flap of its envelope. To his left was a smaller, untidy heap of what must be completed invitations. "I'm sorry about this, Fingal, but it's urgent." Damn it, Barry'd just stood up to Bertie Bishop, and he wasn't going to let Fingal O'Reilly get away with yelling just because he was feeling grumpy. Barry sat along the table to the man's right, and set the bag on the table.

"Christ on a crutch, what's urgent?" O'Reilly lowered his voice a little, lifted his shaggy head, and pointed to the uncompleted cards. "I have to get this bloody lot finished tonight and then I've to go up to Belfast to see Cromie and Charlie about the reunion."

"It's not bleeding-to-death or having-a-heart-attack urgent," Barry said. "I only need a quick bit of advice, but I'd like to get it sorted out now."

"Can't it wait?" O'Reilly sighed. "I do have to finish this bloody paperwork." He blew out his cheeks. "I'd rather muck out the Augean Stables."

Barry saw a way to divert O'Reilly. "Heracles's, or if you prefer Hercules's, fifth labour, I believe, before he went off to kill a lot of birds and then start up the ancient Olympic Games."

"You're right, and his fifth labour didn't count because he got paid for it. Not like me scribbling away." O'Reilly chuckled and, speaking normally, said, "I'm sorry. I growled, Barry. I wasn't really angry." He smiled. "It's a long time ago, but I still remember getting anxious and a bit short-fused immediately before my first wedding—"

No question, Barry thought, Fingal O'Reilly is mellowing, or he's come to trust me a lot more. Six months ago he'd not have apologised or confessed to that.

"I think prenuptial collywobbles must affect every groom-to-be. Marriage makes a hell of a lot of changes in people's lives . . . and it will in my life too," Fingal said, finally laying down his pen and sitting back in his chair.

"But you're looking forward to it, aren't you?"

"Like a kiddie to Christmas morning." He fished out his pipe. "And on the subject of romance, it's really none of my business, but how are things going with you and Sue?" O'Reilly struck a match and puffed.

Barry hesitated. For years, ever since they'd been boarders together at Campbell College, Barry had only ever exposed his deeper feelings to Jack Mills, his best friend, but Fingal O'Reilly, Barry'd come to learn, was the kind of man in whom confiding was natural. "We'd a row last Tuesday." He pursed his lips. "Stupid misunderstanding about her civil rights work."

"I'm sorry to hear that." O'Reilly lit his pipe.

"Now that Kinky's able to answer the phone in the evenings, I'm going to take Sue to the Inn tonight. Candlelight, bottle of wine—"

"Good for you. Kinky can find you if you're

needed." O'Reilly let go a blast of blue tobacco smoke then asked, "You in love with the girl?"

Barry sat back. He'd not been expecting O'Reilly to be so blunt. Was he? Was he in love with Sue Nolan? Certainly he'd not been swept off his feet, not the way he had been with Patricia Spence, but yes, he was feeling a very great deal for Sue and it was growing every time he was with her. Perhaps it was more solid than his earlier infatuation. And yet—

"I think I could be, Fingal," he said very quietly, "but I'm not sure how she feels."

"Go on," O'Reilly said.

"First time I took her out she was late because she had been at a CSJ meeting."

O'Reilly shrugged. "Being late's no great sin."

Barry frowned. "I thought so too, but then—" He shook his head. "The Saturday she came down here to keep me company she said something that I took lightly at the time." He inhaled. "It's silly. Probably means nothing. Forget it."

"If it's bothering you, it's not silly. Come on, spit it out. You'll feel better."

"Well, she'd cut a sailing class to be with me, and she said being with me 'beats skinning your knuckles on a banjo bolt.'"

"A *what*?"

"A banjo bolt. It's a hollow perforated bolt that's to transfer oil in maritime diesels and it's used in hydraulic systems . . . Fingal, you're laughing!"

O'Reilly was pursing his lips and doing his best not

to laugh but smoke was seeping from his mouth and suddenly he let out a loud guffaw and coughed. "I'm sorry, Barry, I'm not really laughing, it's just that, well, oh my, it's not the most romantic thing a woman can say to a young fellah." O'Reilly bit down on his pipe. "So what did you say to her?"

"Nothing. I changed the subject."

"And now you're wondering if you're important to her or not?"

Barry nodded.

"Have you asked her?" O'Reilly said.

"Whether I matter to her? No. But I'm going to tonight."

O'Reilly leant forward and put his hand on Barry's arm. "I'm sure it'll be fine," he said, and his words comforted Barry. He half-turned. Lady Macbeth had leapt up on the sideboard and was slinking along, belly low. As she came abreast of Barry's bag, she hunched her shoulders, thrashed her tail, and sprang, missing the bag because as she leapt it hopped and then slid up the table to dislodge the pile of finished invitations.

"What the hell's going on?" O'Reilly, pipe clenched between his teeth, grabbed the cat and set her on the floor, then picked up the envelopes, straightened, and pointed. "Is that bag possessed? What in the name of the wee man's in there?"

"I almost forgot . . . it's what I came in to get your advice about, Fingal. It's Colin Brown's ferret."

"How the hell did it get in there?"

"I'm afraid *it's* the white animal that's been getting Bertie Bishop's pigeons. I was checking on Colin after his cast was removed, and Bertie arrived like a one-man execution squad demanding Butch . . . that's the ferret's name—"

"And you pulled a quick Scarlet Pimpernel." O'Reilly chortled. "Well done."

Barry grimaced. "Maybe in the short term, but now I need advice. Where can I find a home for the wee creature?"

"Hmmmm," said O'Reilly. "Colin must be heart-broken. I suppose he'll get over it in time, at least I hope so. Kids seem to recover from all sorts of disap-pointments." O'Reilly scratched his head. He frowned deeply, and nodded at Barry's bag. "At least you were thinking on your feet to whisk Butch out from under Bishop's nose." He tapped the stem of his pipe against his front teeth. "We can't keep the beast here, though. Her Ladyship—" O'Reilly pointed to the cat, who was staring fixedly at the bag and thrashing her tail. "—won't stand for it. Not even for one night."

"I don't think Arthur will either," Barry said.

O'Reilly's face split into a huge grin. "Arthur. Fer-rets," he said. "Got it."

Barry wondered if O'Reilly was about to wander off on another of his apparent non sequiturs.

"My brother Lars in Portaferry has a handyman, chap called Jimmy Caulwell. He runs ferrets. Arthur tried to help Jimmy dig one out of a rabbit burrow when I was there ten days ago." O'Reilly looked at his watch. "Could you see a patient at six?"

"I suppose." Barry was meant to be picking Sue up at six.

"Good. It's Tom MacKelvey. You've seen him before."

Barry frowned. "Lawyer. With piles?"

"That's him. Seems they're troubling him again. I told him I'd see him if he popped in at six on his way home from work in Belfast. It won't take long. Have a look. Make sure they're not strangulated. Give him some Proctosedyl oint—"

"Fingal, I have treated piles."

"Sorry. Of course you have. Meanwhile, if I get my skates on, it's five now. Forty minutes from here down to Portaferry. Find Jimmy. Shouldn't be hard in such a wee place, and if I can't I'm sure Lars will look after Butch overnight and give him to Jimmy in the morning. Fifty minutes to Harberton Park in Belfast to meet Cromie and the Greers. Noreen Greer's making dinner for seven, but if I'm a little late, Noreen's a doctor's wife, she'll understand. This is an emergency, Ballybucklebo style."

"Sue's not my wife," Barry said, "not by a long chalk, but I hope she understands when I have to tell her I'm going to be late. That patients always come first."

"She's bound to."

Barry smiled. "I hope so." He shoved his bag closer

to O'Reilly. "There's one thing," Barry said. "Could you get a box from Kinky? I might need that bag tonight."

O'Reilly laughed. "Course." He cast a disdainful eye at the invitations. "They'll have to wait . . . and I'm not one bit sorry. Right, I'm off." He lifted the bag and headed for the door.

Barry said, "Fingal, Colin doesn't seem to have any trouble handling Butch, but he's bound to be a bit upset right now. He's been stuffed in there, jiggled about—"

O'Reilly laughed. "Never worry. I'm good with animals. I'll give you your bag back in a jiffy."

As Fingal left, Barry heard scratching coming from inside the bag. He went to the hall and dialled Sue's number.

It was answered on the first ring. "Hello? Peter?" She sounded excited.

Barry tensed. Peter? Peter who? "Sue, it's Barry." He wanted to ask about this Peter, but not now, and not on the phone. "Look, I'm going to have to pick you up a bit later, say seven? A patient's—"

"Oh, Barry. I'm sorry. I was expecting Peter Gormley to call or pick me up."

"The CSJ committee bloke?" Barry relaxed. Peter Gormley was a surgeon whom Barry had met and was far too old for Sue. It would have to be business. He'd been too quick off the mark suspecting a competitor, but perhaps that should be telling him something about how he felt about Sue Nolan?

"That's right, I was going to phone—"

Barry heard a bellow from the direction of the kitchen. What on earth was that?

"You still there?" she asked.

He'd missed the sound of her voice. "Yes, Sue. Sorry. Go on."

"Something's come up. I'm going to have to cry off tonight and go to Belfast."

"What? Why?"

"It's to do with my civil rights work. They've moved up next week's meeting to tonight. Barry, I'm sorry, but I have to go."

Kinky went charging past and disappeared into the surgery.

He took a deep breath. "Pity," he said, "I was really looking forward . . . look, Sue, I know you're secretary, but surely someone else could take notes? Just for one night."

"I can't. I'm sorry. Please try to understand."

"All right. I understand. It's important to you," he said. He cleared his throat. "I'd not want to stand in your way." He knew his voice had become formal, despite his attempt to sound natural.

The sound of her doorbell ringing came over the line.

"Barry, that must be Peter."

"Fine," Barry said. "Off you go."

"Please don't be like that, Barry." The bell rang in the distance. "Barry, when can I see you again?"

"Honestly, Sue, at the moment I'm not quite sure.

Work—" He didn't want to speak. "I'll give you a ring. Maybe see you at the Yacht Club next time I'm racing." And that was nine days away. He sighed. Just like the advice Jack Mills had once given Barry about Patricia. Leave her be for a while. See if she makes the first move. He hoped Sue would.

As Barry turned from the phone O'Reilly appeared in the hall carrying a box sealed with Sellotape. Airholes had been punched in the cardboard. The sounds of scrabbling came from inside. O'Reilly held up a finger with a brand-new elastoplast. "Bloody thing bit me," he said, looking aggrieved.

I did warn you, thought Barry, but instead said sympathetically, "I hope it's not too sore."

"Nah," said O'Reilly. "Hurts like bedamned at the moment, but it's not that deep. I'll get over it in time." He went out and closed the door.

Not that deep, Barry thought, feeling hurt himself. Patricia Spence's career had been too important for her to make time for romance. She'd told him so when they'd only been going out for a few weeks. They had made up, but she'd eventually dropped him for another man. Perhaps he should have seen the writing on the wall much earlier.

And maybe Sue's remark about the banjo bolt hadn't been as simple as he and O'Reilly had thought. Sometimes a seemingly trivial symptom could be the clue to a serious underlying disease. Maybe he wasn't as important in her life as he'd like to be. If this dinner he'd arranged this evening could be so easily brushed off in favour of another committee meeting— Barry bit his lower lip, grimaced, and headed upstairs. Well, he thought, I've been getting over Patricia. He only hoped that in time he'd get over this too.

36

That Reconciles Discordant Elements

"Any more for anyone?" O'Reilly asked. Then, as if daring Barry or Kitty to say yes, he nonchalantly encircled the pie dish with his left arm, a pie dish containing the remnants of Kinky's orange dessert soufflé.

Barry said, "Not for me, thanks."

He'd only toyed with his food and O'Reilly knew why. Earlier this week the lad had confided that it looked as if things between him and Sue Nolan had gone bust on Tuesday night. It seemed unfair to O'Reilly, in light of his own happiness, but he was wise enough in the ways of the world to realise that all might not yet be lost and that Barry's best tactic was to let the hare sit for a while. Which is what he'd been doing for the past three days.

O'Reilly turned to Kitty. "What about you, dear?"

She shook her head.

"Shame to waste it," O'Reilly said with a grin and helped himself. Kitty was a good cook, but Kinky was definitely in a class by herself, particularly when it came to pandering to his sweet tooth. And despite her ongoing attempts to cut down his calories, she'd been doing more desserts recently, in part, he was sure, to demonstrate just how indispensible she was. While she did seem to be more comfortable with the notion of having Kitty around, the Corkwoman still kept things formal between them.

"Who said, 'Moderation in all things'?" Kitty asked, staring at O'Reilly's tummy.

"Haven't the foggiest," O'Reilly mumbled, his mouth full of the last morsels.

"I believe it was that Roman dramatist, Publius something or other. Terence for short," Barry said. "He's also the bloke who said, 'Charity begins at home.'"

"So let's have a bit of charity in this home about my appetite. It's been a long time since lunch," O'Reilly said, and stifled a burp.

"I'll grant you, Fingal, that soufflé was out of this world, but—"

"Thank you, Miss O'Hallorhan," Kinky said, coming in with her tray. "And yourself, sir, should go easy on the seconds. Your fiancée is right, so."

Lord preserve me, O'Reilly thought, from the "monstrous regiment of women." Not for the first time he realised that it was entirely possible Kitty and Kinky might gang up on him once Kitty moved in. Oh well, it would be good for him to lose a bit of weight, and it had forever been a good tactic to get Irish people to forget their differences and form alliances against a common foe, in this case his waistline. A small price to pay for harmony between the women in Number One.

"It was wonderful," Kitty said. "Mine always collapse."

"If you wish, Miss O'Hallorhan, I'll be happy to show you how I make them, so."

"That," said Kitty, "would be wonderful, and there is another thing, a favour I'd like to ask you too."

O'Reilly saw Barry looking quizzically at Kitty and watched the expression change on Kinky's face from a puzzled frown to—"Welllll—" and the beginnings of a smile. "If I can be of assistance, Miss O'Hallorhan," Kinky said, putting her tray on the sideboard.

Go on, Kitty, Fingal thought, and slid his foot under the table to nudge hers for encouragement. When Kitty had put the suggestion to him yesterday, he'd said it was bloody brilliant. Now it was time to see how it was going to work.

"Doctor O'Reilly has arranged who will be his best man and who will make up the groom's party. He's enough men, five including himself, to form the first two rows of a rugby scrum."

"And rightly so," O'Reilly said. "After all, Charlie Greer and I were the second row for Ireland once."

"Indeed, but you outnumber my side, Fingal." She faced Kinky. "My best friend Jane Hoey's going to be my maid of honour, and an old nursing school friend, Virginia Currie née Treanor, is coming up from Dublin." Kitty looked Kinky in the eye and smiled. "Mrs. Kincaid, I'd be truly honoured if you'd consent to be one of my bridal party too."

O'Reilly watched.

Barry's jaw dropped then he smiled. Kinky frowned, crossed her arms, pursed her lips, and looked down. Clearly she was making up her mind, and not without difficulty. O'Reilly shuddered to think of the implications if she said no.

"Please, Kinky," Kitty said in a voice that would have melted Pharaoh's hard heart.

"Miss O'Hallor . . . Miss Kitty, it would be a great pleasure to me to stand with you on your big day, so."

Barry surprised O'Reilly by applauding and O'Reilly joined in. He laughed then roared, "Good for you, Kinky Kincaid. Wonderful."

Kinky frowned. "But I do see a shmall-little difficulty, so."

Oh, Lord, O'Reilly thought. Now what?

"Perhaps I'm being too literal, but I'm wondering what you'll be calling Mrs. Currie and myself?" Kinky said with a shy smile.

"Goodness. I'm pretty new at this wedding business," Kitty said. "I'm not sure I understand."

"Well, a bride," said Kinky, "can have as many attendants as she wishes. The bride's 'best woman' is the maid or matron of honour. The other attendants are the bride's *maids*. But we're a little old to be bride's *maids,* aren't we?"

Whoops, O'Reilly thought, and saw Kitty looking at him. "I knew getting married late in life would be an adventure, but I didn't appreciate how truly tricky it could be until this moment," O'Reilly said with a laugh. "But it's only a name, Kinky," he said, "and I think I might have a solution."

"Please go ahead, sir, for I would like to do this for Miss Kitty, so," Kinky said.

"For starters, we're not having a completely traditional wedding so I don't think we have to stick exactly to protocol and use all the old titles. I've always been partial to the early nineteenth-century expression 'my particular friend.' I see no reason why Virginia Currie and you, Kinky, couldn't be referred to as 'particular friends' of the bride." He waited.

Kinky's smile was vast. "Oh, I do like that. I do like that very much, so."

"So do I," said Kitty.

"Then that's taken care of," O'Reilly said, and felt himself relax.

"And now that it is, Fingal," Kitty said, "seeing Helen's still answering the phone on weekdays, could Kinky have Monday off? I really could use help picking my wedding outfit and some of my trousseau. Jane is working that day and it's much too far for my old mum to come from Dublin. I would so appreciate Kinky's help. There's the outfits for the maid of honour," she grinned and nodded to Kinky, "and for *my particular friends*. Brands and Norman's have some beautiful stuff." She turned to Kinky. "I'd love to have your advice."

Kinky nodded. "If that would be all right, sir, I could get the train to Belfast."

"Of course," O'Reilly said. Better and better. He must stop worrying about whether the two women were going to get on. Kitty and Kinky were very much alike, really. Capable, intelligent, and for once, when there was a problem to be solved in Ballybucklebo, he hadn't had to come up with the answer. Kitty herself had put things to rights with Kinky.

O'Reilly leaned back in his chair, folded his hands across his full stomach, and sighed with contentment. It was going to be very pleasant having someone else to share the load when it came to sorting out non-medical things in the village.

"And I don't want to contradict you, Miss Kitty," Kinky said, "but I do believe the very best shop for wedding outfits is Robinson and Cleaver's."

"We'll try both," Kitty said, "and I'll take us to Isabeal's for lunch. And you'll not need to take the train up. I'll be staying here until Monday so we'll go up to town together after we've been to see Alice Moloney. I'm going to live here soon so I'd better get in the habit of doing my shopping in the village and I know Alice keeps some lovely things."

Masterful, Fingal thought, and more so because of

Kitty's obvious sincerity. Well done, Kitty, my love. Now let's see what Kinky says.

Kinky's words were measured, chosen it seemed with great care. "That is a very thoughtful thing to do, bye. Miss Alice will be pleased." Kinky cocked her head to one side. "I do believe, Miss Kitty," she said, "that you are going to fit into Ballybucklebo very well. Very well indeed, so."

37

Whose Dog Are You?

"Morning, Connie," Barry said as she joined him in a short queue in front of the newsagent's counter where Phyllis Cadogan was serving. "How's Colin?" Barry was on his way to a nearby home to see a little girl with what, over the telephone, had sounded like German measles. June was late for these kinds of infections, which were usually seen in the spring. It wasn't an urgent case, and Barry, while he was en route, was picking up a tin of Erinmore flake for O'Reilly, who was taking this morning's surgery.

"Och," she said, "his body's rightly mended, but his wee heart's broke, so it is." She switched her wicker shopping basket to her other arm. "He's done nothing but mope since Butch went away last week, you know. Mind you, he's powerful grateful to youse, sir. Colin and me both know that if Mister Bishop had got ahold of the wee craythur—" She drew a finger rapidly across her throat then pointed in her basket to show Barry a comic book with a garish-looking six-armed alien pointing a ray gun at an Earthman wearing a space suit complete with goldfish-bowl helmet. "Colin's been daft about science fiction, so he has, ever since he seen *Doctor Who* on the telly."

"I'll bet he was excited a couple of weeks ago when that American astronaut walked in space."

"That was dead amazing, so it was. You'd not get me out there in a space suit. Next thing you know them Yankees or maybe the Russians'll be putting a man on the moon. Unless—" She giggled. "—it really is green cheese. Anyroad, I thought a couple of these here comics might cheer Colin up when he gets home from school. He says when he grows up he wants to be an astronaut." She grinned at Barry. "I told him if he did he'd better be very good at his sums and do his homework."

"Good for you," Barry said. "I hated maths at school, but I wanted to be a doctor, so I stuck with it."

" 'Bout ye, Doc." Barry recognised Billy Brennan, a chronically unemployed labourer, who clutched a packet of ten Woodbine cigarettes. "Morning, Billy."

The queue inched forward.

The next man, having paid, moved aside. "Morning, Doc."

"Morning, Malcolm," Barry said to Constable Malcolm Mulligan, who was not in uniform so must have the day off.

"I'm glad I'm not working there, so I am." He showed Barry the front page of *The Daily Mirror* for Monday, June 21—a picture of a huge plume of black smoke and a banner headline screaming RIOTING IN ALGERIA. "Aren't we brave and lucky to live here?"

"We are that," Barry said. "Enjoy your day off."

As he spoke, Cissie Sloan left the counter with this morning's *Belfast Newletter* and a copy of the most recent *Woman's Own* under her arm. "Morning, Doctor."

"Morning, Cissie." Barry could see Cissie taking a deep breath, ready to launch into some conversational gambit, but fortunately Constable Mulligan was still speaking, so Barry paid him attention and she left.

"I will, so I will," said the constable. "I'm getting well rested for Doctor O'Reilly's wedding, so I am. I think, by the number of folks that've told me they'll be going to the party after the church, I'll need to have a wee word with my sergeant about getting more officers for crowd control, you know." He laughed. "There'll likely be a bigger mob than you'd get for a Glentoran, Linfield match at Windsor Park."

"Oh, I think you can handle us on your own," said Barry with a wide grin. He was still smiling after the constable had left and Phyllis said from behind the now-free counter, "Morning, Doctor."

"Morning, Phyllis." He put the tin of tobacco on the counter. "And two ounces of jelly babies, please." It was a trick he'd learned from O'Reilly, having a bag of sweeties in his pocket. They often made paediatric consultations much easier, and little Joyce Cunningham might enjoy a jelly baby despite her German measles.

Phyllis took down a large glass bottle from among a shelf of similar bottles, each containing unwrapped sweets—brandy balls, butterscotch, dolly mixtures, and liquorice allsorts. She used an aluminium scoop to ladle jelly babies onto a scale before decanting them into a paper bag and crimping its top. "That'll be two and nine altogether," she said.

Barry counted out the coins, a half crown and a thruppenny bit. "Thanks, Phyllis."

"Brave day, the day," she said. "I hope it'll be as lovely a day for the wedding. Miss O'Hallorhan popped in this morning with Kinky. They were on their way to see Miss Moloney, and then on up to Belfast. Miss O'Hallorhan wanted a magazine for Kinky to read on the train on her way home. She's very polite, that Dublin lady, so she is. I think we're going to enjoy having her living here. Mind you," she lowered her voice, "we'll have to get used to her *southern* accent."

"Don't you be so pass-remarkable, Phyllis Cadogan," Connie said over Barry's shoulder. "She's going to make a lovely Missus O'Reilly, so she is."

"Don't I know that, Connie?" Phyllis said. "And there's no harm in noticing her manner of speaking."

Barry, not wanting to linger and quite happy to leave the ladies to their debate, said, "I'd better be running along."

"And I hear you'll be running further soon," Phyllis said. "A wee birdie told me you're going to be leaving us?"

Barry had learnt months ago that going to any shop here was as much a social outing as a buying trip, and a glance at Connie assured him she wasn't in a hurry. "That's right, I'm going to Ballymena to take more training."

"Och, well," Phyllis said, "maybe you'll come back to us when you've finished?"

"I might," Barry said.

"I think you should. If you don't, that nice Miss Nolan's going to miss you." Phyllis winked at Barry.

"Well . . . I . . . that is—" Barry blushed. He'd not heard from Sue since last Tuesday.

"Run you on, Doctor dear," Phyllis said, "sure I'm only pulling your leg." She turned to Connie. "More of those comics? You'll have wee Colin's head turned. He'll be seeing Martians dancing round our Maypole next, so he will."

"Och," said Connie good-naturedly, "if he does, he'll likely think they're leprechauns. Martians are green, you know."

Barry heard the two women laughing and the little bell on the door tinkling overhead as he left the shop.

He had only gone a few paces when he bumped into Maggie and Sonny Houston.

Sonny lifted his homburg.

"Good morning, Doctor Laverty, dear," Maggie said, and smiled.

Maggie had her false teeth in and was wearing her usual long skirt and boots. Her flower of the day in the band of her straw boater was a red geranium.

"Morning," he said. "Good to see you both."

"And you, Doctor," Sonny said. "And how is that nice Miss Nolan? I've some very interesting news for her."

Barry shrugged. "I've not seen her for a few days. She's very busy with some work she's doing for civil rights."

"Would that be that new group, the Campaign for Democracy in Ulster?" Sonny asked.

Barry shook his head. "No, it's the Campaign for Social Justice." And they're more important than having dinner with me, he thought, trying not to feel bitter.

"I wish them all well," Sonny said. "I do hope that both groups can succeed here in the north. I've been getting much more optimistic about the overall future for the two Irelands ever since Sean Lemass, the Taioseach, came up from Dublin and had lunch with our Ulster prime minister, Terence O'Neill, back in January."

Maggie tugged at Sonny's sleeve and said, "Sonny Houston. I'm sure Doctor Laverty is on important business. He's not got all day to stand here, both legs the same length, colloguing about politics. And we've a clatter of beef heart to buy at Campbell's butcher's and then we've to take a run-race down to Bangor to the pet shop."

Sonny smiled at his wife. "We do indeed." He turned to Barry. "You'll remember our Missy, who was expecting a litter of puppies when you and Miss Nolan visited at the end of May?"

Barry did recall the rotund little dog. "I do."

"She dropped her litter the same day you and Miss Nolan came round," said Maggie. "Four lovely wee puppies. They're wee dotes, so they are. We started weaning them a couple of weeks back."

"Five adult dogs and four pups eat a lot," Sonny said. "Tom Campbell gets us beef hearts for next to nothing and we get puppy feed in Bangor."

Barry glanced back through the door of the newsagent's. He could see Connie and Phyllis still in deep conversation. "Have you found homes for the pups yet?" he asked.

Sonny frowned. "Not yet, but they won't be ready to leave their mother for another week and a half."

"Can you wait for just one minute?"

"Aye, certainly," Maggie said. "If you can, sir."

"Back in a tick." Barry headed for the newsagent's and had just reached for the door when it opened. "Connie," he said. "I'm glad you're still here. It might be a daft notion, but would you like a puppy for Colin?"

She frowned. "I never thought of that. Boys-a-dear, I know he'd love one, so he would."

"You know Sonny and Maggie Houston."

"Och, sure, Doctor, everybody does." She waved at them.

"Their bitch has just whelped. Come and say hello." Together they walked the few paces.

Sonny tipped his hat. "Good morning, Mrs. Brown."

Maggie grinned.

"I've been telling Connie about your pups."

"My wee boy, Colin," Connie said, "he just lost his—" Connie glanced at Barry long enough for him to give a small warning shake of his head. The fewer people who knew about Colin's ferret the better, he thought. "Och, it's a long story," she said, "but I know he'd love a puppy."

"And we'd be quare nor happy for to give him one . . . or two. Their ma's just a wee dog, so she is," Maggie said.

"I'd surely like one," Connie said, "but I'd have to ask his daddy, you know. Lenny'd have to make a kennel, and a pup would have to be looked after proper. Colin's going on ten, but he'd need our help, and Lenny's dead busy just now, you know."

Barry glanced at his watch. German measles wasn't a life-threatening emergency, but it was time he was getting on. "Can I leave the three of you to sort out the details?" he said.

"Of course," Sonny said, "and Doctor Laverty,

when you and Miss Nolan are free, please bring her round. I got my cross bearings yesterday and I'm close to being certain I know where to find a Neolithic structure not far from here."

38

The Wreck of the Hesperus

"Staaaarboaaaard!" The helmsman of the little red-hulled racing dinghy shouted across the choppy waters of Ballyholme Bay.

Barry turned and yelled from where he'd been sitting on *Glendun*'s deck, peering past the bows. "In case you didn't hear, skipper, he's letting us know he has the right of way." *Glendun*'s skipper, John Neill, was going to have to give the smaller boat sea room and Barry, Barbara Orr, and her husband, Ted, and the rest of the crew would have to be ready to change course. The "rule of the road" was absolute if collisions were to be avoided.

As John changed *Glendun*'s direction, Barry felt the heeling lessen, heard the sails flap as they spilled wind and the boat slowed. Now the sail no longer shaded him from the sun and he had to squint to see in the glare.

A gorse-scented breeze was coming across from Ballymacormick Point and according to the wind gauge was blowing at ten knots, gusting to fifteen. The short choppy waves were limned with white. Barry felt the sting of spray on his cheek and could taste the salt.

The whole of Ballyholme Bay was alive with yachts of various shapes and sizes, multicoloured sails jockeying for position, trying to be first across the start line when a miniature cannon signaled the start of each class's race. Thursday, June 24, was a racing night.

Spray flying from her bows, waves slapping against her, the little red-hulled dinghy's course never varied, tearing toward *Glendun*. Barry could see the class symbol, a bell, and her number on the mainsail. The little boat's helmsman and crew both lay backward, their feet in inboard straps, bodies out over the side of the boat as they used their weight to counter the force of the wind. The small craft heeled alarmingly. Barry remembered with fondness his own dinghy, *Tarka*, which he'd sold shortly before he qualified in order to raise the money to buy his secondhand Volkswagen. He grinned. He'd tipped *Tarka* over more than once, but capsizing was part of the dinghy sailor's lot. And serious racing sailors had no time for the encumbrance of bulky, kapok-stuffed life jackets. You had to be a good swimmer or trust in nearby boats.

"Fair winds, Dennis," John bellowed. It was then that Barry recognised Dennis Harper's *Wave Dancer*.

With spray flying in iridescent sheets from her stem, *Wave Dancer* sped past the bigger yacht's bows and Barry caught a glimpse of Sue Nolan. Locks of her hair had escaped from under a toque and were streaming aft, telltale indicators of the wind's direction. He swallowed. All through this past winter and spring she'd been taking a learn-to-sail course with Dennis, a lawyer and a friend of her older brother. Now she was crewing on *Wave Dancer*. Barry wondered, a little bitterly, if Dennis had taught Sue about banjo bolts recently. Then he remembered O'Reilly trying not to laugh when he'd been told about Sue's remark. Barry had laughed—then, but somehow couldn't bring himself to smile now.

"Wake up, crew," John roared.

Barry was dragged back to the present by the sharp command and the flogging of the sail. Now that Dennis's dinghy had passed, John had put *Glendun* on course again so she could pick up speed, but for her to do that her foresail must be properly trimmed. By Barry. "Sorry, John." Barry hauled on a rope and as he did the sail flattened and stopped flapping. *Glendun* heeled and moved forward.

"Five minutes to start," John called. "On your toes, everybody."

Barry looked ahead, but from where he sat, *Wave Dancer*—and Sue Nolan—were hidden behind the sails. It might be hackneyed, he thought, but the old expression "ships that pass" seemed singularly appropriate. Just nine days ago, he'd been wondering aloud to O'Reilly about whether he meant as much to Sue as she was starting to mean to him. He'd planned to get an answer that night over dinner, but her refusal to forgo a bloody CSJ committee meeting— He shook his head. He'd said he'd call, but he'd been hoping she would take the lead and call him. She hadn't and now he was beginning to realize that he probably wasn't ever going to be more in her life than a friend. A friend whose company could be enjoyed—unless something more important came up.

The wind whipped John's next order away, but there was still lots of time to the start. Barry let his thoughts return to Sue Nolan. He'd not, as he'd hoped, seen her in the clubhouse earlier today and might not get a chance later. He sighed. Ships that pass—and perhaps it was better this way? He could cut his losses before he became any more involved. He ground his teeth. As with a patient in limbo before getting a definite diagnosis, it was the uncertainty that was the killer.

"Barry," John roared.

Bugger. Barry had missed the order to change course and hadn't let his sail cross the boat. Now the helm was telling the boat to go one way and the sail was demanding she go the other. The opposing forces had stalled the yacht, which was beginning to drift backward.

Bang. That was their start gun. Shite.

By the time the manouevrings were finished to get

Glendun on course and across the start line, the other six Glen class yachts all had a five-minute lead.

Barry was furious that his preoccupation with the young woman had cost his crew a good start and blunted his enjoyment of what would be his last day's sailing for some time. He did not know if what he felt for Sue was love, let alone true love, but he did know that whatever it was that he was feeling, its course, like *Glendun*'s, was not running smoothly.

An hour later *Glendun*'s crew had worked the boat to her limits, but because of Barry's early inattention had not managed to catch up. They were trailing behind their competitors and were the last keelboat heading for the finish and home.

On the final leg, the wind freshened. The big boat carved through the waters, making an audible hiss as water streamed along the hull. Barry, legs spread wide, had to jam his feet against the side of a deck hatch. *Glendun* was heeling so much the mast was at thirty degrees to the sea and he was nearly vertical. The wind combed through his hair, standing it on end, and he had to duck as a wave broke into the cockpit. He came close to whooping his exhilaration out loud.

He looked ahead to the dinghy fleet speeding past their slower big sisters. That had been fun, he thought, when I used to do that. The small boats had started later than the keel boats, and unlike yachts with fixed keels could, if the wind and seas were favourable, plane on their flat bottoms like surfboards with sails and reach amazing speeds.

A voice followed by a deep laugh came over the water. Dennis Harper's red-hulled *Wave Dancer* was tearing past. Her skipper proffered the end of a rope. "Need a tow, John?"

"Bugger off, Dennis," John roared back with a grin. "See you in the clubhouse. You can buy my crew a round."

Sue Nolan waved and Barry hoped it was at him. He waved back. He knew the course well. At their present rate of sailing, an hour should see *Glendun* across the finish line, at her moorings, and her crew taken off by the club launch to go ashore. The dinghies would be home even sooner, but at least as John had now arranged to meet Dennis, there was a chance Barry would see Sue. Would he get a chance to talk to her alone, and if he did, what was he going to say? He'd an hour in which to make up his mind, but, damn it all, he wanted to know for sure whether he was wasting his time with this vivacious, very lovely schoolmistress. Would it be worth trying to put their differences about politics behind them and see how deeply their feelings went for each other? Give things another chance? He smiled. Maybe he'd have to become more of a political activist if that was what it would take to win her back. Maybe—

Barry had to clutch a winch as a sudden gust made *Glendun* heel away from him until her masthead seemed as if it might scrape the water. He tingled. With the weight of the keel, there was no real chance of capsizing. But the yacht should be brought up to a more vertical position. Another wave broke green over the bows. Barry ducked, but felt the chill water trickling under his oilskin collar and down his back. He needed no bidding to slacken sail. "'A life on the ocean wave / a home on the rolling deep,'" Barry sang off-key. This excitement, the sudden rush of fear that was mastered, wind in the rigging, water tearing past the hull, this was why he loved to sail. He filled the yacht's canvas as the gust passed. "'Give me the flashing brine / the spray and the tempest's roar—' Oh, shite."

Ahead, that same strong gust of wind had caused the smaller *Wave Dancer* to shudder, and rear. Helmsman and crew hurled themselves backward, straining to lever the dinghy upright, sails thrashed in a desperate attempt to spill the wind and reduce the pressure. But Barry knew, because he'd done it before, that the little boat was capsizing. "Man overboard," he yelled, and waited to obey John's orders as any thoughts of racing were banished. The skipper immediately began to set *Glendun* to bring her alongside the capsized vessel in case they needed help.

"Everybody," John yelled, "man overboard drill. You all know what to do. We've practised often enough."

Glendun began to come abreast of *Wave Dancer*. The dinghy's sails were flat on the water. Dennis

had clambered onto the side of the hull and was cling-
ing on, already trying to right the boat. But where
was Sue? Barry scanned the water carefully. Where
was she? The dinghy was slipping downwind, away
from where she had capsized. Where the hell was Sue
Nolan?

Ten yards away from where the boat had originally
been overturned, Barry spotted a commotion in the
water. Arms thrashed. Spray whipped away downwind. A head appeared and borne on the wind was a
reedy "Heeelllppp."

She couldn't swim.

"Ted," Barry called, as he pulled off his sea boots
and threw aside his oilskin jacket and his sweater,
"take this line." He handed over the end of the rope
controlling the jib, grabbed his life jacket from where
it lay beside him, stood up, and ignoring John's yell
of "Don't do it," cleared the guard rail, going head-
first overboard in as shallow a dive as he could
manage. Before he hit the water he glimpsed Sue
resurfacing ten yards away. He knew well enough that
the golden rule was *Never leave the ship for someone in the water.* But that was a rule for sailors, not
physicians. He'd forgotten how cold the waters of
Belfast Lough were. Already he could feel the icy fingers clawing at him. They'd probably not have to be
in the water for more than half an hour, but early hy-
pothermia would already be starting by then. Didn't
matter. Even if it was a stranger out there drowning,

Barry must try to help, and besides, who else but him knew about mouth-to-mouth resuscitation? And it looked like it was going to be needed long before the crew of *Glendun* could pluck Sue Nolan from the water.

Barry surfaced, hauling air into starved lungs. He oughed when a wave slapped in his face and he inhaled spray. He kicked both legs hard and forced his head and trunk upward so he could see over the intervening waves. The spray of Sue's next resurfacing was a beacon. The seas were too much for Barry's preferred freestyle, so he set off with a dogged breast stroke hampered by the life jacket, but he refused to let it go. He sensed the bulk of *Glendun* as she went past. Come for us soon, John.

Barry ploughed ahead, breath burning in his lungs, fingers and toes growing numb, muscles aching. He crested a wave and there in the trough, beneath the surface, he glimpsed something copper.

Two more strokes and he was over the spot. Barry exhaled so over-full lungs would not impede his descent and used the strokes of one arm to make himself sink, holding the waist-tie of the life jacket in his other hand. He was at the fullest extent to which he could submerge without letting go when he clutched something fibrous. With what felt like the last of his strength, Barry kicked toward the silver above, following the last of his own racing bubbles upward.

His head broke the surface and he inhaled a great

breath to the depths of him before dragging on Sue's tresses until her head broke water. He wrestled one of her arms through a loop of the life jacket and, ignoring the second loop, simply tied the waist strap tightly to her other arm across her chest so she'd float face up.

As they bobbed together on the waves, Barry could see *Glendun*'s mast and sails starting to come back. It took time to turn a big keel boat.

"Sue. *Sue.*" Not a sound. Her eyes were closed. Water trickled from a corner of her mouth. Barry forced her mouth open and let more water out, took a deep breath, pinched her nose, put his mouth over hers, and blew out his breath. Then he squeezed her chest as best he could and inwardly blessed the American doctors who had publicised their findings in 1960 about the value of direct artificial respiration. The Holger-Neilsen method he'd learnt in the Scouts and that had been taught to all other sailors in the club would have been useless here in the water. He repeated the process, his own lips as cold as hers. Again and again, the waves tossed them up and down, spray breaking over them.

He knew he was getting weaker, but then he saw a flickering of her eyelids. Her eyes opened and when she tried to inhale she collapsed in a paroxysm of coughing, but then managed a real breath. He tapped a new reservoir of strength. Thank goodness she was breathing on her own. After his resuscitative efforts he was winded.

The sun was blotted out by *Glendun*'s hull. Ted was leaning over the side bawling, "Grab this." A rope splashed into the water and Barry clutched the loose end. He struggled, had to let Sue go, dived and surfaced, having succeeded in running the rope under her armpits. He paused, caught his breath, then somehow, fingers trembling, managed to tie a bowline.

A second rope splashed beside him. "Grab on to that," Ted bellowed.

Barry let Sue go now that she was securely attached to the boat, and wrapped the rope round his waist. "Get her on board," he yelled. "I'm fine." He tied a knot and watched as Sue was hauled aboard like a drowned calf, water streaming in a cascade from her copper hair.

Barry waited for his turn. Dear God, let her be all right. He felt the rope tighten around his chest and bite into his armpits. He put both hands on it as he was dragged up the yacht's side and lowered into the cockpit beside where Sue lay, eyes wide, hair spread round her in a fan, chest heaving as she pulled in lungful after lungful of air.

He instinctively took her pulse. A hundred and ten, too fast, but regular and beating strongly.

He looked up. *Glendun*'s mainsail had been dropped. John was helming, Barbara handling the lines as the foresail filled and John pointed the yacht for home. "Where's Ted?" Barry asked.

"Below getting towels and blankets and putting the kettle on," John said. "We'll hoist the mainsail again when he's back on deck. I want to get you two ashore."

Barry looked ahead to where the red dinghy was scudding for home under mainsail alone. Dennis, as an experienced dinghy sailor, had been able single-handedly to right the small craft, but with less crew had reduced sail.

Barry saw Sue looking up at him. She mouthed, "Thank you, Barry." He smiled back and despite the chattering of his teeth, his heart swelled and he was warmed inside.

Ted appeared on deck. He held on to a couple of blankets and handed a bath towel to Barbara. "Get Sue out of her wet clothes, dried off, and wrapped in a blanket. Barry. Here." He handed Barry a second towel.

As Barbara worked on Sue, Barry peeled off his sodden clothes, no time for modesty, towelled himself dry, then accepted and gratefully snuggled into the folds of a heavy blanket.

By the time he was sitting on a bench opposite a blanket-swaddled Sue, the crew had hoisted sail and *Glendun* was well under way for home.

Ted, who'd vanished below, reappeared carrying two steaming mugs. He handed one to Barry and one to Sue. "Tea," he said, "with lots of sugar. Get that into you."

Barry sipped. God, but the drink was wonderfully warming. He raised his mug to Sue. "This is good stuff," he said, "but when we've got ashore and into dry clothes, Sue Nolan, I'm going to prescribe the O'Reilly cure."

"What's that?" John asked.

"Large hot whiskies for two." And, he thought, to be taken somewhere in privacy now he'd fulfilled his Hippocratic obligations and was simply a young man who wanted to know where he stood with this young woman.

Sue managed a weak smile and a laugh. "Whatever you say, Doctor."

"Good." Barry wanted his nagging question answered.

"And Barry," she said quietly, "thanks again."

She was regarding him solemnly with those emerald-green eyes, and her copper hair was starting to dry into long, wavy plaits. He wanted to be alone with her, to have her accept another invitation for dinner or lunch this coming Saturday. It would sure as hell be a good time and a good place to start getting that answer.

39

He That Seeketh Findeth

"W-day minus seven," said O'Reilly. He was finishing a plate of scrambled eggs garnished with fried tomatoes and mushrooms and a rasher of bacon. Pity Kinky had stopped serving the usual plate of porridge to start breakfast and had cut the number of pieces of bacon down to one, but she'd become as serious about his calories as a trainer about the feeding of a thoroughbred racehorse. He was beginning to think that when she and Kitty had gone shopping for bridal outfits five days ago they had decided on a united front to wage war on his diet. He helped himself to a second cup of tea. "I must say I'm looking forward to next Saturday, Barry. Big changes coming for both of us."

"I know," Barry said. "I'll be starting my new job next Thursday."

O'Reilly buttered a slice of toast. "There's bugger all point you charging off to Ballymena in darkest County Antrim and haring back down here for my wedding three days later. I spoke to Professor Dunseath yesterday. He's agreed to have you start on Monday, July fifth, not Thursday, so you can stay here until Sunday, then drive up."

"That's a lot more convenient. Thanks, Fingal." Barry held out his cup.

O'Reilly poured, and ignored the thanks. "I'm relying on you as my best man," he said. Just, he thought, as I've come to rely on you in the practice. With complete confidence.

Barry, who was behind in the scrambled egg stakes, looked up and said rather than sang, in a poor imitation of Stanley Holloway, "'Oim gettin' married in the mawnin'. Get me to the church on toime—'"

O'Reilly laughed and said, "It is a bit daunting. I can empathize with Alfred P. Doolittle—"

"Character in the Shaw play *Pygmalion* turned into a musical, *My Fair Lady*—"

"Ah, but did you know that Ovid in his poem *Metamorphoses* described a sculptor named Pygmalion who fell in love with the sculpture he had carved?"

Barry choked on a piece of scrambled egg, held up one hand, grinned, and finally managed, "Okay, okay, I submit. I always thought Ovid had something to do with eggs. God, but I'm going to miss working with you, Doctor Fingal ·Flahertie O'Reilly, M.B., B.Ch., B.A.O. Duelling quotes games, chucking malingerers into rosebushes, 'Never let the customers get the upper hand,' talk to patients in a language they understand, Jameson's instead of sherry. With all due respect, you are definitely, absolutely, and as Donal would say, tee-totally one of a kind."

O'Reilly smiled. "Actually, Barry, my friend, we all

are. Every single one of us. And over the last year I've seen you come to realise it, and above all that's what makes you a damn fine GP. It's the individual patient who counts. The disease is secondary."

"You've taught me that . . . thank you, Fingal." There was sincerity in the young man's voice.

"Rubbish," O'Reilly said. "You're a quick study, that's all, and if we don't have time in the next few days, because this whole wedding thing's getting to be like a snowball rolling downhill—" He held out his hand, which Barry shook. "—I want to thank you now for all the help you've been here for the last year and wish you the very best of success if, after you've sampled it, you do decide to pursue specialising." O'Reilly knew he didn't have to remind Barry that if he didn't like obstetrics and gynaecology, the job here would be his for the asking until January 1966—and he sincerely hoped Barry would take up the offer to come back.

"Thanks." Barry lowered his head. "I'm going to miss Number One and all the folks here in the village." He looked up and smiled. "And speaking of folks in the village, I've a bit of good news."

"Oh?"

Barry grinned. "I saw Sue at the Yacht Club on Thursday. Well, to be honest, I fished her out of Bally-holme Bay—"

"Good heavens. Is she okay?"

"She's fine, just fine. I've not had a chance to tell you, but I'm taking her for lunch today."

O'Reilly smiled. "I take it your heroic rescue means things are looking up?"

"They might be," Barry said.

"More power to your wheel. I'll keep my fingers crossed for you," Fingal said. "I hope it does work out." It was delightful to see Barry back to his own cheerful self.

"And you, Doctor O'Reilly dear," Kinky said, coming through the door, "are *not* going to have things work out if you miss your appointment with Miss Moloney."

O'Reilly saw Barry looking puzzled. "Kitty has asked me to wear my naval dress uniform. I tried it on. I was younger the last time I wore it. It's shrunk."

"By four inches at the waist, so," Kinky said, and raised an eyebrow, "but Alice is a fine seamstress and you've an appointment this morning for a fitting, sir." She began clearing the table. "I'd appreciate it," she said, "if one of you gentlemen could acquaint me with your call system for this weekend and for the days to come. It does seem to have become what I hear English folks call 'ad hoc.'"

"Sorry, Kinky," O'Reilly said. "I'm doing this weekend. It'll be my last for a month." He chuckled. "Kitty's coming down here later. Says she's things to do in Belfast this morning." He glanced at Kinky.

"She does. In Robinson and Cleaver's, and when you see what she's bought there I think you'll be very pleased, sir." Kinky's smile was one of deep satisfaction. "But you'll have to bide until next Saturday. It does be very unlucky for the groom to see the bride's wedding outfit before the ceremony, so."

O'Reilly pretended to be disappointed. He grunted, then said, "At least I've been let in on the secret of my honeymoon. Feherty's, the Bangor travel agent, is making the arrangements. We're going to Rhodes."

"Getting another Colossus, are they, Fingal, in a let-out uniform?" Barry said, and both he and Kinky laughed.

"Less," said O'Reilly, "of your lip," but he joined the merriment. "And there's a nice young lass, Doctor Jennifer Bradley, who's been doing locums for a couple of years. She'll be starting this Wednesday as your replacement, Barry. We'll need to show her the ropes before you leave and I head off to the Med. She's experienced enough to cope on her own until I get back. July's not usually a busy month."

"So it'll be yourself this weekend, sir," said Kinky. "Grand, so." She turned to Barry. "And what will you be up to today, Doctor Laverty?"

"I'm going to pick Sue up," he said. "I'm taking her to The Widow's in Bangor for lunch then Sonny Houston has a puppy for Colin Brown. Connie says her husband's given the go-ahead, spoken to Sonny, and asked him to pick one. It's all to be a great surprise for Colin, but I'd like to nip out to the Houstons, cast an eye on the beast."

"You do that, Barry," O'Reilly said, and thought, By God, I do hope you come back in January, son.

You're getting to be so like me. This damn place is getting under your skin just the way it got into my heart. You could start filling my shoes tomorrow, he chuckled to himself as he rose to go and see Alice, but not my bloody let-out trousers. But then, Barry hadn't had the benefit of nineteen years of Kinky Kincaid's cooking.

Barry parked on the road outside the cast-iron gate in a low stone wall. "Just a minute," he said to Sue as she started to open her door. Thursday evening, after the race, the crowded clubhouse had not been a place for a heart-to-heart. She'd been all smiles when he'd collected her today but had kept the conversation at a superficial level during lunch. He wanted, now they were completely alone, to talk about *them*.

She turned to face him.

He put a hand on each of her shoulders, looked into her eyes, bent, and kissed her. When they parted, he said, "And that's because you are very kissable, Sue Nolan." He felt as excited as a sixteen-year-old who had, for the first time, kissed a girl. "And you're a damn sight warmer than the last time I put my lips on yours."

She returned the kiss, then said, "I never thought I'd be grateful for getting myself half-drowned." She glanced away. "You know, Barry, I'd, well, I'd pretty much made up my mind that I really couldn't . . . and shouldn't . . . be bothered with a man who refused to see the injustices all around. So I'd simply let things fade between us."

"I'm sorry," he said. "I did try to explain that night at your place. I just don't think doctors should take political sides." I hope she's not going to start preaching another sermon, and I hope she's not going to say, "Thank you for fishing me out, but I still couldn't care for you."

She smiled. "I can accept that. And it's hard to get cross with someone who's saved your life."

Barry lowered his head then looked at her and said, "Sue, it's not very romantic to tell you, but I'm not a knight in shining armour. I did what anyone should have."

She looked back at him and shook her head. "Not true," she said. "I've taken the sailing course. They drummed it into us . . . never, never, never go into the water even if someone is drowning."

"All right," he said, "I did what any doctor should have."

She smiled and reached over to kiss him again. "And I understood that, and I think that's when I realised that doctors aren't always like other people. You risked your life—"

Barry smoothed his tuft, blushed, and started to say, "It wasn't—"

"It was, Barry Laverty. You could have been drowned. Somebody who takes their professional responsibilities so seriously is entitled not to become too partisan in Ulster if that's what they honestly believe they should do. If they've a reason for being that way. It's not that they don't care."

"Your friend Peter Gormley's a surgeon. He's on your side."

"I know," she said. "That's why at first I thought you were wrong, were sitting on the fence, but you've convinced me that you're the kind of man who doesn't make a fuss, simply practices what he believes. I respect your professionalism, Barry." She kissed him again, a light, lingering kiss that left him breathless. "I have done ever since you looked after that little lad with skinned knees."

"Art O'Callaghan," he said, remembering the boy who'd fallen in the schoolyard a couple of months ago. Barry felt as if shackles had been struck from his ankles. He was free to skip, run, tell her how happy he was. "Thank you, Sue," he said. "Thank you very much."

"I could," she said, "start getting fond of you, Doctor Laverty."

"And I you, Miss Nolan." He kissed her, drew away, and said as he opened the door, "Come on. Let's go and see a man about a dog . . . literally."

"Stay, Max," Sue said to the springer in the backseat.

"One thing, Sue," Barry said. "I know your kids start their summer holidays on Wednesday. Could you possibly stay for a few more days before you go home to Broughshane? I'd like to take you to Fingal and Kitty's wedding."

"I'd enjoy that very much," she said, "and my land-lord's pretty decent. He knows I'll want the place back in September. I'm sure he'll let me stay."

"Great," Barry said. "Now let's go and see Sonny."

They walked along the garden path, through air perfumed with a mixture of mown hay and lavender, which grew in wild profusion in flower beds bordering the low stone wall. Overhead a flock of green plover crying *pee-whit, pee-whit* staggered across the sky. The clicking of Sue's heels on the flagstones was nearly drowned out by the humming of honeybees.

Sonny straightened up from where he was clipping a tea rose from a bloom-burdened bush. "Doctor Laverty. Sue. How lovely to see you both. Here," he said, offering her the flower. "Please take this," and as she accepted, he bent, clipped another, and said, "And this one's for Maggie."

"Thank you," Sue said.

"We've come to see the pups," Barry said.

"In that case, let's go round the back first. I've built a run for mother and her litter. The other dogs keep trying to pinch the puppies' meals."

They skirted the house and Sonny's car.

"I think I've more to show you, Miss Nolan, than pups. I believe I'm on to a remarkable neolithic find not far from here."

Whatever Sue said was drowned out by a series of yips and barks coming both from inside the house and from a roomy enclosure with a low chain-link fence and a green-roofed kennel. The bitch lay on her side on the grass giving suck to two pups while the other two wrestled and snarled and yapped, stumbling over their too-big feet. Their coats were a short-haired mixture of black and deep brown. As far as Barry could tell, they were part Labrador, part terrier, and possibly, if their oversized ears were anything to go by, part beagle.

"They're adorable," Sue said.

"And nearly ready to leave their mother," Sonny said. He leant over the fence and lifted a squirming bundle. "I think this is the one for young Colin. Full of spunk."

"Just like Colin. He's in one of my classes, Sonny," Sue said. "At least he *was* a feisty little lad until his ferret had to go away." She reached out to pat the little dog's head and was immediately rewarded with a frenetic licking of her hand. "I think this fellah'll put a smile back on Colin's face and divilment back in his soul." She laughed and Barry revelled in the music of it. "That American was right," Sue said. "Happiness *is* a warm puppy." She raised one eyebrow and took his hand. "Among other things."

And Barry looked at her smile and thought, True. He hugged the thought.

The other pup was standing with its front paws on the wire, yelping and thrashing its tail as if to say, "Me. Me. Pay attention to me."

"All right," Sonny said, "here's your brother back." He set the little dog in the pen and immediately the wrestling match went to a second round. "Let's go in," he said, leading the way. "I'm sorry Maggie's not here, but I drove her into the village. She's gone for coffee with Cissie Sloan and Flo Bishop at Aggie Arbuthnot's."

Barry's moment of joy was pricked. Poor Aggie. For all Barry's good intentions he still hadn't helped her find work. There was some comfort in the "Big Doctor" being an old friend of O'Reilly's and having agreed to bend the rules and give Aggie another fortnight on "the sick," but then what? And Barry had precious little time now to do anything before he left.

"Come in. Come in," Sonny said, ushering them into the kitchen. "And if you give me your rose, Sue, I'll just be a tick popping it in water with Maggie's." Sonny smiled. "I give her one a day as long as the bushes are flowering."

A red rose for true love. One a day. What a beautiful idea, Barry thought, and wished it had been him who had given one to Sue.

"Done," said Sonny. "Now to business."

He took them to the dining room where a large map was spread on the table. "I'll not bother you with my primary sources, but suffice it to say I have confirmed that Sanctum Lignum was founded by Saint Lairseran, son of Nasca. Your tip was most helpful, Sue."

She smiled. "I'm delighted. So it *is* modern Holywood and you already know your site is three miles east?"

Sonny nodded furiously. "And it's getting even better.

In the papers of Bangor Abbey I unearthed two more references to the structure I'm looking for and its distance west of Bangor Abbey. And they both refer to it by name. Dun Bwee. The yellow fort, so it must be a *lios* or a *ráth*. I've plotted them on this half-inch-to-the-mile, Sheet Four, Ordnance Survey map. Look."

Barry and Sue craned forward. Taking their centres from the site of the abbeys in Bangor and Holywood, two circles, each the distances to scale that Sonny had gleaned from his references, had been pencilled on the map with a geometry compass. He'd drawn a cross at the spot where the arcs briefly touched.

"X," said Sue, "marks the spot."

"I believe it does," said Sonny. "I did try statute miles and the arcs overlapped, but when I took 153 yards off both measurements the circles just kissed."

"How exciting." Sue's eyes shone. "You must be feeling very proud."

Sonny shook his head. "Not yet, my dear."

"Why not?" Barry asked.

"So far, it's all supposition until a properly conducted archaelogical dig can be arranged." He smiled. "I've got an appointment with the people at the Ulster Museum next Tuesday. I must say the chap I talked to on the phone sounded very enthusiastic."

"I really do hope you're right, Sonny," Sue said.

"Me too," Barry said. He leant forward. "And as a matter of interest, where exactly does 'X' mark in today's County Down?"

"There," Sonny said, pointing. "Between the limbs

of that awful hairpin bend on the main Bangor to Belfast Road. I've been there. It's an old cottage with a thatched roof and a sold sticker on the for-sale sign. There's a mound in the back garden. I'm sure that's what I'm looking for."

"And you said it was called Dun Bwee?" Barry said, taking another look at Sonny's map. There it was, a large X directly over the centre of the land bordered by the hairpin bend. "Sonny . . . you just may have given Doctor O'Reilly a *very* timely wedding present."

40

Who Reads Incessantly

"So that's the setup, Doctor Bradley," O'Reilly said to the young woman sitting beside him in the car. "Barry showed you how the surgery works, and you've had the grand tour of the village and the townland this afternoon, seen a couple of the customers in their homes. Grand mal epilepsy and pyelonephritis . . . not the most common things we're called out to see."

"But interesting cases," she said and smiled, "and, the second one? I've never been inside such a lovely cottage."

"It was there before the 1845 potato famine," O'Reilly said, "but by local standards it's one of the newer developments. The townland was apparently inhabited in the Stone Age."

"Amazing," she said, "and your patients and their families were delightful people." Her accent was definitely from the Upper Malone Road where the better-off Belfast people lived. O'Reilly knew her father, Norman Bradley, a retired GP himself. He'd practiced on the Stranmillis Road. "It's been most interesting," she said, "and I'm sure I'll be able to find my way about soon. I do enjoy country practice. I spent the last six months in Ardglass, Doctor O'Reilly."

"You'll find Ballybucklebo much the same, and if you're not sure about anything ask Kinky. And except in front of the customers it's Fingal, Jennifer. We're not terribly formal here."

"Actually," she said, "I prefer Jenny."

"Jenny it is." He eased the Rover into the garage across the back lane. He got out and appraised the young woman while she walked round the car. Twenty-six, twenty-seven, five foot six, blonde hair cut with bangs, or what the locals called a donkey fringe, low on a smooth forehead and sweeping inward to curve under her jaw. Blue eyes with a hint of mischief, small nose, curved lips.

Her navy blue suit exuded a no-nonsense, business-like look. He noticed that she wore no jewellery and very little makeup. Her stethoscope stuck out of one jacket pocket and she carried a battered-looking doctor's bag in one hand. It had probably belonged to her father.

"Let me take your bag," O'Reilly said. Gentlemen were expected to carry loads for ladies.

"I can manage," she said and smiled, "but thanks for offering."

O'Reilly opened the back gate. Arthur Guinness yelped happily and trotted over to welcome the boss home and greet the newcomer. "Meet Arthur Guinness," O'Reilly said. "Be careful he doesn't beat you to death with his tail."

"He's very friendly," she said, patting Arthur's head. "I like dogs."

"So do I," said O'Reilly, "especially that great lummox." He opened the kitchen door and stood aside to let her go in.

Kinky was lifting a tray of sausage rolls from the oven. As ever her kitchen smelled delicious. "Doctors," she said, putting her burden on the counter. "I'm starting to get organised for Saturday afternoon, so, and Doctor Bradley, dear, I have your room made up and your things taken up. It'll be yours until Sunday and then, so as you can have the landing bathroom to yourself, we'll be moving you to the attic bedroom after Doctor Laverty leaves." She shook her head. "It does not seem like a whole year, at all, since he moved into it, so."

O'Reilly detected a wistful tone and knew how fond Kinky had become of the young man.

"I'm sure I'll be very comfortable. Thank you, Mrs. Kincaid," said Jennifer Bradley.

"And where's Barry?" O'Reilly asked.

"Upstairs," said Kinky, "champing at the bit for yourself to get home, sir. I know you've important visitors coming."

"We have," said O'Reilly. He spoke to Jenny. "Barry and I have a meeting with a man from Belfast and, I think, a local councillor." That's what McCluggage had agreed to when O'Reilly had phoned the man on Monday with an offer to save him money—provided he brought any partners along. "We'll be meeting in the lounge, so I'm going to have to ask you to wait in your room or the dining room until it's over, and if there are any calls deal with them. We're pitching you in at the deep end, I'm afraid, seeing you've only been here since this morning."

She smiled, laugh lines at the corners of her eyes. "Deep end? I'm quite a good swimmer, Fingal," she said. "I've been doing locums for two years. I'll be fine."

It was simply a statement of fact, not a boast, and it impressed O'Reilly. "Fair enough," he said, "now come on up to the lounge where you can take the weight off your feet. No need for you to leave there until my guests arrive." He led the way.

They met Helen in the hall. She had her coat on, and his copy of Dickens's *Our Mutual Friend* tucked under one arm. "Helen Hewitt," O'Reilly said, "this is Doctor Bradley. She'll be moving in today and getting to know the place. Taking over from Doctor Laverty."

"Doctor Bradley, pleased til meet you," Helen said.

"How do you do, Helen?"

"Helen's been working as our receptionist," he said, and, he thought, almost certainly following in your footsteps, Jenny Bradley, when medical school starts in September. He'd know for sure by tomorrow. "She'll be leaving us on Friday," he said. "We're going to miss her."

"And I'm going to miss Number One," Helen said. "And I don't want to make no fuss about going, but thank you very much for the work since May, sir." She grinned. "It'll not be as much fun behind the counter in a sweetie shop, but the wages aren't bad."

"I'm sure something better will show up soon," O'Reilly said, and kept his voice level and his face expressionless.

Helen smiled.

"I just wish it was Kinky'd said that." She lowered her voice and said seriously to Jenny, "Mrs. Kincaid has the sight, you know."

"Really?" said Jenny. "How unusual."

O'Reilly detected no hint of Jenny being patronising. Good. "She is a most unusual woman," he said. "You'll come to see that in the months ahead."

"I'll be running on," Helen said. "Doctor O'Reilly, I'll be sure to get this here book read before I leave on Friday." She showed it to Jenny. "It belongs to the doctor. He's been very generous with his library, but I don't want to take advantage."

"You can't go at Dickens like a bull in a china shop. Take all the time you need. Away off now and we'll see you tomorrow, Helen," O'Reilly said. "Come on, Jenny." He headed upstairs, remarking as they climbed, "Kinky's not the only unusual woman here. Helen has been fielding phone calls, doing housework, job hunting, and systematically going through my entire collection of Dickens novels since she started with us in the spring." He chuckled. "She's even made a few side trips into the vagaries of X-ray crystallography. She's not one to let the grass grow under her feet."

"I'm impressed," Jenny said.

"So," said O'Reilly, "am I." He stood aside at the doorway.

Barry, cozily ensconced in an armchair, *Times* cryptic crossword on his lap, rose immediately she entered.

"Sit down please, Barry," she said.

"Thank you." He returned to the chair, taking a quick glance at the crossword.

"Actually, Fingal," Jenny said, "if you don't mind, I'll head on up to my room. I've some letters I want to write. Good luck with your meeting."

"I think, Doctor Bradley," O'Reilly said, "you are going to fit in at Number One; fit in very well indeed."

"I hope so. I'm soon going to be looking for a partnership," she said, regarding O'Reilly levelly.

She's certainly not backward in coming forward, O'Reilly thought, and admired the way she'd got to the point. He saw Barry's eyes widen, his forehead crease. It's a bit Machiavellian, O'Reilly thought, but it won't hurt to let Barry know there could be competition. "And I've got used to having help." He smiled at Barry, whose frown deepened, and said, "So I might be looking for a partner a year from now, but I have to be honest, Jenny. I'm not sure how the country patients are going to take to a woman. Usually they mistrust what they call 'lady doctors.' We'll have to see how you are accepted here." And I'll have to see how I get on as the only man in a household of three women, he thought.

She laughed and said, "I've lived through nine years of that mistrust since I started medical school. It doesn't bother me, and you'd be amazed how quickly most of the patients realise that us 'lady doctors' don't have horns."

"Good for you," O'Reilly said, "but that's not the only constraint, and so there's no misunderstanding, I've promised Barry the job in January if he finds he doesn't like being a specialist."

"I understand," she said. "I'll still do the best I can."

Barry's frown faded.

O'Reilly, warming to this self-sufficient young woman, said, "I know you will, but at least for this evening I hope the phone is quiet and you can get to your letters."

From below, the front doorbell rang.

"Thanks, Fingal. I'll be off," Jenny said, and left.

Kinky's footsteps, then a familiar voice roaring, "Where the hell's O'Reilly?"

"Please go upstairs, Councillor," Kinky said. "He's expecting you."

Perhaps not expecting, more like hoping, although he couldn't remember a time when he'd truly been hoping to see Bertie Bishop. This was a first. Still, his presence was as good as a signed and sealed confession that their tenuous suspicions were right. Given the way the man bellowed, though, how he was ever a "silent" partner was beyond O'Reilly.

41

They Lose It That Do Buy It

Barry stood with O'Reilly to greet their guests. Bertie led the way, and he did not offer to shake hands. He was accompanied by a stranger. The man of about forty was as skinny as Bertie was rotund, had a bowler hat perched on what looked to Barry to be a completely bald head, small ash-coloured eyes, and a dark, pencil-thin moustache on a narrow upper lip. He whipped off his hat.

"I'm Doctor O'Reilly and this is Doctor Laverty,"

O'Reilly said by way of introduction. "Pleased to meet you, Mister McCluggage. Won't you both please have a seat?" He indicated the two armchairs.

For the first time in the year he'd been here, Barry noticed, invited guests had not been offered a drink.

McCluggage smiled, it was an open smile, and replied amiably, "Likewise," and sat.

Bertie scowled and dumped himself into the other armchair.

As previously arranged, Barry took a third chair facing the two men. O'Reilly stood leaning against the fireplace.

"You let me do the talking, Ivan," Bertie said. "I've had dealings with these two before."

McCluggage narrowed his eyes. "All right." He crossed his legs and set his bowler on his lap.

"First things first, O'Reilly," Bishop said. "I want this on the table here and now. Youse told Ivan you'd not say nothing unless he brought his partner. That's me, but we want no word of that getting out, do you hear? Not a whisper."

Barry noted that O'Reilly inclined his head but didn't speak.

"Right. Youse phoned Ivan and told him youse could save him a brave wheen of money. Let's hear what you'se've to say." He folded his arms across his chest. "And it had better be bloody good, so it had."

O'Reilly made a show of lighting his briar.

"Och, Jasus, would youse get on with it, O'Reilly?" Bertie hunched forward in his chair.

"It's true," O'Reilly said. "There's a lot at stake. Mister McCluggage, may I first ask you a few questions?"

"Aye, certainly." The man's voice was a pleasing tenor. "Fire away."

"Are you trying to purchase a cottage I once thought was Dawn Bwee but now know is called Dun Bwee?"

McCluggage glanced at Bishop before saying slowly, "Aye."

"Have you put down a deposit?"

"Aye. Three hundred pounds."

This man is not going to win any competitions for loquacity, Barry thought. Typical Ulster businessman.

"And will you be completing the deal soon?"

"The morrow."

"I'm glad we've got to you in time. I'd strongly advise you not to."

"And lose my deposit?" McCluggage half-turned his head away and regarded O'Reilly sideways.

"Pay you no heed to him," Bishop snarled. "He's only trying to get youse to back off so a local layabout can buy it. If you back out we'll lose a profit of seven hundred pounds—"

"I know *exactly* what we'll lose, Bertie. I'm not stupid," McCluggage said, "but if we go ahead there's another one thousand seven hundred to pay. I'd like to hear what the doctor has to say."

Barry thought the man sounded quite calm, but that "*we'll* lose," and "if *we* go ahead" was interesting.

"Buy it and you'll be throwing good money after bad," O'Reilly said quietly.

"For God's sake, O'Reilly—"

It was as far as Bishop got. McCluggage held up one hand. His voice was measured with a touch of steel. "Wheest, Bertie," he said. "Go ahead, please, Doctor."

Barry recognised that not only was Bertie a silent partner, for all his bluster, he was the junior partner too.

"Have you ever seen the property?"

McCluggage shook his head. "It was just a business deal." He looked across at Bishop. "Bertie thought it would be a good buy for a quick resale. I wasn't going to live in it."

More pieces are starting to fall into place, Barry thought.

"I've been there," O'Reilly said. "There's a big mound in the back garden."

"And what the hell does that have to do with the price of turnips?" Bishop demanded.

"Nothing," O'Reilly said, "but it has a very great deal to do with road straightening."

Bishop sneered, "I doubt you've ever seen a bulldozer at its work. It'll go through your mound like a hot knife through butter." Barry had a sudden urge to grin. Bertie was probably right that Fingal hadn't seen a working bulldozer, but the councillor was going to meet the equivalent of one head on. Right now.

"Correct." O'Reilly took a long count before continuing, "But it's common knowledge that the council wants to straighten the road—"

"And that was brung forward *after* Mister McCluggage put in his bid," Bertie rushed to add.

"I know that, Bertie," O'Reilly said, "but to come back to bulldozers, you're quite right, I've never seen one at work, but I *have* seen compulsory purchase orders stayed."

Bertie went scarlet. "What? Stayed? How? Why? What in the name of the sainted Jasus *and* all the saints are you talking about?"

"I'd like an explanation too," McCluggage said, "and Bertie, houl' your wheest and try to listen."

Bishop spluttered.

O'Reilly said levelly, "A local archaeologist has good reason to believe the mound contains important Stone Age artefacts. The Ulster Museum will be organising a dig."

Bishop leapt to his feet. "What? I don't believe a fecking word. Your head's a marley, O'Reilly. There's no feckin' Stone Age rubbish within fifty miles of here, so there's not."

"'Fraid there is," O'Reilly said, and inclined his head to Barry, "and you don't have to take my word for it."

Barry took his cue. "That's right. I've seen the evidence, it's pretty convincing, and I know the folks at the Museum are considering excavating the site right between the arms of the hairpin."

McCluggage pursed his lips. "That's a turn up for

the books." He stared at the councillor. "Bertie, I'm inclined to believe the doctors."

O'Reilly faced Bishop and said, apparently ignoring McCluggage, "Does the expression 'cease and desist' ring a bell, Bertie? There'll be no compulsory purchase, no big profit for the owner of the house. The house and property'll be made a historic site, which means very little can be done to it, besides changes for maintenance."

"I see. Thank you, Doctor." McCluggage turned on Bishop and said coldly, "You told me it was a sure thing."

"It was," Bertie blustered. "I knew it was. I'd arranged—" There was a pleading tone.

"If I were you, Mister McCluggage," O'Reilly announced, and Barry knew he was stirring the pot, "I'd wave good-bye to your deposit. It'll be cheaper in the long run."

"It'll not cost me a penny, Doctor," McCluggage said calmly.

Barry frowned. How could that possibly be?

"You got me into this, Bertie, you and your 'It's a sure thing as long as we keep our traps shut. Don't let people know we're partners. We'll split the cost of purchase and split the profit after the council buys the place to straighten the road.' When I put *our* money down I made sure that half that deposit's refundable. Guess whose half that's going to be?" He turned to O'Reilly. "I'm not sure *why* you've done it, Doctor

O'Reilly, but you've surely done me a big favour, so you have."

O'Reilly inclined his head.

Barry grinned, and not only at Bishop's discomfort. Two days ago O'Reilly had spoken to Dapper Frew, who had cleared things with the vendors, all hush-hush of course until after this meeting. They'd agreed that as they would be keeping the nonreturnable £150 from the deposit, they'd accept £1,550 from Donal and Julie instead of the £1,700 they'd originally offered.

Bertie said sulkily, "But half of that refund's mine. I should get seventy-five pounds."

"You can go and whistle for it, Bertie. Whose name's on the offer? Who's the refund cheque going to be made out to?"

"But . . . but—"

"And I'll tell you one thing more, Bertie Bishop. You told me before council met that you'd slipped Councillor Wilson fifty quid for proposing the roadworks so you could play the innocent and I could put in the offer on a sure thing."

Bertie was squirming in his chair like a fresh lugworm that had been impaled on a fisherman's hook.

"You can foot the bill for that too."

So Bertie had set the whole thing up. Knew in advance it was a shoo-in for him and McCluggage to make a quick substantial profit. "But that means I'm going to lose two hundred pounds," Bertie said.

Barry thought he sounded like a man on the verge of losing his firstborn child.

"Bertie," O'Reilly said, not unkindly, "if I were you, I'd swallow your loss gracefully." He nodded at Barry. "I have a witness to your scheme. I've no idea what the penalties are for breach of public trust, failure of fiduciary duty, bribing councillors for profit. Could be jail. And it wouldn't do Councillor Wilson any good either." He tutted. "I don't think making it common knowledge would help your next election campaign much, but perhaps that wouldn't be such a bad thing."

Bishop stuttered, "B-b-b-b-but you said at the very start today that not a word of this would get out."

"Sorry," said O'Reilly, "but did anybody hear me say that?"

All Barry remembered was a small inclination of O'Reilly's head.

After a suitable silence, Bertie seemed to rally. "Now, hang about, O'Reilly, youse doctors can't give out confidential information about your patients, so youse can't. I know that for a fact and I'm your patient, so I am." He held up the finger from which O'Reilly had drained pus last July. A smile started.

"True," O'Reilly said. "Very true."

"So," Bertie said smugly, "youse can't say nothing about me. I've got you, so I have."

It was as if this partial triumph over his nemesis almost made up for Bishop's impending financial loss. Bertie's expression was that of a small boy about to stick out his tongue and say "So there. Nyah, nyah, nyuh, nyah, nyah."

"Indeed, Bertie," said O'Reilly, "you are our patient and doctors must keep all *medical* information in confidence. But we're not Catholic priests after confession. We have no obligation not to divulge your worldly sins."

"Och, no," Bertie said, jerking an arm in front of his face as if to ward off a blow. "Och, no, youse wouldn't. Would youse?" His smile had vanished.

"Doctor Laverty?" O'Reilly asked.

"We could be persuaded to say nothing," Barry said.

"I hope so," McCluggage said. He scowled at Bertie. "I've my reputation to think of too, you know. I should never have let you talk me into this swindle."

Barry said, "You two are partners in the shirt factory?"

"Aye," McCluggage said, clearly ignoring Bertie's scowl. "Bad cess to it."

"And eight weeks ago you fired a woman called Aggie Arbuthnot?"

McCluggage nodded and said, "And you're the doctor who wrote her a line, asking if she could have a job sitting down?"

"I am, and I'm going to ask again." Barry watched McCluggage's face as he must be digesting the deeper implications of what Barry was suggesting.

"And if I say yes, you two'll keep your mouths shut about—?"

"Naturally," Barry said. "As long as there are no reprisals and you promise to treat her properly."

"I'll do that." McCluggage hadn't hesitated for a second.

Bertie snarled, "How can you, Ivan, you eejit? Where's the money coming from, for God's sake?"

McCluggage's pencil moustache went up at one side as his lip curled. "That's not a problem, Bertie." His voice was a low hiss. "As managing director, I've just made an executive decision, and seeing the secretary's my wife, you're out-voted." He turned to O'Reilly. "Doctor O'Reilly. You said you came to save me money. You have, and you've made me see what a greedy, unprincipled skiver I've been. I'm sorry. I owe you one, sir. Doctor Laverty, you needn't worry about Aggie. She's a bloody good worker. Been with the firm for years. I didn't want to let her go, but money is tight. All those man-made fibre shirts coming from overseas, you know." He scowled at Bertie and Barry understood who had made the decision to fire Aggie. "She can have a job as a buttonholer. I'll need to train her, but once she's ready it'll pay a bit more than a folder and she can work sitting down."

"Jesus, Ivan, where the hell are we going to get another hundred and eighty pounds a year? Use your loaf, for God's sake," Bertie said.

"I have," McCluggage said. "I told you I'd made a decision." His voice became pontifical. "Due to falling revenue, but the pressing need for a buttonholer, the junior director . . . that's you, Bertie, is reluctantly going to offer to take a pay cut of two hundred pounds a year, and the rest of the board, that's me and the missus, is going to accept his offer . . . or we'll vote him off the board. You and your bloody 'It's a sure thing as long as we keep our traps shut.' You're a right regal bollix, Bertie Bishop, so y'are. I'm only letting you stay on at all because I don't want to spend months feeling guilty about firing you. And we do need your capital in the company."

Barry watched Bertie turn puce, but keep his counsel. There was nothing more he could say.

"Now," said Ivan McCluggage, offering his hand first to O'Reilly and then to Barry, "we've a deal. Can one of you tell Aggie to come in on Monday?"

Barry nodded.

"And you'll say nothing about the house that we're not buying anymore?"

"You have our word," O'Reilly said. "As long as you withdraw your offer first thing tomorrow."

"I'll speak to your man Frew."

"Which'll save us the trouble, Doctor Laverty. Dapper'll know what to do." O'Reilly smiled.

"The vendors can keep half the deposit . . . one hundred and fifty pounds," McCluggage said, and looked at Bertie. "No skin off my nose."

O'Reilly turned to Barry. "Thank you for your help too," he said. "Now Bertie, Mister McCluggage, if you'll excuse us, Doctor Laverty and I were going to pop over to the Duck, but we'll not be offended if you don't join us. I'm sure you'll have other matters to discuss."

"Come on, Bertie," McCluggage said. "It's time we were going, and thank you both again, Doctors." McCluggage bowed to O'Reilly and Barry in turn, then strode from the room, Bertie scuttling behind like a chastened hound at its master's heels.

O'Reilly collapsed into an armchair beside Barry and took a huge puff from his pipe, said, "Thanks be, but that all worked out very agreeably. And Donal and Julie won't even need to know who fixed it. I prefer it that way."

"The Lord," said Barry, "and Doctor Fingal Flahertie O'Reilly both move in a mysterious way their wonders to perform."

"More or less by William Cowper, 1731 to 1800," O'Reilly said as he led the way to the stairs. "When are you going to tell Aggie? She'll be coming to the do on Saturday. You could speak to her then."

"If you don't mind. It's your big day after all." He went downstairs at Fingal's shoulder.

"Och," said O'Reilly, "wait 'til then, Barry. Probably not a bad idea to get things confirmed from Dapper that McCluggage is a man of his word before we tell her. Wouldn't want to get her hopes up before we're absolutely sure. Tell her at the wedding. There'll be enough happiness to go round." He waited then said, "How do you feel?"

"About what?"

"That's the second nonmedical problem you've fixed all by yourself since you came here. Saving Butch was the first."

Barry mulled that over, then said, "Very good. So good in fact," he held open the front door, "that when we get to the Duck, I'll let you buy the first pint."

42

Use the Gods' Gifts Wisely

Barry rose when he saw who Kinky was ushering into the dining room. Jenny Bradley remained sitting.

"Doctor Bradley," O'Reilly said, rising, "may I introduce you to Lord John MacNeill, marquis of Ballybucklebo?"

Jenny, blushing, scrambled to push back her chair and stand.

"Please, sit where you are, Doctor," the marquis said. "It's a pleasure to meet you."

Jenny subsided into her seat, bowed her head, and said, "My lord."

"May I?" The marquis indicated the last vacant chair.

"Of course. Today's the first of July. I take it you

are going to give Helen the scholarship, John? I've been on eggs for the last three weeks."

So had Barry, ever since O'Reilly had confided the news about Helen's chances for the MacNeill Bursary and told Barry to keep it to himself. He said quietly to Jenny, "Doctor O'Reilly's trying to get Helen a scholarship to study medicine."

Jenny said, "Good for him. We need more women in the professions."

"I came to put you out of your misery," the marquis said. "I'm happy to interpret 'By July the first' as meaning past midnight of June the thirtieth, last night. You two medical men will attest that the candidate 'is of sufficiently robust spirit'?"

"We can manage that, can't we, Barry?" Fingal said, and grinned.

Barry laughed. "I don't think the question, my lord, is can Helen 'stand the rigours of the aforesaid faculty.' Can the faculty stand the rigours of having Helen. She is a very determined lady."

"She'll have to be," Jenny said quietly.

"It's hers," the marquis said.

"You," said O'Reilly, "the most honourable Lord John MacNeill, marquis of Ballybucklebo, are a gentleman and a scholar, and the more so for coming round in person to tell us."

"Least I could do," the marquis said. "Now do sit down and don't let me interrupt your luncheon."

Barry sat and watched as O'Reilly danced a little jig. He was beaming. "Thank you, John. Thank you so very much," he said. "I'll have Helen in in a minute. Let you tell her." He sat. "In the meantime, would you like a cup of tea?"

"Thank you," the marquis said. "I'll help myself, and this, Fingal," he handed O'Reilly a parcel wrapped in silver embossed paper, "is a little something for you and Kitty."

"Thank you, John." O'Reilly gave the package a playful shake, smiled, and then looked round.

Barry could tell his friend, for he no longer thought of Fingal Flahertie O'Reilly in any other way, was searching for somewhere to set the gift. Barry rose. "If you like, I'll trot it upstairs."

"Please do," said O'Reilly, handing it over, "and while you're at it, ask Helen to come here. And there's a brown paper parcel in the bay of the right bow window. Bring it too like a good lad."

Barry went into the upstairs lounge where Helen was dusting. "*Another* prezzy?" she said.

"Aye," said Barry, and set it on the carpet beside the brown-paper-wrapped one he was to take to Fingal. "Doctor O'Reilly would like you to come downstairs for a minute, Helen. He's got something to tell you." As Barry lifted the parcel he had to struggle to keep his face expressionless, his voice flat, but he didn't want to spoil the surprise.

"Fair enough," she said.

Barry followed her into the dining room.

Helen curtsied and said, "My lord." She glanced at O'Reilly as if seeking reassurance.

O'Reilly said, "This is Helen Hewitt, sir."

"I'm delighted to meet you, Helen," the marquis said.

Barry could see that she was quite overawed.

"His lordship has something to tell you, Helen," O'Reilly said. "Please come and sit here." He indicated what had been Barry's seat.

She sat as if the chair were made of delicate porcelain and not sturdy bog oak.

"Doctor O'Reilly has told me, Helen, that you have the necessary entrance requirements and you'd like to go to Queen's medical school."

Jenny Bradley whispered, "Good for you, Helen."

Helen nodded and said, "Yes, sir. I would."

"He also tells me, and please don't be embarrassed, that money is holding you back. That's a shame, but I can do something about it."

Barry watched Helen's smile flash and as quickly be replaced by a frown. She took a deep breath and brought both hands up to lie on the tablecloth, one clasping the other so tightly that her knuckles blanched. Dear God, she's going to refuse, he thought. He knew how fiercely proud Helen was.

She said levelly, "That's very generous of you, my lord, and no harm to you, and I don't mean to be rude, but, aye, it is true we are short of cash." Barry could understand how she must be struggling. Finally she said, "It is very kind, but I couldn't accept your money, sir. My da would kill me if he thought I'd taken charity."

O'Reilly started, "It's not like—" but the marquis leant forward and put his hand over hers. "Helen," he said, and he spoke to her as if there was no one else in the room, "I can understand how much you want to go. Your trying to refuse charity is one of the bravest things I've ever heard, but no one is offering you that."

Her gaze never left his. "I . . . I don't understand."

"I am able to award a MacNeill Bursary to qualified residents of County Down. You will receive sufficient money to pay your tuition and cover your living expenses. Here," he offered her a buff envelope, "that's the certificate of award."

She frowned, drew back like a cat sensing danger. "So, it's not you, personally, being generous, sir? I've heard of lordships doing kind things like that. It's the estate, like?"

He chuckled. "I wish I was so rich. But you're right, Helen, it is the estate," the marquis said. "It is in what's called 'the gift' of the head of the family. And that's me. My great-great-grandfather, Richard O'Neill, set up the bursary in 1849, but in 1899, my great-grandfather, William MacNeill, changed it so it could be awarded to young women as well as young men. He was wounded during the seige of Sevastopol in the Crimean War and was extremely impressed by the work being done in the barracks hospital by Florence Nightingale and Mary Seacole. He thought they should be doctors."

He advanced the envelope. "And so, in that fine

tradition, Helen, you have earned this by your own efforts, and your candidacy has been advanced by someone I trust. It is *not* charity."

Barry looked at Fingal, who was studying his fingernails.

"Well done, Helen," Jenny said quietly.

Helen screwed her eyes tight shut, blew out her breath, and opened her eyes. "I don't believe it. Me?" She pointed at herself. "Wee Helen Hewitt from Ballybucklebo's going to Queen's for to study to be a doctor?" She grinned and accepted the envelope. "Dear God," she said, "it's a miracle, so it is." She beamed at the marquis. "I never knew about a thing like this, and I never asked no one, so I didn't." She stared at the envelope. "Why me, sir?"

Barry saw O'Reilly put his index finger over his lips and look at the marquis, who shook his head. He turned to Helen. "You come recommended by Doctor O'Reilly. That's enough for me."

"You done this, sir?" She turned to O'Reilly. "Thank you very, very much."

He shook his head. "No, Helen. You did. You stayed on at school. You worked hard. You passed the exams. I merely spoke to his lordship."

Not quite, Fingal, Barry thought. I know you chased your surgical friends for information, pulled all the strings you could, but the knowledge goes no further than me.

"And . . . and I can go to Queen's this September

and study medicine? Just like that?" Helen's smile at O'Reilly was radiant.

The marquis chuckled. "Not quite," he said. "You'll have to apply, show my letter to the right people, and I'm not quite sure how the actual application to the faculty—"

"Excuse me, sir," Barry said, "I had to do it in 1957. Doctor Bradley started in 1956. The procedures won't have changed much, will they, Jenny?"

"I don't think so," she said. "It was pretty straight-forward. Fill in forms, show your exam marks, pay a registration fee—"

The marquis said, "The scholarship takes care of it."

Barry said, "No time like the present. If it's all right with you, Fingal, and you don't mind covering, Jenny, if I can have the afternoon off?" He looked at O'Reilly.

"Of course."

"Fine by me," Jenny said.

"I'll run you up to Queen's, Helen. We'll have to see the bursar, get the forms filled in. Show him his lord-ship's certificate. Maybe I can speed things up a bit."

Helen looked from face to face, tears streaming down her own. "I don't know who to thank first."

"Huh," said O'Reilly, "you can thank me—"

Barry was startled. His boss always shrank from profuse thanks.

"—by passing every exam first go. Not like some people I once knew."

Barry wondered what that was about.

"I will, sir," she said, and sniffed. "I feel such an eejit blubbing like this, but . . . oh dear—" She dashed her hands across her eyes. "Thank youse all. I don't think I've ever been so happy in all my whole life."

"Not quite," Jenny said. "You'll discover that feeling when you open the letter telling you you've been accepted. It's still tougher for women to get in."

"You mean—" Helen's face fell.

Barry frowned at Jenny.

"I'm sorry," she said, "I didn't mean to spoil things, Helen. I can remember the waiting to hear. It could take a week or two. That's all."

The marquis said, "The bequest is very specific. The bursary is for the study of medicine."

"Thank God for that," Helen said. "I'd break my heart if I got turned down now."

"Please don't worry," the marquis said.

Helen stood, darted at O'Reilly, and planted a firm kiss on his cheek. "I promise you, sir, I will pass every exam first go and when I get to be, och, I don't believe it's true, but when I get to be Doctor Hewitt, I'll try to be as good a doctor as you, so I will." She kissed him again.

You can try, Helen, Barry thought. So can I, but we'll both be hard-pressed to achieve that goal. And, he noticed O'Reilly looking flustered, I don't think in the face of thanks I could ever be so reticent. Time to change the subject. "Helen," he said, "have you got a coat? It's bucketing outside."

"I have."

"Here, Fingal," Barry said. "You asked me to bring this down." He handed O'Reilly the parcel.

"Helen, before you go," said O'Reilly, "when I was a medical student, the dean of our faculty said that no matter how hard we studied we should, without fail, read at least some nonmedical books every week if we were to be educated physicians, but you'll need textbooks as well. These are for you." He handed her the parcel. "Open it."

Barry expected her to rip the paper, but she used a fingernail to peel off the Sellotape, carefully unwrap the package, neatly fold the paper, and set it on the tablecloth. "Och," she said, "they're beautiful." She held up one leather-bound tome for everyone to see. *The Complete Works of William Shakespeare.* The second book was even heavier.

"I struggled with that one," O'Reilly said. "And the subject matter hasn't changed since it was written."

Barry recognised *Gray's Anatomy,* the vast volume that he along with all his classmates had discarded for a much slimmer work, *Johnson's Synopsis of Anatomy,* which leant itself better to the learning of the absolutely vital anatomical facts. He'd advise Helen later.

"Thank you very much, Doctor O'Reilly," Helen said. "We done—" She corrected herself, "we did *Twelfth Night* at school." She held up the Shakespeare. "And *this,*" she said, placing the *Gray's Anatomy* on the dining room table and patting its maroon cover with gilt lettering, "I can start studying right now, so I can."

"You do that," O'Reilly said.

The marquis said, "Allow me to be the first to congratulate you, Miss Hewitt, and to wish you success."

Helen bobbed. "Thank you, my lord. Thank you very much."

Jenny applauded and everyone joined in.

Helen blushed.

Barry said, "Let me congratulate you too, and my lord, Fingal, Jenny, if you'll excuse us? It's time for me to run Helen home to pick up her A-level science and Junior Latin certificates to show to the bursar."

"Can you get back here for six?" O'Reilly asked.

"Of course."

O'Reilly turned to the marquis. "I'm a bit old for a stag session, but I'm taking my groom's party to the Causerie this evening for a bite. If you'd like to join us—"

"I'd love to, Fingal, but I'm seeing my sister. Myrna's really looking forward to Saturday."

"So am I," said O'Reilly. He turned to his new temporary assistant. "Deep end again for you, Jenny," O'Reilly said.

"It's no trouble. You two enjoy yourselves."

Helen said, "I still don't know how to thank you all, and you want to get going, Doctor Laverty, but could you wait just a wee minute? I have to tell somebody or I'll burst so I want to see Kinky."

"I can wait," Barry said as he held the door open

for her to leave the room and thought, On you go, Helen Hewitt, and it's a great pleasure for me to be able to help you take the first steps on your journey to a new life.

囧

"It's a cosy spot," Fingal said to Barry as they climbed the stairs.

Barry looked around the snug little room. A bar stood to one side. Behind it, bottles on shelves were reflected in a wall mirror. Mister Greer and Sir Donald Cromie were already seated and Mister Greer was waving to them. The other six tables were occupied and a soft hum of conversation rose along with curls of tobacco smoke. Cutlery chinked on china.

A waitress greeted O'Reilly. "Hello, Doctor O'Reilly, sir. Nice til see yiz back."

"Good to be back, Peggy." He nodded to Barry and said, "This is my friend, Doctor Laverty."

Barry liked that, "my friend." It mirrored what he had thought about O'Reilly only a few hours ago.

"Pleased til meet yiz, sir."

"Peggy." Barry heard bursts of raindrops rattling off the windows.

She shook her head. "It's a dirty night outside, so it is. The wires is shaking."

"They are that, but it's snug enough in here," O'Reilly said, shrugging out of his damp raincoat.

She took his and Barry's. "I've pints on the pour for your other friends."

"Barry?"

"Please." A year ago it would have been a small dry sherry.

"Two more, and start one for my brother when he arrives, please."

"Right, sir." She left.

"Sure, 'A pint of plain's your only man,' " Barry said.

"From *The Working Man's Friend* by Brian Nolan, also known as Flann O'Brien and Myles na gCopaleen," O'Reilly said. "I'm going to miss playing the quotes game with you, Barry. Come on, let's see how that pair of old reprobates are doing."

"You two know Barry," O'Reilly said when he reached the table. "One of the best young GPs in Ulster."

"Och," said Sir Donald, "as the old cock crows so the young cock learns."

"I'd a very good teacher, sir." Barry glowed at O'Reilly's compliment.

"And it's not 'sir.' Just Cromie, Barry," Sir Donald said, "just like this broken-down old rugby player is Charlie to his friends, aren't you?"

Charlie Greer said, "And any friend of yours, Fingal O'Reilly, you great bollix, is a friend of mine."

"When it comes to bollixes, it takes one to know one, Charlie Greer," O'Reilly said with a grin.

"More lip out of you, Fingal Flahertie O'Reilly, and I'll remodel your nose again."

The three older men chortled.

It was, because of their seniority, going to take a little time to get used to, but Barry recognised in these three men the same comfortable, irreverent leg pulling that was universal among friends in Ireland.

"Charlie and I used to box—" said O'Reilly.

"And the sudden juxtaposition of my glove with Fingal's schnozzle in '36—" He laughed.

"I understand." And Barry had a sudden picture of his first meeting with O'Reilly a year ago and surmising back then that the big man's bent nose and cauliflower ears must speak of a history in the ring.

"Now quickly," O'Reilly said, "if you'll excuse us for a minute, Barry, we've a little business to transact. What's the state of play for the reunion?"

Charlie answered. "Since we met back in June we've had a great response from the class. They want a meeting in September '66 in Dublin. Burrows Wellcome, M&B, and Ortho Pharmaceuticals have agreed to pay for the lunches and a couple of banquets. You said you'd look after the hotel, Fingal. And I think we should have one function in Trinity itself."

"Agreed. I'll arrange the Shelbourne when I get back from Rhodes. Speak to the Trinity folks."

"I've spoken to Professor Micks and Professor Synge," Cromie said. "They'd both love to come—"

Barry let the conversation flow round him and speculated about whether twenty years or so from now he and Jack Mills, by then an eminent surgeon,

and Barry, a—he shook his head, time would tell—
and a couple of others from the class of '63 would be
sitting discussing a reunion.

"Here yiz are, sir." Peggy started setting five pints
on the table. "There's one for Mister Lars too. He's
gone to shed a tear for the old country—"

That was one way of expressing that he'd gone
to the toilet, Barry thought, and more polite than
remarking, "He'd gone to shake the dew off the lily."

"When he comes back, I'll bring the menus." She
left.

Cromie raised his pint. "Even before your brother
gets here, Fingal, a toast. To Fingal, and Kitty. There
never was an old slipper but there was a stocking to
match. Good health and good luck to you both."

Barry raised his glass and drank. "To Fingal and
Kitty."

"Thank you all," Fingal said, "and while I'm at it,
I have to thank you, Charlie. You were right about
that scholarship and we found out today it's going to
a great lass from Ballybucklebo."

"I'm glad to hear it," Charlie said.

"Not entirely for certain," Barry said. "The bursar
was pretty sure this afternoon, but he has to have it
ratified by the dean of the faculty."

"I'd not worry," Charlie said, "John Henry's fair
when it comes to scholarships."

Barry well remembered the students' belief that in
a reversal of the usual hierarchy God sat on the right
hand of Professor John Henry Biggart, always known

colloquially as "John Henry." Helen had left the bursar's office discouraged this afternoon and, as Jenny had said, nothing was certain until an applicant was able to clutch their letter of acceptance.

"Gentlemen," said a tall, moustached man who now stood beside the table.

"Lars, good to see you. Have a seat. Our table is complete, gentlemen. Good drive down from Portaferry?"

"Thank you, Fingal, yes, very pleasant."

"You know everybody except Barry."

"But I've heard a lot from my brother about you, Doctor Laverty, and I'm very grateful that you are going to be his best man. I hate making speeches." Lars sat and offered a hand, which Barry shook.

"I'm happy to stand up for Fingal," Barry said and, emboldened by his ready acceptance by his senior colleagues, continued, "and when it comes to hearing about me, wait until you hear *my* side."

Everyone laughed.

"I assure you, it was nothing but good," Lars said. He lifted his glass and drank. "And you'll be glad to know that my friend Jimmy says Butch is getting on well in his new home . . . and his new occupation."

Barry was pleased and sat and listened while Fingal gave Cromie and Charlie the saga of Colin Brown's ferret. Colin was in for a surprise on Saturday afternoon.

"Excuse me, Doctors, but here youse are." Peggy

placed menus on the table. "And will youse be having wine?"

"I think," said O'Reilly, "we'll stick to the pints for the moment until we see what everybody's going to eat."

"Fair enough, sir," she said, "so I'll give yiz a wee while til pick."

Barry studied the menu. Good straightforward Irish cooking. He made his choices and looked up to see O'Reilly waving at Peggy and holding up five fingers. What the hell? Why not have another pint? Barry Laverty was going to sit back, enjoy the company; the honeydew melon slice with ginger; filet steak medium rare, with champ, carrots, and corn on the cob, and profiteroles and coffee to follow; another pint; and all the rest of whatever came to pass on what he had once heard referred to as his "antepenultimate" evening as assistant to the redoubtable Doctor Fingal Flahertie O'Reilly, the ogre with the heart of corn who in one short year had gone from being Barry Laverty's terrifying mentor to his friend.

Barry lifted his glass. "If I may?"

Heads nodded. Glasses were lifted.

"To you, Fingal. To you."

43

Let's Have a Wedding

A perspiring Fingal O'Reilly ran a finger under his starched white collar. Was it the warmth in the little church or his anticipation of the step he was about to take—was happy to be taking? He could feel a frown creasing his forehead and tried to relax. Still, it was understandable after all those years as a widower. *This*—he looked around at the church—was quite the leap. He smiled and stared ahead from his place to the left of Barry to where Mister Robinson, the black-robed Presbyterian minister, prayerbook open in both hands, stood in front of the choir in their stalls. The man's benificent smile was directed at the men to Barry's right, where Lars O'Reilly was flanked by Charlie and Cromie, all four in tail coats and pin-stripe trousers, sombre as penguins.

Jane Hoey, Kinky, and Virginia Currie sat across the aisle. Robinson and Cleaver's had done a remarkable job of softening Kinky's contours with a beautifully cut outfit. She, Jane, and Virginia wore hats of the same colour as their straight, below-knee dresses and collarless, three-quarter-length-sleeved jackets in a pale turquoise embossed silk. Each woman carried a bouquet of cream roses in her kid-gloved hands.

O'Reilly listened to soft harmonium music. Cissie Sloan was playing "*Prélude à l'après-midi d'une faune.*" Her hat, looking like something designed by Cecil Beaton for the Ascot scene in *My Fair Lady,* fluttered in time with her pumping of the bellows.

O'Reilly, with Kitty's approval, had picked the music and she'd been quite happy with some other changes he wanted to make. He chuckled. Mister Robinson had initially balked at the suggestion for the bride's entrance march, but had eventually come to see the reason O'Reilly asked for it.

"My wedding is going to be a ferociously happy day from the minute Kitty comes into the church and I'm not having any old dirge set the wrong tone. It's going to be something fresh, jubilant, and never heard at an Ulster wedding before."

"How about 'The Prince of Denmark's March' or something from Handel's Water Music?" the minister had suggested.

O'Reilly would not be swayed and Mister Robinson had agreed—and with a smile that had put the often dour minister well up in O'Reilly's estimation.

Cissie, when told, had laughed like a drain and said, "Boys-a-dear, thon's a quare powerful number, so it is, but I'll have it down pat by the day, sir, never you worry."

O'Reilly took a surreptitious glance at his watch. It was about time for Cissie to be swinging into the music for the bride's procession, but he realised she was starting the Debussy for a second time. He wished

Kitty would get here, but then, pursing his lips, he thought, Eejit, wasn't she entitled to be a little tardy? Hadn't he kept her waiting for more than thirty years? Good God, why such a wonderful woman hadn't been married off to any one of what must have been a swarm of suitors was unbelievable, but the only time he'd asked her that question, all she'd said was, "Because I was in love with *you*, Fingal." Humbling, he thought, humbling and somewhat bewildering. Not for the first time he wondered why, this time around, it had taken him so many months to recognise how deeply he loved her.

But he still wished she'd get a move on now.

O'Reilly fidgeted then inclined his head to Barry and whispered, "Got the ring?" Silly question. Of course he had. Hadn't he showed it to O'Reilly just before they'd left Number One?

Barry grinned and fished it half out of a pocket of his black waistcoat so O'Reilly could see the flash of gold that, more than the diamond with the slight flaw that he'd bought her in April, would symbolise and cement the love he felt for Caitlin O'Hallorhan, Kitty to her friends. And wasn't she his best friend too? Course she was.

He took a deep breath and was soothed by the scents of mixed cerise and cream orchids from Lars's greenhouse decorating the first six rows of mahogany pews. Their aromas masked the usual fustiness of the centuries-old building. The late-morning sun streaming through stained-glass windows above the chancel had glanced from dust motes and cast, as if from a kaleidoscope with a missing mirror, irregular lakes of soft colours over the aisle and the pews where a small invited congregation sat, all the gentlemen in their best suits, the ladies gloved and hatted as befitted one of Ballybucklebo's grandest occasions.

He glanced down to where the light accentuated the blue of his Royal Navy dress uniform, all gold braid, brass buttons, and a plain silver cross hanging on his left breast to the right of a number of campaign medals. Its ribbon had one white and two blue vertical stripes. It was regulation that when dress blues were worn, decorations must be displayed, but Queen's Regulations be damned, he was *not* wearing a bloody sword. He vividly recalled a friend from his navy days tripping over his at a wedding. O'Reilly could hear the clattering yet. Robert might have recovered his poise if he hadn't grabbed at the chaplain and brought him down too. Most unfortunate that the man of the cloth as he tumbled had yelled, "Oh shite."

There were going to be no slipups today.

O'Reilly dusted his lapel with the back of his hand and remembered the last time he'd worn this rig. Nineteen forty-six at Buckingham Palace, where King George VI had decorated Ma with the Order of the British Empire for her war work and her support of a charity for unmarried mothers—gone seventeen years now, God rest her.

His reverie was interrupted by rapid crashing chords. Good for you, Cissie. O'Reilly knew everybody, except those in on the secret, would be expecting the stodgy *dum-dum-di-dum* of Wagner's "Bridal Chorus." It was traditional at Ulster weddings for the bride's entrance, but he was having none of this "Here comes the bride, short, fat, and wide" rubbish. Instead, the rousing theme from the 1958 Western *The Big Country* rang out triumphantly. Cissie was swaying like a rock-and-roll player in time with the music. Let her rip, Cissie Sloan. Let her rip. He winked at Mister Robinson, who smiled and nodded.

And none of this "the groom will face the front until the bride arrives." O'Reilly had waited long enough. He spun to peer down the nave.

The congregation was rising with a rustling of women's dresses as the notes soared to echo in the ceiling's barrel vaults. He saw surprised looks turn to grins. Helen Hewitt gave him a thumbs-up and a beaming smile. He briefly wondered if she'd got her acceptance letter yet.

He glimpsed Kitty's eighty-two-year-old mother leaning on the arm of Kitty's distant cousin Brendan in the first pew to the left. Behind her in the second pew on the bride's side, Archie Auchinleck gazed fondly at Kinky, who smiled back, dimples deepening, before Archie turned to face the rear of the little church, looking past two more pews of Kitty's family and friends.

O'Reilly's breath caught in his throat. Coming from

the narthex were Kitty and the marquis, tall, silver-haired, with the unmistakable bearing of a career soldier measuring his pace to accommodate Kitty's shorter one. Her A-line below-knee dress of sapphire raw silk accentuated her slim figure and long legs. It, like her attendants' outfits, was three-quarter sleeved and she wore matching satin gloves. Cream roses cascaded down from a larger bouquet than those of her attendants. A half-veil hung from a pillbox hat.

God damn it, Kinky had been right, as usual, that he'd approve of the bride's choice of outfit. Wasn't she the most beautiful, most desirable woman in the whole of Ireland? In the world? It was all O'Reilly could do to stop himself rushing down the aisle to take her in his arms.

She was gazing down, less from modesty, O'Reilly realised, than from making sure one of her high heels didn't disappear into the cast-iron grating in the floor. It ran the length of the aisle and was part of the central heating system.

The couple passed the fuller pews of the groom's side and O'Reilly looked at his old friend, the marquis of Ballybucklebo. He had forgone dress blues for a morning suit clearly well pressed by his valet-butler Thompson. O'Reilly picked out more friendly smiling faces. Father O'Toole in his cassock. He wore no other vestments today because he was not here in his official capacity. Colleen Brennan, the district nurse, and Miss Hagerty, the midwife, were here. Myrna MacNeill, the marquis's younger sister, sat beside Sonny and Maggie Houston. And immediately behind Barry, just as Archie stood behind Kinky, was Sue Nolan. Things had been a bit strained there for a while, O'Reilly knew, and he truly hoped the youngsters were working it out. But then, as old Willy Shakespeare had remarked, "The course of true love never did run smooth." O'Reilly grinned. He should bloody well know that, but, as Kitty drew ever nearer, his love for her now felt more like a calm bottomless pool. O'Reilly shook his head. Time would have to tell for young Barry. He wanted Barry to be happy. Today O'Reilly wanted everybody to be happy. Clams and pigs in shite were down-in-the-mouth, whingeing mopers when compared to how he felt, and he knew he was grinning like a mooncalf, an *omadán* of the first magnitude for everyone to see—and he didn't care.

Her delicate perfume nearly overcame him as Kitty, still on the marquis's arm, arrived at O'Reilly's side.

Cissie held the last triumphal chord, stopped, and mopped her brow. The harmonium made a grateful gasping noise and subsided into exhausted silence. Mister Robinson waited, then said, "Dearly belovèd, we are gathered here today in the presence of God Almighty and of this congregation to witness the joining of Caitlin O'Hallorhan to Fingal Flahertie O'Reilly in holy matrimony. Please be seated."

The congregation sat, quietly, reverently, but Fingal could imagine how some of the ladies would be nodding and cocking heads in silent approval of Kitty's outfit.

O'Reilly waited patiently through the minister's homily and the reading by Kinky of the passage from First Corinthians, chapter 13. Looking straight at Archie Auchinleck, she finished with the familiar words, ". . . and now abideth faith, hope, and charity, these three. But the greatest of these is charity."

Charity. He knew that the Greek word *agape,* which was often translated as "charity," could also mean "love" in English. Faith, Hope, and Love. But Kitty had been adamant. She wanted no deviation fron the King James Bible. I admire that traditionalist streak in you, Kitty O'Hallorhan, and as her perfume filled his nostrils, another Greek word for love forced its way into his mind. *Eros.* Behave yourself, Fingal.

The choir and congregation gave a lusty rendition of "Joyful, Joyful We Adore Thee" and O'Reilly joined in:

> . . . all who live in love are Thine,
> Teach us how to love each other, lift us to the joy
>   divine.

That, he thought as they finished, was a bloody good sanctified shout.

"At this point," Mister Robinson continued, "it is customary for the minister to offer a short sermon of advice to the bride and groom. My lord, ladies, and gentlemen . . . it is a braver man than I who would attempt to advise our Doctor O'Reilly. It is easier for a camel to go through the eye of a needle." He waited until the laughter subsided. "So, we'll forgo that portion of the proceedings and move on. Now it falls to me to invite you to rise . . ."

There was a clattering of feet on the floor and the rustling of women's dresses.

". . . and me to ask, 'Who giveth this woman to be married to this man?' "

The marquis said clearly, "On behalf of the O'Hallorhan family, I do," turned, and stood beside Kitty's mother, who smiled at him.

"I must ask if anyone knows of any just impediment why this man and this woman should not be joined?"

O'Reilly harrumphed. He knew there was more to that passge about "coming forth or forever holding their peace," but he suspected that Mister Robinson was using the same guiding principle he'd invoked when avoiding advising O'Reilly about the matrimonial state. It would take a villager with the courage of a VC winner to have the temerity to suggest any such thing.

"Let us pray."

Heads bowed. The prayer ended and heartfelt "Amens" were uttered from many mouths.

The ceremony rolled on until finally Mister Robinson asked, "Do you, Fingal Flahertie O'Reilly, take Caitlin O'Hallorhan to be your wife? Do you promise to love, honour, cherish, and protect her, forsaking all others and holding only unto her?"

Fingal began his response but to his surprise found that his throat was dry. He started again, "By guh—" realised that here, of all places, was where he should not blaspheme and simply intoned, "I, Fingal Flahertie O'Reilly, take thee, Caitlin O'Hallorhan, to be my wife. To have and to hold, in sickness and in health, for richer or for poorer, and I promise my love to you." His grin was mammoth yet his voice was soft.

Now it was Kitty's turn. Her voice was firm, clear, and confident, and her gaze never left his eyes as Kitty plighted her troth.

"The ring?" Mister Robinson asked.

O'Reilly watched Barry rummage in his waistcoat pocket. The thing was stuck. He blushed, fiddled, went even more red.

Mister Robinson whispered, "Take your time."

Barry tugged. The ring popped loose and flew skyward before falling and heading for the floor's central heating vents. He managed to grab it as it fell. The marquis was an avid cricketer and his, "Oh, well held, sir," which he would have called to a fielder catching a batsman out, was audible throughout the church. A sentiment echoed by O'Reilly.

"Here, Fingal. Sorry." Barry surrendered the ring and smoothed his tuft.

The putting of it on Kitty's finger took but a moment. "With this ring I thee wed—"

Mister Robinson then delivered the words ending

in ". . . I now pronounce you man and wife. What God hath joined together let no man put asunder. You may kiss the bride."

Kitty threw back her half-veil and O'Reilly looked deep into those grey eyes flecked with amber. Like a drowning man, in that moment his life ran in fast motion before his own eyes. Kitty, a student nurse. The two of them together in the tearoom of Wynn's Hotel, him telling her he had to study, hadn't time for both her and the hours of medical school. Her forgiving him just before he qualified. Her tears years later when he'd told her about Deirdre. Her waiting patiently when they'd met again last year, understanding his reticence until in April he'd at last found the courage to tell her he loved her.

O'Reilly embraced Kitty as a grizzly bear might, and a hungry grizzly at that. Her lips were soft on his. He stood back, still holding her. "I love you, Mrs. O'Reilly," he said, "and I will love you . . . now and forever."

"And I've never stopped loving you, Fingal, and I never could."

As she spoke he wondered why those few simple sentences were not sufficient to bind them forever, but the ritual must go on.

After the benediction, the minister asked, "If you will come with me?" As he led O'Reilly and Kitty, Barry and Jane to the vestry, Cissie Sloan, after a few preliminary pants and wheezes of the harmonium, launched into Pachelbel's "Canon in D Major."

By the time O'Reilly and Kitty had signed the register and had their signatures witnessed, Cissie had switched to Beethoven's "Ode to Joy" from the Ninth, "Choral," Symphony and O'Reilly was happily singing along, *"Freude, schöner, Götterfunken . . ."* He finished, bowed to Mister Robinson, said, "Thank you, your reverence. Thank you very much, and Barry, and Jane. Now, Mrs. Fingal Flahertie O'Reilly," he offered Kitty his arm, "it's time for us to face the multitudes outside, get back to Number One, and kick off the festivities. After all that talking, my tongue's hanging out for a pint."

44

Fall In with the Marriage Procession

By all the saints and martyrs, we've done it, O'Reilly thought as he and Kitty left the church ahead of the marquis and Kitty's mother. The bridal party followed and the congregation brought up the rear.

With the sun high in a cloudless sky, he felt as if he were in a Turkish bath. "Lord," he said to Kitty, "it's even hotter out here."

"You must be sweltering in that uniform," she said.

"But thank you for wearing it, Fingal. You look so handsome. Just as I remember you during that New Year's Eve dance at Trinity College, Dubin, thirty years ago. That's where I started to fall in love with you," she said, smoothing his lapels and darting in for a kiss.

"Now who's the soft-soaper?" he said. "I'm thirty years older and two stone heavier, but today I feel twenty-five again." He'd worn the heavy uniform because Kitty had asked him to. And he'd worn it to his first wedding too, so had hesitated for a minute before granting Kitty's request a month ago. But hadn't he also decided at that time that Deirdre would have approved of their happiness? Bless you, Deirdre, *requiescat in pace*.

"Fingal, you're looking solemn. We'll get you a pint soon," she said, squeezing his arm.

His step faltered and his breath caught in his throat. If there was a more beautiful woman in the six counties he'd eat the silver medal and blue and white ribbon of his Distinguished Service Cross.

"That dress suits you, darling," he said. "You'd take the light from any fellah's eyes and I think that lad's serenading is for you alone." High in one of the churchyard yews, a song thrush poured out his heart in coruscating trills. "And in case I don't get a chance to tell you for a while," O'Reilly waved his free arm at the welcoming multitude waiting outside the church gate, "I love you, Mrs. Kitty O'Reilly. I truly do."

The crowd began to applaud and Kitty had to shout to be heard. "I love you too, Doctor Fingal Flahertie O'Reilly."

Donal Donnelly and the estate agent Dapper Frew, both in the uniform of the Ballybucklebo Highlanders, began blasting out "Marie's Wedding" in two-part harmony on the bagpipes.

Clouds of confetti fluttered down, pink, and white, and silver, and pastel blue.

Kitty threw her bouquet. It fell into the hands of Mary Dunleavy, the publican's plump daughter. Her squeals of delight were clearly audible over the cheers of her friends and thrumming of the drones and the chanters' high-pitched notes.

Donal and Dapper led the procession. Fergus Finnegan and Eamon Cadogan stood in the middle of the road holding up traffic so the bridal party could cross. There was no impatient honking of horns today.

Fingal noticed Doctor Jenny Bradley waving from one of Number One's upstairs bow windows. She'd come down for the party and left the kitchen door open so she could hear the phone if it rang.

Another small blizzard of confetti settled on the moving mass of people. The crowd parted as the pipers headed for the back lane past the marquee that had been erected yesterday in O'Reilly's back garden. Its sides were rolled up. One table served as a bar. A paying bar. He was happy to provide drinks for the guests who'd been invited to the ceremony, but he wasn't bloody well made of money and by the size of the crowd the whole village and townland had turned up. Willie Dunleavy was at his post. He grinned and pointed to a keg of Guinness. There would be champagne for all the churchgoers for the toasts, but nothing, in Fingal's opinion, quenched a thirst like a pint and there'd be time for one while he waited for the multitude to be seated and the speechifying to begin.

He nodded, pointed at Kitty, and mouthed, "Gin and tonic," to Willie, exaggerating the words. He knew he couldn't be heard over the row.

Willie lifted a bottle of Gordon's gin.

Fingal looked at the other catering arrangements. Kinky had done a magnificent job of mobilising the cooks of the village, and she herself had not been idle.

Two tables groaned under tureens of chilled soup, glasses of prawn cocktails, platters of raw oysters, roast hams, chickens, cold roasts of beef, whole poached salmon, boiled lobsters, crabs, and shrimp, smoked trout, salads, bread rolls, wheaten bread, soda farls, butter . . . he couldn't make out all of the dishes, but was content that no one was going to go home hungry on Doctor Fingal Flahertie O'Reilly's wedding day.

He and Kitty went through the back gate, the turf springy underfoot. Donal Donnelly had mowed the lawn yesterday and the smell of freshly cut grass lingered.

Donal and Dapper, playing a quick march, "The

South Down Militia," stood flanking the gate, a two-man guard of honour for the entering throng. Good old Arthur, sitting beside Donal, joined in the music-making with his head thrown back, ululating, and chewing at his own notes as they escaped.

Fingal led Kitty the length of the garden. "Useful lot, the Rugby Club," he said as they passed rows of folding chairs and tables covered with red tablecloths. "Kinky organised the loan of this furniture. We honestly couldn't have managed without her."

"I'll let you tell her," Kitty said. "She'll appreciate it."

"I already have done," he said, "and she did."

As they neared the house, he pointed to several sets that were close to a trestle table beside the house. Its tablecloth and those of the front row were pristine damask Irish linen. Along the top-table's side nearest the house were place settings, and at intervals on it and on the other tables were vases of orchids, bright-coloured floral gems. "Having special cloths, place names, and centrepieces for the invited guests was her idea too. It's free-for-all at the red-topped tables."

He walked round the end of the top table. "I've been to Lord knows how many weddings. I know what I like."

She smiled. "And you've told me what you *don't* like and I agree. I think it's a lovely idea to have a small head table and guest tables. Gives everyone a chance to blether with their neighbours."

Fingal glanced to the last and most peripheral group

in the front row; Doctor Ronald Hercules Fitzpatrick, Bertie and Flo Bishop, and Cissie Sloan and her husband Hughie and their son Callum. It surprised Fingal not at all that Cissie, who was well known for her ability to talk inconsequentially on just about any topic, was in full cry and that Fitzpatrick was having difficulty stifling a yawn. "I see what you mean," he said, pulling out a chair. "Kitty?"

She sat, and he sat to her left. The rest were already taking their seats. Sue Nolan then Barry were to Fingal's left, Jane Hoey to Kitty's right beside Mrs. O'Hallorhan and the marquis.

Fingal had first met Irene O'Hallorhan and her now late accountant husband in the '30s. She sat erectly, a smile from time to time crossing her lined face. She wore a neat maroon suit with a roll lapel jacket and fur-trimmed cuffs. A string of pearls hung beneath the wattles of her thin neck. Her silver hair was done in a tight bun and her eyes, grey with amber flecks, held the same depths as Kitty's. For a moment he wondered if Kitty would look as well in her eighties, but shrugged. She'd always be young to Fingal.

"Here yiz are, Doctor and Mrs. O'Reilly," Willie said, depositing their drinks.

By God, but that "Mrs. O'Reilly" sounded good, Fingal thought. "Thanks, Willie," he said. "Look after everybody else up here and those other tables at the front with flowers on them. And when you get a chance, bring a bowl for Arthur." Fingal turned, lifted his glass to Kitty, looked into her eyes and said, "To you, my love."

"Thank you, Fingal," she said. "Thank you very much." She touched his hand and sipped.

This was their day and the best way to celebrate it was to make sure everybody had a hell of a good time. It was going to be a ta-ta-ta-ra that would be remembered for years to come. And not because some eejit had made a fool of himself in public. "You don't mind we're cutting down on the speeches?" he asked her. Speeches? Jasus, he thought, a pox on them.

"Of course not, Fingal," she said.

"I've lost track of the interminable ramblings I've had to sit through; coy innuendoes, shaggy dog stories that fell flat, a proud father full as a goat and embarrassing everyone by going on about his daughter's potty training." Fingal cringed. "The worst had been a best man with a stutter who had wanted to 'Tell the bride to fuh-fuh-fuh-fuh-*focus* her attention on her husband.'"

Kitty spluttered then said, "Fingal. That's rude." She laughed.

"Not a bit," he said. "*Honi soit qui mal y pense.*" He laughed with her. "And I can't believe you'd think evil thoughts."

He felt a quick kick to his shin under the table. "Eejit," she said.

"Never mind blue speeches." Fingal chuckled. "I've even been to country weddings where sufficient offence had been caused that in the immortal words of the old folk song, 'Finnegan's Wake,'

> . . . Shillelagh law was all the rage
> And a row and a ruction soon began.

"But we'll be having none of that today. I'll have to say a word or two, but I'll be brief, and I've given the other two speakers strict instructions, 'Stand up, speak up . . . then shut up.' "

"I have no doubt you have, Surgeon Commander O'Reilly," she said as she touched the three broad gold rings on his cuff and chuckled. She lowered her voice. "I know how much you want today to be perfect for us. Thank you, Fingal."

"I do." He glowed inside, swallowed a third of the remaining pint in one go, and said, "By Jasus, I can feel life returning." He drank again. To the tune of "A Nation Once Again" he sang, "Rehydration once again," and took another pull.

The pride of the Ballybucklebo Highlanders roared into "The Miller's Daughter," a strathspey that by tradition would be followed by a reel. Children's happy cries punctuated the piping.

Fingal looked over his garden. "Filling up well," he said to Kitty. He glanced at the marquee. Mary was helping her dad and so were Gerry Shanks and Charlie Gorman. Lines of men were queuing to buy drinks. "By the time the next pipe tune's over I think we might get the meal started and the formal part of the afternoon under way and over." He gasped and wiped sweat from his brow and said, "And then as soon as that's over I can nip inside, get out of this bloody monkey suit, and come back and enjoy the hooley." Sue, who must have overheard, said, "It is warm, but I think you're going to have a lovely party."

"Glad you could come, Sue," O'Reilly said. "He's a good lad, young Barry."

"I know," she said. "I do know." And she smiled.

"I'll miss him," O'Reilly said, "but he'll be a damn fine doctor whatever choice of career he makes."

She half-turned to Barry, who was saying something to her. "Excuse me, Fingal," she said.

He felt a pushing against his shin. "Lie down, lummox," he said. Arthur's pink tongue lolled as he panted and flopped to the grass. "I know it's hot. Your Smithwick's coming." Fingal looked up. The tune was now "The Walls of Limerick," a rousing reel and, as he'd predicted, nearly everyone who was coming had arrived. It was harder to hear the pipes over the steadily rising noise of conversation.

He picked out some faces from among the invitees at the front tables. Helen Hewitt was sitting with Doctor Jenny Bradley. Other folks he didn't recognise, Kitty's family and friends from the south, kept them company and overflowed to other places. Father O'Toole was deep in conversation with Sonny Houston and Maggie. O'Reilly grinned. From Maggie's hat, two fresh red roses and a large ox-eye daisy waved from the hatband of what must be a special creation for the day.

The rest of the garden was packed with friends and well-wishers. Laughter, voices, even a shout rising above the hubbub. "Jimmy, make it three pints, aye three, and a brandy and Benedictine for the missus."

Willie was heading toward the head table with a tray of Moët Chandon bottles and a bowl of Smithwick's for Arthur. Ice buckets were stategically placed.

"Good man-ma-da," Fingal said to Willie, who had given Arthur his beer and was popping champagne corks. He finished his pint, listened to a happy slurping from under the table, and said to Willie, "When you get that done, nip back with another pint for me and when you notice Arthur's bowl's empty?"

"Right, Doc," Willie said.

"And give you and your staff a jar on me."

"I will, so I will." Willie left.

The pipe music stopped. Fingal heard the ringing of a spoon on a glass. Mister Robinson was on his feet at one of the front tables. As silence fell over the garden, Fingal heard the far-away lowing of cattle, the distant notes of a cuckoo up in the Ballybucklebo hills, a ship's siren out in the lough, and Mister Robinson saying, "I have been asked to compère. We intend to keep things simple." He pointed to the marquee.

"There will be three courses, starters or soup, main, and pudding. And there'll be only three speeches—"

Fingal thought it might be Constable Malcolm Mulligan who yelled, "And keep them short." A man after my own heart, he thought.

"We will. Two between the courses and the last after the dessert. After that, feel free to wander around, greet your friends and neighbours, and have a good time."

"We'll do that all right, your reverence," a voice called from the crowd.

"I'm sure you will, Alan Hewitt. We'll maybe get you to give us a song later, and anyone else who wants to do a party piece, but for now I'll ask the head and first tables in sequence to go to the marquee for their starters and then each table in order of the numbers on your tabletop."

Fingal's stomach growled and he began to rise. The thought of the feast awaiting was making his mouth water. Then he remembered and sat quickly in time to hear Mister Robinson say, "But before we put our trotters in the trough," he gave O'Reilly a sideways glance and was rewarded by chuckles, "I call upon Father O'Toole to say grace."

The tall priest rose, bowed his head, and said in his soft Cork brogue, "On this wedding day of our dear friends, Fingal and Kitty O'Reilly, may this food restore our strength, giving new energy to our limbs, new thought to our minds. May this drink restore our souls, giving new vision to our spirits, greater warmth to hearts already warmed by the love here today. And once refreshed may we give new pleasure to Thee who gives us everything. Amen."

The chorus of amens sounded heartfelt.

Well said, Fingal thought.

"Now," Mister Robinson said, "if the bride and groom will—?"

Fingal rose, helped Kitty to her feet, and headed for the marquee and the wedding feast, Ballybucklebo style.

45

In a High Style and Make a Speech

The first course of the feast was disappearing and the garden was noisy with *craic,* laughter, and kiddies' shouts. Exactly as it ought to be, O'Reilly thought. That chilled homemade tomato soup had been refreshing. A grand wee sample of what was to come. He and the crowd had then sat respectfully through a succinct speech of welcome by the marquis to the bride's family, wedding party, to all the women who had so generously provided the sumptuous re-past, Willie Dunleavy and his helpers, and all the other attendees.

Then came the main course.

"Funny," O'Reilly said, surveying the wreckage on his plate of the remains of cold salmon, roast ham, roast chicken, a lobster tail, potato and green salads, and two hard-boiled eggs, "I don't think Alice Moloney let out my waistband far enough. These bloody trousers are still too tight."

"Must be the heat," Kitty said, and laughed. "Don't worry, you'll be out of them soon."

O'Reilly was going to say something risqué, thought better of it, and quaffed his second glass of champagne. Not a bad drop, but to be honest he'd have preferred another stout.

It would soon be his turn to get up on his hind legs. He felt Kitty's hand, cool and smooth, creep into his. He squeezed and she squeezed back. Fingal, Fingal, he thought, you may be fifty-six going on fifty-seven, but Kitty makes you feel twenty all over again.

The minister jangled his spoon, stood, and was concluding, ". . . and after that wonderful main course, our next speaker is the groom, Doctor Fingal Flahertie O'Reilly."

Fingal rose to a respectful hush. "My lord, ladies, and gentlemen, it falls to me on behalf of the O'Reilly family to offer words of thanks, and to toast the gracious lady who is now my wife, Mrs. Fingal Flahertie O'Reilly." He could barely bring himself to look at Kitty, so full of her was he.

"I would like to thank my father, Professor Connan O'Reilly, and mother, Mrs. Mary O'Reilly O.B.E.

Regrettably I cannot, but they loved Kitty from the moment they met a young Caitlin O'Hallorhan in Dublin before the war." And although I'll not confess to it in public, he thought, I like to believe that wherever they are, they are looking on today, hearing my thanks and smiling. "My brother, Lars O'Reilly, orchid breeder—those are his flowers you see today—wildfowl conservationist, and my oldest friend, has delayed his annual departure to Villefranche to be here. Bless you, Lars." Fingal inclined his head to his brother, who smiled back. "To the rest of my supporters, Sir Donal Cromie and Mister Charlie Greer, old friends, good friends, thank you. No groom could have been more ably supported." He hesitated, then continued, "And I can only applaud the loveliness of the bride's party, Mrs. Maureen Kincaid, Mrs. Virginia Currie, and Sister Jane Hoey." He beamed at the folks sitting at the head table and in the front row. "And finally, what groom could make it to the altar without a best man? Doctor Laverty has performed his duties admirably, not only today, but all through this year, as many of you can attest."

The applause was even louder and longer lasting.

In the moment of silence that followed, a child, Fingal thought it might be Angus Shanks, yelled, "I want to go potty."

There was a sympathetic outburst of laughter and while a blushing Mairead hustled her son to the house, O'Reilly scanned the crowd and found Alice Moloney: Barry had done a masterful job of diagnosing her obscure tropical disease. Two tables over was Colin Brown: Barry had sewn up his hand, understood his role in a ringworm outbreak, arranged to have his broken arm set, and rescued his ferret, Butch. Then there was Fergus Finnegan, the jockey: Barry had cured his eye infection. And Aggie Arbuthnot: Barry had dealt professionally with her deep vein thrombosis and would be telling her later that he'd helped get her job back. The young man had learnt that there was more to being a country GP than simply dealing with the aches and pains of the body.

The laughter died.

"And now," said Fingal, "are your glasses charged?"

"They're not charged to you, sir," a voice said. "We'd for til pay for them ourselves, so we had."

"Jasus, Jeremy Dunne, for a man who had an ulcer, you should be on orange juice," O'Reilly countered.

"And the doctor's not made of money," Donal chipped in.

There was a mumbling of agreement.

And a row and a ruction then began, O'Reilly thought. "You bide, Jeremy," he said, "and Donal? Houl' your wheest." He'd try to thank Donal later privately for his support. Country GPs weren't rich no matter what some folks here might think. "So fill your glasses."

There was a great clinking of bottle necks.

"Grand," he said. "Now rise with me and toast my family and the wedding party."

He watched everyone get to their feet except Bridget

Doherty, whose arthritis kept her chairbound. A couple of chairs were overturned, but a myriad voices roared, "To the doctor's family and the wedding party."

A single voice yelled, "May they be half an hour in heaven before the divil knows they're dead," and among general laughter and murmuring of voices everyone was seated and eventually silenced so he could continue.

"I've been saving the best for last, of course. It is my privelege to thank the girl I met in Sir Patrick Dun's Hospital in 1934. The lovely woman who came back into my life last year, to whom I proposed in April, and who, God bless you, Kitty, consented to becoming Mrs. Caitlin O'Reilly, my wife. With no disrespect to any of the other lovely ladies here, will you all please rise again and raise your glasses to Kitty O'Reilly, the true shining Star of the County Down?"

The crowd rose and the response chased a flock of starlings from one of the elm trees. Arthur stuck his head out from under the table to see what was going on, muttered, and retreated to his second bowl of Smithwick's.

Fingal bent and firmly kissed Kitty and tingled from head to toe when she flicked her tongue on his and said softly as they parted, "I love you, Fingal Flahertie O'Reilly. Thank *you*."

As soon as most of the crowd had finished dessert, Mister Robinson again signalled for silence. O'Reilly surreptitiously undid his top trouser button. That sherry trifle—Kinky's he was sure—had been blissful. With just one speech, Barry's, to go it wouldn't be long until he could get out of this damn uniform.

"It is time for me to call upon the best man, Doctor Barry Laverty, to propose the health of the bride and groom."

Applause as Barry rose and pulled papers from his inside pocket. "My lord, ladies, and gentlemen," said Barry, glancing at his notes, "it is the task of the best man to toast the bride and groom. Nothing could give me greater pleasure. I've been here for one year, and no young doctor could have asked for a better teacher. For this I must thank Doctor O'Reilly. Where else could I have learned that the correct treatment for a sprained but dirty ankle is to hurl the patient bodily into a rosebush?" Chuckling started.

"Who else could have taught me that the term 'The quick and the dead' might be applied to unwary cyclists who don't know to take avoiding action and head for the ditch when a certain doctor is driving by?" O'Reilly joined in as the chuckling grew into roars of laughter.

Barry softened his voice. "Who, but Doctor O'Reilly, aching to watch his belovèd rugby football on the telly, would ignore that and rather than wait for an ambulance load a little girl with appendicitis into his car," O'Reilly heard the affection in Barry's voice, "and run her up to the Royal?"

Jeannie Kennedy was sitting with her parents, smiling at him.

"Or wait the night through at that hospital to be sure a patient with bleeding into his skull was going to be all right?"

The laughter had gone and remarks like, "Right enough," and "He's a sound man, our doctor," could be heard. "You should buy himself a jar, Jeremy, so you should."

Fingal recognised Dermot Kennedy's voice.

"And contrary to popular belief, Doctor O'Reilly *can* admit he's wrong. Last year I advised him research suggested smoking is dangerous. He pooh-poohed that and on the same day went wildfowling. He'd run out of matches so he took the gunpowder from a cartridge, put it on a flat stone, stuck his pipe in it, struck a spark from a flint . . . and blew his eyebrows off. When he came home, looking like he'd just spent the weekend mining coal in Wales, he had the courtesy to say to me, 'Begob, Barry, you might just be right. Smoking can be bloody dangerous.'"

The laughter was so deafening that as it subsided not only was Arthur howling, but at least ten other dogs were joining in.

Eventually all was calm enough for Barry to continue. "Doctor O'Reilly, you may not be gentle, but in my book you are a perfect knight—"

A nice twist on Chaucer's "He was a veray parfait gentil knight," O'Reilly thought.

"And every knight errant must woo and win a fair lady. You, Doctor O'Reilly, have found her. Since last year I have been privileged to know the woman who was Kitty O'Hallorhan. She is lovely, as you all can see—"

There was quiet applause and at least two wolf whistles.

"As fine a nurse as there is anywhere in Ulster—"

"In Ireland," Charlie Greer roared. "And I should know, she works with me."

"And a complete woman, who as a skilled oil painter has her *Shannon in Flood* hanging in the Royal Hibernian Academy in Dublin. Her *Donegal Peat Bog* series graces the Ulster Museum." He looked straight at O'Reilly. "You, Doctor Fingal Flahertie O'Reilly, are a very lucky man."

Be God I am, and be damned to the throng. Fingal leant over and planted another kiss on Kitty's lips.

"Fingal, to cite sixteenth-century writer John Ford, 'The joys of marriage are heaven on earth, life's paradise.' May it ever be so for you both." Barry raised his glass and said, smiling at Fingal and Kitty, "Will the company charge their glasses, rise, and with me drink the toast, 'Long life and happiness to the bride and groom, Doctor and Mrs. Fingal Flahertie O'Reilly.'"

The toast was so loud and the applause so strenu-

ous that not only did the starlings, which had reset-
tled in the elm tree, take wing once more, but the
azure sky above the Ballybucklebo Hills was alive
with the cawing of startled jackdaws and rooks.

46

Parting Is Such Sweet Sorrow

T hank goodness that was over. Barry sat and took
a deep breath. This public speaking was not his
idea of the best way to enjoy a party. He could sym-
pathise with Lars. Barry'd spent hours poring over
O'Reilly's *Oxford Dictionary of Quotations* to find *les
mots justes*. He hoped his speech had been all right.

One look at Sue Nolan told him that at least one
member of the audience had thought it was. "You
were wonderful. I'm proud of you." Her face, beneath
the tiny pillbox hat that perched on her upswept
copper hair, was made lovelier by a wide smile, and
her eyes sparkled.

"Thanks, I'd like you to be." He smiled back at her.
He meant that. This schoolmistress had struck a chord
with Barry, one he'd not fully recognised, even before
Patricia had announced that she was finished with

him. He was beginning to understand why since their dates had become more intimate after her near drowning. There were real depths to Sue Nolan, and that they ran under a sexy exterior was no hindrance to his increasing feelings. He was looking forward to having time alone with her after the party, but for now he'd have to bide.

"I think that's it as far as speeches go," he said, "and with a bit of luck we can take it easy now, but I need to have a word with one or two folks first. Tie up a few loose ends." Barry looked round to see Fingal on his feet.

"I'm going in to change," he said. "Back in a minute." And holding his jacket closed in front made his way to the back door. Kitty had turned and was deep in conversation with Jane Hoey.

Barry said to Sue, "Can you do without me for a wee while? I do need to speak to a patient, Aggie Arbuthnot. She's a few tables back. I'll not be long."

Sue smiled at him and shook her head. "Do you never stop thinking about your patients?"

Barry thought for a moment. "Fingal never does," he said.

Her smile broadened. "Off you trot," she said. "I'm quite content to sit here and watch the world go by . . . as long as you don't abandon me for too long." She cocked her head and blew him a kiss.

"I promise," he said, and set off, and before he passed the first row of tables he saw Helen Hewitt waving and holding a thumb up. He called, "See you in a minute, Helen," but he was standing right beside Doctor Fitzpatrick's table. Noblesse oblige, he thought, and stopped to exchange a few words with the lugubrious medical advisor who tended to the sick and suffering of the Kinnegar, just up the road. "Good afternoon," Barry said, noting the sun glinting from the man's gold pince nez. "Lovely day."

"Indeed. Indeed," Fitzpatrick said, his prominent Adam's apple jerking as he spoke, "and a beautiful bride." Barry thought the man may have sounded a little wistful. "I knew them both years ago. Fingal and I were students together, you know." He cleared his throat. "I wish them every happiness."

The air was rent by the sound of pipes. A space had been cleared at the back of the garden, folding tables and chairs propped against the fence. Dapper Frew tore into a double jig in 6/8 time and two sets, men with their jackets off, women now hatless, were dancing away.

"And so do we," said Flo Bishop, who was sitting at the same table, "don't we, Bertie?"

Bishop grunted. Barry could understand why.

Flo nudged the councillor and raised her voice again. "Don't . . . we . . . Bertie?" She thrust her face closer to his.

"Every happiness," he said as if each word was a tooth being drawn without the benefit of an anaesthetic.

"I thank you on their behalf," Barry said.

"Doctor Laverty, dear. I think the doctor and his

wife make a lovely couple, so I do." Cissie Sloan was not to be denied. She looked past Barry and he followed her gaze as it settled on Kinky and Archie. "And I think Kinky's taken a shine to Archie. Archie's a good man, so he is, and Kinky has a heart of corn—"

"She has that," Barry said, and smiled. "We're very happy that—"

"And no harm to youse, sir, but I think, we all think, don't we, Flo? That youse and Miss Nolan make a lovely couple too."

Barry cleared his throat. "I thought," he said, trying to change the subject, "your harmonium playing was terrific."

She glowed. "I've always loved music. There's a great wee song, so there is. It's fit for today." She threw back her head and, ignoring the pipes, began in a clear contralto,

I have often heard it said by me father and my
    mother,
That going to a wedding has the makin's of an-
    other . . ."

Dapper's pipes gave counterpoint.

"That's lovely, Cissie," Barry said, searching for an escape route. "Your singing's as tuneful as your harmonium playing. Now, if you'll excuse me?"

"Pay you no heed to Cissie," Flo said. "You run along, and Doctor? We all wish youse well, and everybody I know wants yiz to come back, don't we, Bertie?"

"Och, aye," said the councillor, and Barry heard all the enthusiasm of a heretic anticipating a consultation with the Spanish Inquisition.

He moved on, smiling at folks he recognised, accepting their good wishes, thanking them, shaking hands. Funny, he thought, in one year I've gone from being an only child to having a family of hundreds, at least that's what it feels like. I *will* miss them.

"Aggie," he said when he arrived at her table, "how are you?"

"All the better for seeing yourself, Doctor dear," she said. "The oul' hind leg's no bother at all now." She lowered her voice. "And youse must be a miracle worker. The Big Doctor's keeping me on the sick until the nineteenth of July. It's going to make a powerful difference."

And hadn't O'Reilly sometime in the past year remarked that making differences in small ways was what country general practice was all about?

"Mind you," she said, "I've still not found another job."

"You don't need to worry about that, Aggie—"

"Because," and she laughed, "because I'm for going til meet a rich man here today, get swept off my feet, and taken away to the Casbah?"

She's seen too many Errol Flynn films, Barry thought, but said, "I don't know about that, but

Doctor O'Reilly and I did get a word with Mister McCluggage—"

"And?" He heard the hope in her voice and saw a smile start.

"He wants you to go and see him on Monday morning. He won't give you your old job back—"

Her face crumpled.

"—but he's going to train you as a buttonholer."

Her eyes widened, mouth opened, and she drew in a deep shuddering breath before whispering, "Me? A buttonholer? My God." She frowned. "Honest? Honest to God? You're not codding me, sir?"

He shook his head. "I'd not make fun of you, Aggie. Actually we didn't think Mister McCluggage was such a bad fellow. He told us that you're a hard worker, and he was sorry to have had to let you go."

She sniffed. "About as sorry as Pharaoh was to see the back of the Israelites after all them Egyptians got a bath in the Red Sea, I'm sure."

"He did say he was sorry, and Mister McCluggage understands why you have to sit down at your work," Barry said. "Doctor O'Reilly was there too."

She cocked her head. "If you say so, sir, but, oh Lord, I'm all overcome. A buttonholer? That's dead on so it is. Wheeker. And buttonholers make seventeen and six a week more than folders. Thank youse and Doctor O'Reilly very, very much."

"There's no need for thanks," Barry said. "It's our job. I'm just sorry I'll not be here to see you settled into your new post."

"We'll all miss you, Doc," Aggie said. "Good luck til yiz, sir."

He smiled. "Thanks." Someone was tugging at his sleeve. He turned to see Mairead, and Angus and Siobhan. "Have youse a wee minute, Doctor?" Mairead asked.

"Of course."

"My Gerry's coming over from the bar."

Gerry arrived, clutching a pint of Guinness. "How's about ye, Doc?" He offered the pint, which Barry accepted. "We want to say Cheerio," Gerry said, "and that there pint's a wee thanks for taking care of Mairead here. She's all better now, so she is."

Barry drank. The Guinness was warm, but satisfying. "Here's to you having number three very soon."

"Och," said Mairead, "it would be nice." She tousled Angus's hair. "But we're quare nor happy with the two we've got, so we are. Good luck til you, sir."

Barry inclined his head. "That's kind of you."

"Look," said Gerry. "I'm only a riveter—"

"There's no 'only' about it. It's as skilled a job as any."

"Right enough, mebbe it is, but I reckon in your trade, sir, you're one of the best. Good luck to yiz, and mebbe once in a wee while you'll think of us here?"

"I will indeed, Gerry. I will indeed." You're going to be hard to forget. I've had a great time here. The place is part of me, he thought, turned and said, "If you'll excuse me, I have to have a word with Sonny Houston, and he's over there."

"Away you go, sir, and good luck." Gerry bent and pecked Mairead's cheek. "I'll have to get back to helping at the bar, love, but Jeremy Dunne'll give me a break in half an hour."

Barry made his way back toward the head table, pausing to say, "Father O'Toole, Maggie, Sonny," and was greeted in return. He leant closer to Sonny. "When Doctor O'Reilly returns?"

Sonny nodded. "The Browns are back there and I have what you want out in the car. It's parked in a nice shady spot. Just you tip me the wink."

There was a sudden round of applause and Barry looked up to see O'Reilly, now in his usual tweed trousers, red braces, and open-at-the-neck collarless shirt, letting himself out of the kitchen and heading for the head table. Barry waved and called, "Doctor O'Reilly. Can you come here?"

Fingal nodded, picked up a fresh pint that Willie had delivered moments ago, and made a beeline.

Barry said to Sonny, "Doctor O'Reilly and I need to have a quick chat with Helen Hewitt, and then we'll make our delivery to young Colin Brown, all right?"

"Right you are, Doctor," said Sonny. "I'll be ready."

47

. . . And Must Bid the Company Farewell

Helen's smile was beatific as she rummaged in her handbag and produced an envelope with the crest of Queen's University on the upper left corner. "It came in this morning's post," she said, showing it to the tight circle of Barry, O'Reilly, and Jenny crowded around her. "I had to get my da to open it I was shaking so much. I'm in. I'm accepted." She stood and threw her arms round O'Reilly's neck. "I know I've already thanked you, Doctor O'Reilly, but—" She kissed him, then stood back. "Thank you. Thank you. Thank you."

Barry and Jenny laughed as O'Reilly rumbled, muttered, scratched his head, took a long pull on his pint, and finally said, "We are all delighted for you, Helen." He fished out his briar and lit up.

"Congratulations, Helen. You've an interesting six years ahead of you," said Barry. "But you'll find it's all worth it, won't she, Jenny?"

"You will, Helen, and if you need any help, as long as I'm here you've only to ask."

"Thank you, Doctor Bradley," Helen said.

"It's Jenny."

And Barry immediately thought back to Thursday

night, when he'd been told by Mister Greer, "It's Charlie." Welcome to the profession as a novitiate, Helen Hewitt, he thought. "And it's Barry," he said, "and you'll be amazed by how quickly the six years will go. Good luck to you."

"And remember," O'Reilly said, "when it comes to exams, the amount of luck required is inversely proportional to the amount of work you've done. We're all counting on you, girl." He let go a puff of smoke and continued, "Now, Helen, you go and thank his lordship."

"I will," she said and, with the envelope still clutched in her hand, started toward where the marquis was sitting.

Barry heard the pipe music grow louder, looked round to see that Donal had joined Dapper. "What's that tune?" he asked Fingal.

"'Drowsy Maggie,'" Fingal said. "It's a reel. And it's about time I took Mrs. O'Reilly . . . by Jasus, Barry, I love the ring of that. Mrs. O'Reilly, I really do. About time I took her for a dance."

"I don't think," Barry said, "in the year I've come to know you, I've ever seen you so happy."

O'Reilly guffawed. "That's because I am. Happy as the proverbial *beatus in stercus porci.*" He looked surprised when Jenny laughed.

"It's the same now as it was in your day, Fingal. We all have to have Latin to get into medical school," Barry said. And Fingal did look as happy as a pig in shite.

"Ooops," O'Reilly said. "Apologies, Jenny."

"None needed," she said, "as long as you're *laetus totus*."

The big man's brows knitted, then he guffawed. "I am completely, teetotally, abso-bloody-lutely happy, and, by God, I think maybe, Doctor Bradley, you're going to make up a lot for Barry's leaving."

Barry felt a moment's jealousy, recognised it for what it was, put it away, and said, "If you can wait a minute before you head off to kick up your heels, I think I may be able to make you even happier."

"Oh?" said O'Reilly.

"I want you and the new Mrs. O'Reilly to see something, but I need to speak to the Browns first."

"Fair enough," said O'Reilly, and headed back to the head table.

Barry turned and motioned to Sonny, who rose and headed for the back gate.

Barry moved through the crowd, pausing to chat briefly, exchange greetings. The sun had moved round the sky and was shining through the branches of the elms, dappling the lawn, the tables, and the revellers with splashes of light. He could see a tractor pulling a reaper on a nearby hill. The smell from the mown hay hung sweetly amid the salty tang of the lough. As he passed a rosebush, its scent and the humming of bees was overpowering. The blaring of the pipes all but drowned out the overhead squabbling of gulls, the happy cries of children, adult laughter, and snippets of conversation.

"—she *never* did . . ." A woman's voice. "I don't believe *a word* of it, so I don't."

"—away off and chase yourself, Fred. Glentoran'll never win the cup next year. Your head's a marley, so it is . . ."

Barry arrived at the table where Connie Brown and her husband, Lenny, were sitting. Lenny Brown rose. "Doctor Laverty," he said. "Sound day. Bloody sound."

"It is, Lenny," Barry said, recognising where Colin got his penchant for bad language, "and how are you, Connie?"

"Och, grand, Doctor, but sorry that you're leaving us."

Barry inclined his head. "Thank you, Connie. Now, I've one very important job to do before I go. You remember a chat you had with Sonny and Maggie and you said you'd have to ask Colin's daddy?"

Her eyes widened. "Aye. I do, and I told youse Lenny here said it would be all right by him."

Lenny nodded.

"Where's Colin?" Barry asked.

"He's playing blind man's buff with the other kids, but we'll get him for youse, so we will."

Lenny stuck two fingers in his mouth and whistled.

"Is *it* here, the day, now?" Connie whispered.

Barry nodded and pointed to where Sonny was coming in through the back gate. He was concealing something under his jacket.

Colin came dashing up to them, one sock as usual

crumpled round the little lad's ankle. Barry noticed his bare knees were stained green from falling on the grass. "Yes, Da," Colin said.

"Say hello to Doctor Laverty," Connie said.

"Hello, Doctor Laverty," Colin said. "How's about ye?"

"I'm fine, Colin. I'd like to borrow you, if that's all right with your folks."

"Och, aye," said Lenny, smiling, "for a wee while."

"It'll only take a moment," Barry said. "Coming, Colin?"

Colin drew back. "There's no needles nor nothing like that?"

Barry shook his head. "I promise." He bent his head to Colin. "A little bird told me that Butch is happy where he's living now." Barry held out a hand, which Colin took.

"I'm dead glad to hear that, so I am. I still worry about him, you know." Colin took a look at his mother, then said to Barry, "If youse's taking me somewhere, can we go now? It's my turn to be 'it' soon."

"Come on, then," said Barry, feeling Colin's warm, sticky hand in his. He led them toward the front of the head table and inclined his head to Sonny, who followed, accompanied by Maggie.

They arrived between the head table and those for the invitees. Barry let go of Colin's hand, and said loudly, "Excuse me, excuse me." With the pipes and the dancing and the general buzz of conversation it would have been impossible to get the attention of the whole crowd. But he did want to make sure that those folks in the bridal party could share in Colin's forth-coming happiness. When he was sure he'd got every-body's attention, he said, by way of explanation for the Dublin contingent, "This is Colin Brown. A few weeks ago he lost his pet ferret."

Barry heard a number of "aahs," and "ochs," and, "the wee mite."

"Today Sonny and Maggie Houston have a surprise for the young man."

"For me?"

"There you go, Colin," Sonny said, and from under his coat he drew a wriggling, squiggling furry ball. A six-week-old, Lord-knows-what puppy. Its coat was short-haired, mottled black and brown. Its feet were two sizes too big for its body, and its ears drooped past its chin and nearly hid a red leather collar. The animal made squealing, yipping noises and its tail thrashed.

"He's for you, Colin," Maggie said. She was wear-ing her best teeth today and as she bent to Colin, the ox-eye daisy in her hatband swayed like an angler fish's lure.

"Me? Me? For real, like?" Colin's eyes were wide. He accepted the pup, which at once began licking the boy's face. "He's lovely and warm, and all cuddly," Colin said. "And he's really for me?"

Sonny nodded and Maggie cackled.

"Thank youse, Mister and Mrs. Houston. Thank youse ever, ever so much."

Barry glanced up. O'Reilly had his hands clasped above his head like a triumphant prizefighter. Sue was smiling at Barry. She blew him a kiss. He grinned back.

"Here," Barry said, and produced a lead. "You'll need one of these. It's my going-away present to you, Colin."

The boy took the leash, tucked the pup under one arm, and this time, it was Colin who held out his hand to Barry in a solemn, grown-up fashion. Barry took it and shook. "Thank youse, Doctor Laverty, for all youse've done for me. Mammy says you're going to Ballymena for a while. I hope you'se'll be as happy in that bit of the country as you told me you-know-who is in his." He half-turned, stuck his tongue out at Bertie Bishop, and, praise the Lord, Barry thought, the councillor did not notice. Colin turned back with a radiant smile. "Can I go and show my wee pup to Mammy and me da?"

"Off you go," Barry said, "and take good care of him."

"I will," said Colin.

Arthur Guinness appeared from under the table, sauntered over to Barry and Colin, and proceeded to give the puppy, still in Colin's arms, a good sniff. The puppy yipped, wiggled, and nipped at Arthur's ear. The big Lab looked at Barry as if to say, "Nice kid," and ambled off.

Colin frowned. "Doctor Laverty," he said, "how did Arthur Guinness get his name?"

"Doctor O'Reilly named him after this stuff." He held up the half-finished pint he'd been given by Gerry Shanks.

Colin looked thoughtful. "My daddy says thon Guinness isn't a patch on Murphy's stout, and I've seen my daddy drink it. It's the same colour as my pup's black patches." He clipped the lead to the pup's collar, set him on the ground, and said proudly, "Come on, Murphy, come on and meet my mammy and daddy."

There was a ripple of applause from the head table and the immediately adjacent ones, and Barry heard Kinky say, "I'm surprised young Colin would know about Murphy's. It does be brewed in County Cork, so—"

"And it's not the only good thing to come out of County Cork," Archie said. His speech was ever so slightly slurred and he planted a kiss on Kinky's cheek.

She giggled and said, "Behave yourself, Archibald Auchinleck," but Barry saw she was holding Archie's hand. She said to Barry, "Have you everything packed up for tomorrow, sir?"

"I have."

"A bit later I'll have Archie bring the boxes down to the hall," she said, pushing back her chair and standing. "Doctor Laverty, it has been a pleasure to know you, so—"

"And you, Kinky." That lump in Barry's throat was threatening to choke him and nearly did when she enfolded him in her arms. He felt her shaking and knew she was crying.

She let him go, dashed the backs of her hands over her eyes, and said, "And don't worry about lunch tomorrow for your drive." She waved a hand in the direction of the marquee. "I'll make sure you have a lunch fit for royalty with all the leavings from this afternoon, and put them in the fridge, so."

"Thank you, Kinky," he said. "Thank you so very much . . . for everything." Barry Laverty could manage no more. Tomorrow would be here soon enough.

He felt a tap on his shoulder and turned to see Donal Donnelly. The man's carrotty thatch stuck out in bright contrast to the bottle green of his Highlander's caubeen. "Could youse come over til the side of the garden where it's a wee bit more private like? Julie and me'd like to have a wee word."

"Of course." He frowned. What on earth was this all about? He couldn't stop himself from worrying that something had gone wrong at the last minute with the Donnellys' house purchase. "If you'll just give me a minute."

"You take your time, sir."

Barry moved to the head table. He said, "I'm sorry, Sue. I thought I'd finished, but Donal wants me for something."

"Go on," she said, and smiled. "I can wait."

"Thanks."

"Barry," Fingal called, "don't be too long. I'm taking

Kitty for a dance and you don't want to leave a good-looking lass like Sue alone with no one to talk to."

"I wonder," said the marquis, "if you'd care to be my partner in the next set, Sue?"

"It would be lovely," she said.

"Thank you, sir," Barry said, then turned. "Come on, Donal."

Together they set off toward one of the big elms.

"Do you mind the day we met, sir?" Donal asked.

"I do," Barry said. "A year ago this month. I was lost, trying to find Doctor O'Reilly for an interview for this job. You were on your bike and you gave me directions." Barry would never forget that encounter: yellow gorse, drooping fuschia, a blackbird singing, Donal's directions about *not* to turn at a black and white cow, and the man's flight at the mere mention of the name of Doctor O'Reilly. The ogre, Fingal O'Reilly, had mellowed over the past year. Barry knew Kitty had had a lot to do with that, but perhaps, in his own way, Barry had helped too. "It's been quite the year."

They reached a spot where Julie was waiting in the shade of one of the elms, away from the crowd. With only a few days of her pregnancy to go, she looked thoroughly uncomfortable in the heat and, as Donal had been heard affectionately to describe her, "as big as the side wall of a house."

"Julie," Barry said, "can we not find you a chair?" He glanced back. O'Reilly had been true to his word.

He and Kitty, Kinky and Archie, the marquis and Sue, Jane Hoey and her surgical boss Charlie Greer were dancing to a tune played by Dapper Frew. They weren't the only set. Barry scanned the crowd and realised that with the exception of the O'Hallorhan party from Dublin he knew just about everybody at this hooley.

"Don't you worry your head, Doctor. I'm so big I can't seem to get comfortable in any position I'm in," she said, put her hand in the small of her back, grimaced, then laughed. "Anyroad, what we've to say'll only take a wee minute."

So it wasn't the house. That was a relief.

Donal said, "Me and Julie know it's himself and Mrs. O'Reilly's big day, so we don't want to extract from that—"

"Detract," Julie said, and had to stop chuckling before she managed to say, "Honestly, Donal Donnelly, you're hopeless, so you are."

"Right enough, detract, anyroad, Julie and me didn't want youse til go away without something to remember us and Ballybucklebo by. I mind very well what youse said a year ago, in this here garden at Seamus and Mary Galvin's going-away party. We were queueing up for to buy jars and I asked youse, how do you like Ballybucklebo . . . and working for himself?"

"I remember," Barry said, "and I told you I didn't think 'like' was the right word. I said I loved it here."

"And," Julie said, "since youse come, youse and

Doctor O'Reilly have been quare nor good to me and Donal."

Barry held up a hand as if to stop them, but Donal shook his head and continued on. "Youse know me and Julie's going to get the wee house after all, and for even less than we thought?"

"I'd heard a rumour."

"And I suppose it's all because your man Mister Houston found an old Stone Age thing, mebbe under that mound."

"That's what I heard."

"It's dead on, so it is." He frowned. Barry recognised the look of Donal Donnelly wrestling with a grave intellectual conundrum. "And I don't suppose himself and you had anything til do with it, sir?"

Barry laughed. "We certainly didn't bury that Stone Age fort under what's going to be your back garden, Donal. If that's what you mean?"

When she'd finished laughing, Julie said, "Right enough, but we do know what we know, so we do. That there Doctor O'Reilly does all kinds of things behind the scenes and never lets on, and we're guessing he's got you into the same way of going too, Doctor Laverty."

Barry shrugged. He was not a bit ashamed of emulating the older man.

"Well may you shrug, Doctor," said Julie, "but all youse and himself have done for us can't ever be paid back—"

Barry held up a hand. "Thank you, Julie, but honestly, it's part of our job. And it's been my pleasure. I am going away for a while, but I promise I'll come back to see my friends. I'm going to miss you all, and I'll never forget you." He half-turned. "And I'm sorry, Julie, that I'll not be here for your big day, but I'm sure it'll go very well."

"We'll send you a wee birth notice and all, so we will."

"Kinky'll have my address," he said.

Donal had gone behind the tree. He returned with a narrow, brown-paper-wrapped parcel. He said, "Me and Julie would like for youse to have this, sir. Just from us."

Barry accepted the gift. "Thank you," he said. "Thank you very much."

"Will youse open it, sir?" Julie said.

The pipe music stopped as if to mark the occasion.

Barry tore off the wrapping and gasped. "Mother of God." He realised that under the circumstances that was exactly what Fingal would have said. "It's a Hardy Koh-I-Noor, a number seven—" Barry blew out his breath through pursed lips. "I don't know what to say." He shuddered to think what this, the Rolls-Royce of fly rods, must have cost and realised he was trembling. "Thank you, but it's far too much."

"Och," said Donal, "it was my da's and sure I never fish. We think it's going to a good home that's all, like, but we hope every time youse put a fly on the water you'll mind us and Ballybucklebo."

It was all Barry could do to keep his voice from

breaking. His eyes prickled. "Donal. Julie," he said, "I'll treasure this. I'll take good care of it . . . and it won't only be every time that I go fishing—"

He heard O'Reilly's voice booming over the noises of the crowd. "Come on, Dapper. Give us another bloody reel, you great bollix." The remark was greeted by cheers, whistles, applause. The uncrowned king of Ballybucklebo was holding court, his queen by his side, and as he himself would say, "God was in His Heaven and all was right with the world." Fair play to you both, Doctor and Mrs. Fingal Flahertie O'Reilly, M.B., B.Ch., B.A.O., D.S.C.

Barry shook his head in wonder at the scene before him, smiled, and said, "I meant what I said to you, Donal, a year ago. I love it here . . . and if I live to be a hundred I'll never, *ever* forget Ballybucklebo."

AFTERWORD
by
Mrs. Kincaid

Dia duit, tar isteach. Hello, and come in. I'm just back from church meself. Mister Robinson was in grand form today, his sermon was all hellfire and brimstone, but even so it was a bit of a comedown after the wedding yesterday. *That* was a hooley and a half, but there it is now, all done. Another chapter in the Ballybucklebo chronicles. Sometimes I wonder if that Patrick Taylor fellah is ever going to run out of steam. Rather him than me, for I know the telling of these tales runs to hundreds of pages, so. I'm lucky I only have to pen a few recipes and then get on with a bit of tidying up because Archie Auchinleck, bless him, is popping in for tea in my kitchen at six o'clock.

It does be very quiet here at Number One today. That nice Doctor Bradley has gone to see a farmer up in the Ballybucklebo Hills. On the phone it sounded like he'd ruptured himself, but then I'm no doctor. She's taken Arthur so he can have a run after, so. Himself and Miss Kitty . . . although I'd better get used to calling her Mrs. O'Reilly for a while before I get round to plain Kitty, the pair of them left for Rhodes this morning and young Doctor Laverty loaded up his funny shmall-little German motorcar and headed off for Ballymena. I wonder if he'll come back? I know himself would like that and so would I, and this is one question my gift can't or won't answer. I'll tell you one thing, bye. If I'd ever had a son he couldn't have turned out any better than Doctor Barry Laverty. I hope he finds what he's looking for. Time will tell, but I did be pleased to see how well him and that Sue Nolan seemed to be getting on yesterday. They were telling me about their plans to visit the Glens of Antrim soon. More power to their wheels.

And more power to my pen if I'm going to get this job finished.

I've five for you today, lentil soup, Irish stew, cottage pie with champ topping, fish pie, and orange and chocolate soufflé. I'm making one of those for Archie later today. He's like Doctor O'Reilly and has a powerfully sweet tooth.

So, if you'd get out of my chair, Lady Macbeth—thank you—I'll bid you all *slán leat,* hope you enjoy these dishes when you try them, and hope to see you back here soon.

MRS. MAUREEN "KINKY" KINCAID
Housekeeper to
Doctor Fingal Flahertie O'Reilly
M B., BCh., B.A.O.
1 Main Street,
Ballybucklebo,
County Down,
Northern Ireland

• *Lentil Soup*

1 large potato, peeled and chopped
1 stick of celery, chopped
2 medium onions, peeled and chopped
3 carrots, peeled and chopped
2 cloves garlic, crushed
1 tablespoon cooking oil
1 small can tomato puree
330 g / 12 oz. red lentils, washed
1200 mL / 2 pints / about 6 cups vegetable
  stock
600 mL / 1 pint / about 3 cups water
Salt and freshly ground black pepper to taste
A little chopped parsley and a swirl of cream to
  finish

Heat the oil in a large saucepan and sweat the potato, onion, celery, and carrots over a very gentle heat for a few minutes until the onions are soft but not brown. I like to cover this with a sheet of greaseproof paper, which helps to trap the moisture.

Now, add the remaining ingredients, bring to the boil, reduce heat to a slow simmer, and cook for about an hour, stirring occasionally.

Liquidise and season to taste and serve with the chopped parsley and cream to garnish.

This is a substantial lunch soup and goes very well with my Guinness bread recipe, which I'm sure you all enjoy as much as himself does. You'll find that one in *A Dublin Student Doctor*, so.

• *Irish Stew*

1 kg / 2 ¼ lbs. scrag or neck of lamb on the bone
2 onions, chopped small
3 carrots, chopped small
6 medium potatoes, chopped into quarters
1 bay leaf
1 tablespoon cooking oil
A little parsley, chopped
Salt and freshly ground black pepper
Worcestershire sauce

First, you scrape as much meat off the bones as possible and put this to one side. Heat the oil in a large pot and brown the bones for a few minutes. Cover with about 7 pints/4 litres of cold water. Season, add the bay leaf, and bring to the boil. Simmer it gently for about 2 hours. By this time the liquid should have reduced down to about 2 pints. Now you leave it to get cold so that you can remove the fat from the surface. Putting it in the fridge really helps to solidify the fat. Scrape the meat from the bones again and discard them. Now add the rest of the meat to the liquid and cook for about 30 minutes. Then you add the potatoes, carrots, and onions and cook for another 20 or 30 minutes or so when they should be soft and the potatoes start to break up and thicken the cooking liquid. Season to taste and add a few drops of Worcestershire (or other brown sauce).

    To serve, sprinkle with chopped parsley.

• *Cottage Pie with Champ Topping*

450 g / 1 lb. / 2 cups lean mince beef
2 onions, chopped
1 large or 2 small carrots, grated
15 mL / 1 tablespoon cooking oil
1 teaspoon herbs—fresh or dried—thyme, basil,
    oregano (all of these or just one will do)
15 mL / 1 tablespoon chopped parsley
15 mL / 1 tablespoon tomato purée or ketchup
15 mL / 1 tablespoon Worcestershire sauce
15 mL / 1 tablespoon flour
285 mL / ½ pint / 1 cup beef stock

CHAMP TOPPING

900 g / 2 lbs. / 4 cups potatoes
1 bunch scallions (green onions) chopped
1 cup milk
Salt and black pepper
50 g / 2 oz. / 1 stick butter

First you fry the onions and carrot in the oil for a few minutes, add the minced beef, and cook for a further 20 to 30 minutes. The beef will be nice and brown now and will have released its fat. To make this pie less fattening for himself, and Alice not having to let his waistband out more, I like to press the beef mixture into a sieve and get rid of most of the fat. Then I return the beef to the pan and add the herbs, parsley, salt and pepper, flour, tomato puree, Worcestershire sauce, and finally the beef stock. Now simmer it all for a few minutes and adjust seasoning if necessary.

Set aside into a well-greased baking dish and prepare the topping.

Boil the potatoes until soft and mash well. In a separate pan, cook the scallions with the milk and seasoning at a slow simmer until soft. This only takes a few minutes but keep watching it to make sure that it does not boil over. Now add this together with the butter to the mashed potatoes and mix well.

What you have now is called champ and is very popular in Ireland as an accompaniment for other dishes too. But I am digressing, so to get back to what we were doing:

Spread the champ over the top of the cooked beef mixture, dot the top with butter, and put into a preheated oven at 400°F / 200°C / gas mark 6 for about 25 minutes. The topping will have browned nicely. This should feed four very hungry people or six not so.

I am forever being asked what the difference is between cottage pie and shepherd's pie, and the answer is that you use lamb instead of beef to make a shepherd's. This is very good too and reminds me so much of my childhood and a man called Connor MacTaggart, but you'll have to read *An Irish Country Girl* to find out why.

• *Fish Pie*

450 g / 1 lb. mixed fish such as salmon, cod, snapper,
  or haddock
110 g / 4 oz. shrimp or prawns
110 g / 4 oz. scallops
600 mL / 1 pint / about 3 cups milk
1 or 2 bay leaves
Salt and black pepper
15 g / 2 tablespoons fresh chopped parsley
50 g / 2 oz. / 1 stick butter
15 g / 2 tablespoons flour

Bring the milk, seasonings, and bay leaves to the boil
in a pan and add the uncooked fish and shellfish, omit-
ting the shrimp if it has been precooked. Simmer very
gently for about 3 minutes. Cover with a lid and leave
until you have prepared the topping.

TOPPING

You can either use the champ topping on page 411
or make this very simple one.
900 g / 2 lbs. potatoes
150 mL / ¼ pint light cream
25 g / 1 oz. butter
Salt and pepper to taste

Mash the boiled potatoes with cream and butter and
season to taste.

SAUCE

Drain the milk from the fish and discard the bay leaves. Remove any skin or bones from the fish, break into bite-size pieces, and spread over a greased pie dish with the shrimp. Melt the butter in a saucepan and carefully stir in the flour. Cook gently for a couple of minutes without letting the *roux* (a fancy French word for the flour and butter mixture) brown. Now add the milk to the *roux* very gradually with the seasoning and parsley. Bring to the boil and simmer gently for 3 or 4 minutes, stirring all the time. Then pour the sauce over the fish.

It's time now to cover the fish and the sauce with the potato topping, and dot it all over with butter or a little grated cheddar or Parmesan cheese. Bake in a preheated oven at 200°C / 400°F for about 30 minutes or until nicely browned.

• *Orange and Chocolate Soufflé*

200 g / 7 oz. plain dark chocolate
Grated zest and juice of a large orange
5 eggs
85 g / 3 oz. sugar
1 sachet gelatine
55 mL / 2 oz. water
85 mL / 3 oz. cream

Dissolve the gelatine in the orange juice according to the instructions on the packet. Separate 2 of the eggs and place their whites in a bowl to use later. Put the rest of the eggs and the sugar into another bowl and place this over a pan of simmering water. Now you whisk the mixture for about 10 minutes until it becomes thick and creamy. Set this to one side.

Take a third bowl, break the chocolate into it, add the water, and place over a pan of hot water. Stir until the chocolate has melted and become smooth and runny and add the orange zest.

While this is cooling beat the 2 egg whites until quite stiff.

By now the chocolate mixture should have cooled down. However, if it has not, you could accelerate this by placing the bowl into cold water and stirring the chocolate around. When it is cold, you stir and fold it together with the gelatine into the egg and sugar mixture. Now all you have to do is mix the beaten egg whites and the whipped cream carefully through the chocolate and egg mixture.

Pour into a serving dish and chill for 2 to 3 hours.

Decorate with orange segments and grated chocolate.

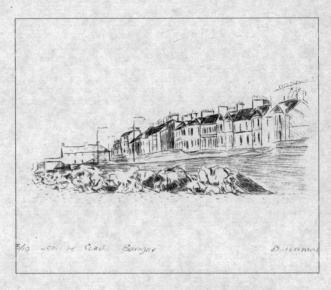

The house to the left facing the reader
is where Patrick Taylor grew up in Bangor.
Original etching by Dorothy Tinman

GLOSSARY

I have tried to be faithful to my characters by setting them as accurately in time, place, and contemporary attitudes as memory and extensive reading allow. Some of my characters' daily speech is the dialect of my native Ulster. While colourful and often highly descriptive, Ulsterspeak can be impenetrable to the nonspeaker. Where an explanation in the text did not interrupt the story I have used that convention, but on some occasions I have had to trust that the context was explanatory. To those I have confused, I offer this glossary.

abdabs, screaming: Diarrhoea and vomiting, severe D and V.

acting the lig: Behaving foolishly.

almoner: Archaic term for what is now called a medical social worker. One of the almoner's original tasks was to distribute charity, alms, to the poor.

anyroad: Anyhow.

asking after: Making concerned enquiries about.

away off and feel your head/bumps: How can you possibly be so stupid?/A reference to phrenology, the study of personality by examining the shape of a head.

backward in coming forward (not): Certainly not reticent.

Bakelite: One of the first synthetic plastics. Used in telephones because of its nonconductive properties.

barrister: A lawyer who by dint of different training than a solicitor (see under S) argued cases in superior and higher courts.

beagle's gowl: The beagle dog's gowl (not howl) or baying can be heard over a long distance. Not to come within a beagle's gowl is to miss by a mile.

bee on a hot brick: Running round distractedly.

bide: Wait, patience implied.

biscuits: Cookies.

bleeper: Pager, usually called a "beeper" in North America.

blether, blethering: An expression of annoyance, talking nonstop trivia.

bletherskite: Someone who never stops talking.

bollix: Testicles, or more accurately the impolite "balls." Used to imply rubbish. Used about a person, "You are a right regal bollix," implies uselessness

bonnaught: Heavily armed Irish mercenary. First appeared in the fourteenth century.

bowler hat: Derby.

boys-a-boys/a-dear: Expression of surprise.

'bout ye/how's about ye?: How are you?

brave: Very.

brave stretch of the legs: A very long way.

brill: Brilliant, meaning perfect.

bullock: Castrated male bovine. Steer.

burroo: Corruption of "bureau," the government department that dealt with issuing unemployment insurance.

bus conductor: Person on the vehicle who collected fares.

can't . . . for toffee apples: Is utterly inept at the described act.

casualty: Emergency room.

caubeen: Soft, floppy brimless bonnet.

chissler/chisler: Infant.

chuffed: Pleased.

clatter: An indeterminate quantity.

cod: To make fun of.

colloguing: Chitchatting.

collywobbles: Rumbling in the guts used often to signify butterflies in the stomach or nervousness.

come on on on in: Is not a typographical error. This item of Ulsterspeak drives spellcheck mad.

coming down with: Having too many of, or being in the earliest stages of, an illness.

council house: Low-income subsidised housing provided by the local authority, usually a city or county council.

cracker: Acme of perfection.

***craic*:** Irish. Pronounced "crack." Fun. Good conversation. A very good time was had by all, often fueled by several drops of the craytur.

***crannóg*:** Irish. Pronounced "crannohg," literally "little wood." Fortified, often man-made island usually constructed with wooden pilings.

craytur/craythur, a drop of: Creature/a drink of spirits, usually whiskey or *poitín*.

cup of tea in your hand: A cup of tea taken informally as opposed to sitting down at a tea table.

currency: In 1965, prior to decimilization, sterling was the currency of the United Kingdom, of which Northern Ireland was a part. The unit was the pound, which contained twenty shillings, each made of of twelve pennies, thus there were 240 pennies in a pound. Coins and notes of combined or lesser or greater denominations were in circulation, often referred to by slang or archaic terms: halfpenny (two to the penny), three-penny piece (thruppeny bit), sixpenny piece (tanner), two-shillings piece (florin), two-shillings-and-sixpence piece (half-a-crown), ten-shilling note (ten-bob note), five-pound note (fiver). Most will be encountered in these pages. In 1965 one pound bought nearly three U.S. dollars.

dab hand at . . . : very skillful at a given action

dander: To stroll, or horse dandruff. To get one's **dander up** was to get or be made angry enough to be ready for a fight.

dead brill: Very brilliant. Perfect.

dead on: A strong affirmative, excited acceptance of good news or a measure of complete accuracy. "I totally agree," "That's marvelous," or "Absolutely correct."

decline (going into a): Becoming depressed.

desperate/ly: Serious/seriously.

doddle: Short walk or easy task.

doh-ray-mi: Corruption of "dough," money.

dosh: Money.

dote (n): Something or somebody adorable.

dote on (v): Adore.

doting (gerund): To be wrong because presumably you are in your dotage.

dulse: Edible seaweed.

duncher: Flat tweed cap.

dunt: Blow with something blunt.

eejit, buck: Idiot, complete idiot.

elected: Everything's coming up roses.

every happiness: Traditional wish on hearing of a couple's engagement. "Congratulations" was not used.

fecking: Euphemism for the "F" word. Liberally thrown in for emphasis, particularly in Dublin.

ferocious: Very severe.

fillums: I have deliberately avoided the phoenetic rendering of words, but two instances are so Ulster I couldn't resist. "Fillums" for films and "northren" for northern.

Fir Bolg: Irish. Pronounced "feer bollug." One of the early races believed to have inhabited Ireland. Probably invaders of the Belgae tribe from Gaul.

fire away: Carry on. Useful except in front of a firing squad.

fit to be tied: Very angry.

fly your kite: I have not the slightest interest in your influence in this affair or, simply, go away.

footering: Fumbling about with.

fornenst: Near to.

full as a goat/ as a lord: Drunk/very drunk.

gander: Look at.

gansey: From the Irish *geansaí*, a jumper (sweater). Used in the Anglicised version by Irish and non-Irish speakers.

gerroff: Get off. Usually said to over-affectionate animals.

Gestetner: An early copying machine dependent upon a stencil technology. Replaced by Xerox photocopiers after 1959.

git: From "begotten." Bastard, often expressed, "He's a right hoor's [whore's] git." Not a term of endearment.

giorria (mór): Irish, pronounced "geara (more)." Hare (big).

glipe: Idiot.

gobshite: Dublin slang; literally dried nasal mucus. Used pejoratively about a person.

good man-ma-da: I approve of what you have done or are going to do.

good skin/head: Decent person.

grand, grand altogether: Well. Very well.

great gross: Very large quantity.

guff: Verbal abuse.

gulder: Roar.

gurrier: Dublin slang. Street urchin, but can be used pejoratively about anyone.

half-un, wee half: A single measure, usually one ounce of spirits, usually whiskey.

hard stuff: Spirits, usually Irish whiskey.

head's a marley, cut: As small and dense as a child's marble (marley), or damaged by having been incised. Being very stupid.

heart of corn: Very good-natured.

heifer: Cow before her first breeding.

hiding to nothing: A "hiding" is a physical beating. To be offered the choice of one or nothing is no choice and hence a complete waste of time.

highheejins: Exalted persons (often in their own minds).

hobbyhorse shite: Literally sawdust. To have a head full is again to be stupid.

hooley: Boisterous party

houseman: Medical intern. Term used despite the sex of the incumbent.

in soul: Definitely.

jammy: Lucky.

knickers: Women's and girls' underpants.

Lamass: Christian religious festival on August 1, introduced to replace the pagan Lughnasa. See *Irish Country Girl*.

laughing like a drain: Laughing uproariously with your mouth wide open.

laughing my leg off: Laughing uproariously.

lepping: Leaping.

leprechaun: Irish, *leipreachán*. A mischevious Irish faery, one of the Tuatha dé (See Tuatha dé Danaan).

let the hare sit: Leave it alone.

like or big as the side wall of a house: Huge (especially when applied to someone's physical build).

liltie: A madman. An Irish whirling dervish.

lug worm: A member of the Phylum *Annelidia*. A ragged-edged marine worm that lives in burrows under tidal sand or mud. Much prized as bait. Harvested at low tide by digging close to the creatures' blow holes in the sand.

main: Very.

matron: A hospital's senior nurse, responsible administratively for all matters pertaining to nursing. In North America the position is now Vice President of Nursing.

Melton Mobray pie: A savoury pork-and-bacon meat pie with a thin layer of aspic between the filling and the buttery pastry. Best eaten cold.

mending, well mended: Recovering from an illness, completely better.

messages: Errands.

Milesians: Invaders from northern Spain who were Gaelic Celts. Some believe they were originally the lost tribe of Israel.

mope: Brood over something, mourn.

muck out: Remove the ordure from stables or a byre.

my aunt Fanny Jane: Expression of complete disbelief.

my belly thinks my throat's cut: Expression of severe hunger. Literally the stomach feels as if the supply route has been severed.

name of the wee man: Name of the devil.

newsagent: Shop which stocked newspapers, magazines, sweeties, and tobacco products.

no dozer: One who has his wits about him.

no great shakes at: Not very good at.

no harm to you, but: Inevitably preceded criticism or disagreement.

no skin off my nose: It doesn't affect me one way or the other. I could not care less.

nose out of joint: Have taken umbrage.

*ochón***:** Irish. Pronounced "ochown." Alas.

on eggs: Worried sick.

on "the sick": Receiving sickness insurance payments while out of work.

out of the woods: Has sucessfully passed through a trying time.

oxter/oxter-cog: Armpit/help along by draping someone's arm over your shoulders to support them.

pass-remarkable: Prone to making unsolicited, often derogatory, comments about other people.

pay no heed to: Pay no attention to.

pelmet: Valance.

pipes: Three kinds of bagpipes are played in Ireland. The great highland pipes, three drones; the Brian Boru pipes, three drones and four to thirteen keys on the chanter; and the Uillinn (elbow) pipes, driven by small bellows under the elbow. There are keys on both the chanter and the drones. If "pipes" is said it usually refers to the first, the latter two are usually specified.

*poitín***:** Irish. Pronounced "potcheen." Moonshine. Illegally distilled spirits, usually from barley. Could be as strong as 180 proof (about 100% alcohol by volume).

poorly: Sick.

pop in/over/round: All mean to drop in unannounced.

price of a pint of Guinness: In 1900, threepence. In

1928, tenpence. In 1958, one shilling and sixpence. In 1964, two shillings and one penny.

pupil: Schoolchild. "Student" was reserved for university undergraduates and only those who had sucessfully completed the necessary university courses graduated.

purler: Tumble.

quare: Pronunciation of the word "queer" in parts of Ireland. Very often succeeded with "nor."

quid: Pound sterling or measure of chewing tobacco.

rain: Rain is a fact of life in Ireland. It's why the country is the Emerald Isle. As the Inuit people of the Arctic have many words for snow, in Ulster the spectrum runs from **sound day,** fair weather, to **a grand soft day,** mizzling, also described as, **that's the sort of rain that wets you,** to downpours of varying severity to include **coming down in sheets/stair-rods/torrents,** or **pelting, bucketing, plooting** (corruption of French *il pleut*), **chucking it down,** and the universal **raining cats and dogs.** If you visit, do take an umbrella.

rashers: Bacon slices from the back of the pig. They have a streaky tail and a lean eye.

right enough?: Is that correct?

rightly: Perfectly well.

road bowling: A game where a twenty-eight-ounce metal ball or "bullet" is thrown or "lofted" over a fixed length of road. The contestant with the least number of throws to cover the distance wins.

run-race: Quick trip.

sidthe: Irish. Pronounced "shee." The burial mounds and hill forts that litter Ireland.

sister (nursing): In Ulster hospitals nuns at one time filled important nursing roles. They no longer do so except in some Catholic institutions. Their honourific, "sister," has been retained to signify a senior nursing rank. **Ward sister**: charge nurse. **Sister tutor**: senior nursing teacher. (Now also obsolete because nursing is a university course.) In North America the old rank was charge nurse or head nurse, now nursing team leader unless it has been changed again since I retired.

skiver: Corruption of "scurvy." Ne'er-do-well.

slag: Verbal abuse. Slagging can be either be good-natured banter or verbal chastisement.

sláinte: Irish. Pronounced "slawntuh." Cheers. Here's mud in your eye. Prosit.

slubbergub: Foul-mouthed person.

snib: Latch.

soft-soaper: Flatterer.

solicitor: Attorney who did not appear in court, a function performed by lawyers called barristers.

sore: Very seriously.

sound/sound man: Very good/reliable, and trustworthy man.

sparks: Electrician. All trades had their nicknames. **Chippy**: carpenter; **brickie**: bricklayer.

stickin' out/stickin' out a mile: Very good/the acme of perfection.

stone: Avoirdupois measure of mass equal to fourteen pounds.

stoon: Sudden shooting pain.

student: Someone attending university. Children at school were referred to as **pupils** or schoolchildren. (Schoolboy/girl.)

sums: Math. Taught initially as counting, addition (the *sum* of two numbers), subtraction, multiplication, and division.

surgery: When used to describe a doctor's rooms, the equivalent of a North American doctor's office.

sweet, sweetie: Candy.

take your hurry in your hand: Slow down.

take yourself off by the hand: Go away (you eejit, implied).

taking a hand out of: Teasing.

taoiseach: Irish. Pronounced "teeshuck." Prime minister.

targe: Foul-tempered person. Scold.

taste: Small amount and not necesarily to be eaten. "Thon creaky axles needs a wee taste of oil."

ta-ta-ta-ra: Party.

tea: An infusion made by pouring boiling water over *Camellia sinensis,* or the main evening meal. "I had a great steak for my tea."

tears were tripping him: He was in floods of tears.

the morrow/day/night: Tomorow/today/tonight.

thick as two short planks: Very stupid.

thole: Put up with. A reader, Miss D. Williams, wrote to me to say it was etymologically from the Old English *tholian,* to suffer. She remarked that her first encounter with the word was in a fourteenth-century prayer.

thon/thonder: That or there. "Thon eejit shouldn't be standing over thonder."

til: To.

'til: Until.

tinker's curse/damn/toss: I could not care less.

took the rickets: Had a great shock, not fell ill from a vitamin D deficiency.

tousling: Roughing up, either verbal or physical.

townland: A mediaeval administrative region comprising a village and the surrounding countryside.

trotters: Specifically pigs' feet, but can be applied to humans.

Tuatha dé Danaan: Irish. Pronounced "tooatha day danaan." One of the early mythical races also known as Cruithne who defeated the **Fir Bolg** and were themselves overthrown by the **Milesians.** (See under M.) The Tuatha were driven to live underground in the *sidthe* (see under S) and became the people of the mounds, that is the multitude of Irish faeries. (See *Irish Country Girl.*)

turn in his eye: Cross-eyed, medically known as strabismus

up the spout: Pregnant, often out of wedlock.

wee: Small, but in Ulster can be used to modify almost anything without reference to size. A barmaid, an old friend, greeted me by saying, "Come in, Pat. Have a wee seat and I'll get you a wee menu, and would you like a wee drink while you're waiting?"

wee buns: Very easy.

wheeker: Excellent.

wheen: An indeterminate number.

wheest, houl' your wheest: Be quiet or shut-up.

whiskey/whisky: The -key suffix is Irish, -ky is Scotch.

wildfowling: Duck hunting.

willick: Mispronunciation of "whelk," an edible sea-snail. Used as a euphemism for **bollix.** See under B.

wires is (are) shaking: The wind is very strong.

workie: Working person, usually un- or minimally skilled.

ye: You. Singular or plural. More common in the Republic of Ireland.

yer honour: Stage Irish respectful address, used sacrastically.

yiz: You. Singular or plural.

yoke: Thingummybob, whatsit. Name for something one does not know the name of.

you know: Larded into conversation as "like" is in North America. Paradoxically it is usually used when the person listening cannot possibly know.

your man: Someone who is not known. "Your man over there. Who is he?" Or someone known to all. "Your man, Van Morrison." (Also, "I'm your man," as in "I agree and will go along with what you are proposing.")

youse: You. Singular or plural.